What others are saying about

The Plum Blooms in Win...

"Linda Thompson attacks the publishing world like a Mitsubishi Zero swooping from the Japanese sky. *The Plum Blooms In Winter* proves a taut, crisp, debut achievement that colorfully evokes the Pacific theater of World War II. Start this one forewarned: it's a stay-up-all-night read."

-Jerry B. Jenkins, 21-time *New York Times* bestselling author (*Left Behind, et al*)

"*The Plum Blooms in Winter* is a poignant story about bitter defeat and the power of forgiveness. With her lovely prose, Linda Thompson sweeps readers away on a journey to Japan and China during and after World War II, crafting a novel about the remarkable beauty and strength that bloomed in the midst of adversity. A brilliant debut!"

-Melanie Dobson, award-winning author of *Hidden Among the Stars* and *Catching the Wind*

"*The Plum Blooms in Winter* is a must read. This story not only portrays actual facts of war, but also long term effects it has on entire families (of both sides) and how they can linger on for years—even decades after it's over. As the nephew of Lt. Robert Meder (a real Doolittle Raider), I witnessed firsthand the effects World War II caused on his parents, my grandparents, and his only sibling, my mother. This story takes readers on a journey into both sides, through the eyes of an American Doolittle Raider and a Japanese civilian woman. Many lose after a war is over, even those on the winning side."

-John Walker, nephew of Lt. Robert Meder, Doolittle Raider

"Pearl Habor is a household name, but what came next? *The Plum Blooms in Winter* shines light on American heroes of the Doolittle Raiders and post-war life in Japan. Even if you've been an avid World War II reader, this unique story is sure to capture your heart and mind, as you follow the journey of two characters on opposite sides of the world (and of the war)."

-Caroline Walker Argenti, grandniece of Lt. Robert Meder, Doolittle Raider

"This is a grand, ambitious story set during World War II that follows the lives of an American pilot and a Japanese young woman after a bomb he dropped hits her hometown. It's a story of impossible choices that lead to terrible regret. It's a story of captivity and freedom, of honor and culture, of revenge and forgiveness. The setting is unique, the peek into Japanese culture is fascinating, and the message of grace is timeless. Linda Thompson is destined to become one of the greats in Christian fiction."

-Robin Patchen, award winning author of *Convenient Lies* and *Finding Amanda*

"Linda Thompson has become one of my favorite new authors! World War II can be too huge to contemplate, but peering into the hearts of two people living through that war brings it home with heartbreak and redemption. I look forward to following these people in their next adventure."

-Hannah Alexander, author of *Hideaway Home*

THE PLUM

BLOOMS IN

WINTER

Brands from the Burning Series

Book One: The Plum Blooms in Winter
Book Two: The Mulberry Leaf Whispers
Book Three: The Cherry Blossom Falls

The Plum Blooms in Winter

Brands from the Burning Series: Book One

By
Linda Thompson

The Plum Blooms in Winter
Published by Mountain Brook Ink
White Salmon, WA U.S.A.

The website addresses shown in this book are not intended in any way to be or imply an endorsement on the part of Mountain Brook Ink, nor do we vouch for their content.

This story is a work of fiction. While the Doolittle Raid of April 18, 1942, the *Green Hornet*'s mission over Tokyo, and the capture and imprisonment of eight Doolittle Raiders are actual historic events, scenes and dialogue and many ancillary events are the product of the author's imagination. All characters and events are either fictitious or are used fictitiously.

Scripture quotations are taken from the King James Version of the Bible. Public domain.

ISBN 978-1-943959-48-8

The Team: Miralee Ferrell, Jenny Mertes, Nikki Wright, Kristen Johnson and Cindy Jackson

Cover Design: Indie Cover Design, Lynnette Bonner Designer

The Author is represented by and this book is published in association with the literary agency of WordServe Literary Group., Ltd, www.wordserveliterary.com.

Mountain Brook Ink is an inspirational publisher offering fiction you can believe in.
Printed in the United States of America

Dedication

"Is not this a brand plucked out of the fire?
...Behold, I have caused thine iniquity to pass from thee,
and I will clothe thee..."
Zechariah 3:2, 4

On April 18, 1942, a mere six months after Pearl Harbor, eighty men took flight from the U.S.S. *Hornet* on a perilous volunteer mission to bomb Japan. The Doolittle Raid was a brilliant military success. But it left fifteen B-25 crews stranded in enemy-occupied China. This novel is dedicated to those eighty Doolittle Raiders, and to the estimated 250,000 Chinese people who lost their lives in retribution for aiding them.

It's my fond hope this book will honor the Greatest Generation. I'll deem it a success if it captures an inkling of the heroism and spirit of sacrifice that earned those men and women the title.

And most of all, I'd like to dedicate this novel to the crews of Doolittle Raid Plane Number Six, *Green Hornet*, and Plane Number Sixteen, *Bat Out of Hell*, whose experiences inspired this work of fiction.

Reader Bonuses

For exclusive bonuses to enhance your experience reading this novel, please visit this special page on my website: www.lthompsonbooks.com/plum-blooms-bonuses/

I'd Love to Hear from You

As an author, I place tremendous value on your feedback! If you enjoy this novel, please consider leaving a review. Reviews weigh heavily with readers when shopping for books. If you leave one you could help another reader experience the power of this story. If you're willing, you can leave a review on Amazon Kindle version by simply swiping left from the last page of an Amazon Kindle book. The bonus page I mentioned above (www.lthompsonbooks.com/plum-blooms-bonuses/) provides easy links to leave reviews in other venues.

Acknowledgments

I'm so grateful my husband, Michael, introduced me to the moving true story that inspired this novel. From the moment he pointed it out to me in a history book, the story has held me enthralled.

I'm deeply thankful to my parents for teaching me to love books. And even more to Michael for continually teaching me new ways to love God. He and my kids have put up with a lot of divided attention as I stole away to write, but they've always supported and encouraged me.

It turns out it takes a whole village to write a novel. I'd never have gotten anywhere with this writing adventure if not for my teacher and mentor, Les Edgerton. Les is leaving a tremendous legacy in the writing community. I'm grateful to my ever-upbeat and highly effective agent, Sarah Joy Freese of WordServe Literary. I'm deeply thankful to Miralee Ferrell, Nikki Wright, and the stellar team at Mountain Brook Ink for taking a chance on me.

I'd like to convey a special thanks to John Walker, Lieutenant Robert Meder's nephew, who has been very gracious with his encouragement and support.

Many others had a big hand in shaping this story. I can't look at a single page without being reminded of a piece of incisive feedback I got from one of you! Diana Beebe, Beth Jusino, and Jenny Mertes, who worked with me as professional editors; Cheryl Hodde, writing as Hannah Alexander, for so much wonderful feedback and encouragement; Kristen Johnson who did an indepth proofread, Maegan Beaumont, Mary Edelson, Katharina Klamt, Holly Love, Janey Mack, Gerald O'Connor and Todd Monahan, who gave me honest feedback and some much-needed pep talks along the way. Wouldn't be here without you! And boundless gratitude to a Japanese reviewer who preferred to remain anonymous. Many of you already have novels on the shelves, and for those who don't, I'm confident I'll see you at your own book signings soon.

I've also been blessed with friends and business colleagues who inspire and support me. Virginia Walker has been a key mentor in business and in life. Koichi Narasaki was the person who originally suggested the character of Miyako to me. Love and thanks go to Myron Wick, Eddie Head, and Brad Bennett. And to Carla, Kimberly, Liz, Terry, and my team of prayer warriors for much-needed "air cover"—you know who you are!

With Love and Gratitude,
Linda

Author Note

While this book is a work of fiction, the bones of the story are true. On April 18, 1942, a mere six months after the attack on Pearl Harbor, sixteen of the Army's medium-weight B-25 bombers left the deck of the carrier U.S.S. *Hornet*—a feat never attempted before or since. They deployed their payloads on Tokyo and other key targets on the Japanese main island. The bombers were too heavy to land on the carrier, so the operational plan called for them to fly on to landing strips in Free China.

While the Doolittle Raid was a brilliant military success, due to a communication breakdown, not one of the planes found its landing strip. The sortie left fifteen B-25 crews—seventy-two of the eighty airmen—stranded in enemy-occupied territory in eastern China. This novel follows the story of two of those crews. While the *Pensacola Payback* is a fictional plane with a fictional crew, the *Green Hornet*'s crew has stepped onto these pages from history.

Dave Delham is an invention, but his spiritual journey was inspired by that of a real (but very different) man—Jacob DeShazer, the bombardier on *Bat Out of Hell*. I have profound respect for Jacob DeShazer and his legacy. While Dave's story follows Jacob's in some important respects, I would like readers to be very clear that my fictional character is not intended as a representation of Jacob DeShazer, or any other person.

I'd also like to issue an important disclaimer around some of the verbiage used in the story. Denigrating slang terms, such as "Jap" (and worse), are included to authentically represent the perspective of the characters toward their military opponents at that point in history. In no way do they represent my perspective, nor do I personally agree with the use of such unkind language. But presenting readers with an authentic journey demands certain liberties.

Finally, if you feel mystified by the use of Japanese honorifics such as -san and -chan, please know you are not alone! Here's a brief introduction. The use of -san after a name is a respectful title, somewhat equivalent to Mr., Mrs., or Ms. in English. The Japanese use -san for both genders, and since Japanese society at that time was structured and formal, -san would be employed in most interactions. In a more intimate friendship with someone who would be considered your equal or perhaps lower on the social scale, less formal honorifics (-chan for women or -kun for men) come into play.

With that, let the story roll!

Chapter One

Saturday 18 April 1942
Osaka, Japan

ALTIMETER STEADY AT FIVE HUNDRED FEET, USAAC *Pensacola Payback* screamed along at two-hundred-seventy miles per hour, right above the steep-pitched roofs of Osaka, Japan. Lieutenant David Delham forced himself to take even breaths and focus on his instrument scan.

Attitude-indicator needles vibrating at level. Twin seventeen-hundred-horsepower engines thundering on her wings.

Straight and level. Straight and level.

His bombs-deployed indicator blinked red. The bomber bucked like a mustang as the third five-hundred pounder dropped.

"Bomb's away." Smith, his bombardier, bellowed confirmation over the interphone.

Dave tightened his grip and yelled into his headset. "Fine work, Smith. Deploy the last incendiary."

"Yes, *sir.*" The fourth indicator glowed red. "Last bomb's away."

At his elbow, his copilot, Watt, let out a piercing whistle that mimicked the shriek of the bomb plummeting toward its target. "Special delivery, Japan."

Dave gave a grim chuckle. He pushed the B-25 into a steep bank and peered over his left shoulder.

Smith blared his elation through the interphone. "Two direct hits!" Flames erupted across the aircraft factory's blue-gray roof.

Four bombs. Two targets smoldering. Three minutes, tops.

The crew broke into wild whoops and yells. Watt strained against his five-point harness and pummeled a fist into the air. "Take that, Jap scum! Now *there's* some payback for Pearl."

Dave hollered along with the rest. "Right on the money, men. We did it!" He, Dave Delham, and his crew had *done* it.

What every American worth his hot dogs and beans had burned to do every day of the four-and-half months since that underhanded attack on Pearl.

Not bad for our first combat mission. Not bad at all.

The bombing run had gone precisely according to the plan their commanding officer, aviation legend Colonel Jimmy Doolittle, had laid out. Next, Dave just had to get them out of heavily guarded enemy airspace and on the ground in one piece.

At that instant, he knew he could do anything.

Vitiollo, in the navigator's pit behind him, shouted over the din of howling engines, shrieking wind and rattling gas cans. "Whoo-hoo! This bird has earned her name."

Dave grinned and patted the dashboard. "Yes, she has."

Pensacola Payback. He'd coined the name, but every member of his four-man crew had shown he was dead set on delivering on it.

Fourteen total hours in flight, according to the mission's operational plan. They'd turned those B-25s into flying gas cans so they'd have the range. Too bad fate had handed them a big wild card that morning when an enemy patrol forced them to launch the attack farther out than planned—by a couple hundred miles.

And two-hundred-fifty gallons of precious fuel.

But fuel concerns would have to wait. A string of distinctive black puffs of smoke bloomed right below them, a few yards ahead and to their right.

His co-pilot's voice went shrill. "Ack-ack. One o'clock. Look sharp."

"I see it." Dave pulled the yoke back. The plane pitched up.

A shell burst in front of the nosecone. The bomber jumped, jostling him in his seat. Smoke whizzed along *Payback's* snout and past the elevated cockpit, pushing an acrid odor into his nostrils.

Watt swore. "Too close. They have our altitude."

Dave gripped the yoke tighter, tension rippling through his jaw line down to his fists. Those innocent little puffs were more than capable of tearing off a wing or punching a hole in a fuselage.

"Evasive maneuvers, Delham," Watt barked.

Guess you think you'd do it better. Watt's attitude problem could also wait. Dave spun the yoke, and they snaked left. He threw the switch on the interphone. "Smith, we're fresh out of bombs. Man your gun."

"Already on it, sir."

Watt peered through the windshield. "We're so dang close to the ground. They could put up a wall of machine-gun fire and down us."

The interphone crackled to life again. "Pursuit," Braxton, the gunner, reported from his vantage point in the turret. "Eight o'clock, high."

"Greetings, dear guests. We've been expecting you." Dave twisted in his seat for a glimpse of the enemy, but he couldn't see them past the fuselage's metal roof. "Cussed gun turret better work, Watt."

His copilot grunted. Those turrets were cantankerous.

"Can you I.D. the aircraft, Braxton?" Dave had heard the Japanese Zeroes boasted a dive speed of four hundred miles per hour. Faster than *Payback* was going to make, especially this close to the floor. *Payback* had no room to trade altitude for speed, unlike the enemy planes above.

"Not sure, sir. They're way up there. I don't think they're Zeroes. They look kind of—uh-oh."

"Uh-oh, what?"

"Two broke formation."

"They coming for us?"

"They're diving."

Dave and Watt exchanged glances. "Straight on. Keep her speed up," Watt said.

"Second Lieutenant." Dave put the emphasis on the *Second.* "Shut up—for once."

Watt opened his mouth to say something, then snapped it closed.

A long, tense moment passed with no word from the back.

Braxton's voice sounded through the interphone. "They're gaining, sir." He cursed, his voice rising in pitch. "They're firing. I can see it."

Fly, Payback, fly! Nothing he could do in the cockpit but

set her weaving and listen to the empty fuel cans rattle.

And wait for the rat-a-tat of machine guns up their backside.

Land of the Gods. Land of the *samurai*. Matsuura Miyako's ancestors had been in the thick of it. Statesmen and generals. Masters of tea ceremony and of sword. *Daimyo* of entire provinces. She even shared her family name with a count.

Watanabe-*sensei*, Miyako's ninth-grade teacher, paced his classroom. "Time for this week's math quiz. Clean sheets of paper, students."

She placed her history book on the stack beneath her desk, running her fingertips along its textured spine. She'd never admit it to the girls shuffling books and papers around her—the tack that sticks out gets hammered, ah?—but when she touched that book, a sense of pride welled up in her. Like an invisible silk cord stretching to the heavens, it lifted her shoulders and straightened her spine.

Full of herself, her friends might say. But they'd say it with a certain deference. Secretly, didn't they all want what she felt when her fingertips brushed those pages? The prestige of a notable family. The sense of noble destiny that sang through her blood.

Of course, she wouldn't be asked to defend any castles like a *samurai*'s wife of old. Or shipped out to war with the Imperial Navy like her father and older brother, Akira-san. Instead of practice thrusts with a *naginata* pike, she spent Sunday afternoons learning to spear stakes of flowers into shallow vases.

Her job would be to make a home and to raise the next generation. Less prestigious—*far* less prestigious—but crucial. Great deeds were for the men. She was tempted sometimes to dwell on whether that was fair, but such thinking accomplished nothing except to put a bitter taste in her mouth.

Instead, she let her fingertips glide across the book once more and felt herself drawn into a steady current of Matsuura family destiny that had coursed along, unrelenting, for more than forty generations. It belonged to her like her blood and her breath.

The sunny Saturday morning was creeping along like a snail in a *koi* pond. She sighed and positioned the paper on her desk.

In the branches outside the window, a bush warbler guarded her snug nest. In the distance a hawk wheeled, mocking Miyako by painting majestic circles in the boundless azure sky.

An ear-splitting shriek shattered the air, jolting her in her seat. Her pencil clattered to the floor.

Air-raid drill—the second that week. Her best friend, Natsue, grabbed her wrist from across the aisle. "It's past 12:15," she whispered, eyes dancing with something more than simple joy at missing a quiz. "We're done for the week, yes?"

Watanabe-*sensei* glared at them. "Girls. Quickly."

She thrust her books into her satchel. The girls joined a mass of crisp white blouses and plaid skirts streaming from the building, along the sidewalk and into the subway station. The blare of sirens faded as they clattered down the cement stairway plunging into the station's bowels. The stale air buzzed with girls' voices.

Natsue huffed. "I don't know why we have to do these drills. We'll never see a *gaijin* warplane."

Miyako answered with breezy confidence. "Our glorious army has always protected us."

At home, she and Mama-san and her little brother Hiroshi had a ritual. Every night since Papa-san and Akira-san shipped out, they knelt around the big radio in its mahogany console and listened to the news. Hiro-chan would race his toy ships across the thick carved rug, and the subtle pinch of worry around Mama-san's mouth would ease as the announcer crowed out the latest victories.

Manila. Burma. The Solomons. Pearl Harbor. The message was clear. Japan was invincible, advancing to fulfill its Heaven-decreed destiny as the rightful overlord of Asia.

Natsue completed Miyako's thought. "Our glorious army protects us. *And* Heaven itself." She leaned toward her, her voice a teasing lilt. "I know something you don't."

"What?" Miyako knew that impish grin. Whatever this was, it was good.

She lowered her voice to a whisper. "It's about my brother."

Kenji-san. A pleasant little shiver chased up Miyako's spine. "Tell me, ah?" Her voice rang at her from the cement wall, shrill and piercing.

"Shh." Natsue smothered a giggle. "He's hoping to see you today."

"He is? You mean—"

"I mean he likes you."

She caught her breath. If Mama-san learned about this, she'd be scandalized. When Miyako was a few years older, her parents would arrange proper *omiai* visits for her to meet young men of the right social class. Appropriate husbands. The sons of old *samurai* families like her own.

Still, picturing Kenji-san's striking oval face and the way his strong shoulders filled out his school uniform made her pulse quicken. She'd never have her mother's delicate beauty, but if *Kenji* thought she was pretty, it would mean something.

"I can't today." She felt the air leak from her chest. "Mama-san wants me to pick up my little brother."

The sirens stopped. Watanabe-*sensei*'s voice boomed from behind them. "You're released for the weekend, class."

Natsue gave her an exaggerated pout. "You can't go five minutes out of the way, ah?"

Miyako sighed and shook her head. Didn't Mama-san wear her down like rain? According to her, one good rumor could kill a girl's *omiai.*

Natsue's eyes went hard with something that looked like real hurt. "I guess my brother's not good enough for you." She spun away and started up the stairs.

According to Mama-san, he wasn't. But her friend's bruised feelings weighed on Miyako like a heavy coat. She hurried after Natsue, touched her arm and whispered, "*Hai.* I'll come."

Natsue gave her a blinding smile and led her out into the sunshine. They turned along one of Miyako's favorite streets. Narrow enough to stay shaded even in mid-summer. Lined with an impossible jumble of wooden two-story buildings—shops with their doors flung open and homes piled topsy-turvy against each other. The air hummed with shopkeepers' musical greetings. Restaurant owners in tidy cotton *kimono* bowed to them, and the savory scent of fried green onions hung on the air.

Three blocks in, the street bent around an old cherry tree. Natsue herded her into its dappled shade. "*He'll* come this way." She gave Miyako a conspiratorial smile.

Thinking about Kenji-san set her heart trilling, a nightingale in full chorus. Broad branches sprinkled with blossoms arched above the sidewalk. A soft breeze carried the subtly spiced aroma of sweet bean paste from the pastry shop on the corner. Petals drifted in the breeze and settled in clusters on the pavement.

Natsue sighed. "The blossoms always disappear too soon, ah?"

She heard it for the first time then. A soft drone in the distance. She shaded her eyes and looked hard at the horizon. Just a blot against the clouds. A plane coming in low, engine noise swelling as it closed the distance.

She watched it for a long moment. "Look. Two tails. I've never seen that."

Natsue waved at it and flashed her dimples. "Our brave pilots. Aren't they wonderful?"

The plane thrummed on toward them, its engines giving out a throaty rumble.

A burst of sound pounded her from every side, swallowing the plane's drone. A piercing whistle. A series of sharp cracks, like summer fireworks but a dozen times louder.

What under Heaven—

A deafening explosion. She felt the concussion in her ears. She pressed her palms over them.

Behind the plane, midnight-colored smoke spiraled from the roofline.

Realization slammed her so hard her world stood still.

The enemy. A *gaijin* dared to drop bombs on the Land of the Gods. Didn't he know every stone was sacred? She stood, transfixed, staring at the plane like it was a dragon coiling and arcing through the sky.

Boom. A new sound eclipsed the rest, reverberating through her chest.

Shrieks and yells from all sides. The crowd thronging the sidewalk scattered in a dozen directions.

Boom. Boom. It took up a bone-jarring rhythm. The Imperial Army was firing on the *gaijin* plane.

The smell of super-heated oil poisoned the air.

Burning. My brother. She picked up her satchel and tugged at Natsue's arm. "Hiro-chan!"

Natsue nodded, eyes wide, but she didn't move.

"Come on!" Miyako tugged harder. Natsue didn't respond. Miyako seized her friend by the shoulders and twisted her away from the plane. "You can't stay here. Come with me."

Natsue moved at last.

The girls pushed through the frantic throng. The throbbing *taiko*-drum boom of the Army's big guns hammered on behind them.

What if I'm too late? Miyako dashed down two long city blocks, pain pressing on her ribs. The satchel banged against her hip, but she felt grateful for that. She clung to the hope that the silk-covered amulet she'd knotted around its strap would ward off modern bombs as well as ancient forms of evil.

She spotted him through the group of jostling shoulders and breathed a thank-you to the amulet. Most of his third-grade class was gone, but his teacher herded a half-dozen children back toward their air-raid shelter.

Natsue hurried along beside her, gasping for breath.

The plane roared overhead. Miyako saw the red circle under its wing—and five white points around the circle. The circle was Japan's. The white five-pointed star was *not*. That insignia wasn't theirs.

Just a few hundred feet away, off to her left, the bomber's belly split open. An object tumbled out, dark against the sky, and dropped between the rooftops. The whistling noise hurt her ears. A woman at her elbow screamed. Sharp cracking sounds echoed along the street, piercing through her like rifle shots.

An acrid chemical odor assaulted her nostrils. Behind a tall fence across the street, tongues of flame began to taste the sky. *The aircraft factory.* If that caught fire, the whole neighborhood could bloom into flame.

Fear sent icy tentacles into her heart. She gave it no room. Nothing could matter but reaching her little brother. "Hiro-chan!" She dashed toward him. He swiveled. She couldn't make out his voice above the din of frantic shouts and booming artillery, but his lips formed her name. He raced toward her, eyes and mouth wide. His crisp sailor collar flapped against his shoulders. His fringe of dark bangs bounced on his forehead.

A fresh explosion rocked the factory complex. A roar like the island splitting pummeled her ears. The ground lurched and a force as strong as the divine wind of legend flung her to the pavement.

Her consciousness drifted, separate from light and time.

An hour might have passed—or mere seconds—before the smell of hot oil and concrete intruded on her senses. She forced her eyes open and pushed her impossibly heavy self off the pavement.

Burning oil and debris strewed the street. Charred wood smoldered where the aircraft factory's fence had stood. Cement dust floated in the air, coating her nostrils and leaving a layer of flat-tasting grit in her mouth.

Hiro-chan? She stared around through the dull gray haze, panic making her breath come fast.

Navy-colored fabric. A square of it, just visible beneath a pile of rubble. A length of heavy-looking metal girder twisted across the pile.

"No!" She ignored her own pain and rushed over. Knelt beside him. She pulled at pieces of fencing, clawed at chunks of tile. Found his cheek, then worked until she got his mouth and nose clear.

Fine gray dust caked his face and coated his lashes. His skin beneath it looked as pale as a *gaijin.* He coughed. "Sister..." His eyes focused on her for an instant before they fixed on something behind her. "Mama...Ma..." His mouth went slack around the word.

"No, Hiro-chan." She wedged her arms under his

shoulders. Concrete ground at her hands, sharp edges gouging her knuckles. "Don't. No!"

He convulsed and fought for one more breath. It choked off in his throat.

She shook him. "Hiro-chan!" No response. She probed at his neck, pressing for a pulse but finding nothing. Her fingertips trailed rust-red blood through the colorless dust on his skin. His blood. Her fingers wet with it. She jerked her hand away. His face had gone vacant.

She felt her heart tear from her chest. A dark rage flooded the aching void it left.

Who'd let the *gaijin* enemy through to lob bombs at Japanese children? Where were the *kami-sama* and the heroes who were supposed to protect their land?

A new anguish leaked in. Wasn't the blame hers? If she'd been where she was supposed to be, they'd have been blocks away from the explosion. If she'd lingered even a minute less beneath that cherry tree, at least she could have scooped him up and shielded him with her own body.

Hiro-chan had paid for *her* disobedience. And what a price.

How could he be gone? That little dark head she'd seen every weekday afternoon, bent with Mama-san's over his schoolwork. His eyes that danced when they followed his kites' maneuvers in the sky. His sturdy practice thrusts with the wooden sword in the bedroom hall. All the sparkle and the promise of him.

Something precious beyond worlds, lost. It could never be recovered. And she was to blame.

Oh, she could never face Mama-san. How would she live with her shame?

Natsue and a few others helped her pry him from the rubble. She gathered her little brother to her chest, rocked him, pressed her cheek against his blood-streaked face.

No. Oh, no.

Dave heard Braxton's voice over *Payback*'s interphone. "Bogies dropping back, sir. Whoo-hoo!"

Watt's face split in a broad grin. "They couldn't keep up

once they leveled out. *Payback's* too fast for 'em. Thank you, Jesus."

That was one thing Dave could amen. He nosed the B-25 right. They skimmed along a shallow valley, crossed a broad bay, and it was all open sea.

He nudged *Payback* into a slow bank a few-hundred feet above the waves, then leveled her out, making certain a narrow blue-green band of Japanese coast stayed visible on the right.

He took a deep breath and thumbed the switch for the interphone. "Well, men, we did our country a big service today. We can all be proud. Shoved it straight in the Japs' teeth and got away clean. But don't let your guard down. The enemy could come swarming off that coast at any time."

His crew acknowledged his order. Watt spoke up beside him. "My turn on the yoke?"

"Why not?" Dave shrugged, trying to release the tension from his shoulders. They were only four hours into the fourteen-hour mission, and his upper torso was one big knot. "Times like this, a fellow really wants a stiff one."

Watt responded with a mirthless chuckle. "You might want it worse later. Not real sure how this is going to play out."

Dave glanced at the fuel gauge. The auxiliary tanks were gone. Watt had switched them over to the mains before they reached Osaka. And they'd burned through all the extra fuel they'd loaded in cans.

He cursed to himself. If that Japanese trawler hadn't discovered them, forced them to launch the raid farther out than planned...

The whole operation had banked on surprise. The carrier U.S.S. *Hornet* stowed its own aircraft belowdecks, so it could carry a group of the Army's ground-based bombers topside. It took a Navy flotilla two-and-a-half weeks to convey their seventeen B-25s across the Pacific and park them a few hundred miles off the coast of Japan.

They'd trained for two months to master the specialized techniques that let them take off from *Hornet.* But once his bird left its nest on the carrier, there was no going back. The B-25s were too big to land on *Hornet.* So with *Payback's* bomb bay empty, it was a matter of avoiding any pursuers—and the antiaircraft artillery—and flying over the Japanese-occupied portion of eastern China. Then finding a landing strip farther inland, in free China.

Fuel was always a consideration. But thanks to that puny Japanese fishing boat it had become a crisis. He'd been doing mental arithmetic off and on all morning. Whether they had enough gas to make it to their landing strip now was anyone's guess.

Yep. I could use that drink.

Doc White had stowed five pint bottles of Navy-issue rye in Vitiollo's nav compartment. One for each of them. "For medicinal purposes," he said. Well, Dave could use a slug of "medicine" now. Get past the taste, and it'd warm the hatch going down and take a little edge off the tension. Too bad it was against the regs.

Vitiollo came up and leaned between their seats. "That was some day's work, eh?"

"Sure was. Once we get Japan behind us, we can relax a little." A shame they couldn't crack out one of those pint bottles. It'd be fitting to toast those five thousand good American lads lying on the bottom of Pearl Harbor. Heck, they'd done the whole *world* a favor today.

He licked his lips. "How many hours 'til we reach our welcome party in Free China?"

"About nine flight hours, sir. With a bit of luck and a tailwind, that should get us clear of the Jap-occupied zone."

Jap-occupied zone. It could be real trouble if they didn't get clear of the Japanese Army. He glanced again at the fuel gauge. *This could be close. Real close.*

Chapter Two

Thursday, December 23, 1948, six years later
Osaka, Japan

SEVENTY YEN RICHER. AND A BAG of black-market groceries weighing down one arm. Miyako had the handles looped twice around her wrist. One could never be too safe from the thieves, ah? That bag made it her best night in a week, and she was going to make sure it came home with her, in spite of the desperate hucksters that infested Osaka's streets.

Best night. Of course tonight was only *best* by comparison to nights like the one before. Men—airmen and Marines—had streamed by the streetcorner where she stood all evening. Appraising what they could see of her and jeering at what they couldn't. She dragged herself home at the end, feet burning like each step fell on embers. Legs that ached from ankle to thigh.

Aching feet and a wet coat. That was all she brought home last night, after working the street for hours.

Tonight was a *best night* because men wanted her. Wanted to slip her cash to do things she had to work hard not to think about later. But the math was simple. Two full hours of those things and she could feed Papa-san and herself and put something aside for the rent and for Papa-san's doctor.

Best night meant yen in her purse, the reek of sweat and whiskey and aftershave in her nostrils, and the grime of their bodies ground into her pores. Which she endured for what? For the contents of the bag that had worn a groove in her forearm. Two small sacks of rice, a pair of sweet potatoes, and packets of dried seaweed and fermented beans.

It was no feast, ah? But it beat going hungry. She smiled a little, picturing how Papa-san's face would brighten when he saw the meal.

A blast of soggy wind battered her from around a corner. She lit a cigarette and huddled into her coat, appreciating more than its warmth. It was a blissful feeling to no longer have her body on display.

She hugged the bag against her chest to keep it as secure as she could and turned into a side street. Or what had been a street, before the *gaijin* bombs. Now it was a strip of cracked pavement lined with crude shacks assembled from anything people had salvaged. It smelled of open fires and rotting garbage.

She passed a hut with a length of canvas stretched across its bare window. Flickering light from inside revealed oil stains and a frayed edge. It was the right faded mustard color for a piece of old uniform.

"Hey, lady. Shine your shoes?" The voice piped from the evening shadows in the alley right past the hut.

"No, thank you." She tensed and hugged her bag tighter.

He stood from the crate he'd been sitting on. He looked about nine years old. His face caught the light and her chest constricted. The way his smooth bangs reflected the glare from the streetlamp behind her. The shape of his chin. If it weren't for the dirt smudged across one cheek and the cigarette dangling from his fingers, the kid could be Hiro-chan.

Something inside her crumbled. She took a deep breath and stopped walking. "You should go home."

"Home." He laughed, took a pull on his cigarette, and studied her. His eyes lingered on her bag.

She dropped her cigarette, clutched the bag and braced herself for him to lunge.

Move on. Move away. She knew she should, but she couldn't take her eyes off his face.

"Leave her alone, Jiro." Another voice, not as shrill, from a few feet farther back in the alley. "She sees what you're up to." She could barely make out the boy this voice belonged to. He was taller than Jiro, but far from full grown.

Jiro gave her a lopsided grin. He picked up the cigarette she'd discarded and wandered off into the shadows. She stared after him for a long moment, the familiar hollow feeling worming its way from the pit of her stomach toward her chest. *Hiro-chan. If only...*

Her memories of Hiro-chan were wearing as thin as that army-canvas curtain. She could no longer hear the echo of his voice clearly. But she could see his bright eyes above the top edge of his favorite phoenix kite. Feel the smooth warmth of his little hand in hers. See the silent agony on Mama-san's face that day, when she came home and choked out the news.

Her late mother's voice breathed from some hidden corner of her mind, soft but insistent as the breeze. *If only what, Miyako-chan?*

Kataki-uchi. Ritual revenge. Since her older brother Akira-san's glorious death in battle, the duty—the *honor*—of avenging Hiro-chan's murder fell to her. A sacred obligation. But how to fulfill it, ah? Several years had passed. So much had been sacrificed. Yet she'd done nothing.

Her helplessness gnawed at her. There were *gaijin* occupiers everywhere. She had a *gaijin* airman as a regular. But you couldn't kill just anyone. *Kataki-uchi* was personal. She had to target the *gaijin* criminal who dropped that bomb—the man the emperor himself had named as a war criminal for his role in that raid. Or the man who ordered it.

She spoke it out loud to her little brother's *hotoke.* "If only I could make it up to you, Hiro-chan."

And then, join you.

Miyako rounded the smoke-blackened corner of Namba Station. About twenty people stood on the platform, queued for the train. Streetlights cast cold shadows down their faces, bringing hollow cheeks and sunken eyes into harsh relief.

Several beggars huddled in the station doorway. An older man with grime-streaked cheeks lay curled in a corner, eyes closed tight as if to ward off the streetlights' glare. He pulled what was left of his navy uniform around him—a captain, about Papa-san's age.

No one left to care for that one.

A deep melancholy washed through her, making it hard to swallow. Out of all their family, she was the only one left to take care of Papa-san.

She studied the beggar and fingered her purse. *Maybe a coin or two.* Then she thought of Papa-san's doctor bills and swore. She needed every *sen.*

A rogue gust of wind pushed an icy blast into her face.

She turned up her collar, choked back her grief, and found something else to look at.

A *gaijin* in a sturdy greatcoat caught her eye. He worked his way along the queue from the far end of the platform, handing out some kind of brochure. He reached Miyako, gave her a little bow—patches of ruddy scalp showing between sparse wisps of straw-colored hair—and held out a copy. "I hope you'll join us, young lady. It's going to be a very special presentation."

She accepted the flier and returned the bow. Courtesy demanded that much.

As she straightened, she caught another glimpse of the Navy captain in the station doorway. The old officer stirred then huddled into his ragged uniform. Five years earlier, his slightest command would have meant life or death for dozens of men. Now he shivered on the pavement among drifts of dead leaves.

She eyed the nubby thick wool on the *gaijin's* collar as the Nankai Line train rumbled into view.

"A week from Sunday." The *gaijin* hurried away.

She shifted her shoulders inside her own second-hand coat with its mended lining. She had no interest in the man with his sturdy wool and his special speaker and his propaganda. Or any further reminders of who'd won the war and who had merely survived it, ground into the pavement by humiliation and defeat.

She jabbed the brochure into the top of her bag, where it would stay out of sight until she found a trash can to hurl it in. But as it folded into the mouth of the bag, the title flashed up at her. A single word in stark white *kanji* characters against a sailor-blue background.

Horyo.

Prisoner. The most humiliating capitulation of all.

She studied the photo beneath it. A *gaijin* soldier, crisp cap at a jaunty angle, looking hale and cheerful and quite pleased with himself. His penetrating eyes arrested her.

This man, *horyo*? The incongruity jarred her. She flipped the brochure open.

I suffered in Japanese prisons for forty months. When I

piloted Plane Seventeen in General Jimmy Doolittle's raid over Japan on April 18, 1942...

She sucked in her breath. Doolittle's raid. April 18, 1942. The raid that killed both her brothers. Her eyes flew down the columns.

...our mission over Osaka...

Osaka. Only one bomber had violated Osaka's skies that day.

Her pulse throbbed against her eardrums. She closed the brochure, fingers trembling so badly she nearly dropped it. She took a long, jagged breath and stared at the photo on the cover.

You. The gaijin *murderer with the bombs. It was you.*

She studied him, and her throat constricted. The outrage of it—the intruder daring to drop those first bombs on Japan. And the ache of it—Hiro-chan's little body buckled beneath a girder, his lifeblood leaking crimson through her fingers.

Her gut twisting, she turned the flier over. The back bore a stamp heralding an appearance by this *gaijin* in Osaka in a little over a week.

The fellow behind her made a "harrumph" sound, and she looked up. The train was at the platform. She hadn't heard it. Passengers mounted the steps, everything going on as if the clock hadn't stopped ticking and the ground hadn't just shifted.

She climbed onto the train. Sank into a bench seat, clinging to the brochure like a piece of fine silk. Sat perfectly still, looking ahead.

Images played through her mind. Precious Hiro-chan, with his fresh-scrubbed face, murdered on the street outside his school. Akira-san, always Papa-san's pride, lost with his ship during the same raid. And Mama-san. She couldn't bring herself to summon a picture of Mama-san. But even a fleeting image of her bore a swish of silk and a whiff of peony.

It was clear enough what she was expected to do. Otherwise, what did it mean, the promise she'd made to Hiro-chan so many times? She was hardly equipped to be an assassin. But she knew her duty. She knew how to honor her dead, and she had the courage to do it.

But how? And what would become of Papa-san—and her own miserable life—afterward?

If she was determined enough, destiny would provide a path. As to the how, Papa-san would have some ideas. He had to.

She tried wrapping her tongue around the *gaijin*'s name. "Delham. Sergeant David Delham."

Six-and-a-half years she'd waited for this—for access to one of the men who had a direct hand in her brothers' deaths. Six-and-a-half years, and this bomb-wielding Delham thought he could come back to Osaka.

Six-and-a-half years, and she'd not had a single chance. Until now.

Chapter Three

Saturday 18 April 1942
Zhejiang Province, China

ABOUT HALFWAY ACROSS THE CHINA SEA, dingy gray clouds began to infiltrate the dazzling spring sky. The weather continued to close in. By evening, when *Payback* reached the Chinese coast, they soared through a blanket of fog. Gusts knocked them around and hurled rain into the windshield.

"Thank God for the tailwind," Watt said. "But this overcast..."

Dave shook his head. "If there's a coastline there, I can't see a glimmer of it. Which means—"

"Which means no way to confirm Vitty's dead reckoning." Watt took a meaningful glance at the fuel gauge.

Dave tried to look at something—anything—else. They were going to have to put their bird down soon. Where was that landing strip?

This wasn't the way his first combat mission was supposed to end.

He craned his neck for a better view. There was nothing beyond the plane's Plexiglas snout but velvety blackness. Either the clouds were dense enough to completely obscure the ground or there was still nothing there.

"C'mon." He yanked his headphone off his right ear and yelled over his shoulder, "Vitiollo, where's Choo Chow Lishui? Where's our airstrip?"

The navigator left his instruments and his tiny steel table littered with charts, compass, slide rule, and battered pencil stubs. He leaned between Dave and Watt. "We should be on top of it now." He raked a hand through hair as unruly as his work surface. "I triple-checked. My math's right. I know it is."

Dave scanned Vitty's face. "Nothing on the radio?"

"Not a thing."

"No homing beacon?"

"No, sir." Vitty turned to Watt. "How much longer can we stay up, sir?"

Dave cleared his throat. "We're not on zero yet, Vitty. Try

the distress signal."

"Yes, sir." The man's thick Jersey accent carried a sharp edge. He returned to his station and threw a switch on the squawk box. "Mayday. Mayday."

Watt's normally relaxed features looked drawn in the instrument panel's ghastly green glow. He spoke into Dave's ear. "The way we're burning fuel, we've got less than an hour." He tapped the main fuel-level indicator. The phosphorescent needle jumped, then settled again just above the 100 mark. "You gotta find us a place to land. Or we'll have to bail."

"Tell me something I don't know."

He had to keep a clear head, in spite of the fear that was getting a chokehold on him. Jumping out of a perfectly good airplane in a raging storm wasn't something he was mentally prepared for. Especially this close to Japanese territory. Neither was leaving a $100,000 piece of advanced Army equipment to fly itself into the ground. This war was supposed to bring him home a hero, not make him a downed pilot on the run.

He yelled over his shoulder, "You're sure this is the spot, Vitty?"

"Sure as I can be, in this soup."

He glanced at the fuel gauge and swore. "This just keeps getting better. We'll circle the area for another ten minutes."

Watt gave him a grim nod.

Dave flew them in widening circles, but no lights broke the blackness below. No sign of the expected airstrip. He watched the final seconds tick away, then shot his assessment at Watt. "I can't see a thing through these clouds, and I don't know what went wrong, but clearly no one's looking for us. We can't spend any more fuel searching for Lishui. I'm moving to Plan B." He banked left. "We'd better hope this will shake us loose from this storm. Then we find a flat spot to land this bird."

Vitiollo was out of his headset and between them before Dave finished. "I still say you should bear south, sir. Give them Japs at Nanchang a wide berth."

Dave felt Watt's eyes on him, but they'd had this discussion. He saw no reason to revisit his decision. Watt was always a little too ready to play to the guys in the back. Hard to believe the man was still so resentful Dave had outscored him in flight school and beaten him out for the left seat. "Let me see that chart."

Vitty gave the chart a couple of deft folds and handed it to him. "We're about here." He trained his flashlight on the spot.

The chart confirmed what he already knew. "Look, if we head south, the coast angles toward us. We'll never get out of this weather pattern if we hug the coast."

Vitiollo inhaled sharply. "But if we go west we'll have to get halfway to Chungking, here, if we want to get clear of the Japs. No way we're gonna make that."

Why do I always have to spell things out—twice? Dave forced himself to adopt his most reasonable tone. "If I can't see to land the plane, we're not going to have to worry about any stinking Japs. And I still don't like the looks of the terrain to the south. Those peaks run right up to the coast."

Vitty's voice rose. "Look. If you keep on due west, you'll fly us right through their front door."

"Thank you for your opinion, Second Lieutenant." Dave turned to his instrument panel. "That's all."

Vitiollo stood behind them for a moment. He turned and moved to his station. Dave caught some mumbled swearing and heard the man's fist thud into the padded fuselage wall as he went.

"Watch yourself, Vitiollo." Watt kept an eye on the man until he resumed his maydays. He leaned toward Dave. "Vitty's right, Dave. I vote—"

"Vote? Since when is this a democracy?"

Watt's voice was forceful but even. "Better dead than captured. That's what we agreed at Eglin, if I may remind you. It's *all* our lives at stake here, Delham."

"You think I don't know that?" Their eyes locked for a moment. "Didn't you see? There's an open-looking patch to the west of where our prize navigator seems to think we are. I believe that's my best chance of getting us out of the sky in one piece, and that's where I'm taking us."

Watt glared. "Who named you Sky God?"

"The Army did. Except they call it 'commanding officer.'"

He firmed his grip on the yoke. "For the love of Pete, Watt, I wish we had better options. Like that airfield we can't seem to find."

None of the choices were good. But he felt in his gut that if he headed south like Vitty wanted, it would be the death warrant for *Payback*. If he headed west, with a little luck he could bring the plane down safely. That had to be their best chance of getting on to Chungking.

He scanned the instruments. "Wanna make yourself useful? You're a religious man. Ask that God of yours for a break in these clouds. And some flat terrain."

Watt shot him a glare. "That's your best idea today." He bowed his head, lips moving in prayer.

Dave snorted and continued his instrument scan.

Thursday, December 23, 1948
Osaka, Japan

The train rattled toward Miyako's station. She stared out the window. The occasional streetlight diffused pallid light over a landscape she saw everywhere now—block after block of shanties thrown up from the rubble. Makeshift slums invaded Osaka like cancer, thanks to this Delham and the thousands of enemy bombers who followed him.

The brochure gave those enemies a single face. Delham's face.

She left the train at Sakai Station and covered the eight blocks home at her briskest walk.

The building where she'd rented a room for the past few months had been a modest hotel before the war. Now it was home to a dozen families.

Most nights, she would climb the stairs softly, take off her shoes outside their door, and slip in, hoping to find Papa-san asleep. She preferred to slide into a simple old cotton *kimono* before she woke him. She relished the chance to get out of her street clothes. Get rid of the smell of the men. She hated carrying her clients' filth around their room. Hated it as much as anything that happened on those stained mattresses on the nights she trolled the streets.

Every time she came home, Papa-san seemed a bit more withered on his futon, like a piece of drying fruit that lost more moisture each day.

He took so little interest in things. Cut himself off from almost everything. Well, she needed him to take an interest in the brochure she carried in her bag. She needed his help with the plan. And besides, she'd like to see the old eager glint in his eyes about something.

Anything.

This would reach some part of him that was still himself, yes? He'd urge her on—she could hear his rasping voice already, reminding her of Confucius' ancient words: *"You mustn't sleep under the same sky as your enemy."*

But if she did it, what about afterward? If they caught her, what was Papa-san going to do? How could she risk leaving him to waste away alone, like the old beggar she'd seen at the station? A shudder ran through her at the memory of the man's grimy hand pulling his ragged captain's uniform around him.

Avenging Hiro-chan. Caring for Papa-san.

What kind of choice was that?

She let herself into the smoke-blackened foyer. Saxophone riffs and drunken laughter filtered through the walls from the nightclub behind their building. The jagged rhythm of the jazz echoed the confused ideas jolting through her mind.

His wretched coughing echoed down the staircase before she reached their narrow landing. Every cough ended with a horrible hacking sound she hadn't heard before. A resonance like bits of lung ripping from the bottom of his frail chest.

She charged along the hall and into their room, barely pausing long enough to kick off her shoes. She dropped the grocery bag just inside the door.

He lay on his futon, wheezing, his face flushed and his body contorted with the coughing. Tanaka-san, their neighbor, knelt on a cushion beside him, holding a damp cloth to his brow. She looked up at Miyako and bobbed her a bow, her kind, round face crinkling with concern. *"Konnichiwa.* He's had a bad day."

Papa-san fixed bleary eyes on her and croaked out her

pet name. "Mi-chan."

"I'm here." Miyako knelt by his futon, noticing again how his skin looked like rice paper. How she could see every vein in his hand. "Papa-san, you'll be so pleased. I got a special bonus at the office, and I brought us a treat. Rice and ingredients for proper *miso* soup. No nasty sweet potatoes tonight."

He grunted, then dissolved into another fit of coughing. He pressed a handkerchief to his mouth. Blood speckled the fabric.

She felt his forehead. More feverish than ever.

Che! Papa-san should be in the hospital. If only she could afford it. But since the Americans had discontinued his military pension and closed the veterans' hospitals...

She bowed twice to Tanaka-san. "*Arigato. Domo arigato.* I don't know what we'd do without you."

"It's nothing. I'm happy to look in when I can. I didn't like the sound of him today, so I stayed. I tried to give him his tea, but he wouldn't take it."

Miyako scowled at him. "No tea, Papa-san? How do you expect to get better, ah? You know Doctor Furuta's instructions. And the tea would warm you—it's so cold in here." If only she had an extra blanket. She slipped off her coat and bent to place it on him. Tucked the wool, soft with wear, around him, then stood and took a poker to the embers in the brazier.

She turned to find his eyes on her. Her nerves always jangled with anxiety when he looked at her that way. Had she fixed her smeared lipstick?

He could *not* know how she kept them in rent money. It would shame him to the core. Children had been disowned for less, and he might be stubborn enough to do it. After all the loss they'd suffered together, the thought of somehow going on without him was the most heartbreaking of all.

"I'm sorry it's so cold in here," Tanaka-san said. "I didn't have any coal I could spare, Mi-chan."

"Don't mention it. You've done so much." She rummaged in the grocery bag and pulled out a small sack of rice. "I brought you something too."

"From your special bonus, ah?"

Miyako supposed Tanaka-san couldn't help the wry tone in her voice, or the way her eyes lingered on Miyako's tight skirt and snug sweater. Not the attire of an office lady. Miyako's eyes sank to the floor. She often wondered whether the story she spun about her office job really fooled her sharp-eyed neighbor.

"Well." Tanaka-san's voice sounded strained. "We're very grateful. We go through our ration so quickly." Tanaka-san shifted on the cushion and gave Miyako a pointed stare. "Are you going back out tonight?"

Thursday. Her stomach twisted. She couldn't stand the idea of leaving Papa-san so sick, but her best client, George-san, had her booked on Thursday nights. She had no way to reach him, and with rent due in two days, she couldn't miss this date.

"I almost forgot. My turn on the graveyard shift." She dropped to her knees next to Papa-san. "I'm so sorry, Papa-san. You know I wouldn't leave you tonight if I didn't have to." She looked at Tanaka-san. "If you could..."

The lady's eyes narrowed, but she gave Miyako a grim nod. "*Hai.* I'll stop by after dinner."

"*Domo arigato,* Tanaka-san. Papa-san and I are deeply in your debt."

Tanaka-san sighed. "Happy to help where I can, of course. But I'd better get home to my own family now."

Miyako thanked her again and bowed her out of the room. She slid the door closed behind her and turned to Papa-san with a deep sigh. "So. How's your chest?"

"Not good. It hurts."

She pulled the handkerchief from his fingers and examined it. Splotches of greenish-grey phlegm joined streaks of blood. She pinned him with a stare. "You didn't tell me you've been coughing up that stuff again."

A reluctant nod. His simple cotton housecoat had slipped off his bony shoulder, revealing a purplish patch of mottled skin. "What's that on your shoulder? Did you hurt yourself?"

"What? No. Stop your infernal fussing." He clawed the housecoat back into place.

She studied him, biting at her lip. That frail hand with

its papery skin. She'd seen another like it earlier that evening. Dirt-encrusted knuckles clenching a worn captain's uniform.

What separated Papa-san from that beggar shivering on the pavement? She did. Nothing else. Leaving him for the night was hard enough. How could she risk being torn from him forever?

Her first obligation was to the living. Hiro-chan would understand that, yes?

A pair of spent incense sticks stood in a small glass holder on a shelf along the back wall—what passed now for their family altar. She looked at it and winced. She couldn't do it. Couldn't discuss the *gaijin* flyer with him. Couldn't ask for his direction when she already knew what he would say.

She whispered to the ancestors, "Please pardon me." Then, putting on the most cheerful face she could muster, she scooped up the bag of groceries. "I'll go start our soup. And make your tea. That will help." She collected her teakettle and the tin of dried herbs Dr. Furuta had prescribed and left for the kitchen downstairs.

She had the room to herself—a relief since she was in no mood for neighbor women with their judgments. Or their chatter about husbands and children while she made a scant meal for two.

She filled the teakettle from the stained sink and placed it on a burner. Measured the herbs into the pot: green tea, kudzu, hawthorn, turmeric. The herbal prescription wasn't cheap. Her belly cried and her feet ached, but she worked carefully so she wouldn't spill a speck.

The music across the alley cranked up again. It was louder here than in the foyer.

She raked and folded the rice until the water ran clear. Put the pot on the burner, took the spear of dried seaweed from its newspaper wrapping—

And stared. Delham's eyes met hers from the newsprint. The same photo as on the brochure. Destiny had put her brother's murderer in front of her *twice* within an hour. What were the odds?

This wasn't chance. This was a message.

A tremor started somewhere above her wrist and moved

through her fingers. Delham was coming within her reach, perhaps only this once. This was an opportunity to make her pathetic life count for something. To accomplish something noteworthy for the Matsuura name. An engraved invitation to greatness. Was she the kind of woman who'd turn it down?

The music segued to a new piece with a driving bass beat.

This thing had to be Papa-san's choice. She needed to put it to him. If he asked her to do it, she'd find a way to drive it forward, inexorable as the bass beat pulsing through the floor.

She carried the tea upstairs to their apartment. She poured it into a chipped cup, her hand so steady it surprised her. She stirred in a few drops of pungent oil to complete the prescription and brought the strong-scented cup to his lips.

He made a face, but he drank, fixing red-rimmed eyes on her over the cup. "*Arigato,* daughter. How was the factory today, ah?"

"It was fine. Orders are steady."

She turned from him and rummaged in the sack for the brochure. "I have something you need to hear, Papa-san. It's important."

He listened well, looking more and more agitated as she read the Doolittle flyer's words. "This *gaijin* bombed Osaka?"

"*Hai.*"

He lifted himself on a frail elbow. "So, the man who slaughtered my second son, ah?" A beat passed while he absorbed this. "He'll be here next week?"

"*Hai.*"

"This is it, Mi-chan. Our opportunity. The one we've burned incense for." He tried to push off the futon but collapsed again, coughing phlegm.

She found a clean handkerchief and dabbed at his mouth. "Papa-san, you must be careful."

He rested a long moment, eyelids screwed shut, breathing labored. When he looked at her, his eyes were moist. "I wish Akira-kun weren't..."

At rest? With the ancestors? This was the first time he'd expressed regret at his firstborn son's glorious death at sea— defending Japan during the raid that slaughtered his youngest. It was the first time he'd given voice to anything other than fierce pride that Akira-san's life ended so early. Ended in a way that would surely see his spirit enshrined among Japan's great heroes. She veiled her surprise. "Shh, Papa-san."

"So it's you and me, Mi-chan. We two"—he took a shallow breath—"must not pause..."

She finished the proverb for him. "...even to retrieve our weapons." She knew it well. Confucius' *Five Classics*, on the urgent duty to avenge a brother.

If Papa-san had breath to speak, she knew he'd go on from there. She'd hear again how even women could achieve lasting glory for their families and themselves. He'd remind her of Yamaji, the handmaid who avenged her noble mistress after the lady had been forced to commit *seppuku*. Or the farmer's daughters of Sendai, another famous pair.

He no longer had the energy. "I'd take this on for you, Mi-chan," he said in a rasping voice. "You're no warrior, ah? But look at me." A cough shook him.

She wedged an arm under his neck and lifted his head and shoulders. "Shh, Papa."

His shoulders heaved two or three times. A moment passed before he was able to speak. "It's all up to you, daughter."

"I know." She glanced at the family altar. The firestorms may have consumed the warlike old portraits that once graced it in their ornate silver frames. But she didn't need photos to sense the count and the general nodding their agreement.

Something in her started to go soft as plum paste. "But Papa-san, what about you? What happens when—"

He reached out to grasp her arm. "You won't have to worry about me much longer."

"Don't say that." She forced the words around the thick spot in her throat. "You're going to get better."

Neither of them believed it.

Miyako hated herself for doing it, but at 7:45, she gave Papa-san one last tuck and forced herself to get ready. She picked out fresh clothes—a snug skirt and a fetching beaded sweater—and headed for the bathroom shared by the apartments on the fourth floor.

She shimmied into the sweater, then pulled several bobby pins off the card. She clenched them between her teeth, took a lock of hair that framed her face, and twisted it around two fingers.

She caught her own gaze in the mirror. Were those the eyes of an assassin?

A week from Sunday, she'd know. If they weren't the eyes of an assassin, they'd be the eyes of a failure—and a fool. A weak woman who betrayed her ancient bloodline, allowing it to die out in shame.

But how to carry out the thing?

She let out a long breath. It did nothing to loosen the coils of tension twined around her chest.

She pinned the twisted hair along the crown of her head, doing her best to keep it a smooth roll. Papa-san's words circled through her mind. *We two can't pause to retrieve our weapons.*

"What weapons, Papa-san?" she whispered at the mirror.

The sisters of Sendai were Papa-san's favorite example. But those girls had formidable help. Their *samurai* master gave them secret lessons in swordplay. Somehow, Miyako had been too busy scrabbling for rent money to perfect her skills with a *katana*. Nor did they own one now—she'd sold Papa-san's heirloom weapon to pay Doctor Furuta.

She opened her box of face powder and patted it on, building up the layers.

How many days did she and Papa-san have to work out their plan? Seven to next Thursday, then three to Sunday night. Ten.

Finally, lipstick. A fashionable blood red. She scooped up her coat and gloves and started out.

Jiro. She was halfway down the stairs when it occurred to her she might encounter the boy in the alley again. The one who'd all but stopped her heart by reminding her so much of Hiro-chan. She turned and retraced her steps.

Papa-san snored gently on his futon. She studied him, at peace for once, then gazed around the tiny room. She'd laid out her futon next to his so it would be ready when she came home. There was barely space to walk around them.

That room contained all that was left to them. The firestorms had taken everything else.

Everything.

Still, it was better than any home Jiro had. Even if she did have to feed Papa-san sweet potatoes when she couldn't afford rice. As long as she could be there for him, it was home enough.

How much longer will that be?

She took a sharp breath, then pushed the question from her mind. She pulled one of the hated sweet potatoes from the grocery bag, wrapped it in a scrap of cotton, and slipped it in her coat pocket. For Jiro.

She reached the alley where she had met the boy and paused, searching the shadows for a glimpse of him. She even walked a few paces in. "Jiro?"

No one there. The desolation she'd been holding back broke over her like a storm surge. She'd missed six years of love and laughter since they'd put the ashes of Hiro-chan's broken body in the family grave.

She turned from the alley, blinking away tears.

Hiro-chan's spirit cried from the heavens for relief. Papa-san's would join him soon. This was worth any sacrifice she had to make.

Chapter Four

Saturday 18 April 1942
Jiangxi Province, China

FORTY MINUTES—AND ABOUT EIGHTY PRECIOUS gallons of fuel—after they missed Choo Chow Lishui, Dave's headphones crackled to life. Smith reported from the greenhouse nosecone. "There's a town down there, sir."

Vitty went at it again with the distress signal. "Mayday. Mayday."

A moment later Dave saw it too. A spray of lights peeping through the overcast in front of them. He looked over at his copilot. "This one better come with a landing strip. We're out of time."

He yelled over his shoulder, "Where are we, Vitty?"

"Somewhere near Nanchang, sir. Which means we're still over Jap-occupied territory." He gave the words "Jap-occupied territory" extra emphasis, as if he thought Dave might not catch the import.

Watt arched an eyebrow at him. "We need confirmation we've got friendlies down there. Unless you like the idea of Japs all over us in a Yankee minute."

Dave snorted. "Vitty doesn't know where we are. If he did, we'd have found Lishui."

"I reckon his guess is better than ours."

"I'm not so sure." He pushed his aircraft into a screaming bank. "I do not want to ditch *Payback*."

She was his first command. And from the day they gave him his pilot-in-command stamp, he knew he was born for that left seat. If he lost *Payback*, would they find him another plane? "She's been a trooper, and she still has plenty of fight in her."

They circled the town. The plane's angling made the spray of lights swing in the dark below them, but there was no runway. No sign of an airfield.

Vitty reported from behind him. "Still nothing, sir. Not a thing."

Watt leaned toward him. "We've got a few more minutes, Delham. Then we ditch, or *Payback* takes us right down with her."

There was no denying the man was right. "All right, Lieutenant. What do you say? Ten more minutes?" Watt's eyes wandered to the fuel gauge. "Five."

"Five, then."

Watt gave him a grim nod. His lips moved again in silent, but clearly earnest, prayer. Of course it made no difference. The storm kept them socked in, knocking them around the sky, with little visibility below. Dave descended as low as he dared, given the uncertainty of the terrain, but he couldn't get beneath the clouds.

Five minutes crawled past. And still somehow ended too soon, with nothing looking any different.

Watt fixed his eyes on him, resignation etched across his features. "That's it."

"I don't believe it."

"You giving that order or not?"

"Of all the rotten luck." At that moment, Dave liked that plane better than most people. At least *Payback* got her job done. Vitty had gotten them lost somewhere, and all Watt could do was take shots at *him*.

His frustration boiled over into a savage punch at the instrument panel. He took a second or two to collect himself, fresh blood oozing from his knuckle. He looked at Watt. "I'm ready."

It seemed Watt spoke as gently as he could, considering he had to shout. "You don't have any romantic notions about going down with the ship, do you?"

Dave didn't address that. "We need more altitude to bail." He pulled back on the yoke until the altimeter showed about three thousand feet, then leveled out and switched on the interphone. "Gentlemen. I never wanted to say this, and I'm sure you never wanted to hear it. But we've exhausted every option."

His next words took all his force of will. "We've gotta bail." *There. Done.* "Make for the hatch. All of you. Now." He tore off the headset and rummaged for his parachute.

Thursday, December 23, 1948
Osaka, Japan

Miyako was a few minutes late to meet George-san. She found him lounging across from the Hollywood Club, leaning casually against a wall, sand-colored hair glistening under the streetlamp. He stood taller than the crowd by a head.

She was halfway up the block before his eyes locked on her in the crowd. He broke into the unabashed grin only an American could muster and pushed his broad shoulders away from the wall. "There you are, Midori." He used her street name. "Now this party can start." He strode to her.

She bobbed him a bow and took a deep breath, steeling herself for what was sure to come next. *For the rent. For Papa-san. That's why I'm here.* Even though Papa-san would never accept it if he knew. "Hello, George-san. Very nice to see you."

He reached for her, the manly scent of his leather jacket mixing with the spicy aroma of his shaving soap. He pulled her into a bear hug and gave her a greedy kiss on the mouth, oblivious to the looks he drew from men and women around them. "Great to see you, doll. I checked us into that Orchid hotel on the next street."

"Checked us in, ah?" She stared at him, surprised. The Orchid wouldn't have impressed her in the old days, but it was several cuts above the Namba Jade, where he usually took her. And that place was nicer than the hotels her other *okyaku* used.

He flashed her that easy grin. "Don't drop your handbag, sweet pea." He cinched his arm around her waist and steered her around the corner and down the next street.

She ducked her head, feeling the weight of people's stares. His broad chest felt solid against her shoulder. It still seemed odd to her, walking next to him rather than following discreetly behind. She stole a glance at him. He was pleasant to look at, as *gaijin* went. But so big. So loud. His voice jarred her nerves. At least she no longer fought a primordial urge to flee. She had at first.

She knew girls who wouldn't take *gaijin*. She understood

how they felt, but it was hard for them. The *gaijin* had the money. Perhaps it was a little easier for her, since she'd studied their language in school. Papa-san had insisted on it. Of course, that didn't make her fluent. But a few clients, like George-san, seemed to enjoy teaching her to say things.

He ushered her up the elevator and into the room. A handsome brass chandelier dangled over the Western-style bed. He switched on the lamp on the nightstand, sat on the bed, and loosened his tie.

She took a deep breath and summoned the most vivid mental picture she could of Papa-san. The way he'd cared for her when she was small and helpless. This was for tea for Papa-san.

George-san's eyes lingered on her curves. "Hit that switch by the door, will you, honey?"

She did, turning the chandelier off. The lamp cast a softer glow on elegant mauve wallpaper.

She settled on the bed beside him and gave him her best attempt at an eager smile.

He pulled her against him for another kiss, then fished in his duffel. He produced a bottle of whiskey and a slim package. He held the package out to her. Tissue paper with an understated cherry-blossom design and a cream-colored satin ribbon.

A twinge of fear ran through her. The last time a *gaijin* had given her a handsome gift, it turned out to be an advance apology for some rough handling. "What's this?" She looked up into his ocean-colored eyes and let out her breath. This was George-san, after all.

A smile played at his lips. "Don't just sit there, silly. Open it."

The paper crinkled in her fingers. "So beautiful, George-san!" She tried to read his face. "So nice to me this evening, ah?"

He cocked an eyebrow and gave her a squeeze. "Open it."

She tugged at the bow and pulled the tissue away. She found herself holding a delicate pink negligee embroidered with chrysanthemums. She ran her fingers over the luxuriant silk. "George-san, I—"

"No need to say anything." He laughed, a rich one from

his belly. "You know how to thank me." He planted a hand on her thigh. His voice went husky. "Put it on for me, babe."

"Thank you! But why, George-san? Why the pretty gift?"

"I've made a decision, Midori." His hand traveled along her thigh. "I like being with you. But I'm not so keen on sharing you with every man in Osaka. And I'm sick of these lousy hotel beds." He squeezed her knee, sending a little thrill of excitement mixed with reluctance through her. "What if we, um...What if I got a place? You could take care of it for me."

Her heart did a stutter step. "Ah." Had she really understood? "I'll be your *onri wan*?"

"Yes." A grin crept across his mouth, making his white teeth flash and carving creases at the corners of his eyes. "You'll be my only one."

His words sunk in, took hold, set her spinning through the air with no more direction than a snowflake.

Why her? Why *now*? Why not a week ago, when she'd have been grateful for such an invitation? Steady money. A way off the street corners. And with a good man, a trustworthy man, even if he was a *gaijin*. She'd felt from the beginning he was different.

This was the best offer a girl like her was going to get.

But Delham's brochure changed everything. Now the thing with George-san was only to keep body moored to soul long enough to achieve *kataki-uchi*. Nothing else could matter. She couldn't let it matter.

She couldn't hold his gaze. "I'm very happy, George-san. But..."

His grin faded. "But what?"

"I have to think. Papa-san..." This would be harder to hide than her few hours on the street.

"Papa? But didn't you say..." He studied her for a long moment, something she couldn't read in his expression. He pulled his hand off her thigh and worked at his own shirt buttons. "Since it's such a tough decision, sure, think it over. You can have some time."

A hint of a break in his voice told her she'd hurt him. "George-san. Please—"

He avoided her eyes. "If it's not for you, I can live with

that. But I'm telling you, I don't want to keep going this way."

Fear of loss ripped at her. There were plenty of girls who'd push their sister to the pavement for this chance. She slipped her arms around him and buried her face in the crook of his neck. "I'll do it. You're my favorite. Of course I will. We just have to take care of some details."

Like how I keep Papa-san from ever having to know.

"There's my girl." He gave her a wolfish grin. "Now put on that nightie. We have something to celebrate."

Miyako woke at first light. She winced, willing the dull ache in her head to go away.

George-san's arm weighed on her, and she started to slip out from under it. He stirred, pulled her tight, and gave her a drowsy, whiskey-scented kiss. "Do you have to go, babe?"

"*Hai*, George-san. Papa-san—"

"He's sick. I know. Hey, why don't you find us a few rooms to look at next time I'm on leave?" He burrowed into the pillow, his words slurring. "If you need money for the train, my wallet's on the nightstand."

She studied him while she brushed out her hair, let her eyes trace the muscles on his bare arm and shoulder and his long, taut torso. *Not bad. Really, not bad.*

How would it be to share a place with him? She tried to picture herself arranging flowers at their kitchen sink while rice simmered on their stove, her pulse quickening at the crunch of his shoes outside the door.

She turned from him, a hint of acid in her mouth. In the Japan that once was, her parents would have considered her barely old enough to start the *omiai*, the formal introductions to acceptable suitors. Just old enough to put up her hair, don a lovely kimono with sprays of hand-painted flowers, and waft on the fragrance of jasmine into some captain's home to meet his son.

Instead she was here. Softening toward a *gaijin* who had the impudence to think he could buy her.

She waited until his snores took on a deeper resonance before she picked up his wallet. She counted out seven hundred-yen bills. More money than she'd seen in one place since much happier days.

The trouble was, he did have the means to buy her. And a couple more like her.

She thrust that thought from her mind. How much could she get away with taking? She studied him, relaxed and trusting in his sleep.

He did owe her for last night. She wadded three bills into her handbag and cleaned out about half his coins.

She slipped out of the room and made her way home through the soul-draining chill of a bleak December dawn.

When Miyako woke the second time, full daylight filtered through the rice-paper *shoji* that screened the window. She closed her eyes again and lay still, grateful that Papa-san had let her sleep so long. He slept fitfully most nights and woke early most mornings.

His breathing seemed more labored, with a new wheezing sound. She rolled over to study him. "Papa-san?"

He grunted. His eyelids fluttered. It took him a long moment to open his eyes.

She sat up. "Are you all right?"

"I'm fine. Quit clucking around like an overgrown hen, ah?"

A smile quirked her lips. "As you wish. I'll find us breakfast, then."

He grunted.

She'd set washed rice aside the night before, so it only took thirty minutes to put breakfast together. She set the tray on the floor and knelt next to him, ready to spoon the rice porridge into his mouth. As always, he waved her away.

"Papa-san, you should let me. You tire so easily."

"Nonsense."

She picked up her own bowl, pushed a spoonful of rice mush around, and set it down. She took a deep breath and plunged in. "You know how determined I am to honor Hiro-chan, yes? And you know I'll always do my duty, for you and Mama-san and our honored ancestors. But..."

He gave her a piercing look. "But what?"

"Papa-san, I'm not sure *how*. I'm no warrior, as you say.

The only weapon I've ever held is a bamboo stake—you know how they made us all drill with those at the...at the end. I don't think I'm prepared."

"You're my daughter, ah? You've Matsuura blood in your veins, ah? You will find the courage."

Courage. She stared at him, stunned, feeling the heat of blood rushing to her head. He thought she lacked courage? He had no idea what she braved daily, for him.

He let his head and shoulders sag onto the pillow and squeezed his eyes shut. "I don't doubt you." But his pained expression said something different. He took a shuddering breath and then another. "Kamura-san."

She bent closer to hear him.

"I got him...that job...instructing at the naval academy, ah? Go see him. Tell no one else." He drifted into mumbling about how Nippon wasn't what it once was and no one respected the old ways.

She lifted her chin and set her jaw. "*Hai*, Papa-san. Remind me, if you please. Which street is Kamura-san's restaurant on?"

Saturday 18 April 1942
Jiangxi Province, China

From the corner of his eye, Dave saw Watt peel his wife's photo off the instrument panel and tuck it in the breast pocket of his aviator jacket. Watt grabbed his parachute and climbed down into the navigator's pit.

Dave held the yoke steady with one hand and, with the other, clipped his floater to the harness around his chest. He glanced over his shoulder at his crew.

Vitty had abandoned his charts and instruments and strapped on his floater. Smith was behind him, strapping on his 'chute. Braxton emerged from the turret and grabbed his 'chute.

Watt squatted to pry up the hatch in the floor. Wind howled through the opening. Nav charts whipped around the cramped cabin like giant crazed moths. Dave pushed one off the windshield in front of him and took another look over his shoulder to check the men's progress.

Vitiollo went first. He pinned Dave with a dark glare for a full second. He mouthed something, then stepped into the hatch and vanished.

Smith was next, but he froze, staring into the howling hole in the floor. Watt shook the man's shoulder and barked something in his ear. No response.

Braxton shoved Smith in the small of the back, along with some choice words Dave couldn't make out. The bombardier dropped to a crouch at the edge of the hole, popped his legs through it and was gone, his wild yell barely audible above the roar of the engines and the shriek of the storm.

Braxton crouched, counted out three seconds, then followed him.

Dave and Watt were alone. Watt looked at him and gestured at the dark hole in the floor. "See you downstairs, Ace. Right?"

Dave forced his reply through a clenched jaw. "Right."

Watt came up behind him, clapped him on the shoulder, and yelled into his ear, "She's been a fine plane, but at the end of the day she's a hunk of metal."

Dave shrugged. "Shame to waste that rye. Give me a pint of it, would you?"

Watt sighed. He squeezed Dave's shoulder, closed his eyes and bowed his head. "Lord, please preserve us, and all our men, this day. Amen." Then he turned and dug around under Vitty's seat until he came up with two bottles. He handed them to Dave one at a time, pivoted, and stepped into the hatch like a fellow going off the high dive. And Dave had *Payback* to himself.

He shoved the bottles into the deep breast pockets inside his jacket.

Hunk of metal. No, she was his first command. And he'd failed her. She deserved better.

Maybe his crew did too.

He caressed the yoke. If this was Japanese territory, what was most likely to tip off the enemy they were there? The smoking hulk of the crashed plane, of course. The more distance he could put between the crash site and his crew the better.

Keep *Payback* in the air. He could do that a little longer. How long did it take the men to bail? Five minutes maybe? *Payback* would have traveled fifteen miles in that time. His men were scattered across half a Chinese province.

He had his orders in the event they went down. Collect the men and reunite with the squadron in Chungking. None of that would happen if the enemy found his crew first. He had to do whatever he could to prevent that.

He held the yoke steady and trimmed the controls for straight and level flight. Eyed his watch, tuned his ears to the sound of the engines and did his best not to think about one key fact. Every second he and *Payback* flew took him farther from Watt and the rest.

One minute. Three-and-a-half miles.

Two minutes. Seven miles. Sixty more seconds and it would be ten.

He swallowed past the constriction in his throat and gave the yoke a pat. "Sorry it had to end this way, old girl."

Thirty more seconds passed. Forty. At the forty-five-second mark, he trimmed her out once more then let go of the yoke. Sprang from the cockpit and made for the hatch.

He stopped short when he reached it. He saw why Smith had trouble. The hatch was barely wide enough for his shoulders. And with no one at the controls, the plane was jumping around like a kid playing hopscotch. He actually wished for an instant that he could share Watt's belief in a benevolent God.

He couldn't bring himself to step through like Watt had. He crouched at the hatch's edge, glad there was no one to see him.

He checked his floater one more time. Gave his pockets a quick pat to ensure their contents—bottles of rye and everything else—were as secure as he could make them. He took a deep breath, put his legs through the opening and dropped into the blackness.

The slipstream struck him like a wall. His cap whipped off as he hurtled into the night sky. He screamed a string of curses.

Right. Count to ten, idiot.

One. Sheer terror. He fought hard to bring it under control.

Two. Still spinning. *Payback*'s lights whirling in and out of view.

Three. He spread his limbs. Glanced up to see *Payback* steady above him, the hatch he'd left the size of a cigarette's lit end. Shrinking fast.

Four. Darkness swallowed *Payback*'s lights, leaving him surrounded by black. It was the loneliest thing he'd ever felt.

Five. Wind shrieked at him, pushed his cheeks back and sucked the tears from his eyes.

Six. What if the rag didn't work? He fought through his panic again.

Seven. Focus, breathe. Keep a steady count.

Eight. How long did it take to fall three thousand feet?

Nine. Good enough. He yanked the rip cord. The floater deployed, the shock of it a slug to the chest. The jolt flipped something out of his pocket. It struck his shoe before it plummeted from sight.

The howling wind calmed to a robust breeze. He drifted, caught his breath. He mopped his face. He was drenched. Cold sweat beneath his jacket, cold rain everywhere else.

The throaty bellow of *Payback*'s engines—his unfailing companion for more than fourteen hours—was gone, with all connection to anything he knew. The cords made a rhythmic swishing noise above him.

He stared past his feet but could make out nothing. He was in a cloud cocoon, with no sense of motion. But physics said the earth had to be rushing at him—fast. How hard would he land?

And what would he find on the ground? If Vitiollo was right, the odds they'd made it to free China were pretty long.

He wasn't a praying man, but it was almost a temptation.

The black clouds beneath him parted to reveal an even blacker rift. Small, but coming up fast. He barely had time to wonder what it was before he slammed into the ground.

With bone-splitting impact.

Chapter Five

Friday, December 24, 1948
Osaka, Japan

DISCRETION TOLD MIYAKO IT WOULD BE best to look for Kamura-san late in the evening, after the dinner crowd left. But she couldn't make herself wait that long. With men that age, who could tell? If his health was deteriorating like Papa-san's, he'd be home in bed long before she got there.

Delham would be in Osaka in nine days. She couldn't risk letting a whole day escape before she learned how Kamura-san would help her.

She walked into Usukitsu, Kamura-san's family restaurant, around three in the afternoon. The polished mahogany hostess desk stood empty. Only two patrons lingered in the dining room—a pair of ladies bent over china teacups near the front window.

A slender girl sat at a table in the back, folding a pile of napkins. The girl invited Miyako to take a seat. She disappeared through the curtains that graced the kitchen entrance. After what seemed like half an hour but was only five minutes by her watch, Papa-san's old friend, Kamura-san, appeared. His face creased in a smile. "Matsuura-san. I'm happy to see you."

She stood and gave him a deep bow. "I'm delighted to see you."

He bowed back. His hair had grayed a bit since she'd seen him last, and he looked less distinguished in a kitchen apron. But he still moved with subtle power, wiry muscles rippling beneath his sleeves.

"How is your father, ah?"

"Not so well. Is there somewhere quiet we can talk?"

He cocked an eyebrow. "Hmm. Not so easy in the middle of the day. Perhaps in the alley. You'll want your coat."

She slipped it on and followed him through the cramped kitchen and out the back door. Pungent odors of rotting seafood and cabbage mingled in the air. Thin December sunlight made it to a few second-story windows but didn't penetrate to the pavement where they stood. She shivered and buttoned her coat to the collar.

He closed the door behind them. "Please forgive me. But if you want privacy, I'm afraid this is the best I can offer. Now, how fares my old friend, Captain Matsuura?"

Her eyes dropped to the broken pavement. Some kind of liquid pooled in a rut, streaked with an iridescent grease rainbow. "He suffers so much with the pneumonia. The doctor told me, with penicillin..." She looked at him. "I can't get it. I've tried everything."

"Ah. This thing is difficult. Very difficult."

"I'm not asking you to take on that burden, Kamura-san. But Papa-san did send me with a request."

"What could be more important than medicine for a dying man?"

She lowered her voice. "The final wish of a dying man. His wish for honor."

"Honor." He spat onto the pavement. "As it goes for your father, so it goes for the nation. Who among us has any honor left?"

"I have a chance to restore his. Ours. But I need your help, Kamura-san."

"*You* do?" He gave her a sharp look. "I'm listening."

She told him about Delham and his appearance in Osaka. "This *gaijin* war criminal took Hiro-chan's life. Yet he's a free man now. Talking to crowds. Coming and going as he pleases. How can Papa-san bear his shame? How can I bear it?"

He sucked in his breath, then let it out slowly, studying her through narrowed eyes. "What do you propose to do?"

"What can I do? I'll kill him with my own hands or die trying."

He was quiet for a long moment, studying her face. "This is certainly what my old friend Matsuura Saburo would want," he ventured at last. "But is it what Matsuura Miyako wants?"

"*Hai.*"

"Are you certain?"

"As certain as the June rains." She stood straight as bamboo. "I want what Papa-san wants, of course. My name is Matsuura, yes?"

He sighed and gave her a grim nod. "So be it." He dropped into a formal bow. "It is my honor to provide the daughter of Matsuura Saburo with what little help I can."

She bowed, pulse quickening with a mixture of triumph and relief. Kamura-san would be a worthy ally. "*Domo arigato,* Kamura-san. You are a true and faithful friend to our family. There is a matter you can help with now."

"What?"

She swallowed hard. "I know when and where I can find Delham. Apart from that, I don't have"—she found this hard to admit out loud—"a plan."

"And no skills?"

Her voice dripped with irony. "No skills in *bushido,* no."

"How much time do we have?"

"Nine days."

"Nine days? Ah, I can teach you a trick or two, young woman, but *bushido* requires work and study. I can hardly make you a master in nine days." He bowed his head in what looked like pained thought. "He's a man, and a soldier. And they will have guards. How do we do this?"

"I must find a way. And if I die for it, I die well."

A beat passed before he looked up at her. "Poison. *Fugu.* You will purchase it in a concentrated form and apply it to the blade. A mere scratch will kill him."

"But is that honorable?" The unsavory story of Takahashi Oden, who'd poisoned her invalid husband, sprang to mind.

He frowned. "You want to risk prison and death for nothing? Your exalted ancestor Matsuura Takanobu didn't become a legendary *daimyo* by going into battle without a strategy to succeed, did he?"

"It's true." She bowed her deepest asking-a-favor bow. "You serve *fugu* here, don't you? Perhaps—"

"Could I find you some discards? That would be more difficult than you imagine."

By *more difficult,* she knew he meant *no.* She stared at him, waiting to see what rationale he could possibly offer.

He cocked his head toward the restaurant. "Come back in, child. I can show you a few things."

They stepped inside. They had the kitchen to themselves. Kamura-san gestured toward a glistening steel counter. "Only parts of the fish are poisonous. The skin, certain organs. Our master chef, Nogumi-san, removes them himself. Always with gloves, and always right here. You remember that poisoning incident with the beggar last August, yes?"

"*Hai.*"

"So, there are new requirements. Now Nogumi-san must discard the poisonous parts here." He gestured to a covered steel bucket under the counter. Soot caked its rim. "And he himself watches while we burn them each night." He lowered his voice to a murmur. "Now you see. Could I sneak out one night with a bit of skin or a liver for you? It would be, as I said, more difficult than you imagine. But difficulty isn't my only concern."

"What else, Kamura-san?"

"Two very real problems, child. First, understand that Nogumi-san is a specialist. Without his training, you're more likely to kill yourself handling the fish than someone else, ah? Second, each fish has a different concentration of poison. It would be very hard for you to prepare it in a way that would guarantee the *gaijin*'s death. So, Matsuura-san, if it's poison you want, I regret to tell you I see only one way." He fixed his eyes on hers. "You must go to the *yakuza*."

"The *yakuza*?" Her pulse mounted, and the familiar tight feeling gripped her ribcage. "Those goons have certainly never done me any favors. And I know I can't afford what they'll extort for it."

"No, it won't come cheaply. But, if you make the right connection, you can buy a prepared extract. Safer for you to handle and guaranteed to kill."

She couldn't say it, but every thread of her being shrank from the prospect of dealing with the gangs. "You're sure there's no other way?"

"I'm convinced this is the best way. And there is one more thing."

"What?"

"Think about this death, Matsuura-san. To remain conscious but unable to move. Unable to speak. To feel muscles lock, slowly until you stop breathing." He placed a hand on her shoulder. "You know some have been buried alive. They lay so still everyone believed them dead. This pilot deserves such a death?"

She pictured her father, gradually losing his own capacity to breathe. "*Hai*, Kamura-san."

"You feel this to your very core, ah? One must live without regrets."

"*Hai*. To my core."

Saturday 18 April 1942
Jiangxi Province, China

Moist earth pressed into the side of Dave's face. The odor of damp soil and rotten vegetation filled his nose.

Did he have to open his eyes? It was so much work. He'd rest just a moment longer.

Something cold and wet burst on his eyelid. He blinked a frigid drop of water away. A second raindrop spattered his cheek.

Awareness grew, and with it, pain. His head throbbed. His ears rang. His body ached in too many places to name.

Passed out. How long had he been here? Seconds? Hours? It was pitch dark.

Images flooded back. Flames licking tile roofs. Watt's face. Vitty's. Arguing over the charts. And then that crazy plunge into the storm.

A sense of wonder filled him. He was still in one piece.

But *Payback* was lost. His gut did a slow churn. His proud war bird, crumpled and smoldering in a hole somewhere miles away. And he was on his own, on a cold wet hillside who knew where.

He groaned and rolled onto his side. Legs, right arm responded. But when he tried to push up with his left arm, pain speared his shoulder. He cried out in surprise.

Something's very wrong there.

He rolled—carefully this time—onto his right side and probed the sore shoulder. It took only a slight touch to send white-hot daggers shooting along every nerve. He gritted his teeth and explored gently. There was an unmistakable bulge at the front of his shoulder. His arm hung immobile.

Dang. What'd I do?

He sat up. Except for that arm, everything moved like normal, more or less. He ached all over, and his head felt like it was in a vice.

It could be worse. Now get a move on.

The shroud lines twisted around his bad arm, across his back and over his shoulders. He tried to untangle himself, but his one-handed efforts accomplished nothing, except to snarl things up even more and send darts of pain that made him gasp.

A fly in a web.

He'd have to cut himself loose. Getting to his knife and flashlight was an awkward process that involved a little twisting and a lot of pain, but he found them. And, to his profound relief, two intact bottles of rye. That would help, anyway.

It was likely to be a couple of days before he found his way to civilization. He patted the breast pocket where he'd stowed one of the bottles. *How long are you two bad boys going to last me?*

He moistened his lips with anticipation. Once he got himself situated, he'd throw back a swig or two. But the rest might have to last him a while.

The crickets and frogs had a regular big-band concert going. This unknown world suddenly felt very large. And he felt small and exposed.

Japs. If Vitty was right, they'd be somewhere nearby.

One of his frat brothers had been a journalism major who subscribed to *Life* magazine. One month they ran a photo spread of the action in China. Pete had shown it around, and an image left an impression Dave couldn't erase.

The camera captured a Japanese soldier at the apex of a forceful lunge, the length of his bayonet buried in a Chinese prisoner's ribcage. A second soldier pricked at a helpless prisoner. The caption explained he was prodding him into position for his final thrust. The victim lay curled up in an effort to protect his torso, but it was clear how the scene was going to end.

There'd been talk in the barracks at Eglin Field too. Grisly reports from Manila. American civilians herded, penned, tossed meals like dogs. Philippine "offenders" lashed to street lamps. Mere children, some of them. Bayoneted, beaten to death for slight infractions.

And from Hong Kong. Wounded British soldiers run through in their hospital beds.

Japanese soldiers were demons, not men. Capture would be a ticket to hell.

He'd been so sure of himself on *Payback*. Thousands of feet above it all, encased in aluminum. But things looked different on the ground. No plane, no crew, no machine guns, and a useless arm. And in bayonet range.

He shivered from more than the cold.

His men were around somewhere, trying to figure out how to avoid becoming shish kebabs. He reached for his Colt. He'd fire a round, see if any of them responded.

Stupid idea. Too much risk of the wrong kind of attention.

Find a hidden spot to wait for daylight. Or was it better to travel by night?

Ha! Travel where? To move by night, he'd have to know where he was going.

The math he'd done on *Payback* came to his mind. His men were scattered miles away, somewhere to the east.

His arm would need a sling. At least he had a ready supply of silk. It took several minutes to cut himself free, follow the cords to the 'chute, and produce a crude sling. He was ready to move out.

Time for a little recon work.

His flashlight presented the same problem as his pistol—it could draw the wrong kind of attention. But he couldn't see a thing in the velvety darkness. He flicked the flashlight on and trained it around.

The beam seemed to soak into the drizzle, limiting visibility to less than twenty feet. He could make out a gentle slope cleared of trees, but clumps of soggy vegetation masked the landscape. A series of hedges crossed the grass. He played the light up and down the closest one.

"Hedge" wasn't the right word. A row of stone slabs.

About three feet tall with arched tops.

An owl hooted its loneliness in the distance. A rustling sound at his feet made him jolt. He caught his breath, took a small jog-step back—sending a fresh wave of pain shooting down his arm and along his shoulder blade—and pointed the beam at the noise.

A flash of motion. A rat skittered into a tuft of grass beside one of the slabs.

He exhaled his relief. *Don't be a girl.*

He switched off the flashlight and stood still, listening for any other signs of life. Nothing. He flicked the beam on, directing it at the ground three feet in front of him.

His relief faded.

The light revealed the base of a stone slab. A cove in its face housed a collection of small items weighted in place with stones. Chinese characters crisscrossed it.

A grave marker. Different from the ones back home, but recognizable. He'd landed in a cemetery. Probably buried his face in some poor Chinaman's fresh plot.

He took an immediate step to the side as adrenaline jolted him once more. He'd been standing on a low mound. *Both feet on a grave.*

He stared around for a moment, barely breathing, ears tuned to the night noises. He wasn't much for superstitions or omens or nonsense like that. But there was something about a graveyard at night that put a man's nerves on edge.

He had to fight a sinking sense that this wasn't mere chance. This Chinese adventure could be fated to end the way it had begun—in front of a gravestone.

Chapter Six

KAMURA-SAN SENT MIYAKO HOME WITH two cartons of hearty fish stew, with rice and a pair of fragrant persimmons for dessert. She felt rich as a baroness carrying this bounty to Papa-san.

She slipped off her shoes in the hall outside their room and slid the *shoji* open. "Papa-san, I saw Kamura-san. And I've got another treat."

No reply. Papa-san lay on his futon, very still. She put down her bags and dropped to her knees beside him. There was a yellow pallor to his skin, a blue tinge around his lips she hadn't seen before.

She shook his shoulder. "Papa-san?"

His only response was that wheeze.

She shook harder. Nothing.

"Papa-san!" She suppressed her rising panic. She cupped his face in one hand, slapped him gently with the other.

No response. She tried again. Same outcome.

Fear choked her. What was the quickest way to get a doctor?

She had to *think*. Dash out to a phone, call Dr. Furuta's office, try to get him here on a house call? It'd take too long.

What about the hospital? She snatched a tin from the cupboard and rifled through her yen. There might be enough of her own money there for the taxi and a payment that would get him seen.

And after that? She pushed away any thought about how they'd get by if he needed to stay there. Or how she'd pay the rent after the hospital got their share of what was in that tin.

She stopped long enough to bow twice to the family altar, then pelted along the corridor. Hammered at the Tanakas' door, entreating her ancestors she'd find them home.

The door slid open and Tanaka-san appeared. Miyako gave her a hasty bow, relief coursing through her. "I am so sorry to trouble you, but I can't wake Papa-san. I need to get him to the hospital right away."

The lady's eyes went wide with concern. "Of course." Thanks to all the deities, Miyako had always been able to count on Tanaka-san's good heart.

Tanaka-san called to her son kneeling behind her at the table. "Ki-kun! Take your father's bike and go for a taxi."

The boy stared at her.

"Hurry. Go!" She gestured Miyako into the room. "Excuse me." She bobbed a bow and disappeared behind a *shoji* partition. Miyako heard the hum of urgent voices, and Tanaka-san emerged less than a minute later with her husband, worry etching furrows across his forehead.

Miyako dashed to her room, the older couple following. The three of them worked together to hoist Papa-san onto Tanaka-san's husband's shoulder. Papa-san moaned. His eyes drifted open, but only for a moment.

Tanaka-san's husband staggered down the stairs and out to the curb. They had to wait for the taxi. Between them, they bundled Papa-san into the generous back seat. Miyako climbed in beside him and cradled his head on her lap.

"I can keep you company for a bit, dear." Tanaka-san took the seat next to the driver.

"*Domo arigato,*" Miyako's eyes didn't leave Papa-san's face.

Tanaka-san directed the driver. "Osaka Hospital, please."

They wheeled Papa-san to the triage area on a gurney. Smelling salts didn't bring him around, but after a few minutes with a mask attached to a big oxygen tank his breathing sounded deeper and more even.

Miyako sat next to him, watching every heave of his chest, her clammy hands twisted in her lap.

Kindly, Tanaka-san placed a hand on Miyako's shoulder. "I'm so sorry, Mi-chan. I'm afraid I have to go. Stop and see us when you get home, please."

Miyako rose and thanked her with a deep bow of gratitude, then turned to Papa-san. Even now, despite those hollow cheeks, there was something noble in his expression. In the set of his jaw, the angle of his cheekbones, there was a strength that hinted of the captain who'd shipped off to war not so many years before.

She heaved a shuddering sigh. Back then, she believed she could do something to protect him. The sacred gift of a *senninbari*, an embroidered sash of cream-colored silk. So much had gone into its making. So many hours spent at the subway entrance. She held out the silk belt to each passing lady and asked her to work a single stitch in the design. A thousand stitches worked by a thousand hands.

She'd do it all again, ten times over, if it would keep him with her. But it hadn't worked then. Plenty of men with *senninbari* hadn't returned from the war—like her brother.

And a silk belt wouldn't help Papa-san now.

She took a fresh towel from the stand and dabbed beads of moisture from his forehead. Tears burned behind her eyelids—she blinked them back. She leaned over him and whispered, "Papa-san, I'm doing everything I can for you. But you need to do something for me. Fight this enemy as hard as you fought for the emperor. And come home to me."

The doctor strode in. An angular man with graying hair and a nose like a hawk's beak, he gave her a slight bow. He plucked Papa's chart from the footboard and rifled through it.

She returned his bow with a deeper one aimed at the crown of his head.

He looked at her over the papers. "Good evening." He squeezed Papa's wrist for a moment, then moved the stethoscope around his chest. The creases on his face grew deeper.

She waited, anxiety mounting, until at last he met her eyes. "I'm Nakamura. And your name?"

"Matsuura. This is my father."

"Ah. Matsuura-san. Well. High fever. Rapid, fluttering pulse. Fluid in the lungs. Your father appears to be a very sick man."

She sighed. "*Hai*, Dr. Nakamura."

"Dr. Furuta diagnosed pneumonia?"

"*Hai*."

"Did your father receive a course of penicillin?"

"No, Doctor." Little old Dr. Furuta had recommended it. And was there anywhere she didn't ask? Any black-market stall she didn't visit? But there was none to be had. They stocked it at the military hospitals for *gaijin* soldiers with V.D. But not for old Japanese with pneumonia.

Dr. Nakamura compressed his lips. "That's a shame. I know it's hard to come by." He stood studying Papa-san's face, nearly as white as the hospital bedding. "I don't think pneumonia accounts for all the symptoms I'm seeing today. His poor color would seem to indicate anemia. Would you say your father bruises or bleeds easily?"

She nodded. "I have noticed that." The night before wasn't the first time she'd seen odd marks on his skin. She wondered how he got them when he spent his days on his futon.

He looked at her intently. "Is it possible that your father has been in the vicinity of Hiroshima or Nagasaki?"

Her chest hollowed. "*Hai*, Doctor. Nagasaki. He was a naval officer."

"When was he there?"

"They sent him in the day after."

He paused, clicking his tongue against his palate, then seemed to reach a decision. "I'd like to order blood tests."

Would George-san's offer be generous enough to pay for all this? "If I could please ask, Dr. Nakamura, what will the blood tests tell you?"

A moment's pause. "Matsuura-san, this won't be easy for you to hear."

The hollow in her chest expanded to fill it.

He sat near the foot of the bed, on her level. "We've recently started to notice an increased incidence of leukemia in people exposed to atomic radiation. Some seem to escape the early symptoms. But we're theorizing their cells may sustain more subtle damage which emerges as blood cancer later." He paused. "I can't know for certain until we have the test results, but some of your father's symptoms are consistent with leukemia."

The temperature in the room dropped. Leukemia? Blood cancer? A painful, lingering death.

He pointed at the purplish area she'd noticed on Papa-san's shoulder the day before. "Look at this."

She bent to get a better view. Tiny scabs formed a honeycomb pattern. A couple dozen of them, accented by several droplets of fresh blood. She breathed a swear word. "*Che!* What *is* that?"

"Pinprick bleeds. The clinical term is *petechiae*." He gave her a searching look then went on in a measured voice. "A frequent leukemia symptom, especially when they present in an older patient. Leukemia can compromise the immune system. That might explain his pneumonia as well."

Papa-san, *hibakusha*. An explosion-polluted person. Everything in the room froze.

She'd seen them after the surrender. Begging on street corners. Swollen limbs and faces, patchy hair, dirty bandages, burns, skin ulcers. Revolting.

Tanaka-san's older son came home from Hiroshima precinct after the bombing, in seemingly perfect health. A month later he started to vomit, and his hair fell out. By the next spring, the Tanakas had buried their oldest son. And the *hibakusha* on the streets had disappeared.

And now Papa-san himself—*hibakusha?*

Dr. Nakamura cleared his throat. She forced her attention back to his words.

"Matsuura-san, your father will need to stay here while we complete the diagnosis and establish a treatment plan. I suppose Dr. Furuta prescribed a traditional *kampo* remedy?"

She had to work to summon her voice. "He did. I've been making the tea Dr. Furuta prescribed."

"Is it giving your father some relief?"

"*Hai*, some."

"I'd advise that he continue it, especially since I don't have penicillin for him. But that's a bit out of our domain. You'll come in and administer it?"

"*Hai*, Doctor." She shifted on the edge of her chair. "But I have to tell you, Papa and I are very poor. I don't know how I'll pay for all this."

He frowned. "You don't feel your father deserves quality care?"

"I do. But—"

"But what?"

What could she say? "Never mind." She studied her hands in her lap.

Saturday 18 April 1942
Jiangxi Province, China

A dog barked somewhere right below the hillside where Dave had landed.

Civilization. Until he was certain Vitty was wrong about this being enemy-infested territory, he needed cover.

His flashlight showed a stand of trees off to his right. He worked his way over, but it was tough going. His feet slipped and mired on the saturated ground. Each time he jerked to regain balance, a fresh shock of pain wrenched him.

He reached the cover of the trees and sat cross-legged in a spot where the ground was flat and the boughs were thickest. Draped the parachute over his head for added shelter and got out the only food he had—a chocolate bar.

Stiff fingers resisted bending around the flashlight. Every inch of his body was wet.

Time for a little of that medicine. To take the edge off the pain—and the nerves. That thought came with a twinge of need. He fished out a bottle of Doc White's rye, vised it between his thighs, and unscrewed the top with his good hand. He threw back a swig.

Every bit as bad as I expected.

He coughed, then sent another one after the first.

Worse. But warmth traveled through his veins, and his anxiety ebbed a little.

The crickets and frogs had resumed—a whole chorus of them. Telling Dave what an idiot he was for sitting on a hillside somewhere in China. Like the chorus of people who'd told him what an idiot he was to enlist. All of them now on the other side of the world. His wife Eileen, his parents, his little sister.

The decisive discussion about his enlistment had taken place at that last Fighting Illini game they'd seen. The U. of I. met Purdue on a breezy September Saturday. Eileen—

who'd been his steady girl since they were high school seniors—had laced her fingers through his and smiled with excitement. The Illini blue and orange in her scarf brought out the color in her hazel eyes. The wind played with the red-gold wisps around her face and tugged at her well-anchored hat.

A vendor worked his way down the bleacher stairs to Dave's right. "Coke here. *Cold* Coke."

He hailed the man and bought a round of sodas. He gave Eileen a subtle wink as he handed her one, then fingered the flask of rum in his pocket. He was itching to break into it. Dad wouldn't care—in fact he'd probably join them. But Dave couldn't doctor the drinks until Eileen managed to herd Mom off to the ladies' room.

His parents had driven from Chicago. Mom was her usual busybody self, bursting with information from home. "You won't believe it, honey. Your old friend Jimmy Schumacher enlisted. And that loud-mouth Brent Casey too."

Dad's eyes stayed anchored on the field, but his angular jaw jutted in indignation. "Still can't believe Roosevelt wants to see us caught up in another foreign war. Those boys could just wait—Roosevelt will see them drafted soon enough."

Mom pulled a compact from her handbag. "We should let the Europeans sort out their own affairs." She checked her powder.

Eileen leaned across Dave so his mother could hear. "You know my friend Josie, right? Her boyfriend went and enlisted. He's leaving the U. of I. I feel so awful for her."

Mom looked at her over the top of her compact. "Why would he do that? It might be a fine thing for that Schumacher kid. You don't expect a boy from that kind of family to amount to much. But for a college man?"

Dave fixed his eyes on his mother. "Some of my frat brothers saw the recruiter. Turns out if you enlist, you can choose which branch you join. If I wanted the Air Corps, for example—"

Dad turned on him, face fierce. "You aren't actually considering this, are you?"

"Yeah." He cleared his throat. "I'm considering it."

All three of them stared at him. Eileen's eyes were widest. "You wouldn't. We've talked and talked about this."

"If they guarantee me Air Corps, maybe I would." He dropped the words deliberately, like round stones into a pool. "With my vision, I can probably get pilot training."

"Throw away three years of college?" Dad said. "For a *probably?*"

Mom pursed her lips. "You know we've made real sacrifices so you can be here."

"You're that desperate to be a flyboy." Eileen's voice had a hollow sound.

"Better a flyboy than crawling through the trenches. Right, Dad?" That was taking it too far, and he knew it. Dad's infantry days in the Great War weren't something the man talked about.

Dad stared at him for a few seconds, mute, his lips a thin line. "That's right. I've been there. Keep that in mind next time you think you know more about war than I do."

"What trenches?" Eileen jumped in. Her voice sounded shrill. "There are no trenches. We just can't get tangled up in another European war."

He shrugged. "If we don't join the war? Uncle Sam shells out for flight school and I get to fly for a couple years."

"Two years?" She recoiled from him, mouth gaping. "If you get drafted it's one year. *If* you get drafted."

He reached for her arm. "Eileen, this might be my chance to do something that will make a difference. And it's certainly my only chance to fly."

His father found his voice—the dramatic courtroom voice he used to bend jurors to his will. "I forbid it. I flatly forbid it."

"Excuse me?" Dad wasn't going to talk to him that way. Not anymore.

"I knew it was a mistake to let you spend all that time with my broken-down battle horse of a brother-in-law. He infected you with the idea you're going to be some kind of hero."

Dave's shoulders went rigid. "Don't say that about Uncle Verle." It was Uncle Verle who'd taken him to the Thompson Trophy Race, where the aviation bug bit him hard. Perhaps it was his first glimpse of Captain Page's Curtiss Hawk, sunlight glinting off her powerful curves. Or maybe even his first whiff of avgas. But whatever the witchcraft was, from that day everything about planes and pilots sent his pulse pounding in a way no one but his "broken-down" uncle ever cared to understand.

Maybe Uncle Verle did drink too much. But everyone knew he had his reasons.

Mom looked a bit pale behind her powder. "Rob, don't start this again."

Eileen tugged at his arm. "Those planes are dangerous enough when someone's not shooting at you."

Chanting swelled around them. "*De*-fense. *De*-fense. *De*-fense."

Mom's lower lip pushed into a puzzled pout. She raised her voice to carry above the crowd. "I thought you were going to law school. It's what your father and I always wanted for you."

His father sneered. "Correct. So you will finish your senior year here. And we'll hear no more about enlisting. Or flying."

The bleachers erupted into cheers. "What a tackle!" someone behind them yelled. People sprang to their feet on every side, and the four of them rose along with the crowd.

Dave stared down his father while the cheering trailed off. "I *am* twenty-one, Dad. You can't actually tell me what to do."

That was something he'd wanted to say as long as he could remember. To prove it, he showed up at the recruitment office the following Monday morning.

And the Air Corps had sent him to a graveyard in rural China.

Dad. Mom. Eileen, who was now his wife. He would sure hate to prove them all right, especially like this. No glory in getting killed running and hiding.

Even less glory in dying so a crazed Japanese soldier could hone his bayonet skills. The truth was seeping into his consciousness. It was possible he'd never see any of them—or home—again.

He couldn't accept that. Couldn't accept not seeing

Eileen again. He had never thought he'd do it, but he did. A foxhole prayer.

Since he wasn't exactly in the habit, he tried Watt's words. "Lord, please preserve me, and all my men, this day. If you're listening. Amen."

He waited for some sense of peace to envelop him from the sky. It didn't come.

He lay down on his uninjured side, using his parachute as both blanket and tent. He propped his arm in the least painful position he could find.

Hunger. Cold. Exhaustion. And fear—gripping, nauseating fear. There was a battle, but in the end, exhaustion won. His last dim thought came with a pang of longing. Eileen's soft body, spooned up against his own.

Somehow, he'd find a way back to her. He had to.

Chapter Seven

Friday, December 24, 1948
Osaka, Japan

MIYAKO SPENT ANOTHER HOUR OR SO at Papa-san's bedside. An officious parade of nurses came and went. Every time someone approached to attend to an I.V. or an oxygen tube, she was sure she could hear the charges adding up, like beads clicking across an abacus rod.

But when the hospital staff left them alone, she dabbed at his clammy forehead and contemplated the hatch-mark pattern of small scabs on his shoulder. The likelihood that her last living family member would leave her soon dug an aching cavern in her heart.

Hadn't the war taken enough?

Eventually hunger got the best of her. She gave him a final tuck and went home. She made a quick meal from the remnants of the feast Kamura-san had sent home with her that morning. She slipped on a nightshirt and eased her weary legs between the sheets. As the cotton caressed her limbs, George-san's face slipped into her mind and the room brightened a bit. At least that would be easier now.

A thought stole in. Maybe Papa-san would even understand that she'd have to accept George-san's offer. How else could she pay for the hospital?

Guilt speared her at the little thrill this brought. How could she find even a second's pleasure in Papa's misfortune? Besides, she was no Japanese Cinderella, and George-san wasn't her prince. Men didn't really care about girls like her. They used them then discarded them. She and George-san weren't destined for any happy-ever-after ending, like in the Western stories.

Especially not now.

She drifted to sleep, her heart heavy with sorrow and her thoughts dark with gloom.

She'd been there before. Many times. A horrid cubbyhole of a room, dominated by a western-style bed with tall posts. Wearing a cheap kimono that wasn't hers. Waiting for something—she didn't know what.

She tried to push the door open. Locked. From the outside. She rattled it. Hammered on it. Screamed. "Let me out! Please let me out!"

There was no answer. She sat on the bed and waited, her belly congealing into a hard knot of dread.

Heavy footsteps, coarse laughter in the hallway. A key clicked in the lock. The door swung open.

Three big men and a whiskey bottle—American soldiers. They advanced into the room, the tallest one taking a swig. Watching her over the bottle, brass-colored eyelashes framing unnatural jade eyes.

Predator's eyes.

He was enormous, with hair like a rusty nail. He said something to the others. They surrounded her, appraising her. She edged away until the wall pressed into her back.

They laughed. The one with curly dark hair said something she couldn't understand. But there was no mistaking the jeer in his tone.

The redhead handed him the bottle, wiped his mouth on his sleeve. His florid face went slack in a leering grin. "C'mere."

She understood that much.

She scrambled away, across the bed. Lunged for the door. The dark-haired soldier blocked her with a hairy arm, squeezed her against his well-muscled chest. She pounded on him. Struggled and gasped, wrenching her face away from the stink and heat of his breath.

He laughed and squeezed harder.

The redhead clawed at her kimono. He stared at her with bared teeth and a demon's burning eyes. "First time, Jap girl?" He pulled three slips of paper from his breast pocket, fanned them in front of her face. "Three tickets. Paid for, see?"

That's when she woke, every time. Heart pounding, breath short.

A quick glance at her surroundings brought Miyako back to the tiny room she shared with Papa-san, lit with a gray pre-dawn light. Relief washed over her as she realized it had been a dream. *That* dream. Again.

She anchored her eyes on her teakettle, secure in its place on the shelf, grateful for waking before she had to relive any more of her first night as a comfort woman.

She sat up. No matter what it cost her, the time had come. Someone must pay a blood price for all the war had done to her family. To Hiro-chan. To Akira-san. To Papa-san and Mama-san.

To her.

Maybe when she was done with Delham she'd have poison left to kill herself.

Miyako woke the next morning with a surge of adrenaline. How many days did she have before Delham's talk? She ticked them off on her fingers.

Eight days. Eight days to train with Kamura-san, come up with money, get the poison. All on top of seeing to Papa-san at the hospital.

Kamura-san had given her a name and address on a slip of paper. A certain Tsunada-san, well placed in the Sakaume gang. "You'll find him a bit intimidating. But I know the man, ah? He'll deal with you in a straightforward way."

A straight-dealing *yakuza*? That would be a wonder.

But first, there was Papa-san.

Miyako walked through the hospital's oversized entrance doors a few minutes before 8:45. She carried a newspaper under her arm. Her handbag held the vial of oil and the packet of herbs she'd measured out for Papa-san's tea, along with the slip of paper with that all-important name and address.

The receptionist told her where she could find Papa-san. "Fourth floor. Cancer Ward. To your right off the elevator. Visiting hours start at nine."

Cancer Ward. Her chest tightened.

She took a seat and scanned the days' headlines fitfully.

Eight days with George-san. This room search he'd suggested was meaningless for such a short time, but she had to keep up the charade. She fished a pen from her purse and opened the paper to the classifieds, circling home rental listings that looked promising

Some might say eight days are better than nothing. The thought brought a sharp twist of pain.

A Japanese man walked in, about her own age, and strode to a chair. A fresh-faced and very pregnant young woman in a pink lace shawl followed a few feet behind him. She gave him a soft smile and settled on the chair next to him. His face brightened as he looked at her.

Miyako's heart folded in on itself. His wife. That woman's path could never be hers now.

How fortunate she'd felt the night she and George-san met. He and two buddies had just rolled out of the bar, down the sidewalk from where she stood. The tawdry neon lights reflected off their aviator jackets. The brown-haired airman put an elbow in George-san's side and cocked his head in her direction. "That one." His slurred words boomed over the noise of the crowd.

George-san glanced at her, then took a longer look. Then flushed and turned away.

His friend elbowed him again, this time with a jeering laugh. She couldn't hear what he said.

She forgot about the friend and focused on George-san. On reeling him in. There was a certain art to handling the shy ones. You had to make it easy for them, but you could scare them off if you came on too strong. She tried giving him a shy smile and a little wave. She called out to him. "Hello, there."

He shrugged, shot her that magnetic grin of his for the first time, and walked over, adopting a bit of extra swagger. He stopped in front of her, devouring her with those gray-blue eyes. "So"—he hesitated, biting his lip—"how does this work, exactly?"

She moved in and toyed with his lapel. Gazed up at him with her most seductive eyes. Gave her shoulders a little shimmy for good measure. There was plenty of whiskey on his breath—that always helped. "You want to get alone with me, ah?"

He glanced over his shoulder at his loud buddy, who gave him a big thumbs-up. He looked back at her, a smile softening his blunt nose and cleft chin. "I suppose I could be talked into that."

Got him. He wasn't bad looking. He had to be new, to be so shy. "What's your name?"

"George."

"Nice to meet you, George-san. I take you somewhere. Leave that to me."

She slipped her arm around his waist and led him to her usual place. The one with the sign that read "Rent by the Hour" in English and in Japanese. But he'd balked at the looks of it.

"No. Not here." He glanced up and down the street. "How about that one." And in a moment, a "short service" turned into all night. And while there was whiskey on his breath, there was an uncertain tenderness to his touch. It had been clear she'd taken him into new territory, and he'd made his appreciation every bit as clear.

She woke the next morning to find him squinting at her through one bleary eye. "Buy you breakfast, if you can hang around a little longer."

"Breakfast?" That was the first time she'd had an offer like that. And with the hollow in her stomach, it was tempting. But so much daylight was filtering in through the chinks in the curtains. How would she explain this at home? "*Arigato.* So nice!" She ran her fingers along his jawline, stopping beneath the cleft in his chin. "But I'm sorry. I must get home to Papa-san."

He gave her an endearing pout, and that first night turned into every week when he was on leave. A regular like him was as good as gold. Or as good as food on the table.

Of course, it wasn't all fun. There were times when he lapsed into a moody silence, and things he wouldn't talk about. But if they saw each other more, that could change, ah?

She doodled an extra circle around the most promising listing—the one that was closest to her own room. And closest to Papa-san, if he came home from the hospital.

If. And what would happen to him at that point, if she went through with this thing?

A lump formed in her throat. She reminded herself that

the decision had been his—she'd given it to him to make the day before, hadn't she?

Confucius' proverb ran through her mind, in Papa-san's rasping voice. *We two must not pause, even to retrieve our weapons.* And then—*It's all up to you, daughter. Hai.* The old warrior had chosen their path.

The pregnant woman and her husband stood. Miyako glanced at her watch. Nine o'clock sharp.

My George-san deserves happiness. Maybe when she was out of his life, he'd find it. With the kind of woman he could take home to his blue-eyed, fair-skinned mother.

She clenched the pen and stabbed it through the newsprint. Folded the paper and thrust it under her arm. She climbed the stairs to the fourth floor, and turned right as the receptionist had directed.

She paused for an instant at the double doors labeled Cancer Ward. Papa-san, the pillar of her existence, an explosion-polluted person. Disease wreaking havoc on his bloodstream.

She took a deep breath and pushed through the doors into the stark room. She saw him right away, three beds down from the door. His color looked better, but he lay very still. She sat next to his bed and took his hand between her own. "Papa-san?"

He struggled to open his eyes. "Ah. Mi-chan. You're here."

"*Hai,* Papa-san. Do you need anything?"

He gave her a wan smile. "I'll take some of that horrible tea of yours."

Saturday morning passed a lot like Friday evening had. More fluffing, tucking, and mopping. Serving his tea and attempting to feed him thin soup. He was asleep more than he was awake.

Dr. Nakamura stopped by while Papa-san slept. "He looks a bit better, yes? I think he's stable now, but I don't expect the test results for a few more days."

When the nurses weren't in the room, she passed long hours with little to do but watch Papa-san's struggle to breathe. Her mind drifted to Kamura-san's words.

This pilot deserves such a death? One must live without regrets.

She did think about it. She found herself building more and more elaborate pictures of how the poison would work. What he'd think when his limbs weakened, then stopped responding. The struggle to tell someone with a mouth that refused to form words. Then the suffering in enforced silence as death crept toward his chest.

Papa-san coughed. He drew a gasping breath, then coughed again, harder. His eyes fluttered open, fixed on hers, flickered with brief recognition, and drifted closed.

"Papa-san." She stroked his arm. "I'm going to make this right."

Delham determined his death on the day he bombed Osaka.

Sunday 19 April 1942
Jiangxi Province, China

Pain woke Dave. That and a gray dawn light. He rolled over, and daggers shot along his shoulder blade. It had grown worse while he slept. The shock had worn off and his shoulder had stiffened.

This was going to be tough duty until he found a doctor. Which could be a while.

The socks that clung to his feet were still sopping wet. His fingers flexed with difficulty, the tips tingling. He had to get warm, get moving.

Fine. Where? Flooded rice paddies receded down the slope into the morning mist. Each hugged the hillside, a winding band of mirror reflecting the sky. Then a four-or five-foot plunge to the next band of silver below.

It was striking, unlike anything he'd seen. A different world.

He stretched out the kinks as best he could, adjusted his makeshift sling, and struck out on the only path he saw. Paddies spread to his left, dense fir forest to his right.

It seemed likely someone would show up soon to work the rice. He couldn't risk contact—not until he was armed with better information.

The sights might have been unfamiliar, but the place reeked like Packingtown. There was no question what these people fertilized with.

His mind circled like a buzzard. His guys were miles behind him. He wasn't going to find them by blundering around the countryside on his own. But how could he make contact with someone he could trust? Not like he could tell a Japanese from a local by looking at him. It was vital to find out if Vitty was right about this being enemy territory. Or *he* could end up as bayonet practice.

All those briefings on *Hornet*. Had they given him anything useful—anything that might help him get through this alive? Take what he'd learned about Chinese politics, for example. Mao Tse-Tung and the Communists. Chiang Kai-Shek and the Nationalists. A mishmash of local factions he couldn't hope to fathom. But the Nationalists were America's allies. They said, if the plane was downed, to look for a Nationalist guerilla unit. That was supposed to be his best chance of eluding the Japanese and finding his squadron in Chungking.

Assuming his men did the same, they'd connect at a Nationalist garrison somewhere. Then on to the heroes' welcome in Chungking they'd more than earned.

He could think of only two small things that stood between himself and that hero's welcome—several hundred miles, and the Japanese Army.

Chapter Eight

Sunday 19 April 1942
Jiangxi Province, China

THE PATH DAVE FOUND WAS ROUGH, and in the early light it was hard going. The sun crawled up the sky. Every step sent pain jolting through his shoulder blade and along his arm.

The path joined another, broader one. New dilemma. Which way to turn? Either direction could lead him directly into an enemy garrison and a forest of bayonets.

His men were somewhere to the east. But with the sun cresting the sky, which way was east?

He groped in his pockets for his compass. Not there.

Swell. That must have been what flipped out of his pocket when the 'chute deployed.

No compass. No map. And ten miles of rugged, forested terrain between him and his crew.

He made a mental coin toss and headed right. He kept off this new, better-traveled path where he could. But for the most part, the dense trees and thick brush forced him to stay on it.

His canteen got lighter, the rumbling in his stomach more persistent. The last time he'd eaten anything like a meal was on *Payback* fourteen hours earlier. A can of franks and beans.

Don't think about it.

A rhythmic crunching sounded on the path ahead. He stopped short and listened, pulse pounding. *Footsteps.* With murmuring voices. He clutched his dead arm and tore through dense brambles into the shadows behind a boulder, thorns ripping at his skin.

He turned and crouched, motionless.

He eased his pistol from his shoulder holster. Stared into the thicket, barely breathing. The bushes swayed where he'd passed.

They could see that. Decide to investigate.

He needed better cover. The ground dropped steeply behind him. A large fallen log rested on the slope below him, propped between the root of one gnarled tree and the trunk of another. He stepped back and eased onto it.

It flexed under him. For a sickening moment he was sure it would give way and he'd ricochet down the slope, but the log held firm. He flattened himself, flipped his Colt's safety and cradled it against his chest.

He could make out a small square of path through one eye. A foot landed less than four feet in front of him. He had a quick impression of dusty laces. Sturdy soles. Battered leather stretching up the ankle.

A combat boot. It lifted to display hobnails.

He tightened his grip on his Colt. Japanese gear?

The Chinese might wear them too.

The soldiers halted on the path a few feet beyond the point where he'd left it. One of them uttered a low exclamation.

They'd seen him. No question. They'd rush him any second, bayonets poised.

Bamboo creaked. Their voices rose and fell, jabbering on. Japanese or Chinese? That was crucial information. And some hero he was, cowering there and making no attempt to find out.

He levered himself up on his good elbow. Craned for a better look. Pain wrenched his shoulder. Still couldn't make out anything. He gritted his teeth and pushed his torso an inch higher.

His arm slipped. A branch snapped off, bounced and slid several feet down the slope. The sound echoed through the forest.

The soldiers fell silent. One man shouted a few words. Footsteps started his way. Dave flattened, held his breath. Clenched his teeth to hold back a moan.

Boots clattered past him along the path and stopped a few yards beyond his position. Rustling noises came from both directions. What on earth were they doing?

The rustling drew closer. They were beating the bushes with their rifle butts, sweeping in on him.

If they weren't the enemy, why were they looking for him?

He felt a desperate desire to scramble down the slope and away, but he couldn't—too much noise. He was a sitting duck.

They worked the bushes beside the boulder, almost on top of him.

*Lord, preserve me....Lord, preserve me....*Please *be listening!* Sweat trickled down his forehead, stung in his eyes.

The rustling and beating retreated. They regrouped a little past him. At last they moved on.

Thank you.

He clung to the log until he heard nothing but forest. He lay there fifteen minutes longer by his watch before he crawled up on the ledge. His shoulder shrieked. His head spun. He lay panting while his vision cleared.

Lord, thank you.

But how much longer could he last? Pain, hunger, and exhaustion were getting the best of him.

Saturday, December 25, 1948
Osaka, Japan

Miyako stayed at the hospital until a nurse came through and announced the end of visiting hours. She stood for a moment with her hand on Papa-san's arm. He stirred and mumbled something. She let herself imagine it was her name.

She left the hospital and walked toward the station.

The address Kamura-san had given her for his *yakuza* connection was a hotel in the Shinsekai District. "He hosts a card game there on Friday and Saturday nights," Kamura-san had told her.

Tiny raindrops deposited a layer of moisture on everything—her scarf, her handbag, her face. The air had a brisk washed-clean scent that made her want to linger outside. Her heart fell at the thought of facing her empty apartment.

It was a little early for gambling, but she'd give Tsunada-san a try.

She left the train at Daikokucho Station and took a direct route into the Shinsekai district. She walked a few minutes farther. The charred base of the Eiffel Tower-inspired Tower

Reaching to Heaven massed before her. It had been the Shinsekai's key landmark, before the bombing raids left it in ruins. Along with the district's once-sparkling boulevards, and its pretensions of being the Paris of Japan.

After a few more blocks of raucous bars and cheap eateries, she spotted the Imperial Hotel's sign, a blaze of blue-and-green neon. The hotel's entrance door gave way to an unassuming lobby. A broad set of carpeted stairs took up the back third of the room. A dour-looking, muscular man stood at their base. He made brief eye contact with her, seeming to assess and then dismiss her. Who cared about one more prostitute?

She gave him a decorous bow. "I'd like to speak with Tsunada-san, if you please. My father's friend Kamura-san told me he might be kind enough to help me."

The man stared at her like he was made of stone. She raised her chin and stood her ground. At last he nodded. "I bring you up." He cocked his head at the stairs.

She followed him. With each step, her feet felt heavier. *Into the gang's lair.*

At the top of the stairs, a narrow corridor lined with handsome *shoji* partitions ran the length of the hotel. The man cracked one of them open and spoke in a low voice to someone within. He turned to her. "Tsunada-san will see you after he plays this round."

She collapsed into a chair, drained. The distinctive sound of shuffling cards leaked into the corridor from several rooms. She settled in and waited.

A roar erupted in the room nearest her. A man rose to his feet, his shadow creating an enormous silhouette against the thin paper *shoji*. He stomped to the *shoji* and muscled it aside.

Miyako found herself staring up into the glowering square face of a man somewhere in his fifties. She slid to a kneeling position on the floor and riveted her eyes on the mat. "Please excuse me."

"You." He growled his displeasure. "What do you want?"

"Forgive me." She deepened her bow. "I'm here to speak to Tsunada-san."

"I'm Tsunada." His gruff voice bristled with impatience.

"What is it?" He nudged her thigh with a glossy shoe.

She sat up, but a profound unwillingness to meet his gaze kept her eyes glued to his pant leg. Fine, handstitched wool. The hem of it pooled gently against the top of that shoe. The cost of either could have paid her rent for a year. "Please forgive this humble person for troubling you. An old friend of my father's, Kamura-san, told me you're the man who can help me."

He chuckled, but something dark in his tone reminded her that a mere flick of his finger could consign her to a painful end. And no one would know.

He stopped laughing. "You'll make this worth my time, yes?"

"*Arigato*, Tsunada-san. I'll do my best."

He crooked his hand at a man in the game room. "Have them bring *sake* to the small tearoom."

Monday 20 April 1942
Jiangxi Province, China

Dave had walked miles and weathered another chilly night on a pine-needle bed. At mid-morning the burning in his shoulder, the rumbling in his gut, the blisters on his feet—none of it had gotten any better.

If he ever saw Doc White, he'd buy the man a drink. A slug of his foul-tasting rye now and then went down like Olympic elixir, taking the edge off Dave's pain and his nerves. Good thing he'd rescued two bottles from the *Payback*.

He pulled out the bottle he could get to, took a swig, and held it up to check the level of the liquid.

Half gone already. He groaned. He would need to slow down if he didn't want to run dry. Besides, while Doc's "medicine" might be taking the edge off his pain, it probably wasn't helping his thirst. His canteen had been empty for hours. He swallowed, trying to wet his throat, but a rattlesnake probably had more spit.

He rested for a moment then hiked on, doing his best to ignore the blisters.

Find the Nationalists, they'd said. They'd told him what

to do, but not how to do it. And it was clear he wasn't going to get much farther without some kind of help.

He rounded a crook in the road and glimpsed one corner of a battered wooden structure. Until that point he'd avoided all contact, slipping into the forest at any sound of a footfall, real or imagined. Seeing fresh evidence of human occupation made him abandon the road again.

What is that building?

Are there people around?

He crossed his fingers and dared to hope for friendlies.

He edged toward the structure, taking care to stay well covered, every one of his senses tuned. A small break in the foliage revealed it as a tiny thatched hovel standing next to the road. Earth walls, sagging roof. Several chickens scrounged for food in an enclosure near the door.

People actually live in a dump like this?

Could he trust them?

Peasants. Bottom of society's food chain. If this was occupied territory, they couldn't have much love for Japanese.

Shrill laughter piped through the forest. Dave edged back into the foliage. Two small boys in ragged pants and wooden clogs burst into view on the bit of road he could see beside the hovel. They skipped into the tiny yard. Indignant chickens clucked and scattered.

The boys had a game going that sure looked like *Army.* The bigger kid pointed a finger gun. "Pow, pow!" The smaller one crumpled.

Apart from the brown skin and rags, they could be my cousins back home.

Three young men in soldiers' uniforms—billed caps, high-collared jackets, big flap pockets—followed the kids. The sight of them jarred his nerves into high alert.

At least one of the young men was in on the little boys' game. He took a running step or two and threatened the older boy with a finger pistol. The kid giggled, flopped to the ground.

They were a shabby bunch. Not much uniform about their uniforms. Some kind of leggings wrapped their shins, instead of the high combat boots he'd seen on the soldiers the day before. They weren't well armed, either. Only two mismatched guns among the three of them. Apart from the guns and the uniforms, they looked like neighborhood teens. Not ferocious Japanese soldiers.

Chiang's boys? Is this my chance?

His eyes rested on their canteens. The Sahara couldn't be more parched than his throat. He swallowed hard, drew his pistol, and stepped out of the forest.

If things went to hell, he had seven rounds in his Colt .45.

Chapter Nine

Saturday, December 25, 1948
Osaka, Japan

MIYAKO FOUND HER SESSION WITH TSUNADA-SAN more than intimidating—she found it terrifying. But in the end, he agreed to supply the poison for the staggering price of ten thousand yen. Which made the possibility of restoring the Matsuura family's honor tangible, although there was still the matter of the huge sum.

And the matter of Tsunada-san's final warning. He'd puffed cigar smoke at her. "You have an obligation in return for my little favor, ah?"

"Of course. What?"

"*Silence.* You'll reveal the source of the poison to no one, under any circumstance. *Any* circumstance. You understand, ah?"

She nodded.

"If we ever have reason to suspect that you did, consequences will be severe." He spread his right hand—his sword hand—out and held it a few inches from her nose. Rotated it to give her a good look. His ring finger lacked a joint. And there was only a stump where his little finger had been. "We start with the fingers." His eyes drilled into hers. "It doesn't stop there."

She put the memory aside with a shudder. At least she had Tsunada-san's commitment. Her father had friends, like Kamura-san. And if everything else failed—absolutely everything—she had George-san.

It was time to reconnect with Kamura-san. Bring him the news and the problem.

She glanced at her watch. Eight-thirty. It was probably peak traffic at the restaurant now. Her chances of having a private conversation with Kamura-san would be better later. She needed a way to pass some time.

What about Kimi? Her friend worked the Abeno District, prime haunt of the brash independent operators everyone called *pan-pan*. Kimi should be out there by now, and it was on the way. It would be good to see her one more time.

She boarded the Midosuji Line, then connected to the Uemachi Line for the Abeno Station. She left the station in a light drizzle, amid a stream of blank-faced commuters. A long block, then a turn past a lot full of rubble, and she was in the Abeno.

Bar windows reflected jagged rectangles onto wet pavement. Raucous laughter from a dozen drinking parties spilled out onto the sidewalk. Girls—they seemed even younger than the last time she'd been there—clustered on both sides of the street. Their umbrellas arched like rows of brown and gray mushrooms against the backdrop of smoke-blackened walls.

She picked her way over broken chunks of sidewalk. Girls she knew greeted her. A young woman peeped out from beneath her umbrella, then stood up from a crate she'd been sitting on. "Mi-chan? Haven't seen you in ages."

Miyako recognized the gait and the voice. "Kimi, there you are. I'm so happy to see you."

"Where have you been?" Kimi wore the *pan-pan's* uniform: bright lips, high heels, permed hair. A wool coat, strategically unbuttoned, so men could get a sense of the figure beneath. "Got a new man?"

"You remember Sergeant Sanders, yes?"

"The blond guy?"

"*Hai.*"

"Spending more time with him, ah? Since when?"

"Since he asked me to find us a place a couple days ago." She tried not to sound too proud of her acquisition.

"Got a ticket off the street, ah?" It was impossible to miss the edge in Kimi's voice. "How nice for you." She huddled into her coat.

"How's business here?"

"It's picking up. A lot of men are on leave. You know it's their big holiday." She gestured down the street with her chin. "We're in luck, ah? Here come some of General MacArthur's boys now. Aren't you glad you're here?"

"Don't drag me into this. I'm done with it." *And I'm out of it for good, one way or another.*

"Oh, show a little courage." Kimi cut her a sly look.

"Sanders won't know, will he? Or are you too rich to need the cash now?"

The mention of cash was a punch to the gut. Papa-san, pale in bed with his tank and tubes. Getting him checked into the hospital had taken every *sen* she had. But she pictured George-san, the way she'd seen him last. Drowsy and trusting, the hotel pillow crumpled under his sandy-blond head and his wallet open on the nightstand. Her heart did that little lurch. She shook her head. "No thanks, Kimi. I don't want to."

Several girls had already rushed the men. Kimi arched an eyebrow at her, then put on a brazen smile and elbowed her way to the front. "Hello, boys."

But screams from the far end of the street interrupted the fun.

"Police!"

"Cops!"

In an instant, Miyako took it in. The van idling at the end of the block. Trench-coated men jumping out. *Pan-pan* scattering before them like leaves in a winter storm.

A policeman grabbed a girl around the waist and dragged her toward the van. She struggled, struck at him with purse and elbows. "No! Let me go!"

"A raid? *Che!*" Panic sent Miyako's pulse hammering and her feet pounding. She spun away from the commotion and pelted down the street as fast as her peep-toe pumps allowed. She could *not* afford to let them take her. If they did, odds were good it would cost three of her precious days. They'd examine her for V.D. and keep her locked up until the test results came in. And it would be more than three days if she tested positive.

Kimi was right behind her, cursing between breaths.

Police converged from the other direction. Their path was blocked. "Quick, this way." Miyako ducked into an alley. It was a dead end, but if luck was with them they could hide.

She heard a thud and a yelp behind her. Kimi sprawled on the wet street, one foot bare. Her shoe stuck in the crack where her heel had wedged.

Miyako hesitated. *She's lost if I don't help her.*

She started back. But the pandemonium was getting

closer. There was no time.

She scrambled behind a set of trash bins and crouched. She could see the street—and Kimi—through a gap. Her friend sat up and grabbed her ankle. By that time, the police were on her. One of them pulled her up and forced her to hobble back the way they'd come.

Miyako slid her dark coat over her so it covered her completely. She wedged herself farther into the space behind the bins. It was all she could do not to retch at the fetid stench. She choked down the bile, breathed through her mouth, and listened while the screams and scuffling noises subsided.

Heavy footsteps. Adrenaline sharpened her hearing. Sounded like a pair of them, searching the alley. Somehow she made herself even smaller.

"Looks clear to me." The squelch of shoes on the wet pavement faded. The wagon's back door slammed shut. The motor started, and the truck rolled away. Rowdy male laughter and juke-box music resumed in the bars and restaurants along the street.

After a time, she moved the coat enough so she could see the street through one eye. No one. She breathed a sigh of relief.

Sitting here with the rest of the refuse.

Her legs were cramping. She stood by inches and shook them out. She still couldn't quite believe her good fortune.

What a hard break for Kimi. And for Chikako, Kimi's little sister. Maybe she'd look in on her. Make sure she had something to eat.

In the bar behind her, several thick male voices rose in song, slurring out what sounded like a sentimental theme. *"Peace on earth, and mercy mild..."*

Her hand moved out of habit to her purse, groped for her cigarettes. She leaned against the wall and lit up.

Footsteps rushed toward her. "You there!"

Of course there was a second truck.

Monday 20 April 1942
Jiangxi Province, China

The older boy saw Dave first. He jumped up from where he lay on the ground, yelled and pointed. A couple of the soldiers jerked in surprise. They went rigid, hands on weapons. The little boys gripped each other. Their peepers couldn't have gone wider if a white tiger had strolled from the bamboo. Dave and the soldiers stared at each other for a long moment. Dave's finger jittered above the Colt's trigger.

The one who'd played with the kids exchanged a murmured comment with the fellow next to him. He directed some singsong syllables at Dave. Made a show of lifting his hand a few inches off his holster.

"Japan? Or China?" Dave's words came out a hoarse yell.

"China. We from China." A taut smile crossed the young man's chiseled face. He bobbed his head, brought his hands up so Dave could see both palms.

Dave could make out the insignia on the fellow's cap now. A tiny blue ball surrounded by a many-pointed star. Not the Japanese army's infamous five-pointed gold star.

He put his sternest face on and gestured with his pistol at the other two soldiers. They echoed the gesture the first soldier had made, lifting their hands, palms forward.

He looked around at the three of them. The soldier who spoke English wore a frank and open expression. The others looked more guarded. The fellow on the left had a blunt head and heavy-lidded eyes that put him in mind of a Peter Lorre movie villain.

The soldier who knew a little English pointed at his own nose. "Chen." He extended an open hand toward Dave, his face a question mark.

Dave took a deep breath before he lowered his pistol. "Dave."

"Dev?"

Dave nodded.

"Dev. Where from?"

"American. Friend of Chiang Kai-Shek."

"Ahh." It didn't sound like a question, but Chen still looked puzzled.

"Fighting Japan."

"Ah," Chen repeated, with a nod this time, followed by a torrent of discussion among the three.

Dave's eyes drifted to Chen's canteen.

How do you say water in this country? How do you say anything *in this country?*

He pantomimed raising something to his lips.

"Ah." Chen nodded vigorously, pulled the canteen from its pouch, and held it out to him.

To take the canteen, he'd have to put down his pistol. He took a long look into Chen's face. Chen unscrewed the canteen's top. That did it. He slipped the Colt into its holster, reached for the canteen, and took a healthy swig. Tepid water splashed across his chin.

Mmm. Bouquet of rusty pipes. But an iced Coke wouldn't have gone down better. He threw his head back for more.

Chen studied him. "You arm?"

"My shoulder." He gestured toward it.

"Bad?"

He nodded. "Pretty bad. I can't move it."

"How you come here?"

Let's see. Flew a bomber off a carrier. Dropped four bombs over Osaka. Flew another fifteen hours. Ran out of fuel and bailed. He had no language for any of that.

"Airplane." He tried flying his good hand, but their expressions registered blank.

I'll draw these fellows a picture. He knelt beside a patch of muck at the path's edge. Grabbing a stick, he did his best one-handed drawing of an airplane. He added a series of specks raining from its belly with a cartoon starburst below.

Chen's almond eyes went wide with astonishment. He pointed at the starburst shape—which the muck was already absorbing—and mimicked the sound of an explosion.

Dave couldn't help but grin. "Yeah, that's it."

"Where?"

"Japan. Osaka. Then we flew. Fifteen hours." He flew his hand into the ground. "Crashed not far from here."

Chen sucked his breath in and stood in silence. It took a second or two for crinkles to emerge at the corners of his eyes. He turned and jabbered an excited explanation at the others.

Dave sighed out his relief. Maybe a small token of friendship would be in order. "Cigarette?"

The soldiers studied him with puzzled expressions, then looked at one another. Dave produced a pack of Chesterfields from his breast pocket and shook two out. Their features lit. They crowded him, chattering. He handed smokes around and produced the Zippo lighter a Navy fellow had given him for luck. When he flicked it and a flame sprung into being, the astonishment on the ring of faces around him was nothing short of marvelous.

More incomprehensible dialog until the three reached some decision. The fellow who looked like Peter Lorre—Dave decided he'd call him Pete—turned and double-timed off the way they'd come.

"Wait. Where's he going?" Dave wrapped his fingers around the Colt's grip.

Chen eyed the pistol, then looked up at Dave with a bright smile. "Get doctor. Very good Chinese doctor. You sit. After, you come." He gestured toward a small shed behind the house.

Dave almost nodded but shook his head instead. *Keep your guard up, idiot.*

Chen insisted. "You sit inside." He pointed at the sun. "Hot." He gestured at the shed again.

It would feel good to get a load off my feet. Stinking blisters. He relented, let Chen lead him behind the house and into the shed. The young man did his best to make him comfortable, clearing a Stone-Age-looking scythe and a crude plow out of his way. Dave settled on the floor in a shaded corner and sagged against the rickety plank walls. Chen perched in the doorway. The third soldier rested on the ground a few feet away.

Dave shifted his torso and propped his arm in its least painful position. It was cool under the thatched roof, the most comfortable he'd been since he bailed from *Payback*.

The rye. That was what he needed. He started to reach for the bottle in his breast pocket but noted Chen's eyes on him.

Not now. Dang. That precious bottle was one thing he wasn't going to share. He let his hand fall to the shed's earthen floor.

"Very good Chinese doctor," Dave repeated under his

breath. *Well, Chen, hope your doctor isn't as backward as your farmers. Wonder what these people eat?*

He fought to keep his eyes open, but he gradually lost the battle.

Voices outside woke him. His hand flew to the Colt's grip. He sat bolt upright.

A shadow fell across the doorway. Several shadows. The fellow with the Hollywood-villain look was back. With company. And the others looked like soldiers, not doctors.

"China. China," Chen reassured him.

"Mao? Or Chiang?"

"Chiang."

The newcomers bobbed, smiled, and repeated the syllables, along with a lot of other babble. Chen coaxed him to come out of the shed. He took wary steps to the door, the Colt's grip cool against his palm.

Six soldiers clustered around him, all in worn uniforms with leggings and the same blue-ball insignia. They smiled broadly as they filled the air with sing-song talk. A sallow-faced fellow gave Dave's good hand a vigorous shake.

Chen carried on a rapid stream of back-and-forth discussion with the other soldiers. There seemed to be some kind of disagreement. After a long moment, Chen turned to Dave. "We go to doctor. You come."

He looked his newfound friends over. Five guns against his Colt. The odds weren't on his side.

I'd hate to drill a friendly. Sweat slicked his palms.

Chen gestured down the road.

His stomach rumbled on cue. These folks had enough Japanese trouble. They didn't need their allies to parachute in and plug them.

He wiped his hands on his trousers and limped along with them.

Chapter Ten

Saturday, December 25, 1948
Osaka, Japan

THAT EVENING'S ROUNDUP HAD BEEN A big one. In the district office waiting area, dozens of *pan-pan* perched on every surface and overflowed onto the floor.

To get recognized there would be unthinkable. If Papa-san found out, Miyako couldn't imagine how he would react. She bowed her head and pulled the pins from her hair so it fell about her face.

It was difficult to move without stepping on a nylon-clad leg. When a pair of those legs turned out to be Kimi's, Miyako settled next to her. "Now what?" She'd never been arrested.

"Now they interview us. And decide we all need to stay over for V.D. checks tomorrow. Then they keep us here until they get the results."

"All of us?"

Kimi grimaced. "All of us. And it takes three days."

"They're going to keep us all three days, ah? No exceptions? I did nothing."

Kimi snorted. "You were in the wrong place at the wrong time. That's enough."

Kimi was right, of course. Prostitution was legal, but the police still knew how to harass a woman.

Miyako's mind fluttered back and forth, a firefly in a jar. They had to let her go. Tonight, while she still had eight days before Delham's presentation. Tonight, before Papa-san spent a whole day in the hospital, with no one to feed him or fix his *kampo* tea.

Kimi gave her a nudge. "If you can get your sergeant to come here and vouch for us, they might let us go tomorrow. *After* they hold us overnight for the exam."

"He's not going to be able to get off base for that. Besides, I'm not sure he'll believe me." The more she agonized, the bleaker her situation seemed. Caught in the wrong district, at the wrong time of night. No steady work. No family member with the means to support her. No story that would hold up under questioning.

They would assume she was guilty. Short of some gift from heaven—George-san appearing from nowhere, ready to tell them he was her husband—three of her eight days were gone. And what about Papa-san? She'd have to get a message to Tanaka-san somehow, asking her to see to him. She let out an exasperated sigh. She could never repay the debt she owed her kindly neighbor as it was.

And when she didn't show up to pay the rent?

A sergeant motioned her over.

Goddess of Mercy, hear me now. Get me out of this thing and I'll visit you at your Temple of the Wisteria Well. And I'll bring a gift more substantial than a handful of incense sticks this time.

She sat across from the policeman. He introduced himself—Sergeant Shimizu. He poised a pen on a fresh notebook page. "I'm going to ask a few questions for our records. Your full name?"

She gave him her usual street name. "Ishikawa Midori."

He wrote it down. "What were you doing in the Abeno this evening, ah?"

"I just got off my shift at the factory." He wouldn't call someone to verify that story at this time of night, would he? "I try to see my friend Kimi on my way home now and then."

"Always a friend or a cousin or a sister with you women." He tapped his pen on the desk. "Look. Here's the truth. You're going over for the exam no matter how much you lie. So you might as well give me the facts, ah? Now, Ishikawa—if that's your name. How long have you been working the streets?"

"I'm not a prostitute." She snorted and looked away from him.

She met a pair of eyes. An older man, studying her. She ducked her head, thinking the man seemed familiar. She had to search her memory a moment before she placed him. When she did, her stomach dove like a swallow after a moth.

Lieutenant Oda—or at least he was a lieutenant in his Navy days. One of Papa-san's drinking buddies from the academy. Oh, it could *not* be any worse.

Oda-san moved toward them, his cane clacking along the floor. That was new since she'd seen him last, but he crossed the room with the same vigor she remembered. Sergeant Shimizu stood and bowed as he approached. She did the same. "Matsuura-san? You? Here?" His voice seemed to fill the room. *Calm yourself.* She bowed lower to veil her dismay. "Oda-san, how good to see you." She took a deep breath. "It's been some years."

One corner of Sergeant Shimizu's mouth rose in a derisive curl. "Ahh. Matsuura, is it?"

"*Hai,*" Oda said. "Daughter of Captain Matsuura, who commanded the cruiser *Aoba.* Clearly there's been some, ah"—his eyes narrowed slightly—"mistake." He turned to her. "Now, Matsuura-san, if you'll come with me, please."

She followed him across the floor, head high, determined to project a self-assured veneer. But beneath it, she squirmed with shame. Everyone in the room was staring at her, she was sure. Once the protected daughter of a noble family, now just another *baishunfu*—a woman who sold her spring. A whore.

According to the plaque on his door, Oda-san was a police captain now. He ushered her into his office and offered her a chair.

"Where've you been hiding, ah? I looked for months for your family after the war, but you'd vanished. I gave you up for dead. Finding you here..." His mouth curved in a slight smile, but his eyes drilled into her face. "Quite surprising, yes?"

Perhaps she imagined an extra emphasis on the word *quite.* Perhaps. She returned his gaze with the most composed expression she could paste on. "I assure you I'm every bit as surprised."

"You must be overwhelmed. Tea, perhaps?"

"That would be wonderful. *Domo arigato.*"

He pivoted, leaning on his cane. "Everyone's consumed with this infernal raid. I'll have to prepare it myself. I'll be a minute."

"*Domo arigato.*"

He clomped his way out of the room and closed the door behind him.

She perched on the chair, a torrent of emotions washing over her. How disarming it was, the way he was treating her. Like the young lady he'd known a few years ago. A few short years, but a different lifetime. A different Japan. A Japan where she'd had value, beyond the fifty yen a man paid for a "short service." A Japan that no longer existed.

She chewed her lip. Could she turn this to her favor? If she could convince Captain Oda she was an innocent victim of the raid, if she could get him to vouch for her, she could go free—perhaps even tonight.

He returned, followed by a policeman carrying a tray with a basic tea service for two. The man's eyes went wide with surprise at seeing her, but he bowed and said nothing. He left the tray.

Captain Oda sat across from her. "I'm intrigued to know how you managed to get caught up in this raid. You're the last young woman I'd expect to find here."

She lifted her cup and mustered an innocent pout. "I'm afraid it's all a terrible mistake. I only stopped off there to visit with a friend."

"Well, if that's the case we'll clear it up soon enough."

"I would certainly appreciate it." She gave him her sweetest smile. "I didn't know you were with the police here in Osaka."

"My blasted leg took me out of the Navy some years ago." He rubbed one hand absently over his knee. "What's it been since I've seen you? Five years, perhaps?"

"Wasn't it the day Papa-san and my brother shipped out?" She'd never forget that day—the last time she saw Akira-san.

"*Hai*, so it was. And what a day." Oda's eyes lit at the memory. "Quite an accomplishment for your brother, to command a vessel at his age. A credit to your family."

"*Hai*, but—"

"I know, child." His eyes took on a fervent glow. "Akira-kun has joined the honored dead. Your brother's warrior spirit will soon dwell in honor on Kudan Hill, ah?"

She bowed her ascent to this patriotic sentiment. Akira-san was the fortunate one. Wasn't he better off residing in glory with the ancestors than living here in defeat?

"And I extend my congratulations on your honored father's glorious death."

His death? Hope mounted. If he believed Papa-san was dead, he wouldn't look him up. "*Hai.*" Perhaps she responded a little too eagerly.

"So many brave Navy men. So many glorious deaths in battle."

She answered with the expected formula. "I'm sure they wished it above all else."

"And their families in a desperate state. Widows and orphans. No pensions. Getting by any way they can, yes?"

Any way they can. He'd heard how she was living. Already made up his mind about her guilt. All this courtesy was a ploy to relax her guard.

She was a hare in the hawk's shadow.

Monday 20 April 1942
Jiangxi Province, China

Dave and his Chinese honor guard hiked a couple of miles in the subtropical sun. He was a walking bundle of misery. Searing pain in his torso and feet. An aching pit in his gut. Muscles screaming, mind cottoned with exhaustion. Head pounding. Each step required a fresh act of will.

How much farther? He caught Chen's attention. "Need to rest a minute." He settled on a boulder beside the path.

The men grouped around him and exchanged a few comments. Pete turned his back to him, crouched a little, and hitched his arms.

Chen made an odd waggling motion with his fingers that seemed to mean *come here.* "He take you, Dev."

What kind of pansy do they think I am? Good thing he was too drained to roar out loud. The biggest of these kids didn't come up to his nostrils. He took a swig from someone's canteen and stood. "Very nice. But no thank you." He made a pushing gesture along the path.

Chen still wore a frown. "You hurt. Maybe bad."

"Yes. Let's go."

Chen shook his head, but they all hiked on.

Keep walking. One more step. One more step...

The ground tipped up and his knees found the dirt.

Dave came to with a start this time, and a cry of pain. He found himself flat on his back. An elderly Oriental man knelt beside him, probing along his shoulder blade.

Torture. I knew it. He jerked to a sit, sending a lightning bolt of white-hot agony blazing across his shoulder.

Wait—don't they question you first?

"Okay, Dev." Chen stood at his elbow. "This Doctor Liu."

The doctor gave him a curt nod. "Please. You lie down."

Dave took in the room. They had him on a ragged mat on the floor. Just Chen and the doctor—and a few ramshackle shelves, sparsely populated. A single low table with a pair of makeshift benches by way of furniture. A lot of peeling paint. And a nauseating odor of rotting fish.

No immediate threats.

He did as he was told, gritting his teeth. After a long moment the pain returned to a level he could handle.

He must have been out cold. They'd managed to get his shoes off without bringing him around. He noted with relief that his jacket and pistol lay in a neat pile on a shelf. His stout leather shoes stood by the door, anchoring a line of wooden clogs and sandals ordered by size.

Jacket. Pockets. Panic surged. "Where's my whiskey?" He started to sit up again.

"This?" Chen held up one of the bottles. He had a canteen in his other hand, which he thrust at Dave. "Drink."

Dave pushed the canteen aside and groped for the rye. Chen lifted it out of his reach. "Water, Dev."

"All right, all right." He accepted the canteen lying down and took awkward slurps that made him cough and dribble water across his chin.

Doctor Liu, a thick-jowled man with salt-and-pepper hair and a mournful slant to his eyes, watched Dave work at the canteen. The man's yellowed teeth displayed a prominent gap where at least two had gone AWOL.

If that's the doctor, he should meet the dentist.
His new reality seemed too strange to take in. The dingy room boasted a solid-looking roof and walls, which made it a palace compared to the broken-down cottage where he'd met Chen. A few pallets, like the one under his back, lay stacked against one wall—apparently they spread them out on the crude wooden floorboards to sleep. A burlap sack stamped with faded red Chinese characters fluttered in front of the sole window, which had stout bars where glass should have been. Something that might have been a brazier stood in one corner.

Chen followed his gaze around the room. "My father's house," he said with a slight incline of his head.

The door opened a crack from outside. Chen stepped to the door, blocking Dave's view. He directed a few low-voiced comments at the person outside, then turned back into the room.

"My sister." Chen glanced over his shoulder at the door. "If Japs find you, very bad." He drew a finger across his neck.

The implication sunk in.

Chen's sister. Pete. Doctor Liu. Several other soldiers, and two little boys. And whoever the soldiers reported to, or whoever else any of them might have told. How many people already knew about him?

It got hard to swallow.

Doctor Liu spoke to Chen, who nodded and took the canteen. He handed Dave the rye. "Now drink." He snickered a little. "Doctor says drink much."

Those were doctor's orders he was more than happy to follow. Especially since none of this inspired confidence. He raised the bottle to his lips with eager fingers. He got several swigs down his gullet and splashed more than a little of the precious amber liquid on his chin before Chen retrieved the bottle. Chen helped him unbutton his shirt.

The doctor produced a glass bottle with a hand-lettered label from his bag. He dribbled some brown liquid along Dave's shoulder blade. It smelled like Old Spice mixed with turpentine and week-old lawn clippings. The doctor placed his hand on Dave's shoulder and started to stroke the amber-colored tincture over his skin.

Despite all his efforts to be tough, he hollered out loud.

Chen gave an emphatic hiss and put a finger to his lips. "Shh! This good."

Surprisingly, it helped. The light oil produced a fleeting surface chill, then a deep, enduring warmth. Coupled with the effects of the whiskey, the tension ebbed from his muscles.

The doctor sent a stream of Chinese mumbo-jumbo Chen's way.

Chen made a face, then attempted a translation. "Doctor says no." He lined up his fists then made an abrupt gesture like he was breaking an invisible stick.

"Not broken?" Dave said.

"Yes."

Doctor Liu made a fist with his right hand then cupped his left around it. He pivoted the fist away from its resting place in the other hand.

"Oh. Dislocated." Dave nodded to show he understood.

Doctor Liu got to work in earnest. He pulled up his flowing midnight-blue sleeve, leaned forward, and pressed his elbow into the center of Dave's sore shoulder. The doctor actually used the point of his elbow to manipulate Dave's muscles and tendons.

Holy Moses, that hurts! He clenched his teeth hard and screwed his eyes shut. He found himself introduced to a new understanding of pain.

The half-hour that followed was the most unusual massage he'd ever received or heard about. The old gentleman pressed, rubbed, squeezed, and even slapped the back of his hand on Dave's skin with a steady rhythm that set half his body quivering. At one point, the doctor had him sit, circled his arms around Dave's shoulders with Dave's left arm draped on top of his, and rocked Dave's entire torso. Somewhere toward the end of that action, the doctor applied gentle pressure to the ball of his shoulder joint while he manipulated his clavicle. The ball snugged into its socket. The sensation was exquisitely strange.

When it was over, Dave eased himself back on the pallet, spent and slick with sweat. "Thank you. That was..." The edges of his vision blurred. His voice seemed to slur from somewhere far away. "Really something."

Chapter Eleven

Monday 20 April 1942
Jiangxi Province, China

THIS TIME DAVE WOKE TO CHEN jostling his good shoulder. "Eat, Dev. Eat. We leave soon."

Dave screwed his eyes shut. Opened them again. The squalid room was still there. The peeling paint and rustic furniture looked even grimmer in early evening's flat half-light. They'd bound some kind of compress around his shoulder and secured his arm with his sling. Amazingly, the pain had subsided to a dull ache.

"You sit?" The kid was in uniform, tension written all over his face. "Come to table?"

"Sure. Thank you." Truth was, the effort to stand made the room swim, but he wasn't about to admit that.

He spotted his bottles of rye up on the shelf with his other things. That familiar pang of need ran through him.

They'd fired up the brazier. Charcoal smoke and spicy cooking odors helped mask the pervasive fish smell. The waning light revealed a new cast of characters—Chen's family. A wiry middle-aged fellow with black hair like porcupine quills sat on a rickety-looking bench near the brazier. His left leg was lashed to a plank—a crude cast. A handmade crutch straight out of Dickens lay on the floor. A small boy with a cheerful face and eyes that shone like black marbles fidgeted on the bench beside him.

A woman with wayward gray hair looped into a lopsided bun bent over a table, working long strands of straw into a half-formed basket. The wide-brimmed hat of a field laborer rested beside her.

A teenage girl with Chen's features and a braid that hung to her waist stirred a large pan over the brazier. She glanced up at Dave.

All five of them shared the same broad noses, inquisitive eyes, and—except for the little guy—anxious round faces.

Fear looks about the same everywhere.

Chen gestured Dave to the table.

The cooking smells had Dave's stomach rumbling. He grabbed his bottle from the shelf and set it on the table. "Chen, will you join me for some not-so-good American whiskey?"

Chen took an anxious look at his sister, probably to gauge her progress. He gave Dave a curt nod and sat down.

Chen's mother brought over a teapot and a pair of small cups with no handles. She poured for them both.

"Thank you." Dave tried a little bow. Her careworn face lifted in a smile. She responded with a torrent of syllables. He grinned at her. "Ask her if she'd like a little whiskey," he said to Chen. "And your dad."

Chen relayed the offer. Chen's mom nodded and produced three more teacups. Chen's dad stumped over to join Chen on the bench.

Dave poured out a scant jigger each. The discovery that his bottle was almost drained sent a slight tremor to his hand.

This better buy me a lot of goodwill. He threw back his jigger.

The others took tentative sips. Chen coughed, screwed up his face, and put the cup down. But his dad leaned back on the bench. "Ahh." He gave an appreciative nod.

Chen's sister spooned whatever she was cooking into a wooden bowl and placed it in front of Dave. Rice with an oversized poached egg. Duck? Goose?

The way his stomach was rumbling, he'd have eaten cobra eggs.

He fingered the chopsticks. He'd never held one before. He picked one up, skewered the egg, and took a wolfish bite.

Chen's sister giggled. She led the boy to a corner near the fire, sat cross-legged on the pile of sleeping mats, and spun a top on the floor. The little fellow crouched in front of her and chortled.

Of course, big sister would find time for him when no one else could.

Girl's cute. But fifteen, tops. He blinked and, for a second, saw his older sister, holding a toy he'd owned years ago—a metal gyroscope top, painted in circus colors.

Jenny. The usual sense of loss yanked at him.

Feet squelched outside the window. Chen exchanged a glance with his father and stood. He got to the door in two brisk strides, cracked it open, and carried on a low-voiced conversation with a man outside. He turned toward Dave again, his expression unreadable. "We go, Dev. Now."

"What is it? What's up?"

"Japs in next village. They look for Americans."

Dave's adrenaline surged. "How far away?"

"Ten *li*. They have truck."

Ten what? "How many minutes?"

"Road no good. Fifteen minutes, maybe ten." Chen held his jacket out for him. "Come."

Dave cussed and shoved the rest of the egg into his mouth. The young soldier helped him put on the jacket and sling. He was amazed to discover he had limited motion in his left arm.

Chen's sister rushed Dave's shoes over and helped him put them on, then scooped up the little boy. His mother flew around the room, thrusting supplies into a large round basket—blankets and mysterious food items. A few finger-length dried fish dropped to the floor, their heads still on.

Chen grabbed his canteen and backpack and hustled Dave out the door. The women followed, Chen's sister balancing the little boy on her hip. The women took off at a brisk pace along the broken sidewalk that lined a row of two-story buildings with stained plaster walls.

Pete was standing lookout on the far side of the rutted road, next to a small stream that washed through an ancient-looking stone channel. He was equipped with a backpack and his rifle, an archaic bolt-action number. He turned and strode to meet them in the waning light.

The thrum of a truck broke through the orchestra of frogs and crickets. Faint but unmistakable.

Chen muttered what had to be Chinese curses. "Come, Dev." He set off at a lope around the corner of the house.

Dave and Pete followed him around the corner and along an uneven alley overgrown with grasses. They crossed the village's only other street. Through another narrow alley between tall walls, and they were in a broad field of weedy-looking plants that reached to his shins. The lemony color of their blossoms was intense, almost luminous, even in the dusk. Chen's mother and sister had disappeared into the crowd of villagers that dotted the field—a few dozen of them, mostly women and children, running for the forest. Its twilight fringe loomed maybe thirty yards ahead.

The truck noise swelled. Everyone picked up their pace. Why couldn't these people grow something tall, like corn? Something that would hide them? Their dark hair and garments stood out in stark contrast to the carpet of lively yellow blossoms.

Dave's longer legs got him into the forest before the Chinese soldiers. He halted and caught his breath until they ran up.

"Japs—at bridge." Chen spoke fast, between gasps.

A pistol barked from the far side of the village. Chen and Pete froze, stared at each other for a second or two. Chen's face dissolved into an agonized expression. He cocked his head to the right. Pete gave him a slow nod.

Chen led them to a ledge that topped a large rock outcropping just inside the canopy of the woods. It was a superb vantage point. In the waning light, they could survey most of what passed for Main Street. Chen's house stood at the nearest end.

Headlight glare washed across peeling, smoke-darkened plaster. The Chinese boys flopped flat on their stomachs. Dave flattened out as best he could beside them, wincing.

The Japanese truck jolted into view—a dark rectangular mass behind a pair of taped-over headlights that looked like slitted reptile eyes. About a dozen soldiers dismounted, hitting the ground running. Bayonets reflected the scarce light. Truck doors slammed. Guttural commands echoed from stone and plaster.

The officer fired into the air. Dave tensed like a tripwire. Not the way he'd planned on seeing action.

Pete braced his rifle on the firm ground. He aligned his sights on the soldier nearest them. He squinted with concentration, but his agitated breathing had the weapon shaking. The kid was terrified.

Dave knew exactly how the kid felt. But he pushed away his fear.

A few soldiers circled behind the structures. The rest split into four pairs and began a methodical sweep of the buildings, starting from either end of the village. One man, clearly the commander, paced the street from end to end. A vicious-looking curved sword swung at his side.

A pair of Japanese took up stations in front of Chen's house, with a third on guard behind.

Chen and Pete carried on a whispered conversation.

"Where's your dad?" Dave said in a low voice.

"In house. Too slow."

"What're you going to do?"

"Don't know. One gun. Thirteen Japs."

Dave slid his Colt from its holster, set it alongside Pete's rifle. "Two guns." It sounded smart and daring. Too bad he didn't have a smart, daring plan to go with it.

One of the soldiers—the taller of the two—pounded on Chen's door and yelled something.

Pete squinted through his sight.

Chen's door cracked a few inches. The soldier kicked it open. He and his companion burst into the house, rifles at ready.

Commotion erupted. Crockery breaking. Two male voices shouting. A third voice responded in a wheedling tone. A moment passed, then another smashing sound.

Chen reeled off a stream of ugly-sounding syllables.

Dave stared into the village, transfixed with horror. *This is all because I'm here.*

The door to Chen's house swung open. Chen's father appeared, followed by the taller soldier, who propelled him by the scruff of the neck. He stumbled into the street, his gimp leg and handmade crutch tripping him up.

The Japanese soldier pushed him to the dirt in front of the officer.

Chen squirmed and made a sort of whimpering noise. Pete put his hand on Chen's arm and muttered something.

Do they know? Do they know which family helped me?

"We gotta do something, Chen."

"How? So many Japs." Chen's voice had a strangled sound.

He glanced at Pete. The fellow's almond eyes showed

white all around the irises. His hands had a visible tremor.

Fine bunch of heroes—a cripple and a pair of raw kids. Chen was right. They weren't winning any firefights.

The Japanese held a brief conversation. The tall soldier handed something to the officer. The officer trained the flashlight on it to get a better look. The beam refracted through a glass bottle.

My stinking bottle! What was I thinking?

Chen made a gurgling noise.

The Japanese officer glared at Chen's dad. Made an imperious gesture with his chin. The two soldiers dragged the fellow to his feet. The square-built one took a position behind him, bayonet poised at the small of his back.

The officer paced in front of the poor man. Brandished the bottle at him. Chen's dad cowered, edged away—right against the point of the bayonet. That brought him up straight.

The officer ran his fingers over the English words on the label. Gestured with the bottle. Badgered Chen's dad with a torrent of syllables.

Chen gasped and issued a quiet moan.

The officer yelled something in a rising tone. Chen's dad withered but shook his head.

The officer closed his fist around his pistol, hauled back, and slung the full weight of the piece against the older man's temple. Chen's father reeled. He tottered on his injured leg and careened to the ground.

Chen spewed an explosive string of words. He reached over, grabbed Dave's pistol, and racked the slide. It chambered a round with a double clack.

Every trained soldier in the world knew that sound. The soldier nearest them—one of the men guarding the escape route behind the village—swiveled.

Chen's father rolled onto his back, grimacing. Pushing himself up to a seated position, he gave his chin a defiant lift and shook his head once more.

The officer holstered his pistol with a deliberate motion, his eyes not leaving the old man.

Chen took a deep breath, squinted through the Colt's sights.

What happened next came so fast it took Dave a second to register what he'd seen.

The officer whipped his sword from its scabbard. It split the air. And just like that, the old man's head bounced on the street. His body slumped to the ground, like a puppet whose strings were cut. Blood pooled in the dirt.

Chen shouted another emphatic stream of syllables and fired.

The soldier with the bayonet jerked and let out a hoarse yell. He crumpled to his knees, grabbing at his shoulder.

Chen took aim again.

The officer dove for cover behind the truck. The Japanese guard ducked around the corner of a thatch-roofed hovel. He pointed his rifle in their direction and yelled something at the others. Half a dozen of them scrambled for cover, rifles and flashlights trained at the forest.

Chen eyed Dave and grimaced. "Run, Dev. This our fight."

Dave stared at the kid—now fatherless. Just like that. Because of him. "It's my fight now."

"No. We all dead." Chen returned his attention to the scene around the truck. "You run. Get airplane. Kill many Japs. For us."

Bullets ripped through the branches around them.

"Go." Chen gave him a shove. "*Go.*"

It took a beat, but in the end, he told himself Chen was right. Much as he might want this to be his fight, it couldn't be. This was a suicide action where he'd be—again—useless. Die without inflicting any damage.

He dug in his pants pocket and slid Chen the extra magazine.

Saturday, December 25, 1948
Osaka, Japan

The teacup shook in Miyako's fingers. She gave Captain Oda her brightest smile, hoping to distract him, and set it on the table.

He studied her over his cup. "And your mother? She's

still here in Osaka, perhaps?"

Her gaze fell to the teapot. He wasn't the only man who'd seemed a little too admiring of Mama-san. "I'm very sorry to say she was killed. Like so many others, during the firestorms."

His teapot became, for a second, Mama-san's iron *natsume* at home. Mama-san's calm hands placed the pot on the brazier. Coaxed a red linen square into an elaborate fold. Used it to wipe the edge of Papa-san's heirloom tea bowl with infinite care.

Then Miyako was looking at the clawed fingers of a charred corpse.

She started.

He sat back in his chair, took a long breath. "I am truly saddened to hear it. Your mother was a beautiful and gracious lady. Those last months of the war were a horrible time. Tragic."

She swallowed around the lump in her throat.

He gave her a moment, then: "And your grandparents? Are they well?" He must have found the answer in her face. "Them too, ah? I see. Again, I am sorry. Fine people. Such a loss." He set his cup down. "So, you're alone. How are you managing?"

His voice was soft, but his eyes narrowed.

She steeled herself. "It's been difficult. I miss them all so much. But I'm getting along."

"You found work?"

"*Hai*. I've been fortunate."

"Where?"

"The Yamato Steel Works." Her standard story. "I managed to rent a decent room not too far from the factory."

Something shrewd and hard danced around his eyes. "The Yamato Steel Works?"

She nodded.

"I know one of the managers there. Man I served with in the Navy. You won't mind if I call him, then?" He pulled the telephone toward him, eyes drilling into her. "We can settle this thing in a minute, and you can be on your way, ah?"

She groped for a safe answer. "What's his name? I work the night shift so he might not recall me."

"Otani-san. You know him, perhaps?" Oda rifled through his Rolodex file.

"*Hai*, I think it sounds familiar."

"Exactly what is the nature of your work there—so I can prompt his memory?"

"I'm an office girl. I type, file, answer the phone. Keep books and records."

"Well, then. We'll see whether he can place you, ah?" He picked up the handset. "Sumiyashi-ko 4-3-3, please."

The seconds it took for the call to go through felt like an hour. She rested her fingertips on the amulet on her handbag and silently entreated the great Buddha for a miracle. Oda's friend could be out for the evening. Or better yet, he could confuse her with someone who *did* work there.

"Otani-san. Oda here. *Hai*, very nice to speak with you as well. Please pardon the interruption at this hour, but I have a young woman in my office. I need to verify her employment at the Yamato Steel Works." With every syllable he uttered, a new weight settled on her chest.

She folded her hands on her lap in the formal manner, so they wouldn't shake and betray her nerves.

"*Hai*. Her name is Matsuura Miyako." He listened for a few seconds. "*Hai*. I see. What about the night shift?" His eyebrows gathered over the bridge of his nose. "Ah. *Hai*, very good. *Domo arigato*."

He put the handset in its cradle and stared at it for an instant before he looked up at her. "Otani-san tells me they can't get raw materials." His words were deliberate. "Running at a fraction of their capacity. They've let many people go."

She put on a mournful face. "*Hai*, Captain Oda. That's true."

"Do those phones ring often during the night shift, Matsuura-san?"

"No, Captain Oda, not often." She worked to keep her eyes locked on his. "I mostly catch up on the paperwork."

"I don't think there's much paperwork, either." He snapped the words at her. "In fact, Otani-san specifically told me the night clerks were no longer needed. They let them all go." He leaned toward her for emphasis. "Every single one of them, Matsuura."

The trap sprang shut.

Captain Oda stood and moved to the office door. "Shimizu-kun, could you bring Matsuura-san's paperwork?"

Sergeant Shimizu appeared, notebook in hand. He opened it and gave it to his captain.

Captain Oda looked it over. The furrows dug deeper into his brow. "These are notes from Matsuura-san's interview, Sergeant?"

"*Hai*, sir."

Captain Oda looked from Shimizu's face to hers. "Matsuura-san, you've given the sergeant a false name. Lying to a police officer is a serious matter. You know this, yes?"

"Captain Oda..." She regretted the wheedling note that worked its way into her voice. "We both know any woman brought in during these raids is assumed to be guilty. I was afraid of the dishonor, the great *haji* for my family, if it became known I was here."

He paced to the front of the desk and stood over her. "Matsuura-san, you've been telling lies all night." He picked up steam. "You lied about your name. You lied about your profession. And you lied about your reason for being in the Abeno. Am I right?"

She quailed. "No, sir. I stopped there to see my friend, Kimi. She's here. She'll tell you."

"And now I'm supposed to believe one of *you*?" He smashed a savage fist into a pile of books on the desk. They tumbled, scattered across the polished surface like billiard balls. A thick book struck the teapot. It spun onto the floor and shattered at her feet. Porcelain shards exploded across her side of the room, and tea splattered the wall behind her.

He faced her full on. "You were born with a rare gift, Matsuura. The gift"—he let the word roll off his tongue—"of your family's good name. A name carried by *samurai* for centuries. By *daimyo*."

He took another pace toward her, his shoulders tensing like a prize fighter's. "Your beautiful mother. Your honored father. Your noble ancestors." The tendons in his wrists bulged. "To think the last of Captain Matsuura's line would become a shameful woman who would squander such a gift.

"You know, your father and I were closer than brothers,

starting from our academy days. I know exactly what Captain Matsuura would do if he were alive. If he could see what I see now." He sneered in disgust. "A dispossessed woman. A worthless whore. He'd disown you."

This was a shot to the heart. It was true. Papa-san would die of starvation before he would live in *haji*. Papa-san would hold a live grenade to his chest before he would bring *haji* to his family. Many soldiers had done that.

She always believed she'd do the same. Protect her honor, her family's honor at any cost—even the cost of her own life.

But her life was a sham. *Gaijin* counting out their money. Their revolting demands. Over and over. Night after night. For the price of a couple packs of cigarettes each time.

When had *haji* become something she could live with?

She forced her attention back to Oda.

"He'd drive you from his house onto the street, where a woman like you belongs."

There was nothing left but to plead her case. "Forgive me, Captain Oda. But how else are we going to eat? Believe me, if there were any other way, I—"

"Don't make excuses," he thundered. "There's no excuse for what you've become."

He turned away from her. Even from the back she could see his neck muscles work. His breath labored. His hand tightened on the brass handle of his cane until the veins stuck out.

At last, he spun on her, his face as good a mask of fury as she'd seen at the *kabuki* theater. "I would never have believed it, but here it is, right in front of me. Dispossessed. Improper. A smudge on your father's memory. An embarrassment to your family name. Yet you make excuses."

He stepped toward her on his good leg, raised his cane behind his shoulder. It whistled through the air at her. She froze in disbelief a fraction of a second too long. She raised her arm to block the blow, but too late. His cane cracked against her temple.

The room reeled. The floor swam up at her. She might have mumbled something about Papa-san.

The last thing she heard was Captain Oda's snarl at the sergeant. "Get this filthy *pan-pan* out of here."

Chapter Twelve

Monday 20 April 1942
Jiangxi Province, China

DAVE CRAWLED INTO THE TREES UNTIL he was sure he was out of sight. He got on his feet and headed deeper into the forest in a crouching, stumbling run.

It felt wrong to leave those kids.

Strategy. He kept repeating the word to himself. Pawns sometimes had to sacrifice themselves to protect a knight. And he was the knight here—a piece with unique capabilities. It made sense to hold himself in reserve for the day he could inflict real damage. The day he could do what the U.S. Army had trained him to do—what these brave people had risked themselves so he could do. Deliver a payload of death into the enemy's belly.

He was a strategist, not a coward. But if he wasn't a coward, why did he feel like puking?

He managed to get about a stone's throw away before the shooting started in earnest. Chen opened up—Dave knew the sound of that Colt .45—followed by Pete.

Dave ran a few more paces, dove behind a large tree, and huddled into a hollow at its roots. Out of view, but well within earshot.

A ghastly scream echoed from the direction of the village.

Here's hoping Chen found his man.

The enemy's answer came a split second later. Withering fire filled the forest around him. He threw his good arm up to protect his head and pulled his knees up into a miserable, quaking ball. Leaves and twigs and at least one small branch rained down on his back.

A horrific scream erupted—one of the Chinese kids. A moment passed before a muffled cry followed.

The Japanese emptied a new burst of rounds into the trees. He flattened and froze, pulse hammering, until the shooting dwindled to an occasional crack.

Soft moaning filtered into his ears. One of those boys was alive.

He was no medic, but he couldn't walk away and leave that kid there. He pushed himself to a crouch and moved through the woods in the boys' direction.

Now what?

Now those Japs come up here. Enemies would swarm their position in less than a minute. What did he think he was going to do for that kid?

Captured. The *Look* magazine photo sprang into his mind. Japanese soldiers using prisoners for bayonet practice.

He stood, hesitating a second or two.

An explosion lit the forest from Chen and Pete's position. The ground rocked. A monstrous pressure crushed his chest. His feet jarred loose from the earth. His nostrils filled with phosphorous while his head resounded with a terrible shrieking noise. He had a vague awareness it came from his own mouth.

How could there be so much light it hurt? And what was pushing at Dave's ribs?

A babble of voices. They droned on and on. But he couldn't make out anything they said through the buzzing in his ear.

It didn't seem to matter much. He could have ignored it all. Gone right back to sleep. Except—

Pain. It was everywhere. His head, his shoulder, one ear. Something warm and sticky seemed to be pooled there. And the pressure against his ribs graduated into a needling sensation he couldn't ignore.

He cracked his eyes open.

Light. Stabbing, blinding. His eyelids snapped shut on their own before he'd actually seen anything.

"Oh ho." The exclamation came with another prick in the ribs. The voice was more distinct through his right ear.

He twisted away from the new sharp pain in his ribcage. He opened his eyes and, with a determined act of will, kept them open.

The torturous light was a flashlight beam shining straight into his face from three feet above him. Behind it were two faces—angular. Brown skin. Slanted eyes. Sneering lips. And a rifle with a wicked bayonet poised against his chest, where his jacket lay open. Up close, the blade was much longer and broader than he'd pictured. A splotch of blood darkened his shirt where the buzzard had pricked him.

Their peaked caps bore Japan's five-pointed star. Two more soldiers loitered off to one side.

Captured? So this is it?

Disbelief numbed him. He, Dave Delham, was supposed to *do* something in this war. Not wind up warehoused in some prison camp, or worse—a pincushion for Japanese bayonets.

Chen was almost certainly dead. And Pete. Along with Chen's dad. He'd barely known the three of them a day, but the ache of their loss darkened his whole world.

Get airplane. Kill many Japs. For us.

He seethed inside. It couldn't end this way. He had a mission—now more than ever. A village full of pawns had been sacrificed for him, and now he was taken too.

A raindrop hit his temple. One of the soldiers hovering over him slammed his rifle butt into Dave's side.

Four of them, well-armed. One of him, left arm useless, no weapon but his knife. Nothing for it, really. "All right. All right." He sat up, hoisted his good arm in the air.

He put up and shut up while they pawed and searched him. Stripped him of everything of value. Cigarettes, sling, knife—even his watch with his wife's engraved message.

Some hero he'd turned out to be. *Stupid, stupid, stupid.*

A voice deeper inside him answered. *Chicken, chicken, chicken.* He'd lasted on the ground less than two days, in spite of the protection of an entire village. And what a price they paid for it. Every man, woman, and child, on the run for their lives—on his account.

Rain spattered his head and shoulders. A skinny soldier with buck teeth searched his jacket and found the remaining bottle of rye. The fellow opened it and took a whiff. He made a face, guffawed, and handed it to his companion.

One of them stepped behind Dave and put a bayonet point against his back. Even through the jacket, he felt the prick enough that he took a skip-step forward. Mocking voices jabbered on every side.

He began his funeral march out from the trees.

A flash of lightning gave him his first glimpse of the welcoming committee lined up to meet him. Several fierce-looking soldiers with triumph written across grim faces. Their hedge of armaments glistened in the rain. Rifles with bayonets, a long sword, a pistol—all aimed his direction. A pair of flashlight beams pierced the rain-streaked night, seeking him out in the trees.

He stopped short, his pulse rising with dread.

A sharp prick in his back again. He managed not to yelp. He drew a deep breath and hoisted his good arm farther into the air, palm open. He managed to raise his left hand a few inches. He walked out onto the open field.

The flashlights found him at once.

Something solid slammed into his spine, sending him sprawling chest down in the mud. They had him surrounded by the time he got to his knees. Hostile faces confronted him from every side. He stared along the shaft of a long-barreled rifle, its bayonet point inches from his chest.

The officer took a pace toward Dave, stopped directly in front of him. Confronted him with a fierce frown and a glare. He unsheathed his sword—slowly, to prolong the ringing sound, revealing the slender blade in all its deadly beauty. The thing was several inches longer than the man's arm.

Dave closed his eyes. Waited for the strike. Pictured his own head rolling through those weeds.

At least it would be quick.

The officer voiced a war-like yell. His sword whistled as it sliced the air.

It came to a precise stop, its razor edge resting against his neck. A slow trickle of warm blood made a path toward his collar.

Dave stared up the blade. It seemed to telescope as he gazed along its length. Sweat formed at his hairline, stung as it trickled into the cut.

The officer grunted and lowered his sword. "You prisoner of Nippon. You do all things we say. If not, we kill you." He spun on his heel and strode toward the village.

Saturday, December 25, 1948
Osaka, Japan

Miyako's gasp woke her. Acrid gas seared her nostrils, her sinuses. She recoiled, the reflex grinding her head back into a hard surface.

My head. Oh Heavens.

That smell! Awful...

A sledgehammer seemed to be going at her temple. Her left eye watered, and she could barely open it. She blinked away tears. Something sticky matted her hair.

A flesh-colored blur hung over her. She tried to focus. The effort brought agony, the light setting off a cascade of pain through her skull.

The blur resolved into a face. She caught her breath. A Japanese man she didn't recognize, his features twisted in a broad leer.

His mouth moved. His voice seemed to travel a long way to reach her. "Look. She's coming around."

Smelling salts. That's what he had under her nostrils. She moved to push him away, but she couldn't bring her hands forward. Her arms were pinioned above her head, her wrists shackled by something cold. Unyielding.

"Hey!" she said—or tried to say. Something was wedged in her mouth.

She took a deep breath, screamed with all her might. Pain stabbed her temple, reverberated through her head, but the sound came out an inarticulate moan.

Gagged. Bound. A nightmarish feeling set in, but this was no nightmare. She was wide awake. On her back on a table, ankles bound.

A bare bulb lit the room. She stared up into its unforgiving light, mustered all her strength. Tried to scream again. It came out a thin, strangled sound.

She twisted. *Handcuffs. He has me in handcuffs.* She strained. Arched. Thrashed. Nothing gave.

Exhausted for the moment, she lay still. Focused on his face. He watched her, lips twitching with amusement.

Mercy. What now?

She tried to read his eyes. What she saw sent a lead weight to the pit of her gut.

The impotence of surrender and defeat. The shame of debasement and privation. Sex was something she could handle. But this wasn't sex. She was here to bear the brunt of his pent-up rage.

"Wondering what you're doing here?" He ran his hand across her sweater. "Captain Oda informed us there's no hurry to get you to the hospital. Which means we can have all the time we need."

We. Another man moved into Miyako's field of view. One she knew. Sergeant Shimizu loomed over her, his face painted with malevolence. "Daughter of a navy captain. Guess you had it pretty good. Not so high and mighty now, ah?" A wild chuckle issued from his mouth.

Her vision went filmy with tears.

This time when they're done with me, maybe they'll just kill me.

Male voices wove in and out of Miyako's consciousness.

"Can't take her there, moron. Look at her..."

"...dump her off..."

"Where?"

They're talking about me.

It didn't matter. She drifted on a sea of agony. The tortured pounding in her head, the scrape of air through her windpipe, the dull ache of her bruised limbs. Fierce stinging, blood sticking where the cuffs had scored her flesh.

"What if she tells?"

"She's a whore. Who'll believe her?"

"Who'll care?"

She didn't care. Not now. Not after what they did to her. She sank into merciful blackness.

Warm, wet pressure on Miyako's brow. Something soft under her back. That same infernal sledgehammer at work on her head.

A gray-haired man in a suit jacket bent over her, swabbing her temple with a damp cloth. She flinched away from probing fingers.

"There you are," he said. "How are you feeling?"

The soft light needled her eyes. She squinted and parted her lips, but no words came.

He dipped the cloth in a bowl, swabbed her temple once more. She flinched again.

"Tender, ah? Nasty cut."

"*Hai.*"

"What happened?"

"I—" Something hard cracking on her temple. A fist on her throat. A succession of men's faces, hungry expressions. A jumble of pain, confused shame. "I don't remember." She turned misty eyes to the wall.

"Of course you don't, child." The honeyed voice belonged to a woman she hadn't seen. She stood in the hallway outside the room, her *kimono*-draped form backlit by a window. A cigarette holder dangled from her fingers. Light reflecting from something outside tinted the *shoji* a soft green like stained glass.

The woman glided into the room. "We decided not to take you to the hospital if it wasn't absolutely necessary. I thought you would prefer to keep this private, yes?"

She was right about that. What Miyako could remember was shame enough. But suffer through the grilling she'd get at a hospital exam? Put into words exactly what they'd done to her? Unthinkable. Unbearable. She could never live with her *haji* after that.

"*Arigato.*" Her voice was a grateful rasp.

Where am I? Who is this woman? Do I know her?

"You're welcome." The woman gave a graceful bow. "May I ask whom we have the honor of hosting?"

"Mats...Ishikawa." It hurt to speak. "Ishikawa Midori."

"Pleased to meet you, Ishikawa-san." The woman's eyebrows tipped up. "I am called Imai Ayao. And this is Doctor Ogata." She looked to the doctor. "What do you think, Doctor?"

"The cut will require a few stitches. I'll examine her to

assess the concussion." He turned to Miyako. "Can you sit? Slowly, young lady."

She tried, but nausea and dizziness overwhelmed her. She slumped onto the futon.

"Ah, be careful. It's all right. Relax. How many fingers am I holding up?"

She mustered all her focus. "I think—two."

"Keep your eyes on my fingertips." The doctor watched her intently as he moved his hand across her field of view. He looked at Imai-san. "I've seen worse. I'll check on her again, ah? My guess is she'll recover in a few days. But with such cases, one can't always tell."

A few days? But there is something I need to do. Something critical.

If only she could remember what it was.

"You mentioned other wounds? I need to examine those as well."

A pained expression crossed Imai-san's face. "*Hai.*" She called over her shoulder. "Yamada-san, bring a sheet, please."

A stout gray-haired woman bustled in. She and Imai-san held a sheet across Miyako's chest to hide her face while the doctor examined the lower half of her body. He parted the cotton housecoat they'd wrapped her in and sucked his breath in sharply.

"*Hai*," Imai-san said. "Brutes."

Miyako had no clear memory of the doctor leaving. Maybe a short time later, a girl knelt beside her with a bowl of broth. Miyako's gut heaved and sent bile up her throat. She waved the broth away.

What is it I need to do? I know there's something. Something important.

Hushed voices came and went—some in the room right next to her, some in the hallway outside the *shoji*. She supposed they were talking about her, but it made no difference. Her consciousness was a *chokibune* boat drifting, pilotless, on its moorings.

Chapter Thirteen

20 April 1942, Jiangxi Province, China
First Day Captive

ROUGH HANDS JERKED DAVE TO HIS FEET. A jeering soldier stepped forward and cuffed his wrists in front of him. Another produced a length of rope and trussed his elbows at his sides. They put the bayonet at his back—this was mandatory, apparently—and a goon on either side. They prodded him toward the village. With his ear still ringing and the ground unstable beneath him, he swerved down the slope.

Flashlight beams crisscrossed the field. For the first time, he had a chance to appreciate the work Chen and Pete had done. A pair of corpses sprawled on the carpet of grass. The path to the village brought them right past one. The young soldier had died clawing at a gaping hole in his chest. His vacant eyes stared into the rain.

He didn't look that different from Chen.

The soldier next to Dave stopped and trained his flashlight on the corpse. He turned and glowered at Dave. The guy behind him uttered some emphatic syllables and rammed his rifle butt into Dave's back.

They entered the village. The truck's headlights cast pallid light along the main road. The man the boys had shot in the shoulder was on the ground between the stream and the road, moaning. Another soldier leaned over him, applying pressure to his wound. There were no Chinese in view—at least, none living. Chen's father lay where they'd cut him down. Dave couldn't help himself. He stared at the corpse. Blood had soaked into the mud, leaving big dark blotches.

That blood might as well be on his own hands. Along with Chen's and Pete's.

He looked away. His eyes landed on his whiskey bottle, lying in the mud.

His stomach roiled. Heaved. And then, in spite of his best efforts to choke it back, he bent double and retched. It took him a moment to regain his composure. He looked up to find the officer watching him, his face the picture of abject scorn.

"He helped you, ah?"

Dave found no words.

The officer spat on Chen's father's chest.

They loaded Dave onto the open truck, in the middle of a bench seat, Japanese butchers hemmed in around him. The smell of rotten fish and sweat—and the taste of his own vomit—made him want to throw up again.

That truck ride was the worst nightmare he'd ever had or imagined.

Except I'm not gonna wake up.

He had no way of gauging how long they jolted across China. Hours, probably, spent jostling and thirsting and fuming. Hemmed in by Japanese murderers who were no doubt finishing off his rye. *His* rye. While his mouth felt dry as gravel, and he had nothing to dull the pain that tore through his shoulder with every rut in the road. And there were plenty of those.

But all of that paled beside the new set of images that cycled through his brain. Chen's dad prone on the dirt. Chen's grim face as he left him. The explosion that no doubt killed both those kids.

His own whiskey bottle in the officer's hand.

Every one of those people would've stayed safe in their cozy little houses if Chen hadn't tried to help him.

Raindrops beat a tattoo against the truck's canvas roof.

Get airplane. Kill many Japs. For us.

There had to be some way his war wasn't over. *Lord, if you're listening, get me back in this war.*

They eventually lurched into an area where the road seemed smoother. They exchanged the bewitching scents of rain on forest for the stink of human waste and discarded food and dirty asphalt.

The truck rolled to a stop. The men unpacked themselves around him.

"*Toridase, horyo.*" He found out the hard way what that meant. A rough arm, or more than one, gave him a shove along the bench seat and a push out over the tailgate. He landed on his side on the wet asphalt—hard—his trussed-up arms useless for breaking his fall.

Laughter above him. Three different combat boots slammed into his back. Rough hands jerked him to his feet.

He staggered forward. A heavy wooden door swung on squeaky hinges in front of him. He tripped up a cement step, across a threshold and onto tile floor. The door behind him thudded closed. The sound reverberating off the floor bore the ring of finality—a clear message.

Prisoner of Nippon. Any control over his own life—gone. And he'd seen how these butchers operated.

Someone peeled off his blindfold and untied his elbows. His lifeless arms flopped against his sides. Two of them grabbed him by the upper arms, hustled him down a side corridor, and shoved him into a bare little room. A key turned in the lock from the outside.

He sank down on the wood-plank floor, let his head droop into his manacled hands. Took shallow breaths while the pain from his shoulder ebbed.

Thirty-some hours earlier he'd stood in front of a grave marker and asked himself if he was looking at an omen.

He had his answer.

Monday, December 27, 1948
Osaka, Japan

Miyako sat bolt upright, ignoring the colony of bees buzzing in her ears.

Papa-san.

How long have I been out? Has anyone been in to look after him?

George-san. I need to see George-san. That thought came with an ache in her chest.

And something else. Hiro-chan. Something to do with Hiro-chan.

"Lie still, please." It wasn't Hiro-chan's voice, but she saw his face. His thick fringe of eyelashes against smooth skin. His round cheeks.

She started, but then the horrific memory flooded back. Hiro-chan was dead.

The face that hovered next to her belonged, not to her

brother, but to the girl who'd brought the broth earlier. She was eleven or twelve, perhaps. A lavender kerchief and sturdy *monpei* pants marked her as a servant.

The girl studied Miyako from eyes hauntingly like Hiro-chan's. "Dr. Ogata said you must rest. Are you hungry now? I can bring you something."

She was ravenous. And thirsty. These physical sensations rooted her. Helped her shake the eerie sense she was talking to her little brother. "*Hai.* But how long have I been here?"

"It's Monday. I found you yesterday morning. In the rubbish heap." She shook her head. "You look awful."

"Monday? *Che!* I have to go see Papa-san." And get a message to George-san. *And something else. What?*

"I don't think so. Not until you eat something." The girl was on her feet. "And not until Imai-san sees you. She wants to talk to you the instant you're awake."

The *something else* struck her like an avalanche thundering down Fujiyama. Hiro-chan's murderer. She'd found him.

She tried to stand but a constellation of stars did a foxtrot in front of her. She sat down and blinked until her vision cleared. She looked around.

Tiny vanity. Mirror. Narrow shelves behind an open drape held a few folded cotton robes—simple, flimsy. Western-style bed. The room just big enough to accommodate the scant furnishings.

It all had a familiar feel. "What is this place?" She posed the question, but something inside her already knew.

The girl looked surprised. "The Tobita Oasis, of course."

No. Oh, no.

A shrill voice sounded from the far end of the hall. "Kawamura!"

The girl gave Miyako a hasty bow and left. Miyako let her head sink into the pillow.

Tobita. "The Oasis." All the women. Tiny room with spartan furnishings—apart from the Western-style bed. A brothel in the licensed district—the blocks inside the infamous red lines on the police department's map. She knew this world all too well.

She wasn't concerned about her physical condition now—pounding head, scorching pain all through her body. Her pulse was taking stutter steps that signaled the start of something worse.

Breathe. She willed it to stop. *Slow, deep breaths. Breathe.*

It's all right. It's been years. I'm free.

She sagged onto the futon, staring around the room. Her eyes lit on the door, then on the lock. The back of the lockbox, more properly. This door locked from the outside. She'd seen that before too.

Laughter. Coarse laughter. Key rattling in the lock. Shoji sliding open. Three men—American soldiers. One bottle. The reek of whiskey and sweat.

She defied the sting of her tortured flesh and pillowed her head against her knees. Her heart thudded, a frightened sparrow in the cage of her chest.

"First time, Jap girl? Three tickets. Paid for, see?"

20 April 1942, Nanchang, China
First Day Captive

Time passed—Dave couldn't have said how much. His mind wandered between Chen and Pete and their village, and his missing crew. What had happened to Chen's mother and sister? And the little boy? Three more lives he'd destroyed. As for his crew...He screwed his eyes shut and hoped with all his might they were well on their way to Chungking.

Don't give up hope for yourself. Even if there seemed to be no grounds for it at that moment. Something would happen—some mistake on their part. And he'd be away to Chungking and back in it.

The creak of door hinges jarred him from his thoughts. A pair of soldiers walked in. One of them scuffed at him with a combat boot. *"Baka. Tachiagaru."*

He lurched to his feet.

What next? His stomach pulled tight with hunger, but he had a feeling a meal wasn't in store.

Hope my men are a hundred miles from here.

The soldiers marched him, limping, down a corridor and into a fair-sized paneled room. Half a dozen Japanese sporting braid and stars anchored their eyes on him from the far side of a long table, across the remnants of a sumptuous dessert.

The ranking officer sat at the head of the table. He was impressive, with an extra spray of braid draped around one shoulder and a cigar poised on his ashtray. He wore a stony expression behind little round glasses like Hirohito's.

All this brass. I must be important. What do they expect from me?

What happens if they don't get it?

There were rules, right? They had to treat POWs according to the Geneva Convention.

But what about that photo from *Look?* Those Chinese prisoners. That sure wasn't the Geneva Convention.

Bowls of fruit and candy stood along the length of crisp linen. A half-empty wine decanter graced one end of the table. But the crowning touch was the amber-colored bottle near the center. It sported a familiar gold label—Chivas Regal.

He moistened his lips. For an instant he could imagine how it would soothe the tension away—bring him to oblivion's door if he drank enough. Oblivion sounded good just then.

Chen's dad flashed through his mind's eye, giving his chin that final defiant lift. It sank in then. Dave would never drink again.

He anchored his eyes on the ranking officer and stood like a soldier.

Never let a bully see your fear. He'd learned that one on the playground.

The one with the grand uniform directed a few sentences at an officer at the table. The man bowed from his chair, leaned back, and looked at Dave.

"Saito-san asks what your name is."

This man's English was the best he'd heard in China. "David Delham. Lieutenant, U.S. Army. O-dash-80073." It was all they were getting.

The interpreter stood and walked toward Dave. He tossed

a plum in the air, caught it, and bit into it with a flourish.

Dave's traitor of a stomach growled on cue—loud enough he was sure the fellows next to him heard it.

"David Der-ham. Saito-san says I should tell you we are very nice people. You answer a few questions and we give you good dinner." The officer's nose crinkled. "And a bath."

A few smirks at the table. Some of them spoke English.

Saito unleashed another flood of language at his interpreter.

The man took another bite. "Maybe you are hungry, David Der-ham? Saito-san asks how you got to China."

"I don't have to answer that. You know it. I know it." He shifted in his chair. "David Delham. Lieutenant, U. S. Army. O-dash-80073."

The ranking officer glowered at him. Gave some order to one of Dave's guards.

A rifle butt smashed into Dave's side. He doubled over and sucked for breath. Burning pain shot from his injured shoulder across his torso.

That still shot from *Look*. What it failed to capture was the savage force of their thrusts.

So much for the Geneva Convention.

A chorus of laughter erupted around him.

Stupid. Coward. Maybe he had this coming. He'd left those boys to die.

He pulled a burning breath into his lungs and straightened his back. He wasn't giving them anything more to laugh about if he could help it.

Saito exchanged rapid-fire comments with two or three other officers. The interpreter inclined his head. "*Hai.*" He pulled his pistol with an abrupt motion and stalked up to Dave.

"Let me explain your situation, prisoner. We know more than you think. You came here in a B-25 late the night before last, after dropping incendiary bombs over Tokyo, Nagoya, or Osaka that morning. You deliberately targeted heavily populated areas. You are not a prisoner of war. You are a murderer and a criminal. And so we will treat you." He clicked the safety off and pressed the muzzle against Dave's forehead. "You choose. Answer our questions or we execute you for your crimes."

Crimes. Everything around Dave came to a sudden stop as he stared past the pistol into the man's face. At his implacable jawline. The fierce glint in his eyes. The room suddenly felt cold.

Disbelief numbed him. If they deemed him a criminal, they could do whatever they wanted to him. No pretense of protection from the Geneva Convention.

Sweat slicked his forehead. "I committed no crimes." He gasped out the words.

The interpreter pressed his pistol against Dave's head. Finally he gave it a push. "Dead." He stepped back. "Think about that tonight, David Der-ham."

Chapter Fourteen

Monday, December 27, 1948
Osaka, Japan

THE WAKING NIGHTMARE LEFT MIYAKO THE way it always did—drained and drenched in clammy sweat.

She released her knees, relaxed her back. Slowly unwound her body from the tight coil she'd made it. She closed her eyes, waiting for the rhythm of her pulse to slow.

What was this thing that happened to her? It always felt so real, like they were right there.

She sat up slowly, to tame the pounding in her temples, and did her best to collect herself. In a brothel, again. They might look a little different—some more elegant, some less—but it was all the same thing. A steady stream of men, each bearing his cursed brothel ticket. And if she said no?

Merciful gods. On the streets, she could go home. In the brothel, they'd smack her around until she did what they wanted.

Her pulse had almost returned to normal. She plucked up the courage to look in the mirror. What she saw ripped her heart out.

A jagged gash on her temple met a cut across her forehead. A swollen lip rendered her mouth a misshapen mass. Bruises ringed her throat. She didn't even want to think about her thighs and midriff. She stared at her reflection, fingertips tracing the bruises.

Damaged goods. That's what she was. What could George-san want with her now? Every time he looked at her, he'd know she'd been violated. Shamed.

She let her eyes close and groped her way onto the futon, tears burning behind her eyelids. Her thoughts gave way to a swirling void of despair.

I swore I'd never—never!—come back to a brothel.

But where else could she go?

They'd taken her in, but everything had its price here. No doubt there was plenty on her ledger already. Imai-san didn't pick her up off the street from kindness. Each day that passed while she recovered would mire her deeper in the brothel's debt.

No! She would not spend the rest of her life here, in what the police called the red-line district. She could not come to consider this place home.

The *shoji* slid open. Imai-san wafted in, a whiff of jasmine floating in with her. "How are you feeling, my dear?" she said, her bell-like voice solicitous.

I'd wager the black widow uses that tone with her mate.

Imai-san settled gracefully on the futon's edge and placed a slender hand on Miyako's forehead.

Miyako's answer came in a voice that was little more than a croak. "Better, *arigato*. Hurts."

"I'm sure it does. Poor thing." Imai-san brushed Miyako's hair from her injured temple. She winced and drew her breath in gently. "I have a salve that does wonders to reduce scarring. A geisha trick I picked up in Kyoto."

How many yen will that put on my ledger?

"What can you tell me about yourself, Ishikawa-san? We couldn't get much out of you yesterday."

The less the better. "Sorry...hurts to talk."

"Will anyone be looking for you? Should we let someone know you're here?"

The last thing she wanted was for Papa-san to know she was here. Or George-san.

She summoned a confused look and shook her head. Imai-san's brow creased with apparent concern. "Still don't remember much, ah? Don't worry. I'm sure it will come back in time. We all want you to feel better." She looked Miyako pointedly in the face. "But there is a rather delicate point I feel I must raise. My girls have bandaged you. Cared for you. Fed you. They've been tireless."

Miyako gave the lady the best smile she could. "*Domo arigato.*" The words grated through her bruised throat.

"You haven't eaten much yet, but I'm sure your appetite will improve. Plus, I've extended myself to cover your medical expenses. The doctor isn't cheap, ah?"

Miyako nodded. She knew all about that. And she also knew where this was going.

"We needn't weigh you down with trivial concerns such

as room and board and medical expenses." Imai-san leaned forward, her delicate heart-shaped face luminous. "The last thing I want is to slow your recovery with such burdens. I have good news. I can arrange a generous cash advance that will more than cover it all."

Wait. How generous? And how much in advance? "Papa-san...in hospital."

"So." Imai-san's penciled eyelids narrowed. "Perhaps you remember a bit more now."

"Some details."

"In the hospital." She sat back. Her eyes were slits. "Naturally, that will be quite expensive."

"*Hai.*" How much would she need to cover doctor bills?

"Well..." Slowly. "I can take that into account. I'm sure a pretty thing like you must have some skills. Some ways to make an evening pass quickly for a lonely gentleman who might be, ah, far from home."

Her pulse began to hammer again. "I'll need time."

Imai-san made an expansive gesture. "Don't concern yourself. I can give you a week or ten days to feel better." She pursed her lips. "Now, what shall we make out your contract for?"

Miyako screwed her eyes shut and considered that question. If she couldn't get the cash in the next couple of days, it meant nothing. But if she could—ten thousand for the poison. How much to keep Papa-san in the hospital a while longer?

She looked steadily up at Imai-san. "Seventy-five thousand? Above what I owe you now." She held her breath, her chest filling with ground glass. It felt like a life sentence. Well, she'd be serving one anyway before she'd ever repay it.

Imai-san arched her brows and laughed a gentle laugh. "I'm afraid your notion of what your services are worth might be a bit exaggerated. I can't possibly go over sixty thousand, however much I might wish it with my far-too-tender-hearted nature. And that would be for a two-year commitment and would include what you owe me."

"I could be flexible." She swallowed, trying to moisten her raw throat. "When can you pay the advance?"

"As soon as you're ready to see clients."

Her stomach plunged like a cormorant after a fish. If she couldn't have the money this week, the amount made no difference, and they might as well spend their time comparing sizes of acorns. "Please. No sooner? You've been so generous."

Imai-san's smile chilled by several degrees. "These are very standard terms, Ishikawa-san." She leaned toward her, eyes taking on a fierce glitter. "If you need the cash, you'll simply have to get better quickly, ah? And don't plan on leaving this establishment until that happens."

"But I'm worried about Papa-san. Is anyone seeing to him? And the hospital—they might want money now."

Imai-san stood and glided to the *shoji,* placing her feet with the precision of a jungle cat. She pushed the panel aside and turned to Miyako. "You simply can't put this kind of pressure on yourself, Ishikawa-san." Her voice was plum wine, but her jaw was firm and her eyes steely. "It's not good for your health. And there is something you need to understand."

"*Hai?*"

"*I* have a business to run. *You* represent a substantial investment. What if you decide to run off on me? Leave me stuck with your doctor's bills?" She conjured a cigarette and her long holder from her sleeve. "No, my dear. Until you've signed your contract and started work, don't talk to me about leaving this establishment."

Miyako stared at the woman. She hardly knew what she'd say to Papa-san now. It would get even harder as the days passed.

Imai-san lit her cigarette. "This couldn't be simpler, my dear. As for your father, you're entering into a contract with me that will enable you to pay his hospital bill. He'll understand that. Even little Kawamura should be able to explain that to him. I'll send her now if you'd like."

"You...you can't...just keep me here."

Imai-san gave her an ironic little smile. "Actually, I think I can." She reached out, plucked at Miyako's thin cotton sleeve. "How sad you don't have any clothes you can wear outside in this weather. And quite apart from that, do you think I'm the only one with a business interest in this place?

Trust me, you'd rather deal with me than my associates. They are not pleasant people."

20 April 1942, Nanchang, China
First Day Captive

The soldiers pulled Dave from the dining room and bound the blindfold on. He barely registered it. Too much to absorb.

Not an ordinary prisoner of war. A murderer and a criminal.

Criminal? The raid was heroic. Exactly what every true-blooded American had been thirsting for. They'd jump up and cheer when they heard about it at home. Probably were toasting him already.

But that was half a world away. Over here in China, it was hard to see how things could get any worse.

Impatient arms tugged and prodded him up a set of stairs. Down another corridor. Something solid—probably another rifle butt—met the small of his back. He stumbled forward. One of them yanked off his blindfold. The door thudded closed behind him.

Dave folded up on the floor.

He'd never been so exhausted, but sleep wouldn't come. Torturing thoughts circled him like ravenous wolves. Chen's eyes on him. The kid's last words to him. *Get airplane. Kill many Japs. For us.*

Lord, if you're listening, please get me back in this war. For them.

The way he'd skulked and hid. Let a whole village of Chinese peasants fight his battles for him. He never lost his nerve in *Payback's* left seat. In her cockpit, between two roaring seventeen-hundred-horsepower engines and with a ton of destructive power in the bomb bay behind him, he could do anything. He was a god. Not down here.

He needed a—

No. No drink.

The officer's pistol, cold and hard against his forehead. *Think about that tonight, David Der-ham.*

He *was* thinking. Would they execute a prisoner of war?

His empty bottle in the officer's hand. And—this image so clear it could have been burned on his retina—Chen's dad's corpse on the rutted street.

Execute me? Sure they would.

Dave must have dozed after all. Voices outside the window ripped him out of it. Daylight flooded the room. He groaned and stretched. His head pounded, and his mouth was dry as a desert gulch.

Shaky legs carried him to the window. It gave him a view down onto the broad steps in front of the building. Probably a dozen soldiers in mustard-colored uniforms surrounded a black truck, rifles at ready. Three men in aviator jackets and handcuffs stood in a line on the bottom step. Two blond heads and a tousled brown mop. Smith, Braxton, Watt.

Vitty emerged from the building, a trio of soldiers prodding him along.

No. They had *Payback's* entire crew. He kicked at the wall. "No, no, no." He punctuated each word with a fiercer kick. The last one sent a plaster chip flying.

A detail of soldiers burst into the room and cuffed him, then delivered him downstairs. His crew—two officers, two enlisted—stood lined up with their backs to him.

But what a difference from the last time he'd seen them. Scruffy. Mud-streaked trousers. Matted hair. Still, each of them held shoulders square and heads high.

His men—not cowed. He stood taller himself as his heart thrilled with pride.

They shoved him into place next to Watt. He took a sidelong look down the line. Watt's jaw worked, but the Texan didn't give him a word or a glance. Vitty gave him a fierce glare, then looked away.

"*Horyo.*" A rifle butt slammed into Dave's solar plexus. It took a moment before the blazing pain subsided and he could focus on the Japanese captain in front of him.

Eyes forward. Got it.

The officer's raging face was the last thing he saw before the blindfold went on.

It was tough to piece together what was going on with

that stinking blindfold on. They pushed and prodded the airmen onto a truck, which rumbled on for a while. He caught the clamor of people and livestock when they slowed. After a few minutes en route, they motored across a smooth surface and stopped. The Japanese unloaded the five of them onto a stretch of asphalt.

His blindfold had worked itself a little looser. A set of narrow metal stairs on wheels moved into the sliver of ground he could see beneath it.

No mistaking the whiff of avgas. A plane. They were putting them on an airplane.

I can fly this thing. I can fly this thing. His heart repeated it with each step he took.

All he had to do was figure out a way to overpower the guards and grab the yoke. And they'd be on their way to Chungking. Right back in it. Sure, it would be hard to fly with handcuffs, but he'd work it out.

The soldiers prodded him up the stairs first. He stepped onto the plane. The cockpit was to his left, but he could see a soldier's boots beneath his blindfold. They'd wisely posted a guard in front of the cockpit door.

Someone grabbed him from behind and twisted him into the narrow aisle. He tried to imagine some way he could fight his way back into it. Get his hands on that yoke.

But there were handcuffs and a blindfold and armed soldiers on every side. A couple of Japs marched in front of him. He could hear more of them shuffling behind. Every step aft took him farther from that cockpit. And there was nothing he could do about it.

They put him in his own row, with Jap guards seated behind him and more in the row in front of him. If they'd surrounded each of the four prisoners in front of him the same way, that would made around a dozen armed Japanese between him and those controls. Versus five malnourished airmen.

His moment of optimism died.

A soldier released one of his handcuffs. His heart soared again—until the man snapped the cuff around his armrest.

Deflated, he slumped into his seat and closed his eyes.

This mission—*his* mission—couldn't have gone more

wrong. The only way he could damage the American war effort further would be to break down under torture. Let them worm critical information out of him.

What would that take?

How much could *he* take?

His head throbbed.

They rolled across the tarmac, turned and stopped. The pilot ran up the engines. She shuddered, straining for the air like a thoroughbred. Like *Payback* used to do. They thundered down the runway and, after a breathless moment, rotated and found the sky.

The thrum of the engines was hypnotic. He fought to stay on the alert, but despite his best efforts he drifted.

The pre-race aerobatic show was on. Dave squinted into glaring sky. The plane was a dark blotch against the horizon, the props' thunder just a hum in the distance.

Uncle Verle clapped a hand on his shoulder. "That's Jimmy Doolittle himself, son. You know what..."

Verle's explanation faded off. The plane made a graceful arc into the air, then shot toward them in a barrel roll, red wingtips clearing the pavement by mere feet. She exited upside down, silver belly bared to the sky, then curved up into a big slow loop-de-loop.

Uncle Verle grabbed his cane and rose from his seat, his face aglow. "Outside roll! Doolittle's trademark move. Take that, Huns!"

The plane's wings sprouted long white feathers. They began a slow beat against the air, pulling her into the heavens.

"She's off and away!" Uncle Verle's fist thudded into Dave's shoulder—

He jerked awake to find himself cuffed to a seat on a Japanese plane bouncing through a stretch of turbulence. All those dreams of aviation glory lay in tatters, and he had to hope his legendary commanding officer was in Chungking by now, carrying on the war without him.

His depression was beyond anything he could put words to.

The blindfold still limited his vision to a thread of light.

He maneuvered to get a thin strip of view out the window. Scattered cumulus clouds revealed an undulating emerald-colored landscape, furred with forest. And then—a mountain. A broad cone with a snow cap and an indentation at the top.

Unmistakable. Mount Fuji.

Japan.

A few minutes later, they banked over a sprawling city that kept a chokehold on a broad expanse of gray bay. He knew it from the maps he'd studied on *Hornet.* Tokyo.

When it came to interrogation, it seemed he'd left the minor leagues.

Chapter Fifteen

Monday, December 27, 1948
Osaka, Japan

SLEEP SPREAD WINGS OF BLESSED FORGETFULNESS over Miyako. She closed her eyes and let it take her.

She woke to raucous laughter down the hall. To her relief, daylight still filtered through the *shoji*. *Papa-san.* She sat up cautiously. She hurt all over, but her head had stopped spinning. And there was so much she needed to do outside the Oasis' walls. Tend to Papa-san in the hospital. See Kamura-san about money for the poison. Find a way to get some kind of explanation to George-san, without letting him get a glimpse of her. She had duties to attend to.

She should still have that packet of Papa-san's tea in—

My handbag. She hadn't seen it here. Oda's men must have taken it. She fought a sense of futility that threatened to wash her under. She had nothing left of worth. She *was* nothing of worth. She coiled her hands in her lap and took a deep breath, fighting the tears that threatened to overwhelm her.

Imai-san or not. Tea or not. She had to go see Papa-san. Make herself useful to someone.

A set of knuckles rapped the *shoji*. A voice she didn't recognize called in a greeting. A woman's voice, but gravelly.

Miyako sat up. "Please come in."

The *shoji* slid aside and a stout older woman entered. Miyako stood and bowed. The woman returned her bow, showcasing gray hair tucked in an immaculate bun.

"*Konnichiwa.* My name is Yamada. I help Imai-san here. I thought I should introduce myself."

"*Arigato.* Excuse me. It's hard to talk."

"That's not a problem, Ishikawa-san."

"Please. You might as well call me Midori." *Since it seems I'm a fixture here—whether I like it or not.*

Yamada-san gave her a crisp nod and a slight smile. "Very well, Midori-chan. There are some details I like to go over with new girls, but since you're not working yet, there's no rush for most of them. However"—her eyes took on a shrewd glint—"I overheard your conversation with Imai-san and I felt compelled to share one piece of advice. Of course you want to see your father. But as Imai-san has informed you, you can't leave without her permission."

"*Hai.* I heard her."

"Good. Then let me caution you to do us all a favor. Don't try to sneak out. Imai-san will catch you. And when she does"—her voice sank to something that was almost a growl— "trust me, your life won't be worth living." Yamada-san fixed her with a stony glare. "Believe me on this. When it comes to potential profits, you don't mess with Imai-san."

A tremor ran up Miyako's spine. At her first brothel, they'd kept a room specifically to "correct" girls who lost their enthusiasm for the work. She'd only had to experience it once.

Yamada-san patted her shoulder. "Now, now." The lizard skin around her eyes slackened. "All in all, you could do worse than Imai-san. She's kind enough as long as you don't cross her."

Miyako gave a deliberate shiver. Maybe looking pitiful would count for something. "She mentioned associates. The *yakuza?*"

Yamada-san issued a dry chuckle. "She pays those goons for protection, all right. Not that it's entirely her choice."

"Which *yakuza* gang? Sakaume?"

Yamada-san gave her an ominous look beneath knit brows. "No. Morimoto."

"Ah." This was mixed news. The Morimoto gang was ruthless. Kodo-san in the Abeno had crossed them, and they'd put him through one of his own shop's plate-glass windows.

But it would have been worse for her if it had been the Sakaume gang. She could hardly rely on Tsunada-san for poison if his gang had an interest in the Oasis. Her collateral at the Oasis was her body. The loan goons couldn't know she was putting that collateral at risk.

Yamada-san was saying something. "Consider yourself

warned, Midori-chan."

"*Arigato*, Yamada-san. I will."

Miyako reflected on Yamada-san's little speech, and it had the opposite effect the lady probably intended. A hint of suspicion prickled her. Perhaps Yamada-san had cautioned her so strongly because there actually was an easy way to gain her freedom.

Her room had a window, screened by a *shoji* on the inside and a carved grating on the outside. She supposed there was a small chance the grating might be loose, or she could snap some delicate feature of the woodwork free.

She pushed herself to her feet, stood on her futon, and thrust the *shoji* aside. That moved easily, but the grating was another matter. She heaved at it, pulled on it, but no luck.

This thing would keep a sumo champion hostage.

She wilted to the futon, breathless. No possibility of escaping that way.

If this brothel was like the one she'd worked in right after the war, there'd be a lounge toward the building's front for mingling with clients, a lounge for the girls, and a kitchen at the back of the building. There might be some opportunity to escape from one of those spaces—some detail Imai-san had missed.

If she rested now, she could look later. She'd learned an important lesson years earlier playing *Go* with her older brother, Akira-san. Sometimes the escape from a trap lies hidden in plain sight.

Sadly, Akira-san had been too busy for *Go* the last few times she'd seen him. The naval academy at Eta Jima hadn't left much time for games with sisters. In fact, he'd barely had time for dinner the weekend he and Papa-san shipped out to war.

Mama-san would have struggled to forgive him if he'd missed it, even though he was her number one son. She and the maidservant outdid themselves that day. All their favorite dishes looked so elegant on the table. Papa-san's beloved hotpot, *sukiyaki*, with generous portions of sliced beef and mushroom, simmered in Mama-san's signature broth and dredged in raw egg. Akira-san's favorite dish, *kaki furai*, oysters fried with crisp breading. And best of all, the dish she craved most—eel, skewered and braised with a tangy sauce. To round out the meal, a *sake* Papa-san declared especially good.

She sighed. How many years had it been since she'd tasted oysters or eel?

That was the day she'd given her men their *senninbari*. She presented the first package to Papa-san, in his place of honor on the cushion at the head of the table. And the second to Akira-san, majestic as a crane in his new officer's uniform. She sank back in her own place between Mama-san and Hiro-chan, so handsome that day in his best little kimono.

Papa-san parted the elegant wrapping paper with a surgeon's precision. He took the folded rectangle of cream-colored silk from the package and unfurled it. He made a careful inspection of the pattern she'd crafted, with the help of all those neighborly hands. The ferocious Japanese tiger alternated down its length with the Matsuura's mulberry-leaf crest. A traditional victory slogan graced its center.

The belts had taken weeks to complete. She'd even sewn in amulets to increase their power.

It was all worth it when he acknowledged her efforts with a solemn bow. "It's magnificent, Mi-chan. The most handsome I've seen." His eyes glistened with satisfaction. "I'll never face battle without it."

How she'd beamed inside. His reaction was everything she'd wished for.

Akira-san's *senninbari* looked splendid against his navy-blue uniform. "*Hai*, little sister. Papa-san and I will be sure victors in these."

How precious those last hours together proved to be! The image of Papa-san standing between his sons, chest puffed with pride, had etched itself on Miyako's memory. If only she could have frozen that moment in time.

Light footsteps sounded in the corridor outside her room, followed by Imai-san's lyrical voice. "Hello, there." The *shoji* slid open. "I took a little break from the evening's business. Have you thought it over, Ishikawa-san? Can we discuss your contract in a serious way?"

She took a deep breath and swallowed hard. *"Hai,* Imai-san. I'm ready." Whatever it took to see Papa-san.

"That's wonderful, child." Her tone was velvet. "I didn't want to get heavy-handed." She settled on the edge of Miyako's futon, her peacock-patterned silks billowing like dusk-kissed clouds. "Let's see. Where did we leave off? Ah. With my generous offer of sixty thousand yen, in return for only two years' work here." She radiated warmth. "Think how fast that will go by. We'll just be getting to know each other."

"You're very kind." Miyako hoped she managed to keep the sarcasm out of her tone. It seemed she had to play along if she wanted any freedom. "I can settle for sixty-five. If I can see Papa-san tomorrow." Since she couldn't have the money this week, the amount didn't matter. But surely Kamura-san with his thriving restaurant would help her. She'd have to figure out a way to get to him.

"I think you underestimate how weak you are, Ishikawa-san."

"It is against my better judgment, but I suppose I could accept your proposal, assuming Yamada-san goes to the hospital with you."

Miyako stared at Imai-san. *Yamada-san.*

Imai-san gave her a thin smile. "Yamada-san is not negotiable, Midori-chan. Let's see how you feel tomorrow. It will all depend on whether you're strong enough."

Oh, she'd be strong enough. Strong enough to see Papa-san. And strong enough to leave her warden behind on some street corner, wondering what happened.

5 May 1942, Tokyo
16 Days Captive

Dave's days and nights melded into an unbroken haze of misery. He rested as best he could in his stifling cell. No air moved through the barred window. No relief from the stench of his body or the wood box on the floor that served as his latrine.

It had to be mid-summer now—at least that's how it felt. Dull but constant pain across his shoulder. Ringing head. Swollen lip. And to top it all off, his head swam from hunger.

When had he slept last? He couldn't remember. Even the lousy excuse for furniture they'd provided—a thin straw mat on the bare cement floor—looked appealing.

One minute. That's all. What he wouldn't give to lie down. His eyelids drifted closed. His head sagged.

Something sharp jabbed at his back. He jolted awake. A guttural voice battered his ears. *"Horyo. Okiro."*

He grunted. "No sleeping. I know." *Miserable guards and their stakes.* His cell door had a narrow slit they used to feed him. The guards would peer like gremlins through it. Jab him with long poles if they found him doing anything off the approved list—including sleeping—any time of the day or night.

Like I'm some stinking zoo animal.

Silently, he renewed the pledge he made to himself a hundred times a day.

Nothing that will help these demons in yellow flesh. No matter what. Nothing that will help them at all.

What about the other guys? Watt, Vitty, Braxton, Smith. How were they holding up?

If someone broke, he couldn't blame them. But it wouldn't be Dave Delham.

Uncle Verle's voice echoed down the hallways of time. "Doolittle! Outside roll! What a dang hero!"

Take that, Huns. If Verle could outlive the German gas and drag his wounded buddy out of range of their guns, David Delham could handle these guys.

Jimmy Doolittle won a dogfight and piloted a plane across the Andes with both ankles broken in spite of pain that nearly blacked him out. If Doolittle could make it through that and go on to mastermind their mission, Dave Delham could take whatever the Japs dished out.

Eddie Rickenbacker lived through that Eastern Airlines crash in Georgia. Crushed, burned, left for dead. If Rickenbacker could survive that ordeal, David Delham could gut it out through this.

Doolittle. Rickenbacker. Verle. They were men. And so was he.

Hobnailed boots struck the floor at the end of the hall. It had probably been two to three hours since his last interrogation session, so they were due to get to work on him again.

A pair of soldiers burst into his cell. He was halfway to standing when they grabbed him and yanked him the rest of the way. They dragged him through his cell door, along the corridor and around a corner before he could find his feet.

Into an interrogation chamber. They all looked the same. Featureless. Windowless. A single door. A wooden table in the middle with various implements laid out. Some of them he knew all too well from earlier sessions.

A pile of towels and several full pitchers. Those would be for the water treatment. Water streaming into his mouth and nose until his lungs burned and screamed. Until he fought them for air with all his might. Until he slipped from consciousness. Then they brought him back around and repeated the process.

A set of sharpened bamboo skewers and a hammer. There were many soft places on a man, and these ghouls found them all.

A bamboo rod about five feet long and four inches in diameter—that was new. His knees went weak beneath him. *What is that thing for?*

He had learned he was in the hands of the *Kempeitai,* Japan's crack secret police. The yellow gestapo. He'd heard reports of their cruelty while he was still on American shores. Those reports had been no exaggeration.

It was the usual scene. Several chairs on one side of the table confronted one lone chair on the other. Four expressionless guards, an officer in charge of the session, and an interpreter. The guards and the officer changed from session to session, but the interpreter, Ohara—with his argyle socks and his cultured accent—was a constant.

Dave knew two of the guards this time. Brutus, and the one he'd nicknamed Ratface for his pinched jaw and prominent incisors. He seemed to be the head guard.

It took real force of will to go sheep-docile and let them shackle him into that chair. He had to battle every instinct he had. But he'd discovered the hard way it was better to save his strength. Endurance was the brand of strength he needed now.

Nothing that will help them. No matter what. Nothing that will help them.

He glanced at the table full of implements. *No matter what.*

Doolittle. Rickenbacker. Uncle Verle. He was going to need them all.

Ohara looked up at him and rubbed his hands together. "Well, well, *horyo*. Here we are again. I don't believe you've been completely truthful with us on this issue." He slammed his hand down on the table. "What is the range of the B-25?"

Showtime.

Chapter Sixteen

Tuesday, December 28, 1948
Osaka, Japan

THE DAY DAWNED GRAY. MIYAKO SLIPPED into Fusako's dress, Tome's shoes and an old coat of Imai-san's and made the trek to the station with Yamada-san. The two women climbed onto the train. After endless starts and stops and stations, and a few more long blocks on foot, she stood at last with Yamada-san in the lobby of Osaka Hospital.

The elevator lifted them to the fourth floor. Miyako's anxiety mounted with it, tightening like a vice around her chest. The way she'd seen him last—his face drawn, his skin papery. Such a struggle to breathe. How would she find him now?

Yamada-san eyed her with concern. "You don't look well."

She shook her head. "If he's awake, I don't know what I'll say to him. How do I explain why I left him alone for so long, ah? And if he's not? I'm so afraid for him."

Yamada-san sighed and patted her arm.

Papa-san wasn't in his old bed near the door. Her breath caught as she scanned the room. Many of the chairs were occupied by older women—devoted family members who'd no doubt been there for hours. Guilt thrust a fresh spear into her chest. Poor Papa-san, no one to see to him all those days.

She walked between the rows toward the back of the room, looking over the haggard faces. Several pairs of eyes followed her. They had to be thinking she was the most neglectful daughter in Japan.

That was when she saw him—the last person she had hoped to find there. In a chair against the far wall, back to a boarded-up window. His face dour. His arms folded in front of the line of silver buttons that marched down his uniform. Braid on his epaulets gleaming in the gray light.

Captain Oda. He stared at her, craggy features twisting with distaste.

She put a hand on a column to steady herself. He'd found

Papa-san. What had he told him?

She made her way toward Oda and the bed next to him, where Papa-san surely lay, with the halting steps of a condemned person. Her pulse beat in her ears. She reached the last row of patients. Papa-san lay quite still, head flat on the pillow. She couldn't see his eyes around the oxygen mask.

A few more hesitant steps and she stood at the foot of the bed. Papa-san's color was ashen, and an ugly bruise stained his jawline. His eyes were open, but he had them fixed on the ceiling.

Oda's eyes drilled into her.

"Papa-san?" Her voice came out a croak. She tried again. "Papa-san, I'm here."

He glanced at her. His brow creased. He frowned and looked away.

In an instant she was around the side of his bed. She dropped painfully to her knees and leaned over him. "I'm so sorry I haven't been here for you." She pinned Oda with a stare across the bed, then looked at her father. "I got robbed on the way home from work. They beat me up—you can see my bruises. Look."

He winced and closed his eyes. Pain dug furrows around his features.

She put out a hand and touched his cheek. He flinched away. Moisture glinted in the crease at the corner of his eye.

Merciful gods. Please let him listen. Let him feel my dying heart.

"Papa-san, I'm sorry. I wanted to take care of you. If I've done anything wrong, I did it to keep a roof over your head."

Captain Oda heaved himself from the chair. His shadow fell across the bed. "That's enough, whore. He won't talk to you." His cane clacked on the floor.

He came around the bed to where she knelt, grabbed her upper arm, and jerked her to her feet. "If you want to do something kind for him, leave. Give him his pride, ah?" He gave her arm a yanking twist that sent pain stabbing through her shoulder. She yelped.

No. That can't be it. That can't be what Papa-san wants.

She pushed an elbow into Oda's diaphragm and fought to

break his grip on her arm. "Say something to me, Papa-san." Her voice broke. "Say something. Please, Papa-san. Tell the captain to leave me alone. I'm your daughter."

Papa-san stared at her, jaw working. Surely he was poised to speak. To tell Captain Oda this wasn't what he wanted.

The captain released his grip. He took a half step back. She dropped to her knees beside Papa-san's bed and leaned toward him, breathless.

He spat in her face.

05 May 1942, Tokyo
16 Days Captive

Sweat sent a chill through Dave's body. These yellow demons were always trying to piece together how the B-25s had penetrated so far into their defenses. That was information he had to protect.

He eyed his opponent. "The B-25's range? It depends."

Ohara nodded at Brutus, who delivered a slap that rocked Dave's head. His ear rang from the blow.

"We expect direct answers, *horyo*."

He glared at the man. "It does depend on several things." He fought the tight little smile that wanted to tweak the corners of his mouth. They could break his body, but they could not break his spirit, and that shamed them, right down to their rotten, soulless cores.

Knowing that kept him going. It had to. It was the only victory he could hope for.

Ohara cocked his head at the table with its implements. "I warn you, *horyo*. One way or the other, we get the truth."

The officer watched the exchange with the intensity of a snake. He gave some direction to Ohara.

Dave's eyes drifted to the table. Which treatment would he get today? He tried to ignore it—the fear that wound its way through his belly, turning it into a cold, desolate pit. A fear so tangible it felt like an eighth person in the room.

But that was another tactic he'd learned. Not to fight the fear, but to resist in the face of it. They could rip his humanity from him in a thousand ways. But as long as he could still resist, could still protect his country, he was still a man.

He was still a man. *Right, Uncle Verle?*

Ohara paced in front of him and stopped. "We'll try the rod today, I think."

Dave's eyes fell on the unfamiliar instrument.

Doolittle could do this. Rickenbacker could do this. Uncle Verle could do this.

Dave Delham had to do this.

He clamped his jaw shut. Locked away the words they were after.

He was still a man.

The pain from the bamboo-rod torture was so intense Dave blacked out. He woke again to a pitcher of cold water in the face. Thankfully he'd lost all feeling in his legs.

The guards holding his shoulders let go. He slumped to the ground, writhed on the floor. He heard himself making noises. Sounds that belonged to a wounded animal. Broken and pathetic.

The four guards watched, impassive. The officer stood and stalked from the room.

Ohara looked down at him with his trademark sneer. "I see we're done for now. We will have more questions for you, *horyo*. Very soon."

10 June 1942, Tokyo
52 Days Captive

The *Kempeitai* were inventive—Dave gave them that much. They knew exactly how far they could take a man without actually killing him. His days passed in unrivaled misery, a mind-numbing cycle of sleep deprivation, starvation rations, questions. Until there was nothing left of him but sheer will.

How much longer would sheer will hold him together?

His mind wandered to his crew—his guys. Watt, Vitty,

Smith, Braxton. He never saw other prisoners, but he had to assume those four were still in this compound somewhere. That sobbing in the distance. Was it one of them? Each muffled cry that battered his ears carried with it a whisper. *You will die in here. With your men. They will pry the truth out of one of you. And you will all die.*

He worked to find some brighter thoughts to keep from drowning in a sea of regret.

Eileen. How gorgeous she'd looked when he presented her with the little velvet box from Hahn's jewelry.

It was the evening after he enlisted. Before he broke *that* news to her, he parked outside her ivy-covered Alpha Phi house, pulled the flask of Bourbon from his glove compartment, and threw back a hearty swig of liquid courage. He knew she'd be outraged, but he had a plan he hoped would counter that. It revolved around that magical little box.

She ushered him into the sorority's formal living room, and he told her he'd joined up. As soon as he managed to spit it out, he dropped to one knee in front of the big stone hearth, slipped that box from his pocket and popped it open.

She crossed her arms, narrowed her eyes and quirked an eyebrow at him. "Really. You're really telling me, after the fact, that you've joined the Air Corps. Then you're asking me to be your little military wife." But she reached for the ring, like she had to touch it to make sure it was real.

He did his best to sound flippant. "Until death do us part."

She looked into his face, her expression unreadable. The flickering light from the flames brought a soft flush to her cheeks and flecks of gold fire to her eyes. She'd never looked lovelier.

But a beat passed. He thought she might actually say no.

Those pliant lips softened into a smile, even if it came with a bit of a sigh. "Fine then. Air Corps here we come."

He hadn't realized how quickly *until death do us part* would come to feel like more than an idle phrase.

Can't happen. I have to see her again. They claimed there was a just God. And Eileen believed it. At least, she went to church now and then.

Lord, if you're listening—

For what had to be the hundredth time, a pair of guards burst into his cell. Dragged him down a succession of corridors. Shoved him into a chair in an interrogation room. Ohara was in conference with the officer *du jour*, that same smug look on his face.

Face to face with that pretentious squint-eyed sadist again. What gave him the right to torment real men?

Simple. The Japanese were armed. He and his men were not. That was it. If he ever met up with Ohara on an even footing he would put a fist straight through the man's face. Wring the life from his scrawny neck. Snap it in two with his bare hands.

Ohara smiled pleasantly. "Shall we begin?"

Dave fixed his eyes on the table, felt his palms go clammy. His mortal enemy, the bamboo rod, was there. Along with some other old friends.

Oh no. Please no. Not the big rod today.

At what point would he finally break? Tell them anything and everything they wanted to know?

The gargoyles had varied the routine this time. They left his right arm free and positioned his chair close enough to reach the table. And something else was new. He stared down at a sheaf of papers bearing neat columns of Jap scribbles.

Ohara placed a pen in front of him. "Sign that."

"You know I can't read your chicken scratch. What's it say?"

"It's your confession." Ohara nodded at Brutus, who picked up a thin bamboo strip.

"Confession to what?"

Brutus whipped the bamboo strip across his wrist. A ribbon of blood trickled down the back of his hand and started a slow drip onto the floor.

The officer shifted in his chair and muttered something.

Ohara drummed his fingers on the table. "Make this easy, *horyo*."

Dave sat back, rubbed trembling hands across unfocused eyes. It was all he could do to hold his gaze steady. "You want me to sign it? I can't even read it."

Ohara nodded at Ratface. He issued a command to the others, then picked up the skewers.

Dave swallowed. His last encounter with those things had cost him days of pain.

Brutus untied Dave's left arm from the chair, keeping a firm grip on his hand. Ratface splayed his fingers and poised the tip of a skewer against the skin between them. Picked up a tack hammer and grinned at him.

"Wait, wait!" Dave fought through a dense fog of weariness to bring Ohara's face into focus. "If I sign it, does this end now?"

Ohara nodded. "*Hai*. If you sign this thing, you go back to China. We have, ah...comfortable prison for you there. Ordinary prison." He snickered, then turned and said something to the officer, who inclined his head and spoke to Dave directly—a first.

"*Hai*. Sign paper, go back China. Ordinary prison."

Ohara gave the guards an order. Brutus released his left hand and they all stepped away.

Was he really going to do this?

It was a deal with the devil. Still...No more sessions with Ohara. No more miserable hours in his cell, paralyzed with fear of the next session. And no more wondering how long it would take them to break him, get something out of him that mattered.

If he signed this paper, he won. He got out, and they got nothing they could use.

What was he signing? His death warrant? They were killing him anyway.

And then again, this might be his route back to Eileen.

He picked up the pen.

Chapter Seventeen

15 June 1942, Tokyo
57 Days Captive

THE DEVIL DOES KEEP HIS DEALS—at least, the letter of them. Several days passed before Dave left his cell again.

He'd read it somewhere. *A prisoner's best chance to escape is in transport.* Maybe, between Tokyo and China, there'd be some oversight. Maybe this would be his time.

Lord, maybe I've made it through the worst of it. Maybe you are listening. Please get me back in this war.

At night, for the first time since his capture, they allowed him the merciful oblivion of sleep. Which was what he was doing when two guards burst into his cell.

"*Toridase. Hayaku.*"

They hauled him to his feet. He stumbled along the corridor, his wobbly legs barely supporting him. They brought him through a pair of heavy wooden doors. He stepped into a sunlit courtyard, blinking like a bat.

A prisoner's best chance to escape...

His men were there, lined up. All four of them. Alive. That was the good news.

But their condition? Deplorable. Bruised, bedraggled, filthy, with bushy beards and matted hair. Grimy uniforms hanging visibly looser.

He'd felt a thrill of pride when he saw them the last time. But one glance at them now and his gut hollowed. There was no chance any of them were going to blend into the civilian population. Even if they were strong enough to attempt an escape.

He was sure he looked every bit as bad.

The Japs pushed him into place next to Watt. An impressive bruise covered the side of Watt's face. He glanced at Dave, gave him a grim nod.

Vitty was on the other side of Watt, but Dave couldn't see his face. He supposed the man had cooled off by now, but it no longer seemed to matter much.

The doors behind them creaked open. He stared over his

shoulder and got a jolt of surprise. A cluster of Japs with two more American airmen. The fellows looked like cavemen.

Who are these guys?

The newcomers joined the line of captives on Dave's other side. The nose of the fellow next to him had been reconfigured into a swollen mass. His eyes drooped with fatigue. Even so, it clicked: Chase Nielsen, navigator from Bomber Number Six, *Green Hornet*.

I'd never pick you out of a lineup.

Dave had to make a conscious effort to close his jaw. Being from different squadrons, they hadn't been best buddies, but they'd spent weeks passing each other in the chow line and rubbing elbows at the O.C. while Colonel Doolittle was getting them trained for the raid.

The American on Nielsen's left had to be Bob Meder, *Green Hornet's* copilot.

The other three guys from *Green Hornet*—Hallmark and the two enlisteds. Where were they? He indulged a fervent hope they'd made it out.

A beat passed. The doors opened once more and big Dean Hallmark, *Green Hornet's* pilot, staggered out between two guards.

That appeared to be it.

The Japs grouped them in pairs, putting him with Braxton. They cuffed his right wrist to Braxton's left. A soldier knelt to manacle their ankles together. The cuffs were sized for Japs and bit at his flesh.

"You sign it, sir?" Braxton murmured out the side of his mouth.

The guard stopped work on their manacles and looked up. "*Damare.*"

Dave gave his gunner a tiny nod followed by a questioning look.

Braxton nodded too.

Their journey back to China lasted several long days. But it wasn't all bad. On the first leg, Dave and Braxton, cuffed together, sat crammed into a bench seat on a local train out of Tokyo. Braxton had the window. Dave sat thigh-to-thigh with a dour-faced guard, positioned between him and the aisle.

The officer in charge popped the door to their compartment open. A skinny soldier walked in carrying a pile of boxes wrapped in newspaper. The aroma of cooked fish and piquant spices wafted through the car. He made his way along the aisle, whistling, and distributed a box to each of the guards.

And, miraculously, one to each of the prisoners.

Dave steeled himself for disappointment. Unwrapped his box. Sat for an instant in reverent amazement at what the torn newsprint revealed—a neat compartmentalized wooden tray with a few pieces of flaky white fish drenched in thick brown sauce, a half cup of rice, some pickled vegetables and sliced peaches.

An actual meal.

The guards had chopsticks, but Dave's box didn't include any. That wasn't going to stop him—or the other prisoners. Braxton shoveled his food into his mouth with dirt-caked fingers. Dave took one more deep breath to savor the aromas, then fell on the food himself. Once he started, an animal urge to cram it into his mouth as fast as possible took over. What if it had been a mistake, or the slant-eyed gargoyles were toying with them? What if they wrenched the box away?

But nothing disturbed his meal. The fish was a little dry, but the mild, sweet sauce made up for it. The vegetables were nothing he recognized. The tangy pickled flavor was a bit surprising, but not unpleasant. The peaches were ripe and perfect. They burst with flavorful juice in his mouth.

It was the most delicious thing he'd ever eaten.

He ate left-handed, since his right hand was cuffed to Braxton. But that didn't keep him from picking every grain of rice and every drop of sticky sauce out of that wooden tray.

The moment ended all too soon. He was licking juice off his fingers when the guard came around to collect the empty box.

Braxton leaned his head up against the window and closed his eyes in contentment. "That was a religious experience."

The guard in the aisle seat glared at him. "No talk, *baka*."
Braxton just grinned and gave his belly a pat.

Tuesday, December 28, 1948
Osaka, Japan

Miyako hit the floor hard in the corridor where Captain Oda
flung her. The double doors to the Cancer Ward closed
behind her, Papa-san on the other side. Inaccessible—
perhaps forever.

She curled up on the hard tile and lay there.

Papa-san. The thought was a long cry of anguish from
her very core.

If she could make herself small enough, perhaps she
could be a little girl again. Run to his arms as he came in
through the front door of the tiny house she'd grown up in.
Burrow her head in his strong chest. Plant her feet in his big
street shoes.

Everything had gone wrong since the day of the bombing.

After a long moment she stirred, but only to sit. She
pushed herself against the wall and wrapped her arms
around her knees. She heard Yamada-san's voice, but it
meant nothing to her.

"Midori. Mi-chan. Come on."

She felt tears on her face, but she was detached from the
feeling. Like the nerve endings belonged to someone else.

"Get up. Let's go home." Yamada-san shook her
shoulder. She produced a handkerchief from her capacious
handbag and wiped the spit from Miyako's face. "We have to
go home now."

Home? The Oasis wasn't home. And without Papa-san,
what did *home* even mean?

Miyako had no clear recollection later of the trip back to
Tobita. She did remember the horrified look on Imai-san's
face. The way it took her three full seconds to lower her
cigarette from her mouth.

"You've been bawling. What under heaven happened to
you?"

Miyako couldn't bear to be in her room. She huddled on the bench in the wintry courtyard, shuffled one foot across the fine gravel, and stared at the stone lantern with its handsome carvings of deer and rabbits. *Prey.* Like she'd always been.

No more.

There was only one path to reestablish her worth. One means to clear her *haji.* Avenge herself on the *gaijin* bomber. Show Papa-san she could restore her family's honor and her own. And if he couldn't see it, perhaps the ancestors would.

She had to get to Kamura-san.

Imai-san stepped out from the building, arranged her fur stole, and picked her way across the stepping stones to the bench. "Midori-chan, would you like to come in for dinner? You could meet the other girls before things get hectic."

Miyako pulled her coat around her and shook her head.

Imai-san studied her. "I trust you don't think your father's unconsidered reaction alters our arrangement?"

"No, Imai-san, it doesn't." Not at all. She was there until she could figure out how to get to the *gaijin.*

"Good. You're wise, child. I'm sure your papa-san will reconsider."

Hai. When eels sprout feet.

Miyako had no interest in food or company that evening, so she went to bed early. Her stomach was rumbling like a freight train by the time the clatter of dishes and the rise and fall of women's voices greeted her the next morning.

It was time to crawl out and meet them.

Her black eye was beginning to turn interesting shades of teal and lavender, but she made herself as presentable as she could. She slipped from her room and followed the voices along the hall toward the building's rear and into a small, bright common room.

The room was cozy, almost cramped, with paneled walls and cheery blue-and-white café curtains. Imai-san and Yamada-san knelt on opposite sides of a square table. A quartet of younger women ringed the table, a tea service spread before them. Their chatter—like magpies quarreling over a rice ball—lapsed to silence when she eased her way in. "Good morning." She bowed to each of them. "Midori-chan, it's wonderful to see you up and about." Imai-san scooted a serving dish out of the way. "Sit here, please."

She knelt at the table, and Imai-san introduced her to the others. Noriko-chan, a handsome young woman, gave her a perfunctory head-bob. Hanae-chan, whose Korean accent belied her Japanese name, stared openly at Miyako's battered face. Fusako-chan, with her soft Kansai accent, and Tome-chan, the curvy one—there was always a curvy one—cast more discreet glances her way.

Haruko-chan appeared with a tureen of soup. It looked and smelled delicious, the savory aroma of mild spices and toasted onion an open invitation. Miyako accepted a bowl with gratitude.

Fusako sipped her tea. "It's good to see you're recovering. When do you think you'll be able to see clients?"

Miyako cringed inside. The idea of entertaining a string of Imai-san's *okyaku* in the confines of her tiny room was suffocating. And with the way her whole body ached? "I think it may be a few more days. Although I certainly need the money." She changed the subject. "Imai-san, there's something I'd like to ask you."

"What is it, child?"

"There are a few things in the room I've been renting I'd like to have." Papa-san's tea no longer mattered, although it hollowed her heart to think so. But George-san's cash certainly did. And she could handle all her other business at the same time. "My own clothes, shoes, lipsticks. Do you think—"

"Absolutely not." Imai-san lowered her penciled brows. "I cannot have you jeopardize your recovery any further with your trivial errands, dear."

She forced herself to eat, but she excused herself as soon as it was polite and retreated to her room.

Yamada-san caught up with her a few minutes later. "About your things. I think I can help. If *I* ask her, Imai-san will probably be willing to send someone to collect them. She'll simply add the amount to your ledger, with an allowance for overhead and expenses, of course. That would cheer you up a bit, wouldn't it?"

Miyako studied the lady's expression. How much of that overhead allowance would she receive? No matter. Perhaps she *could* help.

She put a hand to her throbbing temple. "*Hai*, it would cheer me up. If you could pick up some of my clothes, I'd be very much in your debt. But I have other loose ends I need to take care of."

"Is it something I can do?"

"I trust it won't be too much trouble. I have a friend named Kimi. If she comes to see me here, she can help me get a handle on the rest." Kimi could find out what was happening with George-san. Perhaps get word to Kamura-san as well. "Could you kindly see if you can find her and ask her to come by?"

"Where do I look for her?"

"In the Abeno district. With the *pan-pan*."

Yamada-san pinned her with a look. "You want me to find a *pan-pan* named Kimi. In the Abeno District. You're teasing, right?" She rolled her eyes. "What's the rest of your list?"

Miyako reeled off the items she needed. She debated for a few seconds about the cash. She decided trusting Yamada-san with it was less risky than leaving it in her empty room—which her landlord was sure to rifle when she didn't turn up with the weekly rent.

Yamada-san jotted notes in blocky ideographs. When Miyako finished, she read it back, ticking off the list with her pen. "Blue dress with black lace appliqué. Both pairs of shoes. Your cosmetics box. Lingerie. Bottle of reasonably good whiskey. A tea tin with a bit of cash in it." She looked up and snorted. "And a whore named Kimi. Impressive list."

"I can't tell you"—*really can't tell you*—"how much this means to me, Yamada-san."

Yamada-san tucked her note into her sleeve. "I'll see what I can do. No promises."

"Of course, Yamada-san."

The "of course" meant she understood the older woman's help was going to cost her. The question was how much, and when.

Chapter Eighteen

Wednesday, December 29, 1948
Osaka, Japan

PEARL-COLORED SKIES CARRIED A THREAT of rain for later, but the afternoon was mild enough for Miyako to linger in the garden.

She had the small but peaceful space to herself. The brothel buildings wrapped it on two sides. Tall walls topped by barbed wire enclosed the other two.

"The walls are to keep you girls safe and private." That's what Yamada-san had told her the day before. But as Miyako studied them, something struck her. The struts holding the barbed wire angled *in*. That wire was to keep unwilling girls inside, not to keep intruders out.

She took a long, slow breath. There was no exit from that garden, except through the buildings.

A shed stood next to the building at the back. A pair of big, old yew trees crowded the space beside it. She looked closely at them.

You'd have to be a monkey to get out that way. And given that barbed wire, a determined one.

A door from the brothel building slid open and the curvy girl draped herself against the door frame. What was her name? *Tome.* The one called Fusako stood behind her, peering over Tome's shoulder.

"Want to join us for cards?" Tome's loose housecoat gapped, revealing generous cleavage.

Fusako gave Miyako a welcoming smile. "It makes the day go faster."

Miyako had no desire for company, but she couldn't pass this up. She might learn something useful. "*Arigato.*"

She followed Fusako and Tome into the common room with its paneled walls and perky curtains. The girls had moved the table aside, and Noriko and Hanae knelt beside a clean playing mat.

"Oh, will you join us?" Hanae said in her harsh Korean

accent. The deck of traditional flower cards, small and stiff compared to the deck the *gaijin* used for poker, blurred between her hands. The soft clacking cadence of their shuffling filled the room.

Miyako preferred the *gaijin*'s five-card stud. The flower cards haunted her with memories of lazy Sunday afternoons before the war. "What's the game?"

"*Kabu*, since there are so many of us." Hanae passed the deck to Noriko to cut. "You can bet with cigarettes if you don't have money."

Kabu. A game for children—and gangsters. But it did allow everyone to join in.

The girls drew for the order of play. Fusako elbowed Tome. "I see you drew the *Sake* Cup card. That fits."

"*Sake*'s my best friend." Tome got up to find Miyako a cup.

Noriko shuffled, then doled out a face-down card to each of them. She flipped four cards face up on the mat.

Tome scooped up her card and studied it, fingers unsteady. "I'm glad Midori-chan got Yamada-san sent out on an errand. She takes the game too seriously." She made a pretty pout. "It's no fun."

Fusako gave Miyako a sympathetic smile. "It's not much fun for *you* here, Midori-chan. Is it?"

"You could say that." Miyako picked up her own card. A blazing orange and yellow chrysanthemum card— September, worth nine.

Fusako pursed her lips and compared her card with those on the table. "Don't concern yourself. It's hard for everyone at first. It gets better." She shifted her shoulders so her sequined collar glinted. "At least a girl gets to wear nice things."

Noriko shot her a look. "Yes, but I've seen your ledger. You're as much in debt as when you started. You'll never leave this place." Her lips curved in a tight smile. "You'd better hope you win today. I think that loan I gave you is about due, ah?"

Fusako glared at her across the mat, then glanced around at the other girls.

Hanae averted her eyes. "Don't look at me, dear. I've

bankrolled your notion of style as much as I can afford."

Tome took a swig of *sake*. "Noriko-chan's the only one with tea money to spare. Better stay on her good side."

Miyako tapped a single Lucky from a pack Yamada-san had advanced her and placed it on a card. "You're not in the clear yet, Fusako-chan? How long have you been here?"

Fusako gazed at her card, biting her lip. She put three cigarettes next to the chrysanthemum ribbon card. "Two years."

Tome put her cigarettes on the peony card. "Fusako came over from China after everything fell apart over there."

Fusako's eyes drifted to the mat. "Three days without food can be quite a motivator."

"That's how it was then." Miyako felt a twinge of the ferocious hunger that had knotted her own gut the day she'd let a man in a good suit trick her into the business.

Noriko slapped a new row of cards face-down on the mat. Miyako scooped hers up. Wisteria—April, worth four. Not what she was looking for. She'd have to take another card. "What about you, Tome-chan?"

Tome put two more cigarettes on her card. "They closed my factory, so I went to work as a beer-hall hostess." She tipped the carafe into her cup, her lighthearted smile fading. "A man asked me out after closing one night. Drunken animal. After he was done with me, well, the money was better as a *baishanfu*, so what was the point of holding out? That jerk left me with nothing to lose."

Miyako looked at her in silent compassion. It was true. Once you'd been raped, what was left?

Tome's cup sloshed as she brought it to her lips. "But I'll warn you. Imai-san charges your account for the least little thing. You keep busy every night. Thinking you're making good money. Thinking you're getting ahead. But she shows you your ledger at the end of the month and all you ever do is break even." She slammed the empty cup on the mat.

Miyako looked around at the others. Noriko gave her cards a fixed stare. Hanae nodded, lost in thought. Fusako dropped her eyes, pulled her housecoat tighter.

For a moment, jail didn't sound so bad.

Haruko-chan poked her head in the door. "Was someone

looking for Yamada-san? She's here."

"We can hold the game for a minute." Tome's tone was a shade too perky.

Miyako eased onto her feet and made her way into the front room. Yamada-san was shedding her coat.

Miyako bowed. "Welcome back. Were you able to find Kimi?"

"I stopped by the Abeno. I asked some of the girls. They seemed to think Kimi was with a client, unfortunately. I left your message with a girl named Asagi-san."

Miyako tried not to wince. She couldn't blame Yamada-san, but relying on Asagi to get word to Kimi was hardly a recipe for success.

17 June 1942, China Sea
59 Days Captive

Three days of trains and ferries. Three days of staring at the other airmen and wondering how these guys fell into enemy hands. How much did they tell the Japs? Three days of bellowing guards squelching any attempt at conversation.

More than once, Dave turned to find Vitiollo giving him a dark look. Or maybe his mind was playing tricks? After everything they'd been through, maybe his marbles were a little loose.

The first moment it seemed the guards weren't looking, he whispered to Nielsen, "You guys find the landing strip?"

Nielsen's expression sagged. He shook his head. "Crashed off the coast."

"Your enlisted men. Where are they?"

Nielsen looked away. "Crash was bad. Didn't make it to shore. Neither of 'em."

"Bum luck." He couldn't help glancing at Vitty to see if he'd absorbed that bit of news on how *Green Hornet*'s enlisted men died. But Vitty probably hadn't heard.

Toward the end of their third long day of travel, the locomotive wheezed to a ponderous stop. Guards blindfolded and handcuffed the men, and rifle butts directed them off the train. Glimpses under Dave's blindfold revealed throngs of shoes and ankles—a bustling station.

The guards pushed and prodded them through the crowd, across a sidewalk and into a waiting black sedan. The drive took no more than minutes. They emerged from the car onto a broad stretch of asphalt. The breeze carried a wild tang of fish and salt water. Seabirds screeched.

It smelled like freedom, but it wasn't. Guards conducted them across what had to be a wharf and onto a gangplank. Over the gangplank and onto an expanse of gently rocking steel. Down through a hatch. They removed Dave's blindfold at the entrance to a dank cabin.

No porthole. Not a stick of furniture. Just eight bodies with a stench that soured Dave's stomach, and four steel walls. A pair of latrine buckets sat in the corners opposite the door. The only light came from a bare bulb. He plunked onto the steel deck, slid along the wall and into the corner farthest from the buckets—out of splash range.

The deck above their heads resonated with activity. The engine thrummed to life and the whole vessel hummed. A moment later, the ship swayed. They were off, presumably to China.

The door swung closed. Two narrow slots in the door— exactly like in the cells in Tokyo—spoke to the fact that this cabin wasn't new to brig duty.

The gargoyles had left both slots closed. The prisoners had the space to themselves.

Bob Meder tried to get comfortable on the hard floor. "Look at this," he murmured through a bushy beard that bore no resemblance to the neat mustache he'd sported on *Hornet*. "No guards."

They stared at each other, waiting in silence for someone on the other side of the door to respond to Meder's talking.

Nothing. It was hard to grasp that they might actually be left alone.

Hallmark spoke next, a little louder. "Everyone okay? Any major injuries?"

Watt shifted his weight again. "Reckon I'll make it."

"They haven't killed me yet." That was Braxton.

"My legs are asleep," someone said. Dave joined the rest in a tension-relieving laugh.

The door rattled. "*Damare.*" They fell silent for a moment. But the thirst to hear a friendly voice was overwhelming.

"Thugs break your nose?" Dave stage-whispered to Nielsen.

"No, our landing did that. But a daily fist in the face didn't help."

"*Korah! Damare!*" The door rattled harder, but the bolt didn't move.

Meder gave a low whistle. "I don't think they're gonna come in here."

Grins broke out slowly around the cabin.

"Okay. So here's my question." Dave used a whisper he was confident wouldn't pass through the door. "How do we get through that steel door, past those guards, and take control of this ship?"

Hallmark gave a thoughtful nod. "I like how you think," he whispered. "But how big's the ship? How many Japs on board?"

Watt glowered. "Lousy blindfolds. No way to know."

"Anyone ever pilot a boat?" Meder asked.

Nielsen shrugged. "How hard can it be? Doesn't fly. Only two dimensions to worry about."

Dave leaned forward. "I was serious, guys. We used to keep a boat on Lake Michigan. I can skipper this thing."

Watt elbowed Vitty. "You any good at reading Jap charts?"

Not sure he's any good at reading our *charts.*

Vitty squared his jaw and fixed Dave with a frigid glare. "Now there's some brilliance for you. Where do we take the ship, once we get control of it? We ain't sailing to Hawaii. What happens when we reach shore? Where does your grand plan leave us?" He scowled, picking up steam. "I'll tell you where. Lost, in Jap territory. The same pickle we were in when some idiot parachuted us into this mess."

Meder bristled. "Show some respect to your C.O., Lieutenant."

Watt threw in his two cents. "No disrespect intended, Lieutenant, but Vitty's got a point. Plus, this time there'd be a bigger group of us wandering the landscape. Harder to hide."

The door rattled, louder. "*Damare, baka!*"

Dave brought the volume level down. "We're all here, aren't we? My idiot decision may have saved your life, Vitty." He took an involuntary glance at Hallmark, who'd lost two men to the waves.

Vitty stood and leaned against the wall. A storm brewed across his face. "Sure. Right. We're all here." He exchanged glances with Watt.

Watt picked up his thread. "But look at us. Some great life it is. And we're under a death sentence anyway, for all we know."

"That's my point." Dave kept his voice low but flooded each syllable with conviction. "Yes, there are unknowns on the other side of that door. But I know one thing. If we sit here and do nothing, we'll start dying off anyway."

Hallmark weighed in. "So we get one of them to come in here. We swarm him and grab his weapon, somehow."

"All they have to do is yell, and there are eight more of them right outside that door." Vitty swore and slammed the side of his fist against the wall.

The slot slid open. The guard on the other side roared. "*Korah!*"

Vitty lunged across the small space and hammered at the eye slot. "*Korah* you!"

A command rang out in Japanese. An officer pushed in through the door, grimacing and brandishing a long knife in a brass-tipped wooden scabbard. He swung it and smacked Vitty across the temple with the scabbard.

Vitty roared like a bull. He clenched the weapon and yanked.

Both men froze. Vitty had the scabbard, but the officer still held the knife. The bare blade glinted inches from Vitty's stomach.

Chapter Nineteen

Wednesday, December 29, 1948
Osaka, Japan

AFTER THE GAME, HARUKO HELPED MIYAKO carry the things Yamada-san had brought her to her room.

As soon as the girl left, she seized the tin where she kept her cash. She held her breath while she popped it open. George-san's money was all there. Relief washed over her for an instant before a deep melancholy took its place. As she fingered the bills she saw the soft sheen of his cropped blond hair against the pillow. Heard his sleep-thickened voice.

She knelt to put the tin behind the vanity and her eyes lit on her reflection in the mirror. She caught her breath. The sight of her own battered face still startled her.

Her affair with George-san was over.

"Hello in there." The *shoji* cracked, and Fusako appeared. "We're going shopping." Her voice carried a happy lilt. "Do you need anything?"

"*Arigato*, but no." Miyako sighed. "Must be nice to be on Imai-san's trusted list."

"You'll get there soon. She let you have your own clothes. That's the first step."

Tome spoke up from behind Fusako. "You made a pretty good showing at cards today. Turned one cigarette into five."

Miyako bowed. "Fortune favored this humble person." She straightened and smiled. "But it helps to think through the odds."

"Is that so? You might explain it to Yamada-san." Fusako tittered, her fingers demurely poised across her lips. "She loves to play, but the cards don't love her."

Tome glanced around and lowered her voice. "Here's the true secret of No-chan's success here. She beats Yamada-san at Eight-Nine. That's why she always has cash."

"It makes Yamada-san furious," Fusako added, still laughing.

Miyako bowed and *arigato*'d them down the corridor. How she yearned for the freedom to walk past Imai-san and out the front door.

17 June 1942, China Sea
59 Days Captive

The officer growled something over his shoulder. Two more Japanese filled the doorframe. One of them turned and yelled along the hall.

Vitty grunted. Softened his knees into a fighting stance. Blood trickled from a new gash in his temple.

I don't owe Vitty anything. As this thought went through Dave's mind, big "Jungle Jim" Hallmark stood and moved into a crouch at Vitty's elbow.

Except...as his C.O. It was like someone else's words in his head. His legs moved beneath him, and he found himself standing in a spot behind Vitty's other elbow, facing down the Jap.

Now we're in for it. He'd been praying that the Lord would preserve his men. Perhaps he was part of the answer.

They stood, frozen in place. The deck swayed like a hammock. The officer flitted his eyes back and forth, sizing the three of them up. Dave knew they had to separate the officer from that knife. But he saw no way to do it.

Boots clattered their way. Several more Japs, from the sound of it. So much for the element of surprise.

The deck lurched. Vitty stumbled back and away.

The Jap held his weapon steady, pointed at Vitty. "*Suware.*"

Vitty sank onto his place on the floor, eyes never leaving the man's face. Dave and Hallmark followed suit.

The officer gave Vitty a slow nod. "You be quiet and forrow orders, *horyo.*" He reached forward and wrenched his scabbard out of Vitty's hand. Stuffed it on his blade with a muffled clank. He took one final look around, then—unaccountably, and in contrast to anything they'd come to expect—backed out of the cabin. He swung the door closed behind him.

A beat passed, and then it seemed like they all exhaled in unison. Vitty leaned back, crossed himself, and rolled his eyes to the ceiling.

Braxton gave a low whistle. "Ho-*leee* Moses. How'd you get out of that one alive? You've got more lives than a cat."

"Heck if I know." Vitty ran a hand through his dark waves of hair. His shoulders heaved with something that looked like a cough but turned into a disbelieving chuckle. One after another, the rest of the men joined him.

Watt mused. "That guy wasn't unreasonable. He could have come down on you hard. Maybe we are going to get better treatment in China."

Vitty looked at Dean Hallmark. "Thank you, sir." And then straight at Dave. "And thank *you*. Sir."

That night was a long one. All those weeks of Japanese hospitality had reduced the prisoners to flesh and bones. Their butts gave them little padding on the hard deck, and there was no room to change position.

At least the guards gave up on enforcing the no-talking rule.

Dave turned to Hallmark. "What happened to Dieter and Fitzmaurice?"

Hallmark rocked his head back against the steel cabin wall. "We ran out of fuel. Tried a crash landing in the water, but it was rough. Fitz and Dieter didn't make it."

Dave frowned and looked at his navigator. *Told you that southern route looked dangerous.*

A pained wince flicked across Vitty's features. He crossed himself, then looked straight at Dave.

At least I haven't lost a man.

Yet.

Nielsen gave Hallmark a grim look and took over the storytelling. "We came down hot and hit hard. I remember hearing Dieter holler in the nose cone. And that's all I remember, until I came to, in frigid water up to my waist. I managed to crawl up and out through the broken windshield.

"All five of us got up there on top of the plane with our Mae Wests on. Had to be twelve-to-fifteen-foot swells, with the *Green Hornet* sinking fast. We're all torn up. Bleeding. Dieter can't speak or focus. Fitz has a bloody gash in his forehead. Hallmark and Meder pull the life raft out, but"—a pained look pinched his features—"wouldn't you know it? The CO2 malfunctions. The waves come smashing over and wash us off the plane. Bob manages to grab Fitz somehow, but Dieter was gone."

Meder let out a low whistle. "I was sure we were dead men. I've never prayed like that in my life."

Nielsen nodded. "Same here. Believe me. Once we're in the water, the three of us try to stay together, but soon their voices fade and I'm on my own."

Dave shifted his weight. "How long were you out there?"

"I'm sure it took hours—half swimming, half floating. I was in a kind of daze toward the end. I dragged myself up on that beach with the last ounce of strength I had." He shook his head in wonder. "How Meder got there towing Fitz I'll never know. You were a real Man of Steel."

Red crept across Meder's cheeks. "Any of you would have done the same. Just happened I was the guy who was close enough to do it."

Nielsen snorted. "It was all I could do to get *myself* there."

Meder studied something beyond the cabin wall. "I got Fitz up on that beach, all right. But he was gone."

The door slots slid open, bringing the conversation to a halt. The guard passed in eight small cups of weak tea. Next came rice balls about the size of crabapples, two for each airman. The slots closed.

Vitty brandished a rice ball. "Tonight's gourmet fare, gents. Dig in."

Nielsen lifted his tea cup, pinky extended. "To your health." He took a swig.

Dave took slow sips of the lukewarm liquid that tasted like grass. He made sure he felt every bit of moisture as it trickled down his parched throat.

Meder bowed his head for a few seconds, then crossed himself.

Smith gave him an incredulous look. "You're thanking the Lord for *this*?"

"I'm alive to eat it, aren't I?"

Smith shrugged. "Alive? I guess you could call it that."

Dave contemplated this. Ravenous as he felt, maybe a handful of rice was something to be thankful for. He offered a word of thanks to the Lord, then poised one of his rice balls in front of his face. "I'm seeing a wad of dirty rice, but I'm telling my taste buds it's pot roast."

Vitty groaned. "Don't even think about comparing this mush to food at home."

Dave closed his eyes and summoned the clearest memory he could of the savory taste and rich aroma of Mom's roast. He took a bite.

Braxton spat. "Ugh!"

Dave opened his eyes. Braxton's rice ball lay in pieces on the floor, next to the wad he'd spit out. The man was staring at it like it had sprouted legs.

Meder lowered his rice ball from his mouth. "What's the matter?"

Braxton's cheeks swelled, his throat worked. "Something's moving." He prodded at the rice.

Smith bent for a closer look. "Maggots."

Dave spat out what he had in his mouth and dropped his rice ball like it burned his fingers. Sure enough, several of the rice grains twisted and wriggled. Bile forced its way up his gullet.

Men cussed all around the cabin—all making the same discovery. Vitty roared an impressive string of foul language. Hallmark looked grim. Smith, visibly deflated.

In the midst of all the hubbub, Nielsen sat very still, his rice ball intact in his hand. He held it up and gazed at it. "This, gentlemen, is protein. Amino acids. Essential for life and health. And I am going to eat it."

Dave's gut churned with disgust. "What?"

"You're kidding," Meder said.

Nielsen shook his head. "No, I'm not. My body needs nutrients, and nutrients it shall have. I intend to survive this, so when the war is over, I can see to it these monsters get what's coming to them. Every iota of it."

Braxton cleared his throat. "I don't think I'll last that long."

Nielsen stared him in the face. "That's why you will eat the food, no matter how disgusting. If there is a God, we will win—eventually. And I'm going to do what it takes to be around when we do."

Watt's face was grim. "All right, then. I'll do it if you will." His eyes changed focus to a point outside the cabin. "For you, Yvette." He named his tiny daughter.

Dave shook his head. "What would Colonel Doolittle think if he could see us now?"

Meder lifted his rice ball in the air, for all the world as if someone had proposed a toast. "Our fearless leader would appreciate that we're survivors. C'mon, fellows. Nielsen's right."

One by one, the others joined him—except Braxton, whose rice balls had both disintegrated on the floor.

Dave took another look at his. The maggots were unmistakable—squirming, a little larger than the rice grains, with dark spots on the end that had to be their heads. He couldn't do it. "Here, Braxton. You can have this one."

Braxton laid his head against the wall and closed his eyes. He shook his head. "Thank you, sir. But no thanks."

"Geronimo." Nielsen took a bite. The rest followed his example.

Dave watched the others chew. Morbid fascination took over. *Can you taste the little buggers? Can you feel them?*

Don't ask what you don't want to know. A fresh pang of hunger shot through his belly. He guessed he'd find out for himself soon enough.

Chapter Twenty

Wednesday, December 29, 1948
Osaka, Japan

EVENING TURNED OUT TO BE MIYAKO'S worst time of day. The brothel walls reverberated with tinny music from the bar area and boisterous flirtation everywhere.

She settled in the common room. Its placement toward the rear of the building kept it a little more insulated from the mayhem.

She had to get out of that place.

She crossed to the window on feline feet and slid it open a few inches. Same carved grating in place here as in her room. She threw her weight against it, but it felt as solid as the one outside her window. No surprise. She heaved a sigh and folded her aching limbs beneath her on a cushion by the table, fingers pressed to her ears.

How else could she escape? She looked around the room. Curtains led to the kitchen, which probably had a door leading to the alley. That had potential. The staff might occasionally leave it unguarded. If she watched and waited for the right moment, she might be able to slip out unnoticed. But it would be tough to hang around watching for that moment without looking suspicious.

How about Imai-san's window? *Talk about tweaking the dragon's own beard.*

And she'd seen there was no exit from the garden.

She drummed her fingers on the table. A path would reveal itself if she kept her eyes and ears open. But it needed to reveal itself soon.

Yamada-san strode into the room. She huffed and heaved her girth onto a cushion.

Miyako bowed. "Please, make yourself comfortable. You've earned it. Good business tonight, from the sound of it."

Yamada-san gave a decisive nod. "Very good business, Midori-chan. I think that nice rain might be helping us. Encouraging the men to come in and enjoy some warmth.

Join me for a little *sake?*"

"*Hai.*" Miyako rose to fetch a pair of glasses from the kitchen. By the time she returned, Yamada-san had produced a carafe of *sake* from the sideboard. Miyako knelt across from her and poured for them both.

Yamada-san lifted the cup of clear liquid to her lips. "*Arigato*, child. I understand you came out a winner at Eight-Nine today."

Word travels fast here in the henhouse. She veiled a self-satisfied smile behind a gracious bow. "Fortune favored me. And my older brother taught me a few things before... Well. But that Noriko, now." She gave Yamada-san a sidelong glance. "Rumor has it she's quite the card player, yes?"

Yamada-san glowered. "I know she cheats. I haven't figured out how."

"Maybe she does." She leaned toward Yamada-san. "But between you and me, I'm confident she can be bested."

Yamada-san narrowed her eyes. "How?"

"Like I said, my brother taught me a few things. But he didn't teach me *this* trick." She watched the lady's face. This move could be risky if she'd read her wrong. "I can't guarantee you'll win every game. No one can. But if we work together"—she gave the older lady a level gaze she hoped exuded confidence—"I can boost the odds for you so you'll win out over time."

"What do you mean?"

"How badly do you want to beat her?"

Yamada-san sat back, measured her with her eyes. "Badly enough."

"All right, then. Here's what I propose." A distant sound like rushing water seemed to rise in her ears. "First, we come up with a system of signals. Next, when you see a card, you let me know its number."

Yamada-san jerked up straight and frowned. "And what makes you think I would agree to such a thing?"

Miyako gave her a quick bow. "Please pardon the offense! I'm sure you wouldn't, under ordinary circumstances. But I thought, since you're sure *she* cheats—"

Yamada-san sniffed. "Which she does. Well, go on."

"Then, based on what I know about the cards you've seen

and the cards I've seen, I signal back. Tell you whether to stand or draw. Together, we have better information than she does, and we make better decisions."

"I suppose it could work." The words crept out.

"Not to win every game, of course. But over time."

"The signals would have to be subtle." Yamada-san pinned her with a direct gaze. "What do you expect to gain by this, ah?"

"I'm not interested in the winnings. Let's just say I'm hoping you'll do me the honor of a small favor."

"Oh?" Yamada-san's eyebrows lifted. "What would that be?"

The rushing sound in her ears was less distant now, but she did her best to sound casual. "I need to leave the Oasis for a few hours. A little urgent business I need to take care of in the next day or two. I'm not sure which night yet. Do you think you could arrange that for me somehow?"

"That will be *quite* difficult." Yamada-san sucked in her breath, then pressed her lips into a thin line. "How do I know you'll come back?"

Miyako summoned all her wide-eyed innocence. "I need the money for Papa-san."

Yamada-san still wore that measuring look. "I should be able to come up with something, if you show me that this ruse of yours can really help me beat her."

Miyako bowed. "I'd be honored if you'd consider it."

Yamada-san went quiet, brows knotting.

Miyako lapsed into a musing voice. "Can't you picture her face when she loses?"

A slow smile broke across Yamada-san's lips.

"This will be fun. I promise. We can work out our signals tomorrow."

"I'll find you later this evening. But"—the old courtesan swigged her *sake* and stood, pinning Miyako with a glare— "don't be *baka* enough to think you can pull anything over on me." She bobbed a curt bow and left.

Miyako finished her *sake* next to the brazier, running calculations in her head that made her gut go sour. What she hadn't told Yamada-san was that all her machinations would improve the woman's odds only slightly.

It doesn't matter whether I actually help her win. As long as she wins.

This was going to take some intervention from the ancestors.

19 June 1942, Shanghai, China
61 Days Captive

It seemed the airmen had won themselves some sort of grudging respect. For the rest of their three-day journey by sea, apart from pushing what passed for food through the door, the Japs left them alone.

But once they docked, the guards from the ship handed them over to another unit, and it was back to business as usual. There was a night transfer through the city of Shanghai to a dingy basement prison. The Japanese warehoused the eight of them together in a cage-like enclosure in a basement room. Bamboo poles served as bars. A dim bulb in a filthy glass fixture above the stairs kept the room in perpetual twilight.

They wasted away in that hellish cage for several weeks—torrid summer weeks. The heat was unbearable.

One day, mid-morning, Dave lay curled up in a corner of the cage, doing his best to keep out of the other men's way so he could rest. It had been his and Watt's turn to stand watch the night before, which was a joke, since neither of them was up for much standing. But the men had organized a system to have a pair of watchmen around the clock. The watchmen had two essential jobs—keep the rats off the sleepers and help Hallmark get to the latrine. He was too weak with dysentery to get there on his own.

Japanese voices sounded from above. A dozen guards trooped down the stairs—not the usual trio who delivered their so-called meals. The lead guard produced a key ring. The others clustered behind him.

Nielsen shot him a look that asked *what's this?*

Dave shrugged, his pulse quickening.

"*Horyo. Koi.*" The man opened the door to their cage, gestured at Smith, who was closest to him, then at the floor at his own feet. The guard behind him jangled a pair of handcuffs.

"Oh, no you don't." Watt stood. "Where are you taking Smith?"

The guard made a sweeping gesture, this time incorporating them all.

"Transfer?" Meder muttered. "About bloody time."

Dave dragged himself to his feet. The men around him did the same—except Hallmark, who groaned and stirred. A fly lit on his eyelid. He was too listless to brush it away.

Meder knelt and shook Hallmark. "Time to go, buddy." The lead guard's face darkened. "*Hayaku.*" He waved the guards nearest him into the bamboo enclosure.

Two of them took Hallmark's shoulders. A third pushed Dave aside and grasped the invalid's knees.

Dave filed toward the door, Nielsen and Meder moving with him. He stepped over the threshold and held his wrists out for the cuffs.

Whatever came next, it had to be an improvement. If it didn't kill him.

The guards brought them out to a trio of military trucks. A soldier had to bring a stretcher for Hallmark and the convoy moved.

It'd been weeks since Dave had seen anything besides a prison wall. He craned to look past the guards for a glimpse of landscape.

Each time they slowed, his muscles tensed. Was this his moment? How hard would it be to leverage himself across the guards' knees and vault through the opening at the back of the truck's canvas cover? Roll when he hit the road and come up running. Escape into the twisting alleys of the city or—a few minutes later—dive into the gracefully terraced wheat fields and disappear. Then he'd be on to Chungking and back in the fight.

And finally doing something to be the hero Chen and Pete died protecting. And to get back to Eileen.

Then sunlight would glint off the sharp edge of a bayonet and the fantasy would melt away, leaving nothing but black despair. He'd be back on a hard bench seat in a stifling truck. With several Japanese rifles separating him from freedom.

And more in the trucks behind them.

After an hour or so, a guard tower manned by soldiers loomed to his left, like a giant spider on spindly wooden legs. An all-too-substantial wall—ten feet of cinder-block topped with four lengths of forbidding barbed wire—obscured the last glimpse of golden field and the Shanghai skyline in the distance.

The truck halted. A pair of Japs jumped off and used their rifles to gesture the prisoners out of the trucks.

The guards directed them into a featureless cinder-block building. Unsteady legs took Dave up three cement steps and through a doorway.

Dozens of Japanese thugs crammed the room. They bristled with weapons—rifles, bayonets, swords. A long table stood on a raised wooden platform along the far wall. Five men in flowing black robes sat behind it. Judges, it seemed, who studied the prisoners like lab animals, their faces impassive.

We're on trial? A shudder ran up Dave's spine.

Guards used their standard rifle-butt persuasion to get the prisoners into a line facing the judges. Watt and Nielsen lay Hallmark's stretcher on the floor. Flies covered Hallmark's exposed skin. Vitty wobbled a little where he stood.

The judge in the center—the one with the deepest wrinkles—pounded a gavel. The curls on his ridiculous Dickensian wig bobbed. Those wigs more than offset any dignity the judges' robes might have given them.

A kangaroo court if there ever was one.

An expectant hush filled the room. The judge with the gavel adjusted his glasses and glowered at them. He started a lengthy speech in Japanese. A meaningless torrent of syllables. Like the "confession" Dave signed, he didn't understand a word of it except his own name.

Waves of fever had him alternately beading with sweat and convulsing with shivers. It was all he could do not to keel over.

Stand straight. Be a man.

"Are we on trial here?" Watt spoke up from somewhere at the far end of the line. "What's the charge?"

"*Horyo. Damare,*" the Jap thundered.

Watt's voice rang through the room. "What's your evidence? Where's our defense? Are we on trial?"

Guards swarmed Watt. A rifle butt bashed into his kneecap with a sickening crack.

Dave cringed, feeling the blow like it had landed on his own body. Watt did what Dave should have done—dealt with the threat to the men. Dave had been too focused on his own misery.

The chief judge stood and stared along the line of them. "*Damare. Damare.*" He waited for the commotion in the room to die, then resumed his speech.

Dave couldn't shake his feeling of disbelief. This trial was a travesty. A joke. But their lives might hang on its outcome. And unlike Watt, he hadn't had the presence of mind to lodge an effective protest. For himself, or for his men.

He looked at the judges' impassive faces and the sick feeling returned. It made no difference. The thing was rigged.

The chief judge finished reading. He drilled the prisoners with a glare and a deepening frown.

Soldiers all around the room stirred. Some stood.

That's it?

At Dave's right, Nielsen spoke to the interpreter. "What'd he say?"

"He gave verdict. And, ah, your sentence."

Verdict? Clearly a foregone conclusion.

The foreboding he felt himself was just as apparent on Nielsen's face. "Well, what's our sentence then?"

The officer smirked. "Hata-san say you no be told."

Chapter Twenty-One

IT WAS BACK TO THE MIND-NUMBING solitary routine Dave had known in Tokyo, with two important exceptions. No interrogations, and the prisoners were granted the privilege of morning exercise together. The chance to see the others, and sometimes exchange a few rushed words, became Dave's lifeline.

One steaming August morning he set out, determined to catch up with Meder. He'd been formulating a question for Bob ever since he watched him cross himself over maggot-y rice balls on the ship.

Meder came to a halt in a shady corner and sank down on the sidewalk. Dave seized the opportunity to settle on the ground beside him.

A guard hovered over them. Dave silently went to work pulling weeds. After a moment, the man grunted and wandered off. Dave glanced around to make sure none of the guards were paying attention. They weren't—for the moment.

He spoke in a murmur. "Bob, I have to ask you something."

Bob reached for a weed. "Sure. What?"

"You really buy that fairy-tale stuff they dish out at church? An all-mighty, all-loving God? In the face of all this?" He peered around them at the fence, the cement cellblock building, the guards with their clubs.

Bob stopped his work and looked at him. "With all my heart. It may not always look like it, but God's in charge. We have to believe He knows how to work things out the best way."

Dave took a fierce yank at a weed. "Wonder what Smith and Braxton would say to that."

Or Chen and his village. Or my sister Jenny, in the ground at fourteen.

"Listen, Dave. If seeing how things are over here has proved anything to me, it's this. There *is* one true God, who shows people how to live right. Just 'cause some reject Him doesn't mean He's not there."

The guard had turned back their way. Bob ducked his head lower and spoke through the side of his mouth. "This world isn't running according to His design. But it will."

Dave heaved a sigh and ripped at another weed. "I wish I could believe I'll live to see it."

Alone again in his cell, Dave replayed every memory he could dredge up. He missed everyone. Mom. His little sister Julie. Even Dad. All his fellow prisoners, the *Payback* and *Green Hornet* men. Fraternity brothers. High school friends. Reaching further back, Jenny. Uncle Verle.

And most of all, his wife Eileen, with her porcelain skin and beguiling smile. What was she doing now? Still at her mom's? The telegram would've reached her months ago. She'd know he was missing in action. How long would it take her to give him up for dead and get on with her life?

The two of them had experienced plenty of ups and downs—didn't everyone? But it seemed like it got worse after she joined him in Florida.

They hadn't parted on very good terms. What was that last fight even about? He couldn't remember. But then, that was how it went with a lot of nights when he'd had a few.

He did remember the rage on her features. Her way of knitting her brows over her nose. The shock of her frigid gin and tonic when she dashed it across his face. The sting of it in his eyes.

They'd started out in his Air Corps buddy Joe's kitchen. Joe's wife, Tina, had gotten Eileen all worked up over the new Lombard flick. But somehow the four of them wound up sucking down cocktails at the crummy bar across the street from Eglin Field instead.

Another thing he remembered was all the names she called him that evening.

"You rat. You snake. You—why, there isn't even a word for what you are." She stood and thrust her bar stool out of her way. It slammed against a four-top table and fell onto the floor.

He grabbed some paper napkins and blotted his face. Pulled a few four-letter words out of his own arsenal.

She crossed the linoleum, paused when she reached the door. Turned to face him full on. "All the booze. All the bars. I'm through, David Delham. I mean it. Through." She flounced out into the night. The door slammed behind her.

She always was one for the dramatic gestures. Maybe he did keep drinking that night after she wanted him to stop. And maybe he and Joe were a little obvious about ogling a blonde at the bar. That was no justification for such a big outburst. Was it?

Tina gave them both a disgusted look and went off after Eileen.

Joe elbowed him. "Maybe you better go after her."

He swizzled his Scotch and soda. "Not after a scene like that." A man had to know how to handle a hothead like Eileen.

A few minutes later he was slurping ice at the bottom of his glass. It sank in she wasn't coming back. "You don't suppose she took the car?"

Joe gave him a stricken look.

They left their places at the bar and checked the parking lot. Nothing but asphalt where the Ford had been. "How do you like that?" Dave punched at a trashcan. It clattered against a brick wall, and the top popped off. Cans and greasy newspapers spilled onto the asphalt. Dave kicked at one.

"How'd she sneak the dang keys?"

"You must've left them sitting on the bar." Joe swore. "It's a couple miles' walk."

Dave probably counted to six or seven before he was able to speak again. But he did his best to put a good face on the thing. "Gives a whole new meaning to 'one for the road,' doesn't it?" He turned toward the building. "I say we let them sit at home and stew on this some."

It might have been two for the road before they made their way out again. They passed through the parking lot once more. Joe growled and tensed his shoulders. "There's gonna be hell to pay when I get home."

"You bet there is. I'm not putting up with this kind of treatment."

But when he got to their apartment, there was no purse on the kitchen table. No pearl-buttoned sweater flung across the couch.

No Eileen. And no car.

No silver brush on the dresser. No elegant little flacon of Chanel Number Five. None of those silky, flimsy things she kept in her lingerie drawer.

No stinking car.

There was a note on his pillow. *We need a break. Gone to Mom's.*

And to add insult to injury, when he went to brush his teeth, he found the flask of Scotch he kept in the glove compartment of his Ford in the bathroom sink. Drained.

So that was it? Fine. Sure, he drank hard sometimes, but he worked hard too. So he earned the right. He figured she could come back when she was ready to crawl.

Two days later, the Thirty-Fourth got called out to Sacramento. Apparently, the urge to crawl hadn't quite struck her yet.

That minx might not be ready to admit it, but I know she misses me. She has to.

Still, he couldn't shake the feeling he'd been a pretty big heel. Military life might not have been all she dreamed of when she snagged him. Maybe he couldn't help that. Aviation always held a siren song for him, and he'd finally given in.

But sitting alone in that fetid cell, every fiber in his body ached for her. Ached to feel her silky copper-colored hair between his fingers. To breathe in her Chanel Number Five with its hint of sandalwood, spice, and exotic blooms.

You are a heel. You couldn't look after your wife. Couldn't even speak up for your men at your own trial.

At least he could have taken her to that movie.

How he longed to have Meder's faith in an all-powerful, all-loving God. If there was such a thing, even a heel like him might have some hope for a second chance. Find some way to patch things up and get that sassy smile of hers beaming up at him once more.

Wednesday, December 29, 1948
Osaka, Japan

Miyako sat nursing a cup of tea in the common room. Haruko-chan strode in, serving plate in hand, looking like she'd eaten something sour.

"Midori-san, there's someone to see you. A young woman."

Kimi? Miyako had hardly dared to hope the message would get to her, but who else could it be?

"*Arigato.*" She stood and made her way into the front room.

Kimi had shed her shoes and umbrella and stood in a corner of the room, arms crossed like a *gaijin*, cigarette in hand. The chemical odor of her fresh perm struck Miyako's senses from several feet away. Her flashy red coat looked as out of place in the understated room as a macaque would in a silk dressing gown.

Miyako couldn't have been happier to see her.

Kimi stared at her full out. "Merciful heavens. Look at you."

"I know. I'm a sight." She threw her arms around her friend. "Thanks for coming so soon. It's been awful."

Kimi returned Miyako's hug with a cautious embrace. "It's not a good night for street work anyway." She held Miyako at arm's length and looked her over. "I'm so sorry. I heard how they found you, but I—I wasn't prepared for what you'd look like."

Miyako took her friend's arm. "We can catch up in private." She led her through the room and up the stairs behind. "How are things at the Abeno?"

"Same old story. Asagi tries to run everyone's lives."

"Well, I don't care about Asagi and the rest. They can have the Abeno." She slid open the *shoji* and ushered Kimi into her room. "I got tired of that woman and her games."

"So now you've got this place and its games. I thought you told me you'd never go back to the brothel."

"Shh." She lowered her voice. "The walls are thin, ah? I've done a lot of things I said I'd never do. What's one more?"

Kimi lowered her voice to match. "Let me guess. They're giving you an advance. Hospital bills?"

"*Hai.*"

"Big advance?"

The soft light from the bedside lamp seemed to dim. "*Hai.*"

"So. You *will* be here a long time. What about your Sanders-san?"

"Kimi, I have a favor to ask."

"You want to talk to him. And you need me to find him."

"*No.* I don't want to talk to him. Seeing him is the last thing I want to do—look at me. But"—she studied her feet—"I have to get him a message somehow. He deserves to know why he should find another girl."

"You do have a few things to explain to him." Kimi gave her an impish smile. "But you're so sure about that other girl, ah?"

"*Hai.* Again, look at me. How else could it end?"

"He did come around looking for you." Kimi's voice was a teasing sing-song. "Seemed like he wanted to find you."

"He did? Then it's even more urgent I get a message to him."

"The next time I see him, I'll tell him you'll look for him."

"You're funny, ah?"

Kimi leaned toward her. "Mi-chan, I think he cares about you. Why not give it a chance?"

"Because a man never cares about a girl like me." The pang that ran through her chest surprised her. She took a sharp breath, blinked away a bit of moisture, and put a hand on Kimi's. "Will you take him my message?"

"Why not find him yourself?" Kimi squeezed her hand.

Miyako heaved an exasperated sigh. "Even if I wanted to, which I don't, they won't let me leave. I owe Imai-san big money for patching me up, and you know how it is in these places. The brothel and its games, like you said." She squeezed her eyes shut, then opened them again to look her friend in the face. "Remember last spring, when you needed my help?"

"I haven't forgotten. You got everyone to pitch in the money I needed for the operation—"

"And took care of your sister while you were getting it."

"You're right. I owe you." Kimi settled back on the bed. "What do you want me to say to him?"

"Tell him—tell him I miss him terribly. But you've seen

me. I'm sick, and I don't know when I'll be better. He should find another girl. I'll return the money he gave me when I'm well enough to see him." The last bit was a lie, but she had to say something about the money.

"That's it?"

"That's it."

"You're sure I can't just tell him to come over here and see you?"

Miyako shook her head. "No. For the last time, I never want him to see me like this. And I never want him to see me here. I would die before I would let him think I picked this place over being his *onri wan.*"

Kimi leaned over and gave her a hug. "All right, I'll try. I will."

She wasn't going to trust Kimi with a message to Kamura-san concerning ten thousand yen she needed for poison. That she'd have to handle herself. Somehow.

Yamada-san had better get on her winning streak.

Chapter Twenty-Two

15 October 1942, Kiangwan, China
179 Days Captive

ONE BROODING OCTOBER MORNING, DAVE'S INVARIABLE routine varied. Footsteps sounded in the hall—several sets of them. They shot the bolt, swung the door open.

"*Horyo. Koko ni.*"

He stood on weak legs, wobbled into the corridor. A whole squad of Hirohito's hellhounds filled the hallway, all in crisp dress uniform, bristling with rifles and long swords. One of them stepped forward with handcuffs.

Dress uniform. This is it.

They led him to the room where he'd faced trial all those weeks earlier. About fifteen officers and guards had gathered for the proceeding—whatever it was. He exchanged glances with a grim-faced Nielsen. Meder was there, and Vitty, and Watt.

Their appearance shocked him. Hollow cheeks, sunken eyes, bushy beards that hung to their chests, clothes crusted with filth.

I suppose I look as lousy as those guys. One more scarecrow walking.

But only five of them. Where were Smith and Braxton? What had these butchers done with his men?

And Hallmark? He'd last seen Hallmark on a stretcher.

His teeth clenched so hard he felt the pressure all the way down his neck.

The chief judge moved his gaze along the line of airmen, giving each of them a severe look. He adjusted his glasses and nodded to an officer who stood at his elbow—the same fellow who'd served as interpreter at the trial. The man stepped forward, rifled through a sheaf of papers.

Fever and hunger kept Dave from focusing. But his sense of foreboding swelled. Everything was playing out exactly the way he'd seen it in his most despairing moments.

The officer paged through his documents. He found the spot, started to translate in that reedy voice. "It has been proven beyond all doubt that the defendants, motivated by a false sense of glory, carried on indiscriminate bombing of schools and hospitals..."

He froze in shock. *What? Schools? Hospitals? No. The aircraft factory. The oil refinery.* Direct hits on military targets.

"...machine-gunned innocent civilians with complete disregard for the rules of war..."

Strafed civilians? What?

It took a moment for the shock to wane. He glanced at Watt, steeled himself. *My turn to be the leader.* He lurched forward. "That's not right. Where'd you get that?"

Guards grabbed at both arms and jerked him back, giving his bad shoulder a painful wrench. The muzzle of a rifle pressed into his spine.

This time he was determined to have his say. "We never did any of those things. Where's your proof?"

A rifle butt slammed into his gut. The room melted into a haze of breath-deprived pain.

The interpreter went on. His voice registered as if from a distance. "The military tribunal has passed judgment and imposes...sentences. The tribunal, acting...under the law, hereby sentences"—the interpreter paused to double-check the words on his page—"the defendants...to death."

Death? For what? The interpreter's lips expanded and contracted like a face in a funhouse mirror. The floor tipped, then righted itself.

"Wha...?" An inarticulate groan fell from Nielsen beside him.

Execution? It was one thing to imagine receiving a death sentence—he'd been doing that for weeks. Quite a different thing to hear one handed down.

"But." The interpreter wasn't finished. The head judge pounded his gavel. "Through the graciousness of His Majesty the Emperor," the interpreter read, "your sentences are hereby commuted to life imprisonment, with special treatment."

Life imprisonment. Life. A strange, light feeling took over.

It took a moment for the full import to sink in. Life, yes, but on what terms? He was no longer a prisoner of war. He was a convict serving a sentence.

What do they mean by special treatment?

These were fine people to moralize about "disregard for the rules of war." What about the Geneva Convention?

He took a step forward and yelled at the judge. "Where's Lieutenant Hallmark? Where are Smith and Braxton?"

A group of guards circled him, corralled him toward the door.

He pushed an elbow into the nearest man's ribs. "Where are my men?"

They half-led, half-dragged him to his cell.

Thursday, December 30, 1948
Osaka, Japan

Miyako sat up on her futon and dashed the sleep from her eyes. Her head felt like it was full of cotton—she had to work at clearing it. But after a few minutes, hair brushed smooth, clean robe in place, she headed for the common room in search of tea and breakfast. Especially tea.

Noriko was alone at the table. She barely glanced up from the paper. "Good morning. I'm afraid you've missed everyone else."

Haruko shuffled through the crisp blue-and-white curtains that separated the common room from the kitchen and started to collect the dirty dishes on a tray.

Noriko looked up at her. "You work so hard, Haruko-chan." She gave her voice a cloying lilt. "But don't worry. You're pretty enough, ah? Someday soon, you'll put on a nice dress and make a little money. Play cave-and-eel with the men like a big girl."

Haruko's shoulders tensed.

Miyako pegged Noriko with a glare. "Noriko-chan. There's no need to be cruel." *Or to take out your bitterness on someone more vulnerable.*

She turned to the girl. "Don't pay any attention to Noriko-san. *Arigato* for the breakfast. It looks magnificent."

It did. Delicately scented *miso* soup, stewed prunes. A bowl of steaming rice. Miyako moved to stand. "Do you need help with that tray?"

Haruko gave her a grateful bob. "No, Midori-san. You're supposed to be resting, ah?" She retreated to the kitchen.

Noriko refolded the newspaper sections and placed them in a neat stack on the table. "I'm off to do my nails. Enjoy your breakfast."

Miyako bowed her out of the room, burning with fresh determination to see Yamada-san put her in her place. She put the teapot on the brazier and picked up the front section of the paper. The smell of fresh newsprint filled her nostrils. She lingered over it as long as she could. But there was no sign of Yamada-san. And no one showed up to talk about a game.

She was leaving to hunt down Yamada-san when Haruko reappeared. "Excuse me, Midori-san." She bowed. "Your friend was here. The lady who visited yesterday."

"Already?"

"*Hai.* She left this for you." Haruko dug a bit of crumpled paper from her pants pocket and handed it across the table to Miyako.

Kimi had come through, after all—and quickly. Miyako stifled a twinge of disappointment that her friend had stopped by without seeing her. To be there and gone so early must have been painful for a woman of the night.

She unfurled the paper, fingers trembling with eagerness. A bar napkin, complete with a jagged stain shaped like the base of someone's tumbler. Uneven characters sprawled a ragged line along its right edge.

Decided I won't take your message to your sergeant. I ran across his friend. Aren't you fortunate! You can find them yourself at the Hollywood Club tomorrow night.

You owe me now.

She looked up. Haruko's eyes searched her face, the girl's expression ambiguous. Had she read the message?

Of course she had.

Miyako refolded the napkin in a tidy square, exasperated. Much as she hated to admit it, perhaps Kimi was right. Maybe she did owe George-san a personal explanation. Especially given that, without some kind of divine intervention, she was about to miss their standing

Thursday date.

She had to hope Haruko would stay quiet and the note wouldn't cost her the opportunity to see him the next night. And she had to hope he'd be prepared to see her.

Miyako learned Yamada-san had left to visit a friend. There wouldn't be a game that day. Which meant she would miss her date with George-san. And also meant that everything— winning at *kabu*, Kamura-san, George-san—had collapsed to a single day. The next day, Friday.

She couldn't bear to stay in her room. She wandered out to the courtyard bench. The wintry garden suited her mood, with barren tree branches creating a fretwork of lacy patterns against a restless pewter sky. Her eyes kept drifting to the shed and the yew trees tucked in the corner next to it. Could she make it over the fence back there?

It would have to be a dark night. Windows lined every wall of the buildings. The penalty if she got caught would be steep.

A *shoji* slid aside. Haruko stepped out and slipped into a pair of work shoes. She rooted around inside the shed, emerging a minute later with a rake nearly as tall as she was. Haruko went to work on the dry leaves that had drifted onto the gravel path overnight. A few minutes' effort brought her over to the stone bench where Miyako sat.

"You're leaving, aren't you?" She was careful to keep her voice low and her eyes on her rake.

"What?" Miyako gave the girl a blast of wide-eyed innocence. "No."

Haruko shot her a side-long glare. "Midori-san, I saw what that *pan-pan* wrote you."

"Shh!" She glanced around the courtyard. "No. I'm not leaving. It's just—I've got something I need to take care of. Something important."

Haruko went back to raking the gravel around the bench, which was already pristine. "*Hai*," she breathed. "And it's something that involves meeting an American at a dance hall."

Merciful deities. What's it going to take to buy her silence?

Haruko turned to her, the rake forgotten in her hand. "Please, Midori-san. Take me with you."

Her surprise was real this time. "What?"

"I'm sick of it here." The words tumbled over each other, bursting from her smooth, un-rouged lips. "Mopping up vomit and spilled *sake*. Scrubbing and peeling and carrying all day. Catering to these hussies' every little whim. Especially that Noriko—she's the worst of the bunch. But I know she's right. Soon enough I will be a *baishanfu* like you." The girl dropped her eyes. Tiny beads of moisture glittered on her lashes.

She's only a kid. Miyako's voice went softer, along with her heart. "Haruko-chan, look at me." She waited until the girl did. "You think I know some better way for you to earn money than working here?" She paused, hoping her words would sink in. Noriko was right about that much. "This is a nice place. You have a roof over your head. Charcoal on the brazier. And food you're not going to see anywhere else. Trust me, you could do worse. I've seen girls not much older than you sell themselves on the street for a meal." She was young enough when she started—almost of legal age. But these girls...

Haruko's expression went hard. "If it's so wonderful, why are you leaving?"

"I told you, I'm not." *Unless it's in a police wagon.* "Where else would I go?"

The girl gave her petite toes a petulant little tap. "I don't believe you."

"Honestly, Haruko-chan, it's not what you think. You're right, I am meeting Sanders-san tomorrow, if I can manage to get out of here. But it's so I can ask him for money." This was a half-truth. If he didn't retch at the sight of her, of course she'd look for a way to ask for money.

Haruko gave her a brazen stare. "You think I don't know how a *baishanfu* asks for money? Besides, isn't Imai-san giving you money? A *lot* of money, from what I—" She stopped and put her fingers over her mouth as if she could stuff the words back in.

The girl knew everything. Everything that mattered, anyway. Miyako drew herself up straight. "Is that what you heard? Then perhaps you've also heard about my father's hospital bills."

Haruko blanched and bowed very low. "Please forgive me, Midori-san. I'm sorry I mentioned it. Please pardon this humble person. But"—she leaned toward Miyako, eyes wide with concern—"you must be *very* careful if you go out for your meeting tomorrow. I remember when another girl tried it. Imai-san caught her."

"What happened?"

"It was awful."

"Haruko-chan. Tell me."

Haruko found something fascinating in the gravel by her toes. A beat passed before she looked up. "These men came for poor Yuriko-chan. Tome-chan said they were *yakuza*." Haruko looked away. "I try not to ever think about what they did to her."

Chapter Twenty-Three

Friday, December 31, 1948
Osaka, Japan

TOTAL DARKNESS. SHE PERCHED ON A *mattress. Soft—Western style. Fabric clung to her clammy skin.*
  On edge. Pulse thundering.
  Waiting.
  Miyako strained her eyes. Nothing. Her mind registered shifting splotches of green and purple, but they stemmed from sheer imagination.
  It started. Scrabbling, somewhere outside the room. She'd heard it before—she knew what it was. Enormous talons scraping along the hallway toward her.
  A second set, echoing from a different direction. And another, higher pitched. Soon there were...five? Seven?
  Her pulse pounded like it would burst her veins.
  Whatever it was—whatever they were—came snuffling right up against the thin paper shoji *that divided her room from the hall. Its intense desire to rip her to shreds pressed on her like a physical force.*
  She stood and edged away, eyes riveted on the spot the noise came from. Groped behind her for the wall. Pressed her spine into it, every muscle straining with her desperate need to get away.
  The shoji rattled. The noise of the beast's rooting swelled. The thing would be on her in the dark before she even saw it, sinking its talons into her belly and its teeth into her throat.
  She opened her mouth to scream. No sound came.
  From somewhere behind her, a narrow band of light shot across the bed. It thinned the darkness just enough that she could make out the reptilian claw pushing in through the shoji, *complete with horrid talons.*
  She could also see the scant furnishings. Bed. Small dresser. The band of light struck the single object on the dresser. A large vase, pale colored, with a plum-blossom design.
  She'd been granted a weapon. She lunged for the vase

and dashed it against the wall. Its base shattered, leaving a jagged edge.

The beast snarled from behind the partition.

She faced the shoji *and braced herself.*

The beast ripped at her door. It gave way. The terror burst in.

The last thing she expected, and yet she'd known it all along. The redheaded soldier, blown up to monstrous size. He lumbered toward her, blue-green eyes blazing in eerie contrast to the orange cast of his sun-burnished skin. A blood-curdling snarl issued from his throat. He reached for her with what should have been hands. But in their place, he had grasping claws and rending talons.

And unaccountably, impaled on one talon, three paper tickets.

She clenched her fists around the vase's neck and readied her swing.

One chance at this. It had to count.

He lunged.

She swung. A powerful motion that—

Miyako jerked awake. The scream on her lips died in a gasp. She stared around her.

Mirror. Curtain. Shelves. All normal. Familiar.

Her sheets lay twisted in ropes between her hands. She uncoiled them and mopped her face. Her terror dissipated slowly, like freshly dried ink under running water.

No more sleep for me.

That was what she called the black version of her dream. But the old dream had taken a new turn. A weapon. A chance to escape. Did it mean something? What?

Clattering in the kitchen dragged her back to the brothel. She got up, peeled off her clammy robe, and wrapped herself in a fresh one. She lay down and stared up at the ceiling.

Friday. She *had* to get out of the brothel. It was imperative that she see Kamura-san and deliver her apology to George-san.

The air in the room felt heavy. In the corner farthest from the light, a tiny brown spider worked an intricate pattern in silk. As she watched it she saw herself, brooding over the tenuous web of her plan.

Too tenuous. An industrious spider would lay more silk. *I might as well live in a lacquered jar.* She hoped the lid had air holes.

Miyako decided a cup of tea would do her good. She slid the *shoji* aside and eased her way into the common room. Tome knelt at the table, flipping through the newspaper.

"Good morning, Tome-chan. How was business last night?" Miyako lifted the teakettle from the brazier and checked the coals. "Sounded lively enough."

Tome yawned. "Okay for me, but better for No-chan. She still had a party going when I went to sleep."

"Do you think he spent the night?"

Tome snorted. "I know he did."

"Good for her." Profitable night for Noriko, but she might not be up for hours. "So she'll sleep in. No game until later then?"

Tome lifted her delicate shoulders. "Maybe not."

"Do you think we'll play at all?"

"We'd better." A smile played at Tome's lips. "I'm out of cigarettes."

Miyako's gut balled with anxiety. No game yesterday because of Yamada-san's errands. Possibly no game today. And that meant no chance to keep her bargain with Yamada-san and get the lady's help.

But a few minutes later, Noriko made her appearance, left hand pressed against her temple. "Ah. What a headache. Why is everyone so loud today?"

Tome gave her a sympathetic smile. "Poor No-chan. You look like you've been run over by a horse."

"More like an Eidan Subway train."

Tome brought Noriko *soba* and tea. The teacup jittered as she raised it to her lips. She drained it, then relaxed enough to give Tome an uneven smile. "You're in a kind mood today."

Tome gave her a sweet smile. "Need to get you fixed up for *kabu*. We won't play without you."

"I don't think I'm in the mood today." Noriko rubbed at her temples. "I'm going back to bed."

Miyako's stomach lurched. Today's game had to happen. Tome pouted. "But you have to play. Or who's going to advance Fusako-chan the funds?"

Noriko had closed her eyes again. "Play for points then."

"What if we double the stakes?" Miyako said. "Raise the maximum bet to two hundred yen instead of one hundred?"

Noriko opened her eyes to a squint and looked at her as if she'd noticed her for the first time. "Where are *you* going to get the cash, if I might be so bold?"

"I had a little tea money set aside. Yamada-san was kind enough to bring it to me."

Noriko sat straighter. "I'll play." She produced a cigarette from the sleeve of her cotton robe and positioned it in a holder. "But we'll triple the stakes."

17 October 1942, Kiangwan, China
181 Days Captive

Dave heard guards at the end of the hall. He dove for his plank bench and held his breath, listening.

Two days had passed since the sentencing, and nothing seemed to have changed. Life plodded on according to the same solitary routine. Same rice-glob meals thrust through the slit in the door. Same few minutes in the prison yard by himself each morning. Same stained walls, same narrow window. Same wobbly legs that barely held him up. Same dysentery that never let up.

Same perpetual hunger.

The cell door swung open. Two guards stood in the hall. One of them beat his baton against his palm. "*Koi, horyo.*"

Dave stood and let them conduct him out to the prison yard. The other fellows joined him one by one. Watt, Meder, Vitiollo, Nielsen. What had they done with the other three? Same question he'd asked himself a thousand times.

Prison transfer. That was it. The guards saw how sick Hallmark was and moved him somewhere for medical attention.

Yeah? What about Smith and Braxton?

Two men emerged from between the buildings. The first

was thick-jowled, with the long sword of an officer and the regal bearing and fierce expression to match.

The second man was a surprise. A young Asian, gaunt in a ragged prison uniform, sharp cheekbones jutting over hollow cheeks. Dave had gathered there were other prisoners in a different section of the camp, but he'd never seen one.

The officer strode out onto the grass, then came to a precise halt facing the line of airmen. The Asian prisoner trailed up behind him. The officer gave them a curt bow, spoke a few sentences, then nodded to his companion.

The prisoner ran one hand through his hair and started to translate into heavily accented English. "Warden Tatsuta wants you to understand that you are war criminals. Enemies of the nation of Nippon. Your hostile acts of bombing, shooting, and killing innocent Japanese citizens are proved. You are judged and convicted."

The officer's upper lip curled into a sneer of disgust while this message was delivered. He directed a few more sentences to the interpreter.

"Insignificant as you are"—the interpreter's lips twitched with what looked like an effort to put on a severe expression—"you must be thankful to the emperor for his magnificent goodness. It is right that you are condemned to die, but he has pardoned you. You will spend the rest of your lives as worthless prisoners, understanding that it is useless to try to bring harm to Nippon."

Tatsuta went on, with periodic breaks for interpretation. It was the usual litany about how they should be good prisoners and cooperate. And how they'd be killed if they tried to escape. They'd heard it all before, although Tatsuta's rendition rang with even more scorn than usual.

Once he'd finished, he gave the prisoners one more severe look, then spun on his heel and walked briskly toward the wooden buildings.

The young man gave them a slight bow. "Now your sentence is decided. The Imperial Japanese Army will return your things to you. Please follow Kinoshita-san." He gestured toward one of the guards.

Dave exchanged a surprised glance with Nielsen. But he had deeper concerns than his things. He directed a question at the interpreter. "Excuse me. Could you please tell me what happened to—"

A guard stepped between them and brandished a baton. "*Damare, baka.*"

The young man's chiseled features squeezed into a pained look. He bowed without speaking and walked after Warden Tatsuta.

The five airmen turned and trooped after Kinoshita. He led them into the assembly room where their court proceedings had taken place. Several more guards accompanied them.

The now-familiar long table displayed an array of items laid out in methodical Japanese style. A neat arrangement of wallets. A box filled with their watches and jewelry. Most important, a line of leather jackets, battered with use, arranged by size.

"Eight," Watt murmured. "Eight jackets."

Dave took measured steps over to the table. Six officer's jackets with squadron patches. Three of them sported the Thirty-Fourth Squadron's bold Thunderbird design—his, Watt's, Vitty's. Three jackets bore the Ninety-Fifth Squadron's Kicking Mule. The name bands read Nielsen, Meder, and Hallmark. Two jackets without patches bore the names of the enlisted men, Braxton and Smith.

He stood with a hand on Smith's jacket.

Vitty was going through the jewelry. "Look," he said in a low voice. A set of dog tags dangled from his fingers.

"Whose are those?" Dread narrowed Dave's throat. Dog tags only came off for one reason.

Vitty's jaw worked. "Braxton's."

It was true, then. Dean Hallmark, Peter Braxton, and Robert Smith no longer required their personal effects.

Dave closed his eyes for a long moment. Moisture blurred his vision when he looked up at Watt.

Nielsen's voice resonated with determination. "If the Japs killed those men in cold blood, they'll pay. We will survive this thing somehow, and they will pay."

Dave turned away, speechless. No words would bring those heroes back. And no words could capture the violent rage that swelled through his chest.

Dave studied the contents of his wallet until his cell grew so dark he couldn't see them.

A photo of Eileen. Her bright eyes and engaging smile on the front. Her spidery scrawl on the back.

Dear Dave,
So excited to be your bride!
Love, Eileen
April 1941

He ran a finger over the ink. He'd been a lucky man, once. That must have been a million years ago.

A license to drive the blue Ford coupe she took off in.

A library card. How little he'd appreciated what a treasure that was. How many books did they have in the Cook County library? Thousands? Maybe tens of thousands. What he'd give for even *one* of them now. Wouldn't matter if it was *Nancy Drew.*

About three bucks in coins. Enough for a drink or two. More than enough to take Eileen to that movie she wanted to see. Maybe he could still do it someday.

Lord, are you up there somewhere listening?

Distant as the possibility of taking his wife to a movie seemed, it was more hope than Hallmark, Smith, or Braxton had now. And Dave was determined to cling to it.

Chapter Twenty-Four

Friday, December 31, 1948
Osaka, Japan

TOME WENT TO FETCH THE REST of the girls. Miyako and Noriko cleared the breakfast table. They'd just spread out the playing mat when the others joined them.

Yamada-san bowed her greetings. "Turned a good profit last night, did you?" she said to Noriko.

"*Hai.*" Noriko bowed back. Her lips took on a mocking twist. "I trust you won't win it all away."

Yamada-san snorted. "We'll see, won't we?"

Miyako avoided the quick glance the older woman gave her. This was the craziest thing she'd ever attempted. How many winning hands would the ancestors have to furnish to convince Yamada-san to keep her side of the bargain?

They played the first round through to the last hand—Fusako's. Yamada-san sat with her face stony, holding an anemic total of two. She would need to see either an eight or nine to collect on her bet.

This was a calamity. Miyako took a long pull on her cigarette and looked at anything but Yamada-san.

Fusako dealt herself a card with a soft thwack. A gleaming white moon rising from a verdant field of silver-gray pampas grass. *Hachi*, eight.

Miyako had never been more delighted to see that moon. Fusako held the worst hand in the game. Eight plus nine plus three—*ha-kyuu-san*. It added up to zero. The fabled "bad hand" from which the *yakuza* derived their name.

Yamada-san was going to collect on her two-hundred-yen bet after all. They all were.

Yamada-san's face crinkled into a grin. The woman shot Miyako a glance. She returned an innocent smile, but her gut twisted. Yes, Yamada-san had won. Yes, she *should* be happy. But it was an obvious stroke of luck.

How in the world do I take credit for that?

The dealer's role shifted to Noriko. She fixed a fresh cigarette in her holder and shuffled, her blood-red nails a blur. She snapped the cards on the mat then sat back, a supercilious smile on her ruby lips.

Miyako needed to give Yamada-san some direction. Needed to maintain the pretense she was helping her. But the cards weren't telling her what the lady should do. She closed her eyes and lifted an urgent prayer to the Matsuura ancestors.

Wait. The gift from her dream. The vase with the spray of blossoms. Perhaps that gift would come to her rescue again. She signaled Yamada-san to bet on cherry.

Yamada-san scowled, deliberating. She put down four more markers. She had six smooth white stones—three hundred yen—riding on the cherry card.

Miyako sucked in her breath. The highest bet she'd seen at the Oasis.

"Ah." Noriko gave Yamada-san an appraising look. "You feel fortune is with you."

"I think it's my turn, ah?"

Noriko arched an eyebrow and dealt the face-down cards. "Another card, Yamada-san?"

"*Hai,*" Yamada-san replied without hesitation.

Miyako clamped her mouth shut to keep a gasp from escaping. What was the woman thinking? She hadn't waited for the signal. It took a full second to work it out. Miyako had been biting her lip while she mulled the odds. Yamada-san thought she saw the signal.

Miyako's head spun with disbelief. *Three out of ten.* The odds Yamada-san would improve her hand were only three out of ten.

Despair sank long black talons into her heart. She watched Yamada-san's third card descend in slow motion.

She barely heard Noriko ask her if she wanted another card herself. Barely managed to shake her head no.

With all the cards dealt, Yamada-san flipped up her third card and crowed. "Three cherries. Three of a kind!" She spread her cards out on the mat.

Miyako stared, then broke into a slow smile. The hand was so rare it was an instant winner.

Noriko's jaw gaped like a *koi.* She counted out Yamada-san's winnings, her voice pitched high with disbelief.

Yamada-san chuckled. "I think I'm done for the day." She folded and tucked eight crisp fifty-yen notes into the bosom of her *kimono.*

Miyako stood and stretched, doing her best to look casual.

The ancestors had heard her. The weapon from her dream had proven its worth. But would Yamada-san see it that way?

Yamada-san left the common room, avoiding Miyako's eyes. Miyako checked the old courtesan's bedroom a few minutes later and didn't find her. She wandered along the corridor and overheard Yamada-san carrying on a hushed conversation with Imai-san.

Fortunately for Miyako's sanity, Yamada-san sought her out a few minutes later. She tried to stutter out a few words of explanation, but the older lady preempted her. "It was tonight you wanted to go, ah? Make sure you're ready by seven-thirty." She compressed her lips, turned on her heel, and marched away.

Miyako stared, stunned, at Yamada-san's departing back. What did it mean? The woman had elected to keep her side of the bargain, but why?

It did mean one thing. She needed to get busy.

18 October 1942, Kiangwan, China
182 Days Captive

The square of light from the window had reached it at last— the precise spot on the floor it had to hit before they'd bring around Dave's rice-blob lunch. The cell door's top slot opened, followed seconds later by the lower food slot. Right on schedule. He stood to collect his tray. He took a quick glance into the eyes behind the slot—

And did a double take. The corners of those eyes crinkled with a smile.

He stopped short and stared. All he could make out of the eyes' owner was a broad forehead and a pair of unnaturally strong cheekbones.

"*Douzo omeshiagari.*" The man gave him a slight bow.

Dave wasn't sure what the words meant, but they sounded friendly.

Someone behind the door yelled, "*Damare.*" The slot slid shut and the eyes were gone.

He blinked a couple times, then sat. He balanced the tray and its nondescript contents across his thighs, his gut coiling with anxiety.

Guards didn't smile unless it involved some form of torment.

He took a deep breath to relax, lifted his regulation tin cup and took a sip—a small one, to make the tepid liquid last. He set the cup on the tray and gnawed at the flavorless rice ball. Picked up the cup again.

A tiny triangle of folded paper fluttered from the bottom of the cup and landed on the floor. He almost dropped the cup in his surprise.

On reflex, he looked at the door. Both slots were closed.

He picked up the paper. It felt moist—a bit of spilled tea had glued it to the bottom of the cup. He unfolded it with trembling fingers, careful not to rip it.

Block letters. Pencil. In English. Blurred a bit by the moisture, but legible.

You're kicking the Japs out of the Solomons.
I think the tide has turned.

Questions barraged Dave's sluggish brain.
What?
Who?
And finally, *Is it true?*

Unless the contents of his wallet counted, he hadn't seen an English word in writing since he bailed out of *Payback*. And now here were lines on a snippet of damp paper. Someone reaching out to him.

It took a moment for an image to come to mind. Chiseled features, a gaunt frame. The Asian prisoner who'd interpreted the warden's speech the day they'd arrived at Kiangwan.

Without a doubt, that was the fellow he'd seen through the slot. Who was he and why would he take this kind of risk for a *gaijin?*

The young man had seemed sympathetic—like he didn't buy into the insults he was echoing in his solid but accented English.

Dave read the note again. His hands shook when he threw it into his *benjo.*

The tide has turned. We might get home. His whole being longed to believe it.

Brief messages kept arriving with Dave's meals. Each flashed a strobe of hope into his dismal cell.

Japanese paper reports big battle off Guadalcanal. I think they lost.

And then—

Don't be afraid. You'll go home soon.

Since their new friend always delivered their meals right under a guard's nose, the airmen didnt learn much about him. They code-named him Tom.

Apart from Tom's messages—which meant more to Dave than he could have put in words—weeks went by with little change. It got colder. They all got sicker.

Dave developed a dry cough that wouldn't stop. If he sat too long, he couldn't feel his feet. Frost formed on his windowsill. He chipped tiny icicles from the snarls of his beard when he woke each morning.

It happened with as little explanation as anything else. One day after exercise the guards didn't return them to their cells. Instead, they herded them into a single nine-by-twelve room. Their personal effects had been taken from their cells and piled in one corner of the new quarters, along with a pile of fifteen blankets—three blankets each.

Nielsen looked around. "I guess this is our new home? It's gonna be close quarters."

Watt whistled. "This is their idea of how we're going to beat the cold? Body heat?"

Meder rummaged through their piled-up property. "So what? Sure beats solitary."

This was greeted with, "Yes, sir," "You bet," and a solid "Amen," from Watt.

"Darn straight." Dave felt giddy with relief. Being the ranking officer, he took the lead. "Okay, men. I see five stations around the perimeter. Two against the wall beside the *benjo* and three against the opposite wall."

Watt made a suggestion. "We could do rock-paper-scissors for initial position."

But Vitty sank to the floorboards, a pained expression on his face. He leaned against the wall with his arms around his knees and started a gentle side-to-side rocking.

Meder was quick to crouch beside him. "Vitty, what's wrong?"

"What day is it?"

"I don't know." Meder glanced up at Dave. Dave shrugged.

Vitty stopped rocking and stared at them, whites showing around his irises. "What day is it?" Louder this time.

"Hey, that's what you usually tell us." Meder chuckled a little. Then he went solemn. "Oh. I see."

Dave stared at the two of them, mystified. "See what?"

"Vitty's been keeping that calendar on his wall. On *his* wall. In his old cell. It's gone now."

Nielsen looked at Vitty, brow furrowed. "You don't remember what day it was on your calendar?"

Vitty banged his shoulders against the wall, then bit his lip and gave his head a slow shake. He looked up at Watt. His eyes glistened.

Watt sat on Vitty's other side. "Hey, don't worry, pal. We'll figure it out."

"We will." Meder patted Vitty's shoulder.

Watt scratched his chin beneath his unkempt beard. "Tom passed me a birthday note—December 3. Who knows how he knew, God love him. It wasn't yesterday. Was it the day before?"

Nielsen shook his head in wonder. "The risks that man takes. Unbelievable."

"They'll beat the snot out of him if they catch him. That's

for sure," Watt said. "Wonder if he had anything to do with our getting moved back together."

"Maybe he did." Dave had added Tom to his mental Hall of Heroes.

Meder watched Vitty for a long moment. He stood, leaned against the wall, and looked around at the others. "Do you guys feel like we're all getting a little erratic? The strain of the way we're living—nothing to do, hour after hour, day after day. I think it's getting to us. Lack of focus. Losing track of things. Irritability."

Nielsen grinned. "So you're saying it's not just that Watt's a mean cuss."

Watt growled.

Meder cracked a tight smile. "Well, that's a given." All serious again. "But don't you feel like you're losing your grip a little? Look, Delham, how many presidents can you name?"

"Roosevelt, Hoover, Coolidge...Roosevelt again...Washington, Lincoln, Jefferson...Adams..." He paused, no more names coming. "I haven't thought about it in years."

"Okay, fair enough. Watt, recite the Declaration of Independence for me."

"Fourscore and seven years ago our forefathers...No, our fathers set..."

Bob shook his head. "It starts with *When in the course of human events.*"

"Oh. Dang!"

Nielsen jumped in. "Something about *certain unalienable rights—*"

Watt rattled off the next phrase. "Yes. *Life, liberty and the pursuit of happiness.*"

"Vitty?" Bob's voice was gentle. "You remember any of it?"

Vitty thought for a moment. He shook his head.

"See?" Bob looked around. "That's important stuff. It's what we fought for."

Dave had to agree—he'd felt this too. He glanced at the men. All nodding. All looking to Meder. Dave might be the one with the rank, but Meder was the real leader.

He went stiff. "What do you propose, Lieutenant?"

Bob gave him a crisp nod. "I think we need a mental workout program. Everyone should pick some mental exercise and work on it every day. Consistent and deliberate."

Watt leaned forward. "Like what?"

"I don't know. Something you care about. Design and build something—the more complex the better. Write a poem and recite it. I've started an essay on a problem I heard about in philosophy class that has always intrigued me. I'm writing the essay—and by that, I mean typing it out word for word—on a typewriter in my mind."

"I see." Dave gave a slow nod.

He looked around at the men. Their eyes gleamed cautious enthusiasm above gaunt cheeks and sagging jowls. He stared at Nielsen, and the man's expression summoned a memory—a baby monkey he and Jenny had seen years before at the Lincoln Park Zoo. Bright eyes shining out of a solemn little face, it had studied him for a long moment before swinging up on its mother's back, trusting her to lift it to safety.

The monkeys faded into another image—one he'd seen only in his thoughts. Meder grunting and gasping in the night-black surf, spending his last ounce of strength to tug a waterlogged corpse from the China Sea.

Yes, Dave had the rank, but it was Meder who had what it took to pull the men through this. Rapport. Meder had earned it. What Bob Meder had to offer now—Dave needed it as much as anyone.

Tough to give away what you didn't have.

He took a deep breath, then chimed in to support Meder's proposal. "How about a model airplane? When I was a kid, Uncle Verle and I used to build them. That Camel we put together was a real beaut. Is that the kind of thing you're after?"

"I built one of those." Vitty actually smiled a little. "Painted it fire-engine red."

Meder gave Vitty a nod. "Could you reconstruct her in your mind, strut by strut?"

"Sure."

"That's the ticket." Bob beamed at Vitty. "Any other takers?"

Chapter Twenty-Five

Friday, December 31, 1948
Osaka, Japan

FRIDAY EVENING AT SEVEN-FORTY, MIYAKO finally walked out to the freedom of the street. Damp and dismal as the evening was, she still wanted to skip across the sidewalk and fling her arms around the nearest lamppost.

After descending down an endless flight of cement stairs, Miyako stood on the Midosuji Line platform, Yamada-san at her elbow. The old courtesan ventured a sidelong glance at her. A dry chuckle formed in her belly and gathered strength until it burbled out.

"That was something unexpected this morning. You with all your signals." Yamada-san laughed in earnest. "Oh, I know you didn't mastermind that three-of-a-kind, so don't even pretend."

Miyako opened her mouth to protest, but the glower Yamada-san shot her stopped her.

"Still..." The lady took a handkerchief from her handbag and dabbed at the corner of one eye. "The expression on her face. That one look." She started to laugh again. "That one look made it all worthwhile."

Miyako let herself relax. "*Hai*, it certainly did. No-chan was undone."

"And me eight hundred yen the richer for it." Yamada-san settled deeper into her seat and sighed out her satisfaction. "You said I'd win if we partnered. You didn't say how." She shook her head and mumbled. "Three of a kind. Still can't believe that." She dabbed at her eyes once more and stuffed the handkerchief in her purse.

Miyako gave her a thin smile. And tried to figure out how she was going to leave her behind.

The train rattled up. Miyako followed Yamada-san into the car.

Yamada-san leaned toward her. "So, Midori-chan, we might as well get clear before we set out. Imai-san agreed to let you leave the Oasis on one condition. If you take off, I'm beholden for your debt. Please believe me when I say I'm not going to let that happen. So you might as well tell me what you're doing."

Miyako stammered out something. "I thought I mentioned my appointment with my sick widowed aunt."

Yamada-san huffed. "You can't think I believe you're visiting your sick aunt. Any more than I believe you helped me with *kabu* today. Especially since you told me at the hospital that your papa-san is your only living relative."

Miyako winced. She'd done her best to forget everything that happened that day.

Yamada-san grabbed her arm and squeezed. "You see how I've put myself on the line for you. I expect you'll make it worth my effort. If you're cutting business on the side, I expect a piece."

Miyako stared at Yamada-san, surprise stealing the breath from her lungs.

Some of this just got a bit easier.

"So. We'll see two men tonight," Miyako said.

Miyako debated whether it was better to see George-san or Kamura-san first. Her lover won. It was too early to go to the restaurant—that's what she told herself. But in truth, she had to know about George-san.

As promised, Yamada-san stuck to her side like a barnacle. They made their way along Dotonbori toward the Hollywood Club. Miyako could hear the ruckus there from a long block away. The piano hammered out a syncopated tune while a saxophone riffed around the melody. Applause and catcalls spilled out into the damp night air along with strident bursts of laughter.

The noisy good times within the club made the sidewalk outside feel even more damp and miserable. She huddled into her coat. Now that the prospect of seeing George-san was real, her nerves all but crippled her.

The band rolled into a familiar Glenn Miller number. Male voices joined in, slurred and off pitch. She recognized "In the Mood."

Aren't they always?

The music mounted to a screeching crescendo then abruptly stopped. The door swung open, momentarily blocking the light that glimmered through the glass-block strip beside it. A brown-haired airman stumbled out. He had a Japanese girl by the hand. They were no more than three paces clear of the door when he swiveled her against the wall and kissed her hungrily. She gave a startled yelp, but it faded to an embarrassed giggle, and she draped her arms around his shoulders.

A second airman followed them. His face caught the light. Hair the color of sand, strong jaw punctuated with a cleft chin, blunt nose. She knew that profile—George-san. Her heart did a stutter step, its usual trick when she first saw him. But then her stomach clenched. So much had happened since she'd seen him. Since the night he'd asked her to be his *onri wan*. She was no longer the exquisite merchandise he'd been ready to pay a premium for. She was damaged goods—the kind you sold for half price at the rear of the store. And once he knew, once he understood how she'd been shamed—

She took a deep breath. "That's him."

Yamada-san nodded and faded to an unobtrusive distance.

I knew she'd have to give me a bit more freedom here. Miyako had every intention of taking advantage of it.

George-san said something to the airman with the sweetheart. They all crossed the street toward her. Miyako froze for an instant, a sick feeling congealing in the pit of her belly. Strong as the temptation was to shrink into the crowd, she made herself step into his path. "George-san."

He glanced at her, then stopped and stared. "Midori? Is that you? Good Lord. What happened to you?"

19 April 1943, Kiangwan, China
365 Days Captive

The bitter winter melted into a soggy spring. Dave had completed the fourth model plane in his imaginary collection. Nielsen was busy nailing tiles to the roof of his manor house.

Vitty had abandoned model airplanes for poetry. His recitations were getting pretty decent—at least in English. The ones in Italian were harder to judge, but they appeared to involve plenty of emotion.

Watt was digging the seventy-fifth posthole around the perimeter of his model ranch when the Japanese decided to transfer them again. It took about an hour's flight and another ride in the back of a military truck to reach the new place.

Their new home-sweet-home was different and possibly a little better. It still had the look of a military barracks, with neat rows of identical low-slung buildings and a weedy prison yard, all surrounded by a towering wall with barbed wire at the top. But the buildings were constructed on a more human scale. And there appeared to be an orchard on the far side of the wall. Treetops stirred in the spring breeze above the cement blocks.

Dave glanced at Watt, who gave him an angled eyebrow and a slight nod.

"*Hayaku, horyo.*" A guard shoved him from behind.

They filed into one of the cellblock buildings. The spacing of the heavy cell doors confirmed his worst fears.

They were going back in solitary. And no Tom, no notes. Only long days full of desolate silence.

There was a breed of guard Watt called the "happy Jap." On their fourth morning in Nanking, their most memorable experience with this sub-species began. The guards funneled the airmen through the cellblock door and out into the yard. A pair of them stopped the prisoners at the base of the steps and had them line up. Several others stood around.

They seemed animated. Expectation—of *something*—floated in the spring drizzle.

A round-faced guard with a solid build stepped forward. "Sportsman," he proclaimed, with an index finger on his nose and a broad grin on his lips. "You know Nippon *sumo*?"

They didn't, and the precise rules remained a mystery, but they got clear on the basics fast enough.

The Sportsman tapped Meder's shoulder, led him into

the middle of the yard, and crouched. Meder shrugged and squared off with the man. The Sportsman pushed out his chest, then lunged. Even in his weakened state, big Bob held his own with the grappling. But the Sportsman got tired of that game. He surprised Bob with a series of strikes and kicks that toppled him.

After that, the Sportsman would challenge one of them to a *sumo* match every few days.

On a humid May morning, Nielsen wound up on the losing end of a hard-fought battle. He lay on the ground, grimacing. The Sportsman did a gleeful victory lap around the yard. His fellow guards cheered and applauded. Cries of "*Nippon Bansai*" echoed off the cement-block walls.

While the guards were busy celebrating, Dave and Meder helped Nielsen up.

Dave kept an arm under Nielsen's shoulder, not sure the man could stand. "You okay?"

Nielsen gave him an almost-undiscernible wink. "I'll live," he whispered. "I'm testing something. Did you get actual meat chunks in your broth two nights ago?"

"I did," Dave said. "Small, but recognizable."

Meder's voice registered his surprise. "Same here."

Nielsen brushed grass off his pants. "I have a theory it'll happen every time one of us loses. Watch for it tonight."

Several endless hours droned by in Dave's hot-box of a cell. Dinner showed up at last. He gave his soup a thorough examination. Sure enough, four small chunks of something that looked like chicken floated in the broth.

He chuckled to himself. So it was true.

11 December 1943, Nanking, China
601 Days Captive

The five prisoners sweated their way through a simmering summer—even worse than the one they'd spent in Shanghai. Or perhaps Dave's fever just made it seem that way. The chief upside was that the facility was so new the vermin hadn't found it yet, and he didn't have to share his cell with rats and fleas. The lice, unfortunately, had hitched a ride with him.

The cell was furnished. He'd been there about ten days when a pair of guards showed up with a simple desk and a wooden chair. They nailed both pieces to the floor, so he could only sit facing the blank wall. All the same, to have a place to sit and a surface to put his food on felt like unimaginable luxury.

He still had to sleep on the floor.

The seasons cycled on through a simmering summer and a crisp fall.

Winter arrived. Temperatures plummeted to the point where he had to break crusted ice off the mop bucket they gave him twice a week to clean his floor.

He paused to rest in the middle of that chore one day when a guard's voice sounded in the corridor. "Good morning, Meder-san. How are you?"

It was the guard with the Coke-bottle glasses. The one they'd nicknamed Cyclops. He'd learned a little English somewhere, and he'd been coming by once or twice a day to practice it on Meder.

No response from Meder's cell.

Cyclops rapped on Meder's door. Shuffling noises and a low moan filtered through the wall that divided Dave's cell from Meder's. But no words.

Dave stood stock still, holding his breath. Meder had to be all right. He had to.

"Meder-san?" A beat passed, then Meder's door creaked as the guard pulled it open.

Bob moaned again, but after a few seconds he answered in a rasping voice Dave could barely hear. "Good morning. I'm fine, thank you."

Dave let the breath he'd been holding whoosh out. Still, Bob didn't sound fine, no matter what he told Cyclops.

Another guard came to collect them for exercise. The cellblock doors opened to the prison yard, now a rectangle of grimy trampled slush. Dave blinked like a mole at the gray light that reflected off a thin layer of snow. He clapped his arms across his chest in an effort to warm up.

Nielsen came up behind him. He spoke from the corner of his mouth as he strode past. "Hey, Delham. Your pants are flopping around."

He grimaced. "I could use a new tailor." His pants sagged on his emaciated body like the hide on an elephant's knee. "I think you froze your butt off." Nielsen cackled and broke into a run—or at least a rapid hobble.

Dave launched out after Nielsen as best he could. They rounded the turn before the cellblock, Nielsen a little ahead of him. Meder sat on the cement steps. Back sagging, eyes hollow, his feet and ankles swollen like a Neanderthal's.

Nielsen slowed. Looked around to see what the guards were up to. Sank onto the step in front of Meder, real casual. Pulled off his sandals and made a show of bending over to rub packed snow from between his toes. As Dave approached them, he heard Nielsen talking in a low voice. "C'mon, Bob. For God's sake, walk a lap or two."

Meder focused with effort. "Nah, not today. Might ruin these stylish shoes." He made a sporting attempt at a laugh but stopped to grimace and clutch his gut. He suddenly looked serious. "Chase, remember what you promised me on *Hornet.*"

Nielsen shook his head. "Don't talk like that."

"You'll do it, right? You'll go see them if I—"

"Stop talking like that. Of course I will."

The conversation drew the head guard's attention—a brutal specimen named Aota. "*Damare!*" Aota gave the men a menacing grimace.

"Just pray for me, okay?" Meder said.

Dave's insides went hollow. Meder had never asked for prayer before. In fact, he couldn't remember a pessimistic word ever leaving Bob's mouth.

Aota strode their direction, grasping his baton. A twelve-inch blade swung in a scabbard at his side.

Nielsen bent over and put an arm under Meder's shoulder, helping him stand. From the far side of the yard, Cyclops also started toward them, his features creased with concern.

Dave plastered on his nonchalant look, walked on. But he took a quick glance at Meder as he passed. *Look at him. So weak his legs won't carry him. Feet so swollen they overflow his sandals.*

Beriberi on top of the dysentery. They all had both to

some degree. When Dave pressed on his shins he could feel how his bones were going soft. But Meder had the worst case of them all.

Dave stopped walking. *We are not going to lose Meder. So many good men, dead. We are not going to lose one more.*

Meder needed a doctor. A doctor he would have, if Dave had anything to do with it. He turned toward the cellblock steps. Aota headed for them in full rant. Dave called out to him, "Aota-san. *Sumimasen.* Meder needs a doctor." Doctor...doctor...what was the word? "*Isha. Kudasai. Isha* for Meder-san."

Aota glowered at him. "*Damare, horyo.*"

Cyclops rushed up, saluted Aota, and started to stammer out some sort of explanation. Aota became more and more agitated, issuing a stream of commands in Japanese. Nielsen ignored him, still bent over Meder.

Cyclops turned to Dave. He gestured him toward the cellblock stairs. Dave yelled at Aota as he mounted the steps. "*Aota-san. Isha. Kudasai. Isha* for *Meder-san...*" For? How did that go again? *No tame no.* "*Meder-san no tame no isha. Kudasai.*"

Cyclops gave him a push that might have been a little gentler than usual, in through the crude pine doorframe.

Dave stared over his shoulder. Nielsen had managed to get Meder standing and climbing the stairs. Aota had positioned himself on the top step. He gestured at Meder, his face flushed with rage.

Cyclops guided Dave into his cell. "Solly, Delham-san. Aota-san's orders."

"Try to put in a word for Meder-san, okay?"

Cyclops sucked his breath in past his teeth and nodded. The door thudded closed.

Chapter Twenty-Six

Friday, December 31, 1948
Osaka, Japan

GEORGE-SAN STEPPED ONTO THE CURB beside Miyako. "Midori, I didn't expect to see you here. In fact"—his face clouded—"I didn't expect to see you at all."

George-san's friend and his girl strolled up, her face flushed from the kissing. George-san glanced at them. "Why don't you two head over to the Pearl Cafe? I'll be along in a few." He wrapped a hand around Miyako's arm. "What the heck happened to you yesterday?"

"I am so sorry, George-san! I, ah, had trouble with the police."

"The police?" He studied her through narrowed eyes. "Why?" He shifted her so the light hit her face. "Is that a shiner? Where on earth did you get that?"

She brought her fingertips to her hairline to hide the bruise. "I stopped at the Abeno to see a friend. You know Kimi, yes?"

"Sure." His stare told her *go on.*

"They arrest me."

"Arrested you? For what?"

"For nothing! I wasn't doing anything—I promise."

"They arrested you just for being there. And that's why you stood me up."

The disbelief that rang in his voice made her cringe. "That's what they do to *pan-pan*, George-san."

"Really?"

"*Hai.*"

Perhaps the harsh glint in his eyes softened a bit. "Okay. Let's assume I believe you. Then what?"

"They, ah, took me to the office. Made me stay for V.D. tests." At least, that's what should have happened.

"They held you in jail? For tests? That's why you went AWOL on me?"

"I'm so sorry, George-san." It was jail, in a manner of speaking.

He snorted like a caged bull. "Where I come from, you get a free phone call."

"Not here, George-san. Please forgive me. Kimi say you looked for me. But I couldn't come. They had me."

"And the cops did this to you." He jutted his jaw. "Not our MPs, I hope. Your guys?"

She nodded.

He stared at her in silence for a couple of seconds, pain creasing his features. Then, slowly: "What did they do to you, exactly?"

"They…" The horror of the past week came rushing back. The pain. The humiliation of that hour in the back room. The way they left her. She shrank inside her coat. How could she form words to explain it to George-san? He'd hate her if he knew the full truth—how completely they'd shamed her. But not as much as she hated herself.

"They hit me to get me into the truck."

He studied her, a sinew at the side of his neck working. "That's it?"

Shame choked her. She stared at the pattern of light reflecting from a dirt-streaked puddle.

"There's more you're not telling me." His voice sounded gentler now. "Look at me, Midori."

She did.

"Did they—" He put his fingers under her chin and turned her face up. "Midori, did they, you know…"

If he knows the truth he'll want nothing to do with me. The soft patter of the rain, the smell of stale beer and wet pavement filled the silence.

"They did, didn't they? Someone raped you. And you've been holed up recovering ever since."

She dropped her eyes again and gave him the slightest nod.

He pulled his hand from her chin and shoved his fists in his pockets. "Why didn't you tell me?"

"I thought you…" Tears blurred the pavement at his feet.

"You thought I'd what?" The fierceness in his tone hammered her ears. "Blame you?"

She looked up and found him staring at her, a vicious glint in his eyes. "If you thought I'd blame you, you thought wrong. But if you thought I'd rip them to pieces and spread out the shreds for the seagulls, you thought right."

So he wanted to protect her? It was a little late for that.

"These are important people." She shook her head. "You're so nice, George-san, but this too big fight for you."

"You're telling me someone hurt my sweetheart, and the fight's too big for me?" His fists came out of his pocket and hung poised, loose but ready, at his hips.

"George-san—"

"You know who they are, right? You could point them out in a lineup?"

"*Hai*, but—"

"If you can find these guys, that's all we need. I'll talk to Captain Peterson and we bring them in. We'll make sure they get some good old Yankee justice."

"They'll believe me, George-san? A *pan-pan*?"

"Well, look at you. Obviously something happened to you."

"They can say it was anyone. They can say it was"—she looked straight in his eyes—"you."

"What?" He stared at her and stiffened. "I would never do that."

"*Hai*. But how you prove it, ah?" She gave him a pleading look. "No. George-san. No. Please hear. You don't know what they do." The questioning. The detailed reenactments, living through that hour again and again. The scrutiny—maybe very public scrutiny. Which she couldn't afford. Not that week, with Delham coming. "And how it ends, George-san? I'm shamed enough to die. And they do nothing to those men."

She's a whore. Who'll believe her?

Who'll care?

Her rapists were right.

He folded her in his arms, his expression melting. "You're sure?"

She relaxed against his chest as a lovely warmth flooded her. "*Hai*." As sure as she'd ever been of anything.

"Absolutely sure? One hundred percent?"

"*Hai*. Most men not like you, George-san."

"Okay." He cradled her head against him. "Okay. Have it

your way for now. But you ever show me the guy who did this to you, and I swear—I *swear* to you—I'll rearrange his orifices."

She nuzzled into him, breathing in the smell of damp leather. Was it possible Kimi was right? That he still wanted her? In spite of her marred face. In spite of everything.

He ran his hand along the curve of her back. "I thought I'd go crazy when you didn't turn up last night, babe. I didn't even know where to look for you."

A raindrop burst across her cheekbone. He gave her a relieved grin as he wiped it away. He took her elbow and guided her along the block into a doorway's shelter.

She leaned against him and toyed with his collar. Drank in the clean, manly scent of his shaving soap, his leather jacket, and the beer on his breath. She riveted her eyes on his. "George-san, you still want to look at rooms? Or—"

"Yes. I still want that, baby. In fact, let's put all this behind us. You know that mountain inn you always talk about?"

She stared at him, dumbfounded. "The *ryokan. Hai.*" It was a dream she'd had for years. The *Ryokan* Montei with its beautiful natural hot springs. Private caverns where couples could take the waters together. Papa-san took her mother there that last summer before he shipped out. Mama-san came back glowing. And Miyako had imagined it ever since.

He flashed his easy grin. "I think it's time to plan a little celebration. You and me, some good whiskey, a deck of cards, and that hot spring place you told me about."

"Really, George-san?"

"Why not?"

The warmth she'd been feeling ebbed. A knot at the base of her stomach took its place. There was the Delham thing.

"I'm on leave on Sunday." His grin broadened.

"Sunday?" Delham's presentation. "I can't leave Osaka Sunday. So sorry, George-san." She groped for an excuse that would flatter his ego. "And I want to look pretty for you. I think I need more time."

"I don't care about that, sweetie."

She beamed her brightest smile at him. "When you on leave next time? We go then, ah?"

"Next Thursday it is, baby." He checked his watch, then glanced in the direction Bill and his girl had gone. "But I have to go now."

What? "You go to the Pearl?"

"Yes, I have to meet them."

Miyako stared at him. *Merciful gods. Why?*

"There you go with that look." He shifted on his feet. "I'll tell you the truth. I asked Bill to set me up with someone." He shot her a sidelong look. "You disappeared, you know. With my cash, by the way."

"Ah! I have your money, George-san. It's at home."

"That's a relief." He pulled her closer. "I'd rather be with you, babe. Honest. But I'll never live it down if I don't show this girl a decent time this once. It is New Year's Eve."

A bitter smile wanted to play at her lips, but she smothered it. She had to admit she'd given him some justification.

She allowed a vision of her rival to form in her mind. Wide eyes. Smooth skin. A plunging neckline and pronounced cleavage. A straight line of white teeth with the slightest Lauren Bacall gap in front. Dwelling on that image made it a bit easier to do what she she had to do next.

"I understand, George-san. I take care of everything." She used her softest, throatiest voice. "But the inn, the train, our new apartment. I buy good tickets, so we have the best. It all takes a little, ah, tea money." Could she make it enough tea money to buy the poison?

Kamura-san would cover that, surely. This was insurance.

She went on tiptoes to graze his neck with her lips, breathed into his ear. "I want it to be special. For you."

He rolled his eyes, but then he smiled a little. "How much is that gonna run me?"

"Ten thousand." She held her breath.

"Ten thousand?" He took a step back and stared at her. "Ten thousand yen. You know that's more than a week's pay?" He whistled. "I have missed you, but that is a chunk of change."

She moved to him and coiled his tie in her fingers. "It worth it, I promise."

He looked out at the street a little too long. Was he deciding how he would raise the cash? Or whether he *should* raise the cash? He had to agree to it tonight. She couldn't count on seeing him again before Sunday.

He broke into a smile. "You know, you deserve a nice break, after all this. I'll try. I have some gambling debts I might be able to call in." He grazed her forehead with his lips.

Relief welled up. "I need the money to buy the tickets, George-san. Please. Maybe you have it Sunday?"

"I'll do my best."

"Meet me here? Three o'clock?"

"Okay." He gave her a hungry kiss. "Look, I'll catch up with you then. With the cash for that trip, if I can."

She cringed inside. Surely—*surely*—Kamura-san would come up with the money so she wouldn't need George-san's.

But at that moment, he had to do her one more favor. He had to help her get away. She went up on tiptoes and sought his lips. Lingered there a long moment. Shuddered with practiced ecstasy when his mouth found hers.

"Whoa, babe." He cleared his throat. "I—I missed you too."

"Oh, George-san," she said, in her best breathy tone. "I can't wait for Thursday. The *ryokan* will be so fun. But..." She glanced around and lowered her voice. "Tonight, I need you to do this one thing for me."

"What?"

She looked up at him with her softest smile. "Please take me into the club. I need to leave through the back."

"Why, babe?"

She felt his arms, strong and protective. Saw the concern written on his face.

I could tell him.

For an instant, she teetered on the verge of giving him the truth. Imai-san and the brothel and the mountain of debt that was keeping her there. Not to mention the threat of the *yakuza.*

No. He'd insist on going to the police. Which might work where he was from, but not here. And police scrutiny was something she didn't need.

"I'm okay, George-san. And you need to find that"—she

pinned him with a disapproving glare—"other girl."

He rolled his eyes. "Yeah. She was a mistake, but one I have to live with, at least for one evening. But seriously, babe, if you're in some kind of trouble—"

She laid her fingers across his lips. "I'm okay, George-san."

She could handle old Yamada-san.

11 December 1943, Nanking, China
601 Days Captive

Dave sank to the floor with his ear to the door. Feet shuffled by. Meder's door slammed shut, followed by another cell door farther along the hall.

Nielsen and Meder were quiet as death in their cells. Thinking about the state Bob was in, and that they might lose him—it made Dave itch to break a Jap face or two. And he knew exactly which ones, but they were out of reach.

Someday.

Prayer? That's what Meder had asked for. Sure, Dave would pray. He'd pray every one of these brutes got the journey to Hades they so richly deserved. But first, he was going to get Meder some medical attention.

Three guards—from the sound of them—patrolled the corridor. He stood in front of his cell door and yelled as loud as he could, "Hey! *Isha* for Meder-san."

No response.

He drummed on the door, then hurled himself against it, yelling, "*Isha! Meder-san no tame no isha. Kudasai.*"

Boots pounded along the corridor, converging from both directions. He had their attention.

Someone—perhaps Cyclops—tried to hush him from outside his cell door.

Nielsen, in the cell on Meder's other side, took it up as a chant. "*Isha. Isha. Isha.*" Watt's baritone, now thinner than in their old days at Eglin Field, joined in too.

Dave joined the men's chant. "*Isha. Isha.*" He backed into the corner farthest from the door and knelt. His cell door swung outward and three of them rushed in, each brandishing a weapon. Aota came first with his long knife held high, still in its scabbard. The second guy, a fellow they'd nicknamed Dim, waved his club. Cyclops followed a half step behind. His palm rested on his club as well.

"*Damare, horyo*," Aota thundered.

Dave put his hands in the air and repeated the Japanese word for *please*. "*Kudasai, kudasai.*"

They surrounded him, staring. Aota unsheathed his blade. Dim growled something and poised his club behind his shoulder like a slugger at bat.

They had no power over him. He was past caring what they did to him. "*Kudasai.*" He gestured in the direction of Bob's cell. "*Isha. Meder-san no tame no isha. Isha.*" That moisture around his eyes was back. He bowed to the floor. "*Kudasai.*"

"*Sumimasen,* Aota-san." Cyclops begged Aota's indulgence, then spoke a couple more sentences in an obsequious tone.

Aota's feet shifted, and Dave looked up. The man was glaring at him, but he'd lowered his weapon. After a long moment, he gave Dave a grave nod. He cocked his head at Dim, who shot a savage kick into Dave's solar plexus.

They left him doubled up and groaning. A minute later, a sharp cry pierced the wall from Nielsen's cell. Then a brief scuffle and a yelp from Watt's.

Watt. Watt had developed a ferocious case of dysentery in Kiangwan. The devils had the decency to send some kind of medic then—the sole time the airmen had seen one. He had called on Watt daily and looked genuinely concerned. Watt told them later he gave him injections.

Watt came around. Why not Meder? Out in the yard, Bob had asked for prayer. Dave figured at least he should try, for whatever weight his prayers might have with the Almighty. He pushed himself to his knees, folded his hands and bowed his head.

Dear Lord, Bob's a good man and a true believer in you. And I don't know what we'd do without him. Please bring him through this alive. He kept at this prayer through the afternoon, putting all the feeling in his heart behind it.

Daylight was fading when Dave heard a pair of Japanese

in Bob's cell. Dragging sounds, then a low-voiced discussion. He thought Bob mumbled a few words.

Surely they'd brought the camp doctor. Surely he'd see how sick Bob was.

Bob, you're going to make it now.

Chapter Twenty-Seven

12 December 1943, Nanking, China
602 Days Captive

THE NEXT MORNING, CYCLOPS DELIVERED WHAT passed for breakfast. When the eye-slit opened, Dave strode to the door. "How is Bob?" he whispered.

Cyclops took a furtive glance around before he whispered back. "Don't know. Medic still here."

"He spent the night?" That was a definite first. It had to mean Meder's condition was desperate.

Cyclops' eyebrows bunched with concern behind his thick glasses. "*Hai.* He good medic. But I think he worried." He gave Dave a grim nod and moved on.

Dave slouched at his desk and stared at the featureless wall. He tried to keep his thoughts focused on Meder, but inevitably, his mind drifted into a state of delirium that had become increasingly real to him. The room faded.

Mom. Clear as day. She paraded before him, beaming, with a heaping platter of fragrant turkey. Her hair carefully coifed, a new lavender dress—it was Thanksgiving, and he was home.

Home. Dad at the head of the dining-room table. Afternoon sunlight streamed through the bay window, making lace and china gleam.

Eileen followed Mom with steaming stuffing and green-bean casserole. The works.

He saw himself lifting the fork. He knew it wasn't real, but it felt real. And it sure beat any reality he had.

A sharp thud shredded his reverie.

Sweetheart. Mom. Come back. And he was forced to confront his dismal cell.

The ladies, the turkey, gone.

Another thud. *What the—what* is *that dang noise?* How was a fellow supposed to think?

The racket went on with annoying persistence. He'd heard something like it before—long ago, in a different lifetime. His clouded brain worked to dredge it up.

He finally placed the noise. Hammering. They were building something.

The hammering went on for a while. Reverberating through the building, shattering his thoughts. What in blazes were the ghouls up to?

They sure weren't crafting furniture for his cell.

He paced the room. The floor swayed like *Hornet* on the open ocean, but he had too much nervous energy to sit still.

A scaffold? Nah. The Japs wouldn't hang a man. Not enough blood.

A row of big stakes for a firing-squad execution?

Maybe.

A brooding sky produced gusts of soggy snow that drizzled streaks down Dave's grimy window. The close weather made him feel even more socked in than usual. He spent the morning pacing like a caged lion until his legs wouldn't hold him up, then sinking onto his chair to agonize.

It was well after lunch before a guard swung his cell door open. It was Cyclops—and one glance at his face sent black bands of dread coiling around Dave's heart.

Cyclops inclined his head in something that was almost a bow. "Derham-san. Prease come outside."

Dave took halting steps along the corridor and out the cellblock doors.

A large pine box rested on the frost-hardened earth in the center of the yard.

No.

He took a slow step toward it. Another.

No. No, no, no.

He covered the last few feet at a run, stared into the box.

Meder—or all that was left of him. Irretrievably dead.

Dave dropped to his knees, eyes fixed on what lay in the coffin. The broad shoulders that towed a fellow airman across miles of tossing sea. The eager intellect that challenged them in prison. The unrelenting heart that spurred them on.

Nothing left of any of that but a cold corpse. Not even twenty-seven years old, and his life gone like a mist.

All his faith? All his philosophy? Dead along with him.

The pine box Meder lay in was the biggest piece of kindness the Japanese guards ever showed him.

What kind of miserable human beings were these people? How could a man stuff another man in a cage and stand back and watch him starve? A decent man wouldn't treat an animal that way.

Dave's breath came faster. *Braxton, Smith, Hallmark, Meder. I suppose they think they can keep on killing us, one by one. And no one knows we're here, so no one is the wiser.*

He slammed both fists into the sodden earth. He pushed to his feet, turned to face the guards behind him, and yelled outright. "No! You sick bunch of murderers. Meder was—"

That was all he got out before they swarmed him.

Chapter Twenty-Eight

Friday, December 31, 1948
Osaka, Japan

MIYAKO KEPT UP A VIVACIOUS STREAM of talk as George-san walked her into the club. The mountain resort and its charms. The natural hot springs. The private caverns. Housekeeping details she made up as she went, but that were sure to be expensive.

She glanced over her shoulder a few times. She expected Yamada-san would follow at a discrete distance, but she didn't see her. The key would be to slip through the club and out the rear door before the older, stouter woman could.

She giggled up at George-san, doing her best to act like it was a game, and led him as fast as she could through the jostling shoulders in the bar area.

Yamada-san didn't appear. She must have gotten held up by the traffic light before she could cross the street.

There was a rear door at the end of the narrow hall that led past the bathrooms. A line of women clustered there, waiting. She pressed through them, George-san following.

He held the door open for her. "Don't say I don't take you to the nicest places."

They passed into the alley. She stepped over a broken beer bottle. "They're all nice, with you." Still no sign of Yamada-san. She tried to exhale away her tension.

He took her arm. "Let me walk you to the station. It's on my way."

Anywhere would do, as long as it put distance between her and Yamada-san. "*Domo arigato*, George-san."

Four long city blocks stretched between them and Namba Station. Miyako had to scurry to keep up with George-san's strides, but she was happy to do it. This would put her Yamada-san problems behind her. She kept a sharp eye out, but Imai-san's lieutenant made no appearance.

They reached the station entrance. She got up on tiptoes for a final kiss. "You're so kind, George-san. I can't wait for our trip."

He gave her a parting squeeze. "Same here."

"Sunday at three. Don't forget."

He walked away and disappeared around a corner. It wasn't hard to let yearning paint her face.

An airman and his Japanese sweetheart strolled along the sidewalk, fingers interlaced. How easy it looked, to simply enjoy an evening with your lover. She sighed, and it struck her like a mallet on a gong. How much she wanted that kind of simple romance with George-san.

A dozen endearing memories crowded her mind. Running her hands through his thick, bristly hair. Swigging whiskey straight from his bottle in a succession of hotel rooms. The way the corners of his eyes crinkled when he laughed. The glow on his face when he showed her the pictures from home with his new baby niece.

A dull ache filled her chest, but she did her best to jar herself out of the mood. *One must live without regrets,* in Kamura-san's words. Feelings for a man were something a woman of the night could not afford.

At least she hadn't seen Yamada-san since they'd ducked through the club. George-san didn't know it, but he'd helped her win back her freedom.

It was more than time to connect with Kamura-san—perhaps he could help her keep that freedom. His restaurant was a few blocks away. An easy walk, just over the Ebisu Bridge. She started north.

Revelers thronged the streets, headed for Osaka's chief entertainment district. *Salaryman* with their hats and briefcases who'd gone straight from work to their drinking. Japanese couples out for an evening. American Marines and airmen on leave. A mother with a trio of children, munching on lime-green pastry balls on sticks.

She'd gone about a half block when a powerfully built Japanese man in a brown pea coat crossed the street fifty feet in front of her. He turned up the broad sidewalk in her direction. Maybe she imagined his eyes following her.

A moment later, she heard heavy footsteps closing behind her. She glanced over her shoulder. Another athletic-looking Japanese, this one in a leather jacket. The streetlight gleamed on his slicked-back hair.

Something about the two of them—their decisive gait and relaxed-but-ready bearing, perhaps—set off alarm bells in her head.

Imai-san's associates?

They couldn't have tracked her. But if they had, what could she do about it? Her mind darted like a bat after a mosquito. She didn't come up with much, except to hope there was protection in the crowd.

The man walking toward her passed her. He *was* watching her. No mistaking it. He converged with the man behind her—two pair of footsteps, a pace behind her. A slight head twist gave her a glimpse of the brown pea coat to her left. Leather-jacket-guy strode along at his elbow, behind her to the right.

Merciful gods. Panic spiraled up her spine and made the skin on her neck prickle.

A line had formed along the sidewalk a few feet ahead. A shop was selling *kushikatsu* through a window. She joined the queue. The two men fell in line behind her.

Hai. She had a problem.

She turned and faced them. "You're following me, ah?" she said, in a voice loud enough to carry.

Leather Jacket gave her a crooked grin, his mouth pulled taut by a scar that ran from his neck up onto one cheek. "No, young lady. Enjoying a little evening stroll. Happened to get hungry."

Pea Coat spoke up in a rasping voice. "Why would we follow a girl who just broke a legitimate contract of employment with a fine entertainment establishment?"

The man next to her edged away. The five or six others in line developed a sudden interest in the pavement.

Leather Jacket issued a barking laugh and reached for her arm.

"Legitimate?" She spat the word, packing it with all the scorn she felt. She twisted away and strode back the direction she'd come.

The Coats ambled after her. One of them started up a tuneless whistle.

She ducked her head and picked up her pace—not that it would help. She wasn't going to outrun these men. And strangers on the street weren't prepared to interfere, it seemed.

A beefy hand settled on her left shoulder. She shrieked and shook it off.

The sidewalk was too anonymous. She lunged through the nearest door. One of the Coats followed on her heels.

It was a small eatery. A heavy-set man with grizzled hair worked behind a counter fitted with a commercial grill at the rear. Half a dozen patrons wielded chopsticks around small tables.

She rushed up to the counter, panting. "*Onemai shigasu.* Help me!"

His eyes rested on her for an instant before they fixed on the men behind her. He sucked his breath in sharply past his teeth. He set his spatula on the counter next to the grill, a slight tremor to his hand, and bowed. "Yahiro-san. Welcome. I, ah, wasn't expecting you gentlemen tonight."

Leather Jacket came up behind her. In an instant, he had her clamped against him, his hand so tight on her face she had to work to breathe. "Ah, Negishi-san. We're here to claim a little"—he lifted her so her feet dangled—"lost property."

She squealed, squirmed, and kicked at him. He grunted when her heel found his knee and squeezed her harder against his barrel of a chest. He reeked of sweat and raw fish.

She pinned pleading eyes on Negishi-san. "Help me!" But the paw across her mouth made her words indistinguishable.

Sweat slicked Negishi-san's furrowed forehead. He stood by and watched her struggle, a pathetic look of helplessness on his face.

Pea Coat spoke in the same rasping voice behind them. "*Arigato*, Negishi-san. I'll let Morimoto-san know you assisted us in this matter. I'm sure he'll agree to a few more days' extra consideration on that loan."

She did her best to sink her teeth into the fleshy part of Yahiro's hand. Unperturbed, he lugged her around the counter and through the curtained doorway to the kitchen.

15 December 1943, Nanking, China
605 Days Captive

For Dave, day came to mean delirium. Hallucinations centered around family and friends and long tables loaded with fried chicken and biscuits and crisp summer salads and peach cobbler. And increasingly, night meant nightmares.

Back in Chen's forest. The twilight pulsed with the sound of crickets, bullfrogs. Spying birds trumpeted his every move. Eerie croaking noises he couldn't identify filled the woods in the gloom.

He couldn't see Chen, but he heard him just ahead, rifle jostling and canteen clanking.

A hoarse shout rose from somewhere to his right. A cry for help.

He knew the voice. Meder's.

"Chen. This way," he shouted. He ran toward Meder's voice, pushing through brambles, branches scraping his face.

There was still time after all.

His blood pounded a rapid drumbeat. He forced his way through a thicket and stumbled into a clearing. Meder stood in the middle of it, knees bent in a fighting stance, fists up. A dozen shadows circled him, snarling, glowing red eyes fixed on his torso.

Dave wrapped his fist around his Colt. Seven bullets. Not enough.

Shoot one. The rest will scatter.

The biggest of the shadow-beasts crouched, haunches quivering. On a straight line between him and Meder.

He tried to raise his pistol, but moving his arm was like pushing through a thick wall of rubber cement. It took all his strength to bring it up, cock it, train it on the beast.

His finger grazed the trigger.

What if I miss?

Too late. The monster lunged, all muscle, teeth, and claws. Meder pinned Dave with a last agonized stare as he went down.

Four of the remaining beasts swiveled their heads toward Dave.

Dave's nightmare disintegrated into another gray winter morning. He stared wide-eyed around his cell. Adrenaline ebbed and confused emotions churned. Relief flooded him for an instant before a black depression swallowed it.

Dark dream. Dismal cell. Didn't matter. Bob Meder was still dead.

A bitter wind blew at exercise time. More pacing around the yard in the unending quest to get warm. Flexing and blowing on chill-stiff fingers.

I bet we heat our POW barracks. Unlike the Japanese.

Nielsen was doing his rounds just ahead. Dave picked up his pace. When he was even with the man, he started in the usual stage whisper. "Nielsen—"

Nielsen didn't turn his head. "Shh. The Sportsman's staring."

Sure enough, the Jap's prize wrestler lounged near the cellblock stairs. His eyes bore an eager glint Dave had come to recognize. The Sportsman was ready for a fight.

"Suits me." Dave's pulse quickened. He relished the feel of it. "I'll stick his *sumo* up his—"

Nielsen dropped back.

The Sportsman pushed off the wall, swaggered up, and knocked Dave on the shoulder. "*Sumo!*"

"*Hai.*" Dave pictured putting a fist through that smug face and allowed himself a taut smile.

He followed the Sportsman into the center of the yard and assumed a fists-up fighting stance. The Sportsman crouched and started a slow circle. The other guards and prisoners gathered.

"Go, Dave. Deck 'im good." That was Watt.

"Give it to him, Delham," Nielsen said. "You can take him."

The guards chanted in unison. "*Nippon. Nippon.*"

The Sportsman was a half foot shorter than Dave, but solid. As for motivation, Dave was mad enough to lay on a good pounding. *In a fair fight, I'd have a sporting chance.*

Fair fight. That was a good one. This was anything but. Dave's vision blurred with fever. His fists wove in front of him.

It still held true that rations got better for a few days after the Sportsman won. Dave scanned his buddies' faces. His eyes rested for a moment on Vitty's. The man's eyes burned with the intensity of a starving lion above hollow, pasty-white cheeks. He was wasting away.

No two ways about it. Dave needed to end this round with his butt in the snow. But he wasn't going to let it look easy. If he could, he'd get off at least one good punch first. He took a deep breath, summoned all his focus, and got his feet moving.

"*Hai-ya!*" The guard lunged. Dave teetered out of the way. The Sportsman retreated.

"That's it!" Watt whooped. "Keep 'im guessing."

Back to the wary circling. The Sportsman feinted a lunge. Dave managed to dodge again, and the Jap spectators jabbered. He sucked at the air, the footwork wearing him down.

If I'm going to get a punch in, it'll have to be soon.

The Sportsman leapt at him, this time directing a foot toward his gut. One unsteady step and the kick passed to his right. He turned, planted his left mitt on the guard's shoulder, and cocked his right fist. He pictured Bob, laid out in that coffin and let his seething anger swell. He channeled the energy into his muscles and delivered a crashing right hook to the man's face. It connected with a satisfying crack.

The Sportsman grunted in pain, fell back, and grabbed at his jaw.

It felt good. Real good. But Dave swayed on his feet. It took him long seconds to regain his balance, muster the strength to follow up. The Sportsman was ready for the next punch and blocked it. Dave teetered. The guard bunched his bulk like a rhino readying his charge and came at Dave with a rapid-fire series of kicks.

Time to take one for the guys.

It was over in a moment. Dave on his back on the soggy ground. The Sportsman straddled him, arms high in victory. "*Nippon Bansai!*" He struck a pose, with his hobnailed boot pressing a waffle pattern into Dave's chest.

The guards took up the cheer, celebrating and clapping

each other on the shoulders. "*Bansai! Bansai!*"

There'd better be a lot of extra grub for this. He looked up, found Vitty's eyes. Vitty nodded slowly.

Dave's gut convulsed. *Not now, dysentery.* He forgot his pain, focused on one thing—willing his bowels not to release. A second passed, then two. Three. Maybe there was a God.

Oh, no.

Nothing he could do about it. He grimaced and rolled quickly onto his back. If he gave his pants a good coat of mud, maybe no one would see the stain, and he wouldn't have to put up with the guards jeering over that too.

And maybe, just maybe, they were all too busy congratulating the Sportsman to notice the stench.

Moments passed. He lay perfectly still, eyes closed. His face went hot. His thin cotton uniform went wet and cold.

"*Bansai! Nippon Bansai!*"

His gut churned harder. He opened his eyes.

That was when he saw it, about eight inches from his face. No more than a glint of steel beneath the snow, but at this range he could see it was a nail head.

From Meder's coffin.

A weapon? Maybe with the right opportunity. A thrust at someone's eye. He was burning to get at one of these guys.

What are they going to do? Kill me?

Starving. Filthy. Dysentery ripping holes in his gut from the inside. Lice chewing away at him from the outside. All dignity erased. A shell of the man he'd been.

Pure hatred kept him going. What did he have to lose?

The guards were busy congratulating the Sportsman. He moved his hand a couple inches and palmed the nail.

Chapter Twenty-Nine

Friday, December 31, 1948
Osaka, Japan

YAHIRO SHOVED MIYAKO THROUGH THE KITCHEN door and into the alley. He slammed her against the building's rear wall and used his bulk to pin her there, one hand over her mouth. She thrashed with all her strength, but she was vised between the thug and the wall—two immovable objects.

He growled in her ear, "Calm yourself, or I swear you'll be sorry." He spoke to the other man, who'd followed them out. "Ando, get my knife."

Looking over Yahiro's mitt, she could see Ando's hand work a large folding knife out of Yahiro's jacket pocket. Fear pushed shards of ice into her chest.

Yahiro took the knife, thumbed it open, and flashed it in front of her eyes. "No more fuss. Or you'll feel this."

She froze.

He pressed the flat of the blade against her cheek. "I could kill you. But it would be a lot more fun just to hurt you." He used the knife to move her hair out of the way and put his mouth against her ear. His breath came in heavy pants. She could feel his pulse pound behind his ribcage.

"I like the smell of you." He bit her earlobe. Hard. The sudden pain made her yelp.

"Shh. Or the blade bites too." She felt steel again, this time on the back of her neck at her hairline. He started up that tuneless whistle again.

Ando leaned against the wall beside them and looked her over. "I don't see what the fuss is about. They've got better-looking girls at the Oasis."

"Maybe Imai-san wants to make her an example." Yahiro followed this with a throaty laugh.

Despair welled up, a noose around Miyako's neck. They'd have a painful lesson for her at the brothel—that was certain. But merciful gods. Surely Imai-san would have more sense than to let this monster administer it.

It wasn't long before a dark-colored coupe pulled up at

the end of the alley. They wedged Miyako in the back seat between the two goons. Yamada-san sat next to the driver. She peered over her shoulder at Miyako.

"So, Midori-chan. I see you've met a few of our honored business partners." She smoothed her coat. "You might be interested to know that Yahiro-san has been following you since you tried to run off at the club."

Yahiro elbowed her. He made a point of displaying the knife, open on his lap, and gave her that twisted grin.

Yamada-san waited until their laughter died. "I assure you this girl's not going anywhere." She clamped her jaw shut with an air of finality.

27 December 1943, Nanking, China
617 Days Captive

The weeks crawled by. Dave thought about Bob Meder every waking hour. And those thoughts filled him with a blinding, choking rage. As time passed, the rage chilled to match the winter landscape. But it never went away.

He smuggled a fragment of concrete in from the yard and worked at Meder's nail. Honed it to an ever-finer point. He examined its three-inch shank, tested its point against his palm. Sharp enough to gouge flesh with ease.

Getting there. *For Bob.*

At exercise, Cyclops headed into the middle of the yard, carrying a sack of something. He bellowed an order. "*Horyo. Koi.*"

Dave and the others converged.

Cyclops beamed at them. "This good. You like this. I bought for you in Shanghai." He produced a pile of books from his sack.

Books? "For us?" Dave's voice rose with surprise. "We can have these?"

"*Hai.* Commander-san said *hai.*"

So Watt's letter had borne some fruit after all. Right after Meder's death, Watt badgered the guards into allowing him to write to the commandant. Along with better food and generally better conditions, it begged for reading material.

Something spiritual is what we need most, Watt wrote. *Could you find us a Bible?*

Watt collected all their signatures before the guards made him give back the pen—too bad, it might have worked as a weapon, which in Dave's view would have been the real value of the exercise. He signed but knew it wouldn't result in anything. These gargoyles couldn't care less.

But now, probably thanks to Cyclops, here were books. Five of them. And among them? A Bible. He stared at the silver-embossed black leather, shook his head, then stared again.

Vitty studied the titles. "Guess we each pick a book?"

"By rank, as always," Nielsen said. "Delham, what's your pleasure?"

He scanned the books. Some distraction through all those empty hours would be a great thing.

The Son of God. The Hand of God. The Unknown God. The Spirit of Catholicism. Spiritual reading, all of it. Like Watt had requested. But if it gave the men a little comfort, it was a good thing. At least it wasn't *Little Women.* In his fragile condition he might cry.

He passed on the Bible. No thanks. Something a little lighter to start with.

He picked out *The Spirit of Catholicism.* To honor Meder, and Eileen. "Watt, you're next."

Watt grabbed the Bible with an eager glint in his eyes.

Vitty and Nielsen made their choices.

Dave fleshed out the ground rules. "We'll rotate the books down the ranks. Two weeks enough?"

Watt shook his head.

"Three weeks then. Fresh reading material in three weeks."

Watt took the leather-bound Bible and perched on the cellblock steps. He cracked it open with the enthusiasm of a kid who'd found the key to his big sister's diary.

Vitty settled on the step beneath him, his own book forgotten for the moment. "Where's that one about the shadow of death?"

Watt thumbed through the pages. "That would be Psalm Twenty-Three. Here it is." He read quickly, in a muffled voice, for fear of the guards. "The Lord is my shepherd; I shall not want. He maketh me to lie down in green pastures; He leadeth me beside the still waters. He restoreth my soul."

*Leadeth...restoreth...*The church language took Dave back to Jenny's funeral. The cloying scent of lilies all but choking him. His mother mouthing the words along with the pastor, her red lipstick in stark contrast to her pallid face and black dress. Each syllable she whispered framed in the glossy ruby oval of her lips. His father stone-faced on the other side of her. Dave was eleven.

The Lord is my shepherd. That was the one Mother spouted most in those last tense months before Jenny died. When he came in from school with his little sister, Julie, Mom always abandoned whatever hymn she was hammering out on the piano—she played nothing else during Jenny's sick years—and rushed to the foyer. Hugged them both. Took their wrists and pulled them into the parlor.

"I went to see Jenny today." Red blotches marred her nose.

Dave swallowed hard. Missing Jenny was a constant dull ache. She was the one who'd put aside what she was doing to make time for him when no one else did. Even if it was "boys' stuff"—Tinker Toys and erector sets.

It had been weeks since he'd seen her. They wouldn't let kids inside the sanatorium. "How is she?"

Mom's lips tightened. "She'll be fine. God will heal her— I know He will. We simply have to believe with all our hearts and pray."

But they didn't pray hard enough. Or they didn't believe hard enough. Or Jenny's tuberculosis was too big for God.

Watt was still reading. "Yea, though I walk through the valley of the shadow of death, I will fear no evil; for thou art with me; Thy rod and thy staff, they comfort me."

Vitty's eyes softened with regret. "I should've paid more attention in Catechism."

Watt clapped Vitty on the shoulder. "We all should've paid more attention. Sweet old Mrs. Connelly. I reckon I was the death of her."

Dave kept his mouth shut. After Jenny's funeral, he never walked into a church again until his wedding day.

A guard called them in. Dave made his way through the dank passageway into his bare cell. He placed the brown volume in the middle of the empty desk.

The book wasn't large. He'd be likely to have the thing memorized by the time three weeks were over. It wasn't new, but it was in good condition. There was an inscription inside the cover.

To Samuel, with best wishes for a bright future. May you turn here in days both sunny and dark.
Love, Aunt Cecilia
May, 1931

He looked around his dim cell. It was hard to imagine any darker days than he was in the middle of.

He pictured the Bible and shook his head in amazement once more. *Where do you get an English Bible in China?*

It hit him in a flash. The only possible explanation for a little actual kindness from the commandant.

These guys know they're going to lose this war. Someone up the chain must have gotten nervous that there might be repercussions from Meder's death.

A broad grin spread across Dave's face. The guards were always feeding them fantastical accounts of Nippon's tremendous victories. It was a great day when Nielsen worked out that these "victories" were getting closer and closer to Japan.

He opened his book, flipped past the table of contents, and dove into the first chapter. He was confronted with a discussion of what distinguished Catholicism from other branches of Christianity. He struggled to focus his fevered brain on it. It felt like listening to one side of an argument—one he didn't care about. He pressed his thumb into his thigh and felt the bone give a little. Got up to use the *benjo* and noted how hard it was to get his legs to respond. How the room swam around him.

What he wanted to hear was how he was going to walk through the valley of the shadow of death and come out alive. But if Meder's God was up there, He wasn't giving out any answers.

Maybe Dave had stopped asking.

Chapter Thirty

Friday, December 31, 1948
Osaka, Japan

THE COUPE ROLLED UP TO THE alley behind the Oasis. Yahiro clamped a hand over Miyako's mouth and dragged her from the car. Her foot slammed against the running board and she gave an involuntary scream.

He shook her like a pair of dice, then pressed the flat of the blade into her back. "Open that mouth again and I'll carve my name in your flesh," he snarled.

The three men hemmed her in, herded her into the gilded cage that was the brothel.

Yamada-san opened the kitchen door. Haruko-chan looked up from a pile of dishes she was drying. Her lips parted, and her eyes went round as the August moon.

"Midori-san." She barely breathed it.

Yamada-san scowled at her. "Quit gawking and get Imai-san."

Haruko's mouth pulsed, but she bowed, wordless, and retreated from the room.

The driver plucked a cloth napkin from a pile. "Hold her while I gag her. Wouldn't want screaming to disturb Imai-san's business."

Yahiro grabbed her from behind while the driver implemented his suggestion.

Imai-san stormed into the kitchen, pale beneath her powder, lips pressed into a contrasting red line. Haruko followed in her wake, eyes enormous. Imai-san elbowed Yahiro out of the way. "I'll attend to this refuse." She focused her fierce gaze on Miyako. "You. I see the thanks I get for trusting you." She hauled her manicured hand back and slammed it across Miyako's cheekbone.

Stinging pain ignited the side of Miyako's face. She bit back a cry.

Haruko made a choking sound. Imai-san's eyes rested on the girl, and she jerked her chin toward the kitchen door.

Yamada-san's face softened a bit. She put her hands on

Haruko's shoulders and led her out the door. The girl took a final horrified look at Miyako as Yamada-san bundled her out of the room.

Yahiro leaned against a counter, inspecting the edge of his blade. He looked up at Miyako, something feral lurking behind his gaze.

The driver elbowed him, sneering. "This one's looking worse for wear, Ya-kun. Let's ask Imai-san for two of her good-looking girls."

Imai-san shot the men a dismissive glare. "We'll see to you." She looked at Miyako, and a tight smile formed on her lips. "As for this one, she can spend the night in the shed." She gestured Yahiro over. "If you would, please."

Yahiro rubbed his hands together, then heaved Miyako across his shoulders like a sack of rice. The brute followed Imai-san out onto the garden path.

Imai-san slid the shed door open. Miyako got a glimpse of the woman's face by the light of a paper lantern. No hint of mercy in those icy eyes.

Yahiro pushed a box aside with his foot. He slung Miyako on the rough plank floor and straddled her, pinning her wrists above her head with one hand. He flashed the knife out with the other. He looked up at Imai-san. "You want her punished, yes?"

Imai-san regarded them for a long moment. "*Hai,* but we'll handle it. Come inside. I think I've got something you'll like."

"Fine." He slipped the knife in his pocket and rested his hand across Miyako's neck. "Stay right here, little bird." He caressed her neck, then gave it an abrupt squeeze before he stood.

Miyako wheezed and fingered her throat.

Imai-san stared at Miyako with a stony expression. "You need to learn your place. You can cool off out here while you consider that—and what kind of lesson you'll get in the morning." She shoved the shed door closed and turned a key in the lock.

The odor of dust, fecund earth, and pine siding filled Miyako's nostrils. Pallid winter moonlight oozed through a dirt-streaked window mounted high on the end wall. It illuminated a cluttered space no larger than her tiny room.

She sat up and pulled her wool coat tighter around her. Listened to their footsteps crunch toward the main building, leaving her alone.

She worked at the knot on the gag as her eyes adjusted. She pushed a collection of gardening implements out of her way and settled on top of a burlap bag in a corner. It gave very little beneath her. Whatever it contained had the consistency of fine gravel.

It was going to be a long, comfortless night. And in the morning?

No, thank you. She wasn't staying around for that.

She heaved a deep breath and looked around. The door looked sturdier than she'd expect for a garden shed. And why the lock?

She shuddered as realization grew. The structure must have been reinforced for this purpose. How many other women had sat here, waiting for their punishment?

No, no, no. She got up and slammed her weight into the door. Took a frantic step back and tried it again.

That door wasn't budging. She rubbed her shoulder and scanned the space. From what Imai-san said, she had all night. Something would come to her.

Gravel ground outside in the garden. She froze. The footsteps had a solid ring—a man, not Yamada-san. And definitely not Imai-san.

He started up a tuneless whistle.

Yahiro.

"Che!" She gasped out a strangled little cry of surprise and took a desperate look around for something—anything—she could use to fend him off.

His feet pounded the gravel outside the shed door. "Little bird?" A mocking sing-song. "Are you still in your cage?"

The door rattled.

Moonlight glinted from a length of steel rod on a high shelf near the window. She took a deep breath and nursed a desperate hope that it belonged to something she could use as a weapon.

Yahiro whistled to himself outside the door. Metal grated on metal within the lock box. She listened in horror.

How long will it take him to pick it?

She climbed up on a barrel and grabbed the steel rod. She yanked at it, and was jubilant to discover it was attached to a pair of shears. She pulled them from beneath some other clutter and brandished them. They were the kind professional gardeners used on trees. Lethal looking, with eight-inch blades attached to three-foot handles.

The lock rattled again, louder. She backed into the corner farthest from the entrance, pulse drumming in her ears. She squeezed her fists around the handles, leveled the point at the door, and hoped with all her might those vicious blades wouldn't somehow get turned on her.

She stood, riveted in place, rehearsing the principles Suga-*sensei* had stressed in his wartime bamboo-spear drills for neighborhood women.

Adopt a strong stance.

The lock's mechanism clicked into place. The shed door slid open. Yahiro loomed at the opening, peering into the shadows. He spotted her and broke into a leering grin, eyes and teeth catching the dirty light. "Oh ho." He slipped his knife from its scabbard. "Little bird has a beak."

He stepped into the shed and closed the door behind him. Crouching, he edged toward her, eyes fixed on her weapon. Moonlight glinted off his blade. "You *are* going to sing for me tonight, little bird."

She took a half step away from the wall, breath whistling through her teeth. *Soft knees. Engage your thigh muscles. Use your whole body.*

She took a deep breath and lunged, jabbing the shears point first at his belly. He snapped them aside with a quick forearm block. Twisting his arm around the handle, he grasped the shears midway along the shaft and gave them a yank. She hung on for an instant, but it was tug-of-war and he won. She let go and slammed against the wall.

The fear that hunted her clutched at her again. It was the redheaded G.I. with his tickets. The taloned beast from her nightmare, snarling and snuffling. The police sergeant, squeezing her throat.

But this time it was Yahiro, sick passion fueling a hellish fire behind his eyes. With a bare knife in his right fist and the pruning shears—a weapon as fierce as a *samurai*'s pike—in his left.

Well, she was through being helpless prey. She was going to beat him off this time. Or he would have to kill her.

A sturdy-looking shovel lay along the wall beside her feet. She plucked it off the floor, clenched her fists around the handle, and stretched it like a staff in front of her chest.

He chuckled like a fiend and feinted with the knife. She side-stepped out of his way.

One chance at this. Has to count. Like in her dream.

He edged toward her, his knife threatening from one side. He jabbed the tip of the shears from the other. She stepped back into a crouch and eyed him.

A predatory grin split his face. "Sing, little bird." Excitement throbbed in his voice. He pricked the tip of the shears at her ribs again.

She cracked the shovel's handle down on his elbow, and he cried out. She sprang at him with adrenaline-born power and slammed the blade into his face.

He lurched back, his features a contorted snarl. "You'll pay for that."

Not if I can help it. She brought the shovel up behind her shoulders like a baseball bat and swung. He lifted an arm to block the blade, but the shovel had too much momentum. It struck the side of his head with a crack. He put a hand to his temple and glared at her.

Che! Here he comes. She heaved the shovel behind her shoulders again.

But then he stopped. His eyes went vacant. A fleck of saliva foamed at the corner of his pudgy lips.

She firmed her grip on the handle and lobbed the shovel across his head. He teetered, crumpled against a bag of fertilizer, and sagged onto the floor. The knife slipped between his fingers. He twitched once, then stopped moving.

Her heart ballooned with fierce pride. She'd won.

He looked almost harmless, slack-featured on the floor. She groped in the corner for the napkin they'd used to gag her. She found it in a clump behind the bag of gravel. His head was thicker than hers, but the napkin was just big enough to gag him.

She knelt beside him and looked down—into his eyes. He mouthed something.

She dropped the napkin and sprang to her feet. Forcing down her panic, she picked up the shovel and brandished it above her shoulder. They stared at each other.

If I kill him, the police will come looking for me. She couldn't afford that.

He let out a moan. She held the shovel at ready. *If he so much as twitches my direction, I'll club him to a pulp.*

His eyes rolled back and closed again, and his head lolled to the side. She didn't dare try the gag again. He was out for the moment, but every second was borrowed time. She pocketed his knife, grabbed the shears, and slid the door open.

15 January 1944, Nanking, China
636 Days Captive

Dave was at work honing the nail's tip. Footsteps and guttural voices sounded in the corridor outside his cell. He jammed it beneath his blankets and went to stand near the door.

I'll have my usual.

Right on cue, a guard slid the upper slot open, spied on him for a moment, then opened the lower slot and pushed a small tin tray through. No surprises, unfortunately. He picked up the tray and carried it to his desk. Found his place in the book again and brought the broth to his lips.

But the broth sloshed, slicking his fingers, and he lost his grip on the cup. Soup spilled over his prison uniform. The cup clattered onto the floorboards.

He swore. He wasn't going to get any more soup.

He picked up the cup. And saw crude letters etched across its base.

CONNIE G BATTLES
US MARINES

His hand shook so hard he almost dropped the cup

again. He set it on the tray in slow motion.

Ever since they'd left Tom behind at the Kiangwan camp, the Japs had them so isolated they could have been buried alive. That cup was a fissure in their crypt. There was—or had been?—at least one other American in the camp. If Battles was still here, Dave had a way to communicate with him. A way to get the word out that he and his fellow Raiders were alive. A way to make the Japanese accountable for what became of them.

He let loose a low whistle. How many minutes did he have before a guard came around? He slurped down his tea, then checked the bottom of the teacup. Blank.

He retrieved the nail and sat down with the teacup. His fingers shook, and his pulse drummed in his ears, but working fast, he managed to scratch all their names in tiny letters on the bottom.

WATT DELHAM
VITIOLLO NIELSEN
DOOLITTLE RAID 4/18/42

He put the cup on the tray and took several deep breaths. Willed his pulse to slow.

How likely was it an American would see his inscription before some Jap did?

The more he thought about his odds the less he liked them. But this was worth any risk he had to take.

Over the course of the next couple days, Dave found opportunities to whisper the good news to the men. He encouraged them to check their dishes for messages.

They'd come up with a means of communicating when the guards were out of earshot. Morse code, through the walls. Knock for dot, scratch for dash—Meder's invention, of course. A day or so later, Nielsen knock-scratched some news.

C-U-P...B-A-C-K, Nielsen signaled.

M-A-R-I-N-E-S...G-O-T...M-E-S-S-A-G-E

So Nielsen had a cup with an etched response. And *Marines,* plural. More than one. This kept getting better.

Dave stood and took his best crack at a jitterbug.

The Tincup News Service had commenced irregular operations.

27 January 1944, Nanking, China
648 Days Captive

The cups made their rounds. In due course, the airmen learned some things. Battles was still there, along with six other Americans.

They got some war news, too. US HAS GILBERT ISLES, one teacup headline crowed. RUSSIANS ON GERMAN BORDER came etched beneath another cup.

Dave's heart beat out an unsteady rhythm in his chest. *I might make it through this. If they hurry. Lord, please bring me home from this war.*

One morning, his prison sandal slipped off in the frost-slickened yard. He looked down to shove his foot into it. A tangled pile of twigs beaded with clumps of frost lay on the hard ground beside his foot. They must have blown from the plum trees on the free side of the wall, victims of the storm the night before.

He stooped slowly to pick one up. A dozen buds spread along its five-inch length, their lively pink jumping out against the glaring white frost.

Watt walked up and gave a quiet whistle. "Dangest thing, those trees," he murmured. "The way they bud right through the frost. Almost gives you a little hope."

"You think Tom's right? You think the tide's turned?"

A guard started toward them. Watt cocked an eyebrow and moved on. Dave held onto the twig until the guards called them in.

His legs barely carried him up the cellblock stairs and to his cell. He fell into his chair and stared at his window sill, where Bob's nail lay—out of sight, and out of reach unless he stood on his desk.

I might make it through this. I might make it home.
If they hurry.

Chapter Thirty-One

Friday, December 31, 1948
Osaka, Japan

MIYAKO STEPPED OUT OF THE SHED and closed the door behind her. But that would hardly keep Yahiro contained when he revived.

She looked around. Bamboo and ornamental juniper. Not much cover. Twin rows of windows along the brothel's two buildings faced into the garden.

She needed to get out of sight. Fast. And then get outside that wall.

She dropped into a crouch with her back against the shed. *Stay low and move slow.* A flash of movement could draw eyes. She kept in a deep crouch and inched her way toward the yew trees around the shed's corner, hauling along the shears. She wasn't going to leave that weapon for someone else to find.

She'd almost made it to the corner when she heard it—a cough followed by a gruff sound inside the shed.

Yahiro. She dove for the space beneath the yew trees.

The gardener had been methodical. There was a cleared area about two-and-a-half feet high beneath the bottom branches—no doubt the work of the shears she carried. She pressed into it. Needles stuck in her hair and pricked at her stockings.

Yahiro rumbled to life mere feet away, inside the pine wall beside her. Bellowing like a bear.

She froze, pulse hammering. The way he was shouting, he'd have the whole brothel out to investigate. Why, oh why, hadn't she clubbed him again?

A frantic look around only confirmed what she knew. The only way out was up those trees. And she was going to need both hands. She stuffed the shears into the darkest corner she could reach.

She pushed into the branches and grabbed at one. It folded under her weight.

Yahiro groaned and hollered, his words slurring. "Where are you? When I get hold of you—"

She groped up the tree for a thicker branch. Found one and put her knee on it. It buckled, but held. She boosted herself up. Damp needles dragged at her hair and slapped at her face.

The garden wall loomed beside her, an expanse of smooth plaster. She tugged herself onto a sturdy-looking branch a little higher. She was high enough to put a hand on top of the wall.

Commotion echoed from the main building. Voices rang and heavy footsteps sounded on the gravel. They'd heard him. They'd find her any moment, peel her from the tree, drag her down for more punishment. She had to get over that wall.

The next branch she tried snapped beneath her weight. She half fell onto a thicker branch and grabbed at a limb for balance. She pulled herself up, bringing her shoulders level with the top of the wall. But there were still three rows of wicked-looking barbed wire between her and the street.

She fumbled at the buckle of the fabric belt that cinched her waist, yanked it free and threaded it around the barbed wire. Tugging it as tight as she could, she gathered the wire into a tight bundle—tight enough to step over. She looped the belt into a half-knot to secure it.

A male voice, only a few feet away at the front of the shed. "You lost her? How'd you manage that, *baka*?"

Another one. "Guess that impudent whore got the best of you."

Yahiro growled some colorful curses. Coarse laughter followed.

"Where'd she go?"

"I don't know."

"We'll find her." The second man's voice was a snarl. "Get up. She can't have gone far."

"I'll rip her limbs off this time." Yahiro's voice sounded more distinct.

Sheer terror pushed her up the tree. The trunk thinned as she climbed, and the tree rocked and swayed. Somehow she got her thighs level with the top of the wall.

Footsteps sounded behind her. "I heard something. Over

there!" The undulating tree had given her away.

She flailed for balance, then managed to get her right foot on top of the wall. She tugged herself up by the belt and found a precarious perch for her left knee on the edge. Wrapping both fists around the belt, she eased her way up to a crouch, then a stand. She stepped over the wire and teetered on the wall's narrow top.

The tree beneath her rustled. She looked down to see Yahiro on the ground beneath her, his face a malevolent leer. Another goon stood behind him.

His fist closed on her ankle. "Got you now, little quail."

Miyako shrieked and stomped her heel down on his wrist. He yelped and let go.

The effort sent her further off balance. She clung to the belt with all her strength and slipped backwards, down the street side of the wall. Her legs scraped along the rough plaster and her chest smacked against it.

She dangled for an instant above the sidewalk. Let go of the belt and dropped to the ground.

Free. Now she had to keep it that way. She took a frantic scan around her.

A male voice sneered from within the brothel garden. "She outsmarted you, moron."

Yahiro answered. "Not for long. Give me a boost, *baka*. You come around through the front."

Yahiro's friend was headed for the Oasis' main door to her left. An alley yawned to her right. She sprinted toward it.

Heavy impact and an "Oof." Yahiro hit the pavement behind her.

She glanced back. She had a half-block lead on him—not enough. At least he didn't have the shears.

She drank air in huge gulps, pumped her arms, and pounded along the pavement as fast as panic could propel her. She plunged into the alley and dashed down it.

Footsteps thudded behind her—closing.

A streetlight illuminated a circle of pavement at the alley's far end. She focused every ounce of strength on reaching it.

She could hear him behind her, panting and growling curses.

A few more steps and she'd pop out of the alley. Just a few more—

A pair of American airmen bartered with a vendor on the opposite side of the street. If only she could get close enough to get their attention. She hoped they'd be the decent sort. Two more paces. Yahiro's fingers closed on her arm. She wrenched away, put on a final burst, and stumbled into the circle of light. She gathered her breath and screamed in English.

"Help! Help me!"

Yahiro grabbed at her shoulder. She shrugged him off. "Stop!" she screamed—again in English, for the Americans' benefit.

The redheaded one looked up. "Hey." He put down the trinket he'd been examining and started in her direction.

Yahiro grabbed at her again, cursing.

The second American joined his friend and they jogged over, sizing up the situation. "What's the matter, little lady?" the redhead said.

Yahiro cracked a grin, which made his scar writhe along his jaw. "My girlfriend. We had little fight." He pulled her to him. "Come on, sweetie. No more fighting." He tried to plant a kiss on her cheek.

She pushed at him. "Don't believe him. Lying *baka*." She aimed a slug at his jaw.

Yahiro caught her wrist and held it fast, a lethal fire behind his eyes.

The dark-haired American glared at him and squared his shoulders. "Hey, jerk. Do the lady a favor and take off."

Yahiro's eyes darted around, no doubt observing the dozen or more *gaijin* in plain view along the street. The second gangster came up behind him, a short distance back, still in the shadows.

She worked at twisting her wrist from Yahiro's grasp. "Let go of me. Now."

He squeezed it harder, giving her an oily smile. "Okay, baby. If that's how you want it. But don't worry." He bowed over her hand and grazed her wrist with his lips. He looked up into her face. "You'll hear from me later. I promise." He let her break away.

She wiped her wrist on her coat, then brushed two or three pine needles out of her hair.

Yahiro and his friend slipped into the alley. The redhead watched them go. He circled an arm around her waist. "You look like you've had one heck of a night. My name's Pat. What's yours?"

"Midori." She gave him a bright smile, hoping he wouldn't notice how filthy her coat was. He followed her fingers with his eyes as she unbuttoned it and slipped it off.

She thought she spotted the gangsters in the alley's shadows. She fawned on her new friend for their benefit.

Pat turned to his buddy. "I'd say Midori here needs a beer. What d'you say, Harry?"

Harry laughed, not entirely a pleasant sound. "I'd say several." He gave her a crocodile grin. "Midori. Now ain't that a pretty name?"

She took stock. Entertaining a pair of flyboys was the last thing she felt like doing at that moment, but in view of the alternative—

The longer I keep friendly with these two, the better.

A sharp twinge in her gut reminded her she hadn't had a bite for hours. And there weren't two *sen* in her pocket.

She dimpled up at the redhead.

26 February 1944, Nanking, China
678 Days Captive

Book exchange day. Next up for Dave was the Bible. He'd been doing warm-up rounds with the other Nanking Book Club selections for weeks. Time now to take on the heavyweight.

It was Cyclops who brought it to his door. He slipped the Bible through Dave's food slot, same as the other books. But being bigger and heavier, it slid to the floor and fell open. Like his mother's fell on the floor of their parlor the day after Jenny's funeral. Dad had ripped it from her hands and flung it.

Mom gave a sharp little cry.

"Enough of this idiocy." Dad stared at her, his expression

savage. "Time for you to give up these silly delusions. Your all-seeing, all-knowing, all-powerful God didn't help Jenny. He's not going to help you."

Dave had picked the Bible up off the parquet. Held it in his hands, the void from Jenny's death giving way to a different emotion—cold rage. He couldn't decide who he hated more.

Dad, for treating Mom like that.

Or God, for letting her—and Jenny—down.

Like that day in the parlor, he rescued the Bible from his cell floor. Slipped the smaller book he'd been reading out through the slot.

He thanked Cyclops and opened the Bible near the middle. Psalms. Where was the one Watt read in the yard, about the shadow of death?

It came to him with an ease that surprised him. Psalm Twenty-Three.

He flipped to the passage. *Yea, though I walk through the valley of the shadow of death, I will fear no evil; for thou art with me; Thy rod and thy staff, they comfort me.*

Thou art with me?

He'd never felt more alone. Unless spying eyes through a slot or a few whispered words in the prison yard counted as company.

Fear no evil?

He'd never felt more afraid. Death stared him down from every direction.

All right, God. Show me you're real.

Show me Dad was wrong.

Genesis 1:1. *In the beginning God created the heaven and the earth.*

Chapter Thirty-Two

Friday, December 31, 1948
Osaka, Japan

PAT AND HARRY PICKED OUT A place halfway along the block. "This joint looks all right." Pat shot a quizzical look at Harry, who shrugged, then at Miyako.

A pair of soldiers burst out the pinewood door, giving them a glimpse into the crowded room inside.

"It's perfect." She flashed Pat a smile and followed it with an anxious glance over her shoulder. As she feared, Yahiro and his cohort loitered a block or so behind them. A shudder ran up her back, and she edged a little closer to Pat.

"Mr. Slick there wasn't your boyfriend, was he?" Pat put his arm around her shoulders.

"No. He and his friends were trying to, ah, do bad things to me."

"Well, we can't have that, can we?"

Pat pulled the door open and ushered them into the nightclub. The room was packed with American servicemen with their broad smiles and ringing laughter. More than a dozen crowded the bar. Perhaps twenty more ringed tables grouped around a small dance floor. No chance Imai-san's thugs would follow her in here. The tension faded from her frame for the first time in hours.

A bevy of Japanese beauties buzzed around the men, colorful as hummingbirds after nectar. Dance hostesses flirted and flattered. Waitresses plied them with food and beverages—anything to separate the *gaijin* from their dollars. The jukebox delivered throaty female vocals.

Pat eyed a woman's swaying backside in a pale blue skirt before returning his attention to Harry and Miyako. "How does a guy get a beer in this place?"

Harry cocked his head at the bar. "Belly up, lightweight. It's whiskey for me." He put an arm around Miyako's waist and scooted her toward the bar. "You too, sweetheart."

"Please excuse me, Harry-san, but I'd like to powder my nose first."

Except I don't have any powder. That was in her handbag, which had been lost somewhere between the *kushikatsu* shop and the Oasis' shed. She made her way to the ladies' room, avoiding looking anyone in the face.

She was a disaster—dirt splotched her skirt's hem, mud spattered her shoes, a big rip was spreading up her stocking. She did her best to brush and spot-clean her outfit, but no comb, no powder, no lipstick—not much she could do about her face.

Amazing those men would even talk to her.

She smoothed her hair into place with her fingers, gave her reflection a hopeless sigh, then turned away to rejoin her flyboys.

On her way out of the powder room, she nearly ran into the young woman with the light-blue skirt. "Please excuse me." She bowed, and the woman bowed in return.

Her skin tone's close. Would she? "Pardon me," Miyako said. "My handbag was stolen earlier. I don't suppose you'd consider—I know it's a lot to ask—loaning me your compact?"

The young woman gasped. "Ah! How terrible. Of course." She pulled a compact out of her handbag, handed it to Miyako, and tittered a little. "You're very welcome. Kindly help yourself. You'd like my comb too, yes?"

Miyako found Pat and Harry right where she expected them, at the bar. A half-full glass of beer stood in front of Pat, an empty shot glass and two full ones in front of Harry.

Harry threw his second glass back, slapped it on the wooden counter, and wiped his mouth. "Trust me, darlin'. This is just what the doctor ordered. Now." He handed her the third glass. "Bottoms up."

The amber liquid scorched its way down her throat.

Harry waved at the bartender.

Pat studied her. "Did you have dinner?"

She gave him a wry smile. "No, I did not." Dinner had been the least of her worries.

Pat grabbed Harry's shoulder and spun him toward the dining area. "Give her a break, Harry. The lady's hungry. I could use something to eat myself. Let's have a seat."

They found their way to a table. A few minutes later, she was slurping steaming noodles flecked with whitefish pieces from a large celadon bowl, an American looming on either side.

"This stuff ain't bad." Pat speared a piece of fish. "A fellow could get used to it."

"Speak for yourself. Not a decent burger on the whole cursed island." Harry deposited a forkful of teriyaki into his mouth. "They might have a few tasty dishes, though." He turned to leer at Miyako and slid a glass of beer closer to her hand. "Right, honey?"

Her giggle sounded a little edgy in her own ears.

"New Year's Day." Pat leaned back in his chair. "Should be eating baked ham and listening to the bowl game."

Harry swigged his beer. "We'll catch it on the radio later. We only need to kill a few more hours." He looked over at her. "Next dance, toots?"

"Of course." She gave him a quick bow, then renewed her attack on her noodles until the jazzy rhythms of *Twelfth Street Rag* died out. The jukebox cranked out the piano intro to a more sedate piece.

Pat sighed. "This one always makes me think of Cindy. Wonder what she's up to." He lifted his glass to his lips, a distant look in his eyes.

"Sleeping, lunkhead." Harry planted a hand on Miyako's arm. "C'mon, doll."

A woman's rich alto floated across the compact dance floor. A ballad about lost love. Miyako looked at Pat. He peered into his glass as if he'd found the answer to some existential question there. The rakish angle of his cap spurred a wistful thought of George-san. *Merciful gods.* What would he think if he saw her now, flirting with these two?

A pang of regret speared her. If she'd told him the truth, she wouldn't be in this mess.

Harry maneuvered her around a breathless departing couple and onto the dance floor. He pulled her into a tight hold, his body flush against hers. He led her out in a slow foxtrot, swaying with the song's sinuous rhythm. The whiskey on his breath mixed with the odor of his sweat.

The jukebox continued its warble. His hand strayed down the curve of her back. He drew her in so close his belt buckle ground into her stomach. His lips brushed the top of her hair. "I've got an hour or two to spare. Whaddaya say, baby? Go somewhere?"

She went stiff. *Do I dare give him a flat no? Or do I need to string him along?*

A push from behind knocked her out of rhythm. Harry steadied her, but his attention was riveted over her shoulder.

"Well, look who we found." The voice boomed from behind her.

She swiveled to see the speaker. Another American in an airman's uniform. Fair skin. Short, dark hair. Small, close-set eyes. Big. And three of his bigger buddies flanked him.

The newcomer folded his arms across his chest. "Someone oughta clear this trash off the dance floor."

"Calm down, Bowman." Harry's voice was steady, but she could feel his muscles tense. "We ain't looking for trouble."

"Oh, I think you are, Perkins. I told you what would happen first time I ran across you off base. And see? Here you are." He glanced at Miyako. "You better tell your yellow gal goodnight. Things are probably going to get ugly. In fact"—he reached for her—"why don't I give her a special escort off the dance floor. Find her some place nice and safe."

Harry's arm locked tighter around her.

"Wait a minute." Bowman stopped and looked her over. "I recognize you. Aren't you Sanders' girl?" He peered into her face. "The one that went missing on him." He chortled. "Oh, this is rich. Wait till I tell Sanders where you turned up, and who had his hands all over your butt."

Pat shouldered his way through the crowd ringing the dance floor and took up a post beside Miyako and Harry. "Look, she's not part of this. Leave her be."

Bowman took another swagger-step toward them. "And if I don't?"

Harry jeered from behind her. "That's it. Show us all what a big man you are."

Pat stepped between her and Bowman, jaw set. "I said leave her out of it."

"Fine. My real business is with your friend here." Bowman stared at her over Pat's shoulder, eyes lit like a wolf's. "Be off, Jap girl."

Pat turned and gave her his elbow. "I'll see you to the door. Be right back, Harry."

She took his arm, her heart melting with gratitude. He maneuvered her toward the front entrance. *The gang.* Her pulse raced. "Wait. Please, Pat-san. There's another door, yes?"

Pat gave her a quizzical look but clearly wasn't going to spare it much thought. He turned and marched her through the throng, then along the narrow hallway that led past the bathrooms.

"You'll be all right from here, won't you?" He glanced over his shoulder toward the dance floor. "It's true, what Bowman said? You're Sanders' girl?"

"You know George-san? *Hai*, I'm his girl."

Pat's spine went straighter. "So who was that Jap guy on the street, again? Old flame?"

"What is 'old flame'?"

He folded his arms. "Old boyfriend."

"No. I told you, he's *yakuza*. Those guys were after me for money they think I owe. Please, Pat-san. You've helped me so much, but I have to ask for one more thing."

"What's that?"

"Talk to George-san. Tell him I didn't do anything. I wasn't going to leave with Harry. I needed to stay here with you two, to get away from those guys."

"Sure thing." He started to turn away.

She grasped at his sleeve. "Tell him I'll make it all up to him. When I see him."

A crash sounded from the bar area, followed by loud yells.

"Gotta go, babe." He wrested his arm from her and took off at a run.

She called after him. "Tell George-san. Please."

He was gone.

She huddled into a corner, sucked in air through her teeth, and let loose a racking sigh. What exactly would George-san hear, and who would he hear it from first?

If you'd let him, he'd have kept you out of this mess.
She couldn't help that now. *Live without regrets.* She had enough trouble facing her that moment. How long had she been there? Not long enough to outlast the *yakuza.*
Her pulse picked up pace. She told herself she was safe for the time being. *Calm yourself. Think.* The bathrooms were to her right. The kitchen to her left. The gangsters would watch all the doors.
A thud sounded from the bar area, followed by shattering glass. Confused cries and shrieks arose. A husky male voice yelled, "Call the cops!"
Cops. She froze, pulse pounding. Japanese NPA would be the first to come. She couldn't be there when they did.
No more time to think.
The men's room door swung open. A Marine swaggered out. She bowed. As she straightened, she spotted something over his shoulder. A crude pine ladder propped against the men's room wall.
Storage ladder. Where does it lead?
She checked to make sure the Marine wasn't watching her. The antics on the dance floor had his full attention. She pushed into the men's room. It was open to the rafters. The ladder gave access to the storage space above the kitchen.
She swarmed up that ladder like a sailor. She stepped across the top rung onto a haphazard pine floor. The space was lit only by the bare bulb above the mirror in the bathroom below. She had to pause a moment while her eyes adjusted to the dim light.
Perfect. Absolutely perfect. She sighed out her relief. The tension that had a python's death grip on her gut loosed its hold a little.
The dank space was crammed with supplies packed in every sort of box, sack, and barrel. A tall stack of crates loomed in the farthest, darkest corner. She picked her way to it, the ruckus downstairs masking the creaking from the uneven floor. Heaving and grunting, she pushed the boxes away from the corner until she'd opened a cubbyhole behind them. She toppled a sack of rice into place and, exhausted, dropped in a pile on top of it.
She lay motionless for a long moment, too weary to

think. But the reality of her predicament intruded soon enough.

It was Saturday morning by now. The *gaijin* bomber would be in Osaka the next day. And here she was. Hunted. Destitute. And no closer to her goal.

Hot tears welled behind her eyelids. She blinked furiously, then gave up the battle, balled her fists, and let them come.

Her last waking thought was a fervent hope that no one would need kitchen supplies until morning.

Miyako started awake. Every joint stiff. The storage room was dim, with gray daylight filtering up from below. Rain pattered on the roof above her head and dripped into a bucket near her elbow.

Morning. She had to get out before anyone showed up.

She sat for a breathless moment, listening. No noises in the building. Apart from the rain, she heard only muffled calls from the street outside and a cat yowling somewhere in the distance.

She eased her stiff legs into motion and made her way down the ladder. Slipped into the ladies' room and did what she could to clean up.

She edged into the deserted kitchen. It was a treasure trove. An array of knives glittered on the counter. The full range, from a delicate paring knife to an impressive meat cleaver. She cast an involuntary glance around before picking up the largest knife that would fit in her coat pocket.

The solid weight of the knife brought it home. All the planning, all the running and fighting—it would be over the next night. If she did her duty, all the spirits would rest at last from the weary years spent crying for justice. Akira-san, whom she idolized. Funny little Hiro-chan, whom she adored. Not to mention lovely, gentle Mama-san. She could give them rest. And Papa-san would know she'd avenged them, and he'd see his daughter's worth before he went in peace to his deathbed.

She wrapped the knife in a clean cotton napkin and slipped it into her pocket, next to the folding knife she'd taken from Yahiro. A persimmon and three packets of rice crackers went in the other pocket. She grabbed another persimmon, cracked the restaurant's rear door open, and took a careful look in both directions.

No motion. She inched through the door, still scanning. No sound except the drizzle. No one in sight, save a solitary peddler spreading a display of vegetables on a wet cloth. It seemed she'd actually gotten them off her track.

Of course, she'd thought that before.

She had a day and a half to raise ten thousand yen for Tsunada-san. She was going to need to eat more than persimmons, sleep somewhere, and—she looked at her rumpled, spotted coat—find a decent outfit. And all her cash was gone with her handbag.

Kamura-san. What time did the restaurant open?

Chapter Thirty-Three

IT WAS THE WORST PART OF the day in Dave's airless wooden box of a cell. Several empty hours stretched ahead before dinner, and his book was his only distraction.

The Book. The Bible. He'd skipped around, but now he had the ribbon positioned about three-quarters of the way through, at the end of the Gospel of Luke.

Father, forgive them; for they know not what they do.

He paused and absorbed the words. Ran his index finger under the line of letters.

He rubbed at his aching eyes. Stood and retrieved his pet project—Meder's nail. Tested its fine point against his palm as he considered Jesus' words.

Dave knew a few things about torture, all from the receiving end. Compassion for those on the giving end was nowhere on his list. Jesus' brand of forgivness was far beyond him. How'd Jesus do it—forgive those men?

Why'd He do it? The nail's point glinted in the cell's dim light. If an opportunity to use the thing ever cropped up, Dave knew he'd be ready. Did that make him a sinner?

No. It just made him a man in tune with the hard realities of this world. Jesus' words made for a pretty sentiment, but in real life a man couldn't live that way. Not as long as Hirohitos and Hitlers and Aotas stalked the earth.

He closed the book.

Emphatic jabber started up outside his walls. Scant seconds later, they were yammering at his door.

Speak of the devils. He barely got the nail stashed under the blankets in time.

Aota—who else?—burst in, brandishing a knife. "*Horyo. Koi.*" Before Dave could react, the guard grabbed him, swung him from his chair, and yanked him, stumbling, into the dim hall.

What the—

Seven or eight of them stood crammed into the corridor. Rough hands—the heavy-set guy they called Dim—shoved him up against the wall and held him there. Nielsen hit the wall, hard, next to him. The other airmen got the same treatment.

He winced. So they'd discovered the Tincup News Service.

Aota strode in front of them, wearing a ferocious scowl.

Dave bristled. "What's this about?"

Aota unsheathed his twelve-inch knife. He pointed the blade at Dave's face. "*Damare.*" He gestured at one of his henchmen, who pulled something from a box on the floor.

A tin cup.

"Let me get this straight," Watt said. "This is about a teacup?"

Aota flipped the knife to his left hand. He spun at Watt, hauled back, and socked him in the gut. Watt groaned and hunched over.

Aota stepped back with a self-satisfied little smirk.

You filthy—

Aota reached for the cup. "You dare write lie about Nippon on this thing. Who write this?"

Dave glared at him. "Write what?"

The brute turned the teacup over to display lettering on the bottom.

JAPS PUSHED TO MARIANAS

Dave squared his shoulders. "Never saw that." Which was true—that one hadn't gotten to them yet.

Aota bellowed. "This is lie." He threw the cup as hard as he could against the wall. It clanged onto the floor.

"If you say so," Dave distilled two years' worth of rancor into his voice. "We haven't seen a newspaper since we got here."

Aota strutted up to Dave. Put the point of his knife at his throat. "You lucky captain no see. We *all* in big trouble." He gave an order to the guard with the box, who extracted another cup. Aota took it with his spare hand, flipped it over, and held it in front of Dave's nose. "You so smart guy. What this thing?"

WATT DELHAM
VITIOLLO NIELSEN
DOOLITTLE RAID 4/18/42

Dave swallowed hard. There was no squirming out of this one. Clearly one of the four of them had done it, and there was no way he'd let one of his men take the fall for what he'd done. "Oh, that. That was me."

The tip of Aota's knife dragged horizontally across Dave's throat—the blade so sharp his nerves didn't register searing pain until Aota lifted the knife away.

Aota's upper lip curled. He shifted the blade with a quick move, positioning the tip over Dave's heart. "Your friend? He die because his heart stop. *Beri-beri.* And you, ah? How you heart?"

Firing on about three cylinders. Dave closed his eyes so he wouldn't have to look at Aota. But he couldn't help smelling him.

Aota gave the knife a little push that broke Dave's skin. A trickle of blood started down his chest, racing the blood from his throat. "No more writings. Or I stop heart for you now."

Dave raised his hands in the air. "Okay. You win."

Aota replied with a growl. He cocked his head at the other prisoners and issued some command in Japanese. The guards shoved the other men in their cells.

Aota pushed at the cup with his foot and glared at Dave. "What you do this with?"

His mental gears engaged. There might be an opportunity here. He produced a puzzled face. "What did I use to write it?"

"*Hai.*"

"Lay off with the knife and I'll give it to you." He groaned and clutched his gut. "But I need a minute. *Benjo.* The dysentery."

Aota snarled.

"*Onemai shimasu.*" Dave gave the man his best agonized expression. "I'm sick." Time slowed as he waited for Aota's response.

Aota considered for an instant, then barked at the men restraining Dave. They flung him through his cell door toward his *benjo*. He dropped his pants and crouched over the stinking hole in his floor. Glanced up at the door. The yellow vermin were laughing among themselves and— understandably—paying no attention to him.

Now or never. Two years in prison and this was it. The closest to an opportunity to get even with a guard he'd seen. The closest he was likely to get.

He'd stowed the nail in a hurry earlier, so it was close at hand. With his eyes glued on Aota, he reached for the pile of blankets, fished for the nail. He found it behind the cement fragment. He wrapped his fist around it. A voice—Eileen's, perhaps—whispered something in his ear. Something about keeping his head. Not doing anything stupid. But it was drowned out in an instant by a louder voice—Aota's, railing at him.

He squared his shoulders and stood. Pulled up his floppy prison pants and secured the drawstring. Dropped his right hand to his side and made the nail firm between his knuckles. He knew nothing but the solid feel of the nail. Heard nothing but the roar of his blood in his ears.

Two-and-a-half inches of honed carnage protruded from his fist.

Aota stood closest to Dave's cell door, that twelve-inch blade back in its sheath.

Perfect.

Something in the pit of Dave's stomach went hollow. Aota had no doubt practiced swordsmanship since he was a tot. Dave had never in his life gouged anything with a nail.

He took a deep breath, screwed his eyes shut, and summoned an image of Bob's face, relaxed and joking around aboard the *Hornet*. Then again, gray and swollen in that pine box.

Am I a man or not?

He summoned his strength. Even mouthed something like a prayer for power and speed.

Okay, Aota-san. Your time of reckoning has come, big fellah.

He hoisted himself onto his chair. Took another

unsteady step onto his desk. Paused to let his balance catch up with him.

He braced himself, then whooped out a war cry.

Aota looked over at him. The man's mouth gaped. He launched into the cell, knife drawn and poised over his shoulder. Dim and another goon rushed in behind him, batons at ready.

Aota yelled and thrust the blade. Adrenaline flooded Dave's system. Time stretched. The knife came at his belly in slow motion, glinting in the filtered light. He sidestepped it and struck at Aota's arm behind it. The bony edge of his forearm crashed into Aota's wrist.

The knife point missed his hip by an inch.

His blow jarred the knife loose. It slammed against the wall, dropped to the floor.

Triumph. Disarmed the brute. Dave teetered and crumpled onto the Jap. Drove the butt of his left hand at Aota's nose. The man fell, twisting like a snake. Dave threw a punch with his right that went wild, the nail gashing Aota's scalp. Dave landed on his back, the guard on top of him. His wrist smashed against the chair leg. The nail dropped to the floor, rolled away useless.

Dim and the other man closed around them, clubs raised.

Dave lunged for the nail. The third guard's hobnailed boot came down, hard, on his wrist.

Aota had Dave pinned. He sat up and straddled him, his face a broad snarl. Aota's knees pressed on Dave's thighs. The sole of the third guard's boot crushed his wrist. His heart did a crazy, lurching jig inside his chest.

Dave raged inside. *This can't end now. Not like this.* Impotent on the floor. He hadn't felt this defeated since the night Chen died. He'd been living with those regrets for years.

One last effort. He took a deep breath and drove a knee up into the Jap's backside. Twisted toward the knife. Aota reared back and slugged him on the side of the head. Dim delivered a savage kick to his ribs, then another. Aota settled on top of his legs again. The other two had his arms.

"You finally found fight, ah?" Aota tipped his chin toward the nail. "Too bad your weapon so small thing." His face twisted into a malevolent sneer. "I kill you, *horyo*. But not today."

Aota's next punch was the last thing Dave knew.

Thirst. A wide, blazing desert of thirst. Pain. Head thudding. Wrist throbbing. And Dave's chest—right side burning. Severe constriction when he breathed.

Something had a vise grip on his torso. With his arms bound tight against his side, he squirmed to make space for his lungs to work. Nothing gave.

Feral panic mounted. *Have to breathe.* Even if each breath turned his brutalized ribs into a smoldering firepot of pain.

Dull gray light stabbed through his eyelids. He opened his eyes to a slit and took stock. He was in his cell, crumpled on the floor. Wrapped tight as a mummy in sturdy white canvas—a straitjacket. That's why he couldn't breathe. Straitjacket too tight. The animal panic subsided. He just had to take shallow breaths.

What? Why?

Memory returned in a lightning strike. He groaned.

Failed. Defeated. Again.

Considering his situation made his gut go liquid. These fiends were inventive. The penalty for what he'd done would be severe. Well, that was that. Someone had to stand up to the school bully like a man—and pay the price.

Another breath. Another jolt of agony. He rolled onto his back. Tried to sit but couldn't. A moan escaped him.

The eye-slot slid open. The bolt on the door shot back. The door swung out into the corridor. Aota and Dim strolled in, stood over him, Aota with his trademark smirk. "Ah. You awake, *horyo*. Very good."

He swallowed, wordless.

They rolled him over onto his chest. Someone's full weight landed on his thighs. Something jerked at the back of his straitjacket.

He gasped at the sudden pain. One of the thugs was sitting on him, tightening the straps. He was certain his ribcage couldn't compress any farther, but somehow—eighth inch by eighth inch—it did. If his ribs weren't cracked from the beating they'd given him, they were now. It took everything he had not to let loose a shriek. He wheezed. Got a tiny swallow of air through the burning pain in his side. Wheezed again. Another tiny swallow. Each individual breath came with excruciating effort.

It was drowning without water. His head throbbed, brain cells crying for oxygen. He felt his eyes bug and his nostrils compress. He couldn't form a coherent thought, except about his need for air. He gasped and writhed in an agonized battle for life. Opened his mouth to scream but he had no breath. Nothing came out but a raspy squawk.

His desperate fight for air pitched him onto his side, then his back. The pair of demons in yellow flesh stood over him, watching. Aota wore the same sadistic little grin he'd worn after he slugged Watt. Dim—a study in clinical disinterest—pulled out a stopwatch and started it ticking.

Dave thrashed and strained, drifting from pain to numbness and on to detachment. His body no longer felt like his own. In fact, whatever it was that was *him* lifted away from his body—peeled up like a Band-Aid. He found himself observing the scene from a point near the ceiling, watching with vague interest as Dim and Aota loomed over a twisting figure on the floor.

His focus drifted around the room. His desk below him—the size of a kid's toy furniture. The Bible lay on it, a silver-embossed cross glinting on its cover.

The cross. Did it feel like this? Lifted above the action, watching them kill you?

Father, forgive them; for they know not what they do.

But this was different. That slant-eyed buzzard with his stopwatch. That twin set of smirks. Those two Japs knew exactly what they were doing.

The words repeated in his mind. Insistent. *They know not what they do.* Realization came. *They* included him—the agonized figure writhing down there. This was about *him.*

Forgiveness for what? But he already knew. Up in *Payback.* Roaring props. Avgas fumes. Watt's sweat-slicked face reflecting the instruments' green glow.

"Who made you Sky God?"

I made the best call I could.

Braxton. Smith. Chen. Chen's father. All dead because of his pig-headed "best call."

But I didn't mean to. I didn't know.

The strait-jacketed lump on the floor—his body—gave one more anemic jerk, then lay still. Very still. Was this it, then? Was this what it came down to?

His body was a container. He'd spent his entire life taking care of it, but now it didn't matter much. They'd broken it and his soul had seeped out. He was deathly afraid for his soul. Maybe he wasn't guilty of deliberate murder or torture like these guys. Maybe he'd mostly been a pain in the butt. Arrogant with his men. Self-centered with his wife—all those liquored-up fights. All the time thinking he was a pretty good guy.

He needed forgiveness.

Somewhere far beneath him, Dim conferred with Aota. They bent over the motionless body. Rolled it onto its belly. Worked at the back of the jacket. The pressure released. Air found the vacuum in his chest. He gasped, then gulped oxygen into lungs red-hot with pain.

They hauled him to his feet, peeled off the jacket. He slumped between them, drinking in air.

Not dead. I'm not dead.

Dim snickered and held out a handkerchief.

He still needed saving. From himself. He needed... *Jesus.*

Relief flooded the vacuum in his soul. As forcefully as air had rushed into his empty lungs. And then another sensation—something new. An overwhelming sense of being known through and through, yet unequivocally loved.

He basked in the feeling for a long moment.

He wanted to take the handkerchief and wipe the sweat and spit off his face. But he couldn't raise either arm. He turned and stared Aota in the face, looked past the owlish glasses and the slanted eyes and the malevolent grin. Into the soul that had only been taught that *might makes right.* He had to wait until he could form words before he said it.

"I forgive you."

"Ah?" Aota glared at him for a long moment. His brows drew together as he tried to understand.

Dave slumped against the wall. Slid onto the floor. "I forgive you."

Aota shrugged and curled his lip. He stalked from the cell. Dim trailed him, slamming the heavy door behind them.

Dave took another shuddering breath and looked around. Same nine-by-four cell. Same pile of ragged blankets. Same filthy, stinking *benjo*. Same racking pain in his guts. Same stuttering heart. Nothing had changed in his circumstances. But something hard to define had changed in him.

He was still in solitary, but he wasn't alone.

Chapter Thirty-Four

Saturday, January 1, 1949
Osaka, Japan

MIYAKO DIDN'T HAVE MONEY FOR THE subway. The walk to Kamura-san's restaurant took an hour. Skirting puddles and piles of rubble, she stayed away from main streets and kept a sharp eye out for *yakuza* predators.

A cross-street brought her past the entrance to the narrow alley that led to the old Hozen-ji temple. Rain dripped onto broken fragments of ancient, mossy flagstone. The warm, spicy fragrance of sweet red bean soup hung on the damp air.

She picked up her pace, her chest feeling tight. The smell of that soup always took her back to the morning she'd lost Hiro-chan. To the dappled light under the cherry tree. To that last moment of innocence before she heard the first bomber.

Delham's bomber.

She walked on. Her blistered feet took turns radiating pain after the long walk, but her tension lifted a little. She nourished the thought of breakfast and a few sips of green tea to warm her. Kamura-san would do that much for her—and, she hoped, a great deal more. Perhaps even a warm place to hide.

The entrance to the Usukitsu restaurant stood on a broad, fashionable street. She pictured the paneled dining room with its crisp tablecloths and sparkling china. She glanced at her own damp coat and battered shoes. She'd slept under that coat. Crawled through a garden in those shoes. Knocked a gangster cold in that outfit.

Maybe the kitchen entrance would be best.

She trudged around the row of buildings and turned into the alley behind them. She knocked on the kitchen door and called out a greeting. A boy cracked it open.

"We don't have anything for beggars now." He started to swing the door closed.

"Wait." She put her hand on the door. "Could I speak with Kamura-san, please?"

He looked blank, but he admitted her. "Grandfather, there's a woman here to see you."

She whisked off her grimy coat. The sound of chopping and the savory fragrance of toasted onions filled the air. She breathed in a mouth-watering whiff, then kicked off her soggy shoes and lined them up next to a few other pairs at the door. She wriggled her toes, soaking in the room's warmth.

Kamura-san sat at a small table at the far side of the kitchen, his back to the door. He set an abacus down on a ledger book and turned toward her.

His mouth gaped. "Matsuura-san. What are you doing here?"

She gave him a deep bow. "Please forgive me, Kamura-san. I, ah, I guess I'm a few days late."

He hurried over, shaking his head. "You can't be here."

"Why not?"

He grabbed a large umbrella from the coatrack and opened the door she'd walked in only a moment ago. Cold, damp air hit her face, seeming to shrivel her soul.

"I'm sorry, Matsuura-san. We'll talk outside, perhaps?" He took her elbow and steered her to her shoes. She slipped her blistered feet into them and put her coat on. He conducted her out the door into the rain, popping the umbrella open so it sheltered them both.

She looked up at him. "What is it, Kamura-san? What's wrong?"

Concern creased his face. "You look terrible. What— Never mind." He took a deep breath. "When you didn't come last week, I worried. After a few days, I thought I should investigate this thing. I had my son-in-law take me to your apartment. If I didn't find you, I thought I'd find your father, yes?

"But I found neither of you. Your landlady told me where I could locate Captain Matsuura. I went to the hospital. And he told me everything he'd learned about you." He pierced her with a look that made her heart plummet. "So now I know it all, child. How my esteemed friend's daughter has been sustaining herself these years. Lying to her father." He paused, his mouth taking on a wry twist. "And to me, ah?"

She winced. How many others had she lied to? *If only he knew what good company he's in.* "I humbly beg your pardon, Kamura-san."

"Captain Matsuura is disappointed. I can understand this. But I believe you're a woman of some worth, in spite of"—his eyes rested on a large stain on her shoulder— "appearances to the contrary. I see something more when I look at you."

She shook her head. "What, Kamura-san?"

"The poet said it best, perhaps. The plum is not the showiest of flowers, but when you see its red blossom against the winter snow, you won't soon forget it. Beauty that thrives in adversity is of inestimable value, Matsuura-san. Always remember that."

"Then the women of Nippon must be the loveliest in the world." She did her best to keep the irony out of her voice. "And as for me, I've got the radiance of the moon, ah?" She bowed to mask her impatience. "Kamura-san, are you able to help me?"

"You saw Tsunada-san?"

"*Hai.* And the good news is, he agreed to get the poison for me. But the price, Kamura-san..."

"How much?"

"Ten thousand yen. I negotiated him down from thirteen."

"Ten thousand." He shook his head. "I guess that's not a complete surprise." He watched her for a second, biting his lip. "So you're a *baishanfu*, yes? Can't you get an advance?"

"Of course. But not until I start work. And look at me, Kamura-san. Who's going to pay for me?"

He heaved a sigh. "I see. And this *gaijin* comes when?"

"Tomorrow night."

"That's what I thought." The next sigh seemed to well up from the depths of his lungs. He studied the ground for a moment, then shifted his gaze to her face. "The problem is my son-in-law. He heard your father's story too. Unfortunately, he thinks he needs to hear nothing more. If he learns I've helped you, things will get very tense around here."

If he learns. Kamura-san intended to help her secretly,

then. "*Hai.* I see it would be difficult for me to stay around. But please forgive me for asking, what about the money for Tsunada-san?"

He gave her an agonized look. "I don't have that kind of cash, Matsuura-san. Not that I can get hold of overnight. Ah, if only you'd come to me sooner."

He couldn't help her at all? Her mind hummed with disbelief. "Merciful gods. I tried, believe me. This is the soonest I could get here."

"Forgive me, Matsuura-san. Please forgive me. I pledged I would help you. If I could get to the money, believe me, I would. But as it stands, what can I do, ah?"

The pavement seemed to shrink, as if seen through the wrong end of a telescope. A whirring like wasps' wings rose in her ears. His voice went on, barely audible behind it. "I can spare a few yen from the till. A little won't be missed. But I'm afraid there's nothing more I can do before Monday."

A long moment passed before she could look at him. In spite of the hollow feeling in the pit of her stomach, she gave him another polite bow. "*Arigato,* Kamura-san. I'm grateful for anything you can do."

He pushed the umbrella at her and disappeared into the restaurant.

She paced the alley. Rain clattered on the tile roofs and trickled through the drainpipes beside her. She watched it plink onto the wet pavement, puddling in the network of cracks.

He returned and pressed a wad of bills into her hand. "This should take care of a few days' expenses. I wish I could do more." He gave her a quick hug, and then a very formal bow. "Destiny has dictated your field of battle. Acquit yourself with honor, Matsuura-san. If you should need anything in the future, I hope I can be of more help."

She thought she saw his eyes glisten as he slipped through the door, leaving her standing in the alley, as gutted as the rotting fish she smelled. She aimed a kick at a dented can.

What about the plum that blooms in rubbish? Is that one special, too?

The last time she'd been here, Kamura-san had advised

her to get two things—training and poison. A week had passed, and she had neither. How could she have let this happen?

Everything now rested on George-san. As much as she'd hoped it would not.

20 August 1945, Peking, China
1219 Days Captive

Things felt different at the prison. Kind of eerily different. And they had for several days.

The guards seldom came around. Exercise periods had stopped, and the books were gone. Dave's thoughts drifted in thick, morose clouds, like the smoke he'd seen billowing outside a few days earlier, black as an octopus's ink. With bits of burnt paper floating in it.

The Japs knew something they weren't talking about. He felt it in his gut. The war was winding down. That was why they'd stopped their rounds and why they were burning papers—reams of papers. They'd gotten orders to destroy evidence.

It was a good thing Dave had memorized portions of the Bible. Bits of it floated through his delirium and depression like that paper floated through the smoke—the only thing that anchored him.

Faith as a grain of mustard seed. It took effort, but he gathered all the energy he had left and mouthed the words to that verse. "If ye have faith as a grain of mustard seed...nothing shall be impossible unto you."

Nothing impossible? For Dave to make it home alive seemed impossible. Home, where bellies were full and chairs were soft and people actually cared about you. Humanly speaking, he'd never see it.

Faith as a grain of mustard seed. He didn't know much about seeds, but Jesus said a mustard seed was less than all seeds, so it had to be pretty small. Surely even Dave Delham could pull that much faith together. And he had a mountain that needed shifting.

Pray, then. The words impressed themselves on his

mind. A command issued by something that was almost, but not quite, a voice. He turned to face the door and sank to his knees. That was against the current set of rules, but if the guards beat him, they beat him. This was life and death. And come hell or high water, he wasn't getting up until this mountain moved.

The stifling August heat made him woozy. Still, he prayed.

The mat ground into his bony knees and shins. Chafed on his boils. Still, he prayed.

His hips and knees ached, and his thigh muscles throbbed. Still, he stayed on the floor, praying that he and his buddies would live to see freedom. All four of them.

Boots tromped in the corridor. Dave flinched, his mind flashing to the feel of those boots striking his kidneys. *Do I fear God? Or do I fear the guards?* He stayed on his knees.

The cell door creaked open. He cringed in spite of himself.

The guard didn't come in. Didn't brandish a club or a fist. Instead, he stood in the corridor and bowed. "*Kocchi ni kite, kudasai.*"

What in the world?

He heard another guard at Nielsen's door, repeating the same words. He pushed himself onto legs that wobbled like a young foal's and made his way out of his cell.

Watt joined the two of them in the corridor. Vitty came a moment later, draped over a Jap's shoulder. The guard had to prop him against a wall.

The prisoners looked at the Japs, then at each other, faces creased with suspicion. Dave noticed Watt's knees go soft and his hands ball into fists and realized his own had done the same.

The guards lined up and bowed to them in unison. Not a little bob, but a real, deep bow. The one in the middle addressed them in heavily accented English. "War is over. You go home."

Watt stared at the man, blank-faced. "Go home?"

"It's a trick," Vitty stage-whispered.

It could be. Dave wouldn't put it past these fellows to burst out laughing and turn on them. Pull out clubs and beat them back into their cells. Or worse. Get their guard down, then shoot them all.

He ran wary eyes along the line of guards. But their batons stayed in their belts, and they carried no other weapons. The guy who spoke a little English bowed again. "True. War over. You free now." He gestured with a flourish down the hall. "Bath?"

"Bath?" Dave turned to Nielsen. "Sure, but I had one two days ago. You?"

The guard nodded at them, wearing an ingratiating smile. "You take bath now. Please."

Nielsen fixed the guard with a stare for a second or two, like he could see straight into him. He gave Dave an ambivalent shrug and slipped an arm beneath Vitty's shoulder. Dave got the man's other side. They followed the guard into the washroom, Watt on their heels.

Bowing repeatedly, the guards brought razors and ran water in buckets. The English-speaking guard planted a bucket in front of Dave. He knelt and cupped his hands in the water. *Warm.* That tiny bit of offered dignity was the thing that made him start to believe. He looked up at the others.

"Guys. They gave us *warm* water."

Watt's face broke into a slow grin. "So maybe we're not *horyo* anymore?"

Nielsen shook his head. "It can't be that easy."

The guard bobbed another bow, like that would convince them. "War over. Americans come for you."

Nielsen shot Dave a look. "Just like that? Do we believe him?"

Dave splashed delicious warm water over his face. It trickled into his matted beard. "Things have been different. For days. Haven't you felt it?"

Watt turned to the guard. "Who are you, anyway? What happened to the regular guys?"

The guard gave a quick nod. "Some men go home."

Dave paused his splashing. "See? The Japs are going home."

Watt's jaw dropped. "So we're next? We won?"

And then they were all yelling and hollering.

Nielsen thrust a fist into the air. "No more rice balls!"

Watt's face lit with joy. "No more kill-all order."

"No more dang clubs!" Tears streaked Vitty's dirt-stained face.

"No more stinking lice." Dave felt tears on his own cheeks and realized he was crying too. "Home. We're going home. Thank you, Jesus!"

My mountain moved.

Faces seemed to dance in front of him. Mom. Julie. Dad. Even Jenny and Uncle Verle. And Eileen. Especially Eileen, walking toward him with that radiant smile. Her presence was so real he almost reached for her.

"I can't believe it," Nielsen said. "We made it. Gentlemen, we outlasted this war."

"Thank the dear Lord." Watt's cheeks gleamed with tears. "Annie, honey, I'm coming home."

Vitty threw his arms around Watt, broke down and flat-out bawled.

Nielsen's eyes widened, his voice full of wonder. "Home. Back to the land of the free and the home of the brave."

Dave turned to the English-speaking guard. His face had lapsed into a vacant stare. Dave caught his gaze and the man was quick with a bow and an obsequious smile. But it didn't erase the haunted look around his eyes.

Those other guards. What did they go home to? They'd been taught all their lives that Japan was invincible. How did it feel to find out your entire belief system was a lie?

"What do we do now?" Watt asked the guard.

"Americans come. One hour."

Looking back on their release later, Dave never quite understood it. The day before, the guards had been, for the most part, vicious thugs. Overnight they transformed into kowtowing hosts. When he compared notes with others, he learned this experience wasn't unique to the Raiders.

The best explanation he came up with was this. As *horyo*, the Americans had been a lesser breed—something subhuman in their captors' eyes. But now that they were victors, full human rights and privileges applied.

Dave remembered the days after their release in bits and

pieces. An ecstatic, delirious blur. He and the others had finished washing up, then lingered on the cellblock steps, blissful in their new status as free human beings.

"Hey!" Watt said. "I've got an idea. How 'bout we raid the kitchen?"

"Are you nuts? I'm not touching anything they have in there." Nielsen spat on the ground like he was expelling something vile. "I'm holding out for real food. Steak and ice cream, fellas."

Dave glanced at Vitty, took in his emaciated arms and unfocused eyes. His buddy was in no condition to wander around. "Let's rest till they come for us. I sure don't want to miss that bus." He elbowed Watt. "Hey, you might get to build that dude ranch after all."

Watt grinned. "And you might take home that Thompson Trophy."

Dave stared at the sky above the tile roof across from them. A thunderhead was stacking up. "That'd be a fine thing. I hope they start the air races up again, now that this war is—"

"Over!" The others joined him in hollering the last word. Their voices reverberated from cinder-block walls.

Watt whooped and they all laughed. Poor Vitty nearly toppled over with the excitement.

Three Caucasian men in dirt-streaked prison uniforms strolled across the yard toward them. The men looked as gaunt and ragged as Dave and his friends, but they sported enormous grins. One had commandeered what looked like a table leg. He stumped along, using it as a cane.

Dave riveted his eyes on their faces. Besides his fellow airmen, he hadn't seen a pair of round eyes since the U.S.S. *Hornet.* Three years and four months earlier.

The man in the lead called out to them. "You must be the Doolittle men?"

Dave pushed himself to his feet. "Yes, sir."

The man's grin went even broader. He extended his hand. "Commander Scott Cunningham. Thank God we found you."

Cunningham. Dave had seen that name scratched on tin. He gave the man's hand an enthusiastic shake. "The Tincup

News Service."

Commander Cunningham laughed. "The what?"

"That's what we called it, sir. And the morale boost it gave us helped pull us through."

"I'm delighted to hear it. And your mission, men"—he snapped to attention and included all four of them in his gaze—"may have helped win this war. The impact in military terms wasn't enormous, but I wish you could have seen what you did for morale."

Nielsen broke into a disbelieving grin. "No kidding."

Chen's voice reverberated through Dave's mind. *Get airplane. Kill many Japs. For us.* He'd done exactly none of that. But perhaps their mission had accomplished something worthy of Chen's sacrifice.

He felt tears well again.

Watt draped an arm across Dave's shoulders and sniffled. "Praise God. Praise be to the living God."

Chapter Thirty-Five

Saturday, January 1, 1949
Osaka, Japan

THE RAIN GAVE WAY TO A light drizzle as Miyako retraced her steps toward Ebisu Bridge. The mid-day throng was appearing now, which would be true with any of the bridges. Thankfully, Kamura-san had left her the umbrella. She positioned it so it hid her face as much as possible.

With no plans and nowhere to be until three o'clock the next day, she paused on the bridge and leaned over the railing. Studied the water fifteen feet below. A pair of ducks bobbed on the surface. The drake's iridescent plumage gleamed against the dismal gray-green water.

Was it true they mated for life? She watched the pair, her mood murkier than the water.

She wandered across the bridge to the alley that led to the ancient Hozen-ji temple. This time, the fragrance of red bean soup beckoned. That soup was a favorite of Hiro-chan's on cold winter days. They would eat it together in Mama-san's kitchen after they came home from school. It did wonders to dispel the winter chill.

Why not? Let the memories come. *Che!* Why not wallow in them?

An old cafe stood on that alley, very famous before the war. Sweet red bean soup was its signature dish. It had even given the title to a famous novel, *Sweet Bean Soup for Two.* She turned into the narrow alley, her shoes squelching on mossy fragments of broken flagstone.

That whole district had been leveled, but the cafe was somehow still in business, serving from a scrap-wood shed. A petite woman took orders behind a rough counter. A ramshackle roof stretched over a row of plank tables.

Miyako joined the line of customers that stretched under the string of bright-red paper lanterns.

"Sweet red bean soup, if you please."

She chose a seat at the table farthest from the counter and waited, running her fingers over the tablecloth. It was well-worn cotton, with a pattern of scattered pink cherry blossoms. *Cherry blossoms.* The warm scent of red bean soup. The memories came in a tsunami that swept her back to that horribly bright April afternoon, to the dappled shade and drifting petals—pink snowflakes on the breeze.

Natsue's voice echoed in her ears. *The blossoms always disappear too soon, ah?*

She crushed her napkin into a clump in her fist. *Hai, Hiro-chan. You disappeared much too soon. I swore I'd do my best for you, but it keeps getting harder.*

George-san. It was all up to him and his ten thousand yen.

He'd tasted red bean soup once, on one of their first Thursdays together. They'd passed a small shop on a frosty evening. A shop much less famous than this one. But unlike this one, it had actual walls.

Sampling the soup hadn't been her choice. It had been his. He'd stopped outside the door, his breath hanging on the air. "What is that? It smells good."

She breathed in the rich, spicy aroma and forced back the memories it carried. "Japanese special dish. Maybe you like, ah? It's warm."

His nose crinkled, along with the laugh lines at the corners of his eyes. "I don't mind trying something new." They turned in and joined the queue to order. He stared around, taking in everything, his face lit with perplexed amusement. He pointed at various items on display in the glass case. "What's that?"

Dango, rice dumpling balls on sticks, coated with sweet, sticky sauce. *Mikasa*, pancakes sandwiched around a layer of sweet bean filling. She did her best to explain what they were. But he looked especially dubious at the thick red-brown mixture a woman behind the counter was spooning into bowls. "Is that what we're eating?"

Miyako smiled up at him and stroked his arm. "*Hai.* Trust me, George-san."

A pair of schoolgirls stood in front of them, matching short braids cascading onto frayed white collars. Matching pairs of toothpick legs and scuffed shoes under pleated skirts. The older girl clutched a worn wallet. The younger one studied the pastries in the case with wide eyes, standing so close her breath fogged the glass.

When it was her turn, the older girl ordered two bowls of sweet bean soup.

"Thirty yen," the cashier said.

The girl shook her wallet so her coins spilled onto the counter. Twenty-five yen.

She counted them.

George-san shifted his weight impatiently, his smile fading.

The girl sucked in her breath. "Do you have some coins, Ko-chan?" Her little sister dug in her pocket and pulled out two small coins.

The older one rearranged the coins on the wood-plank counter. "No more money, Ko-chan?"

George-san's eyes widened with understanding. He murmured in Miyako's ear. "She doesn't have enough? Is that why she's taking so long?"

"No. Not enough."

George-san winced.

The smaller girl pushed out a quivering lower lip and shook her head.

The older one looked at the cashier, her expression flat. "One bowl, please."

He took a half step forward. "I'll get that for her." He looked at Miyako. "Do they want that soup stuff? Tell the lady to give them each a bowl, please. And"—he smiled down at the younger girl—"ask if there's anything else they'd like."

It was easy to be generous when you had a full belly and a wallet crammed with bills. That thought lodged in Miyako's mind. But she learned in time George-san was like that. Always free with his cash. So ready to pamper his *onri wan*— hotel room, silk negligee, train tickets. Even ready to protect her. Maybe there was something in him that liked to come to the rescue. Play the big hero.

An acrid taste grew in her mouth. If Bowman had talked to him, he was sure to be feeling a lot less generous now.

The young woman who'd taken Miyako's order came over. She bowed and set a lacquer tray with twin bowls of steaming red-brown soup on the table. Their rich sweet aroma teased at Miyako's senses. "Excuse me. But I'm afraid there's a mistake. I only ordered one."

"Ah. Please forgive me. We only serve them in pairs. His and hers bowls."

She did her best to smile at the server. The woman bustled off, humming.

Of course. That happened in the novel too. But Miyako had always assumed it was fiction. She dropped her gaze to the tray in front of her, a sentence from the novel's climax running through her mind.

It's better to be a couple than alone in the world. True, if you were identical as a pair of bowls. But she and George-san had always been a mismatch. A *baishanfu*, a woman who'd sold her spring, to use the polite expression. Paired with the man who'd bought it from her. A proud daughter of *samurai* on the verge of a historic but ruthless deed. Coupled with an enemy soldier.

Enemy soldier. Enemy airman. Delham had been one, like George-san. Who were the women in Delham's life? What did he mean to them?

Did he like to come to their rescue?

She couldn't bring herself to eat "his" bowl.

20 August 1945
Peking, China

A truck brought Dave and his friends to a swank hotel in downtown Peking. Its towering marble lobby was grander than anything Dave had seen, even in Chicago. A bellman in full gold-braid regalia showed him to a luxurious room. He soaked in a real tub bath and flushed the toilet about ten times simply to watch the water swirl around the gleaming white porcelain bowl.

He had a hazy memory of seeing a doctor, who gave him injections and a bottle of vitamin pills. The man cautioned him. "Go easy on the food, now. Stick to soft, bland meals for a few days. Your stomach's not ready for anything rich."

He had no intention of taking that advice.

He had a very clear memory of that first dinner. Thick,

fragrant Irish stew with big chunks of beef and carrot and potato. Crusty rolls, meltingly soft inside, with actual butter. Dainty fruit tarts for dessert. And finally, coffee with sugar and cream. Dave gorged himself, then furtively stuffed his pockets with rolls and tarts in case the food disappeared later.

After the meal, Watt joined him in his room. He settled on the bed with its red brocade spread. "Sheets, even." He ran his hand along their crisp folded edge. "I think I could get used to this." He sat a moment, then looked at Dave, eyes glistening. "Pinch me, Delham. I still can't believe it."

Dave nodded. "The only thing that would make this better is if the other guys were here. Meder. Braxton. Hallmark. Smith."

"I know." Watt closed his eyes.

A spasm wrenched Dave's stomach, like the doctor predicted. It passed, for the moment, although he suspected worse would come later. But he didn't care. He walked over to the window. Men and women strolled the boulevard three stories below—free men and women, going wherever they pleased.

"I love my country." Watt's voice broke with emotion. "I love that we won this stinking war. I love every one of those boys that fought to set us free."

Dave turned to look into his friend's face—his eye sockets still hollow from hunger, the skin on his jowls still slack, his cheeks moist with tears he was no longer holding back.

"Yes," Dave said, "but no. I don't mean any disrespect, and I'm more grateful for every man's sacrifice than I can say. Especially our friends. But no man set me free. Jesus Christ did that, over a year ago."

Monday 10 September 1945
Washington, D.C.

Walter Reed General Hospital. A meeting room on the main building's first floor. Dave sat at a rectangular table that ran along one end of the room. An Army public relations man,

Chuck Roberts, sat to his right. Nielsen and Watt to his left. Poor Vitty was still too weak to come.

It was a press conference with the remnant of *Doolittle's lost crews*—turned out that's how the free world knew them.

A sparkling glass of water stood in front of him, with actual ice cubes. He picked it up to watch them jiggle.

Newsmen crowded the room—at least a dozen of them. He looked at all the faces, and animal fear pushed his throat closed a little. He took a deep breath and reminded himself that a press of friendly strangers was a good thing. Cameras flashed, and he tensed. Took a few more deep breaths.

A slight, balding man in the front row issued the first question. "The whole world has been in suspense. Tell us your story. What happened after the raid?"

Questions came in a rapid stream—too rapid for him to keep up. He struggled to focus. Thank God Nielsen did the talking.

"What's the best part about being home?" A beefy fellow in a tweed jacket issued that one.

"That's easy." Nielsen broke into an infectious grin. "Six square meals a day."

Laughter rippled through the room.

The door swung open. A sergeant slipped in, clipboard in hand. As it closed, Dave caught a flash of color—burnished copper—in the hall outside.

Eileen? At last?

No. Not her. That color was haunting him. He'd developed an uncanny ability to find a snatch of it in any environment.

"Gentlemen, I'm sure the Raiders are tired. We'll take one or two more questions." The P.R. man nodded to a fellow in the last row. "You, sir."

"I expect you're heading home to your families now. But after that? What's next?"

Nielsen answered first. "I'll keep flying for the Air Force. I figure I might manage to complete my second mission."

More laughter.

Watt nodded in agreement. "That's my plan, too."

"Lieutenant Delham, what's next for you?

"I haven't decided yet. I need to talk it over with my—"

Wife. A pang radiated through him. He hadn't heard from her. Three whole weeks since he'd been released, and she hadn't answered a single letter. Every time Watt or Nielsen got a letter he felt sick. "With my family. I think my Air Force days are done. I have a few other ideas that might surprise you. This'll surprise"—he paused, trying to fathom how Eileen would react to going to Japan with him, if she even cared where he went—"a lot of people."

"A hint, sir. Please."

"I can tell you this." His throat felt tight again. He cleared it and took a swig of ice water. "My experiences over there taught me a big lesson. About Jesus. About the power of His forgiveness. It's a lesson I intend to devote my life to sharing."

Pens scritched over notepads.

Roberts stood. "That'll wrap it up for today, fellows. Thank you so much for coming."

The sergeant at the door held it open. Dave looked through it—and straight into her eyes. *Eileen.* Her perfect oval face arrayed with that bewitching smile he'd pictured a hundred times. Every day.

The conference room, the table, the reporters—they all vanished. He jumped up and elbowed his way out into the hall. "Eileen?" He took her shoulders in his hands and gazed into those hazel eyes with their flecks of gold fire. "It's you. Really you."

She threw her arms around him and burrowed her head in his chest. "Oh, Dave." She took a gasping breath, then dissolved in sobs. "We didn't know if you...They couldn't tell us."

He folded her against him. "Shh. It's all right, honey." Held her, rocking her a little. Exalting in her warmth.

She shuddered against him. "We knew some got executed, but we didn't know who."

For more than twelve hundred days, she'd been a figment of his imagination. A fantasy. But here she was, with her scent of spice and tropical blooms. All his senses were telling him she was real. He ached to believe it. He burrowed his cheek into her luxuriant hair. Let his lips rest against the silk of it.

"It's all right now. Everything's all right now."

She looked at him, face wet with tears, and turned up those sweet lips—an engraved invitation if he'd ever seen one. He planted a lingering kiss on them.

A flashbulb went off, then another.

Dave jerked around toward the newsmen, blinking. Four of the press men had followed him.

"Hello, gentlemen." He tried not to sound too exasperated. "Allow me to introduce my wife, the lovely Eileen Delham."

"Beautiful. Give us a smile, you two." The flashbulbs popped, catching Eileen with a bashful smile and tear-streaked cheeks.

Roberts emerged from the conference room, took stock of the situation, and grinned. "Would this be Mrs. Delham, by chance?"

Dave gave her shoulder a squeeze. "Yes, sir."

"Are these fellows bothering you, ma'am?"

She started to speak, but Dave answered for her. "We would prefer some privacy at the moment."

Roberts put his hands on his hips. "You heard the lieutenant, boys."

"One more shot?" It was the cameraman who'd been at the left of the conference room. "Look over here, please. Smile. That's it."

Roberts herded them away.

Dave pulled his wife against him. "Roberts to the rescue. Now, where were we?" He kissed her until he was breathless. Clung to her, giddy with joy. He could see the curtain opening on a future together. Furnishing a home. Raising kids. Celebrating a long succession of anniversaries and Christmases. All the normal things free people did with their lives. Until that moment, that future had felt like a distant dream.

Could she get used to the idea that their home might be in Japan?

He stroked her hair. That conversation could wait. "There's so much to tell you. It's going to take a long time. But maybe we'd have more privacy outside."

"Outside?"

"The truth is, I can't get enough of looking at the sky."

They laced their way arm-in-arm through knots of people in the lobby and strolled out the front door. Down the broad steps and onto a sidewalk that crossed the lawn.

Eileen pulled away. "Dave, there's something else." She fished in her purse, dug out her wallet and flipped it open to a photo encased in plastic.

He took the wallet. A toddler with shiny, medium-light curls cascading onto a ruffled dress looked back at him. "She's adorable. Who is she?"

A smile bloomed from Eileen's lips, even as she dabbed a fresh tear from the corner of one eye. "Sarah. Our daughter." She sniffed and somehow managed to look both proud and apologetic at the same time. "She's a carrot-top."

"Our daughter?" A sense of unreality settled in. He gazed around at the hospital grounds, surprised that everything still looked solid.

Eileen nodded, all smiles now. "She'll be two years and eight months on Saturday. She can't wait to meet you."

"I'm a dad?" The curtain on that dream life was rising a lot faster than he expected. "When can I see her?"

"She's home with Mom."

"I can't believe it." From the pit to Pharaoh's throne room. Joseph himself couldn't have been more overwhelmed.

He studied his little girl's photo. Bright eyes. A winsome smile displaying even teeth like a string of tiny pearls. Pudgy little hands folded in her lap. Glossy black shoes. And a miniature version of her grandfather's chin. "She's gorgeous." He grabbed Eileen and gave her another kiss. "Like her mother. Oh, darling—" He picked her up by the waist and whirled her around. "You've been alone. All this time. Not even a letter." He lowered her to the sidewalk and squeezed her, the wonder of it flooding him again. "You're so brave. How did you find me here?"

She laughed her musical little laugh. "I got a phone call from General Doolittle himself, no less. He told me you were on the way, and he'd fly me out."

"And you came."

"Of course I came, silly. Did you think I wouldn't?" Concern dimmed that radiant smile. "Oh, Dave. All these years, did you imagine I'd left you for good? Look, those last weeks at Eglin—"

"Stop. I deserved it. I deserved it all. Eileen, I love you so much. And I was so rotten to you."

"I was pretty rotten back." She gave him a rueful look.

He clasped her smooth hand and felt its warmth in his own. Gazed into the mysterious green-and-gold depths of her eyes. "It's all right. That chapter's over."

"Yes, thank God. Oh! I hope you like the name Sarah. We never talked about it."

"Are you kidding? Sarah's a great name. You know Sarah in the Bible?"

Eileen shook her head. "Not really."

"She got to have a baby when she never dreamed she would. And Abraham, her husband? Abraham did plenty of things wrong. But he finally got it right with that little boy."

He sank to one knee, like the evening he proposed. There wasn't much he was sure about in that big free world with all its options, but he was sure about this. "Darling, right now, I'm swearing a solemn oath. You know that guy you ran off on in April of forty-two?"

She nodded, eyes glistening.

"I am not that guy. I promise—I *promise*—I'll get it right this time. I swear before my Lord Jesus Christ that I will learn to be the husband you deserve. The father our little Sarah deserves."

"Your Lord Jesus Christ?" She arched an eyebrow, but her smile returned to full radiance. "Something has changed you."

A thick place swelled in his throat. So many men didn't make it back, but the Lord had given him a fresh chance. Fresh as Sarah's little cheeks. Shiny and new as those tiny patent-leather shoes.

He stood and circled his arm around her. "I bet you're getting cold. We should go in."

They made their way toward the steps. A giant banner hung in front of the monstrous columns enclosing the hospital's veranda. *Welcome Home POWs.*

Eileen squeezed his waist as they walked beneath it. "Well, how does it feel?"

"Which part of it?"

She beamed up at him. "The part where you're the hero you always dreamed you'd be."

He stopped and turned her to face him. "Being everyone else's hero isn't all it's cracked up to be. But your hero? Now that's worth fighting for."

He pulled a silver half dollar from his pocket, flipped it in the air, and caught it. He said what he'd waited more than three years—*very long* years—to say.

"Hey, want to see a movie?"

Chapter Thirty-Six

Saturday, January 1, 1949
Osaka, Japan

MIYAKO DIDN'T GO TO HER OWN ROOM. She had a deep-rooted fear of turning up where anyone might look for her. She knew plenty of cheap hotels. Kamura-san's cash was good for a night at one of those.

She scoured the black-market stalls on the fringe of the Shinsekai for a change of clothes. When evening came, she passed an hour or so in her hotel room practicing. She stood in front of the cracked mirror and opened the handbag's clasp subtly, with one hand. Pulled the knife out with a smooth motion. Followed up with a fierce thrust. She thought she looked dangerous, but without Kamura-san's guidance, who could tell if she'd be good enough?

The poison would be critical.

She sank onto the futon, head throbbing, nerves wound tight as silk in a cocoon.

George-san. Why not forget all this and get on that train with him?

She rolled onto her side and pulled the pillow to her chest. She drifted to sleep imagining her head cradled on his strong chest, the scent of pine in her nostrils.

Sunday crept by with the tedium of a snail scaling Mount Fuji. Until the afternoon, when it was time to catch the Midosuji Line to her meeting with George-san.

She arrived a few minutes early. She stood on the curb outside the Hollywood Club, gnawing at a hangnail.

It was an afternoon worth remembering. One of those clear, crisp winter days—which was a gift, since odds were good it would be her last day of freedom.

The afternoon light brought everything into high relief. The pile of firm apples on display at the fruit stand next to her glowed red and gold. The spicy-sweet aroma of barbecued pork from the Korean barbecue place down the street teased at her nose.

It had to be three o'clock. She tugged at her top. Any minute, he would appear. And with him, the answer to the question that had plagued her since Friday night. What rumors had gotten back to him?

The streets were busy, but there was no mistaking him when he rounded the corner at the end of the block. Cropped sand-colored hair and that familiar confident stride. She took one last tug at her sweater. Was she worth ten thousand yen?

She got a good look at his face as he crossed the street. Mouth drawn in a taut line. Furrows creasing his forehead. Her chest hollowed, but she put on her warmest smile and started toward him, arms extended, before he reached the curb.

"George-san. Finally. I miss you so much." That was the truth.

His lips twitched. "Funny. That's not what I heard."

Any confidence she held vanished like incense smoke in a drafty room. "Why? What you hear?"

He stopped a long pace short of her, folded his arms, and glared. "Don't play me, baby."

"That Bowman talked to you? Stinking liar."

"Not just him."

She sucked in her breath. "What else, ah?"

He strode past her, plucked an apple from the pile, and handed a coin to the street vendor. He faced her, his expression fierce. "To hear Perkins tell it, you were all over some Jap fellow when he picked you up. You flirted with O'Shea. But it was Perkins you couldn't keep your hands off of."

She stared at him, all but spluttering in disbelief. "Pardon me, George-san, but you believe all that?"

The betrayal written across his face told her that, at least at some level, he did believe it.

She took a deep breath. "It wasn't like that, George-san. No."

"What was it like, then?"

"I ran into some Japanese guys I knew from Abeno. They said they would..." She laid a hand on his sleeve. "Bad things.

I was afraid, George-san."

He pulled his arm away and bit into the apple, eyes narrow. "So you thought Perkins and O'Shea would protect you? But when I offered—"

"I am so sorry, George-san. I made a big—how do you say?—mistake. Please forgive me. And I paid for it." *Much more than you know.*

Did his expression soften?

She chose her words with care, revealing as much of the truth as she dared. "I thought if I stayed at the club, those Japanese guys go away. Harry asked me to leave with him. But I wasn't going to. Then the big fight started."

"You weren't going with Perkins, huh?" George-san took another hearty bite of apple and gave her an appraising stare. But without a doubt, his expression softened. "You're a load of trouble. You know that?"

She bowed low and stayed there, eyes on her shoes. "Please, please forgive me, George-san."

He put a hand under her shoulder and pulled her up. "Don't bow like that. You know it bugs me."

That hand rested on her shoulder. Hundreds of men must have touched her there. But there was a steadiness to his grip that made his touch mean something. It reminded her he had every reason to leave her—and didn't. How could she lie to him now, when she'd felt what it meant to lose his trust?

She wrapped her arms around him and nuzzled into his strong chest. He hesitated a second before his arms circled her. A wave of warmth washed through her. "I am sorry to make so much trouble for you. I'll make it up to you, I promise."

The train. The taxi. The *ryokan.* She'd imagined it for years—going there with a man she loved. A man who'd take care of her. Fight for her. Stick with her when others would not.

Was it too late to take that train with this man? Seize this chance at happiness?

She should forget Delham and escape with George-san.

Papa-san. Hiro-chan. Surely they didn't want her to pay with her life for this.

She sighed and leaned into his chest. Her cheek rested on smooth leather, then found a ridge—his squadron patch. He was a soldier, and soldiers had duties. Sooner or later, he'd go wherever the U.S. Army sent him.

She had duties too. If she forgot them, what would it buy her? A month of happiness? A year?

Maybe as little as a weekend.

The dream shattered, giving way to hard reality. A daughter of *samurai* lived for honor, not for passing pleasure. Her duty to her family was eternal. For Hiro-chan. For Papa-san. For the ancestors. This had to be done.

She had to betray him.

She felt a pang of grief that was almost physical—a spear piercing her chest. But she steeled herself and breathed the crucial question. "Did you bring the money?"

He slipped from her arms and fished a thick wallet from his pocket. His gaze rested on her as he thumbed it open, giving her a glimpse of a stack of bills.

She twittered like a nightingale. "Wonderful! I'll buy the tickets tonight. It will be perfect, George-san."

"Not so fast, babe. How much are these train tickets? When do we leave?"

She sent a silent thanks up to the ancestors that she'd thought ahead to detail it out. She shot him a confident smile. "We'll take the 10:10 train to Shirahama. Then a taxi to the *ryokan*. It's an extra special nice one. Two thousand yen for two tickets."

"What's the name of the place?"

"*Ryokan* Montei."

"And what's the rate there?"

"Three hundred yen per night." She searched his face. "All these questions, George-san. You don't trust me?"

"The station's not too far from here. We can go over there right now. Pick up the tickets together." He took another bite from the apple, eyes not leaving her face.

"I, ah, have some things I need to take care of. Today, before the shops close." The words seemed to fight her, not wanting to come out. "If you could please just give me the money, I can pick them up later tonight."

"No, Midori. I'll do this with you."

She made an attempt at a light-hearted giggle. "But it'll be boring for you. No need to bother you with all these detail things. You trust me with them."

"I insist."

She pouted. "You don't trust me."

"I used to. But this is smelling funny, kid." He tossed what was left of the apple onto the sidewalk. "Look, I need to think about it."

"Think about it?" In less than an hour she was to meet Tsunada-san's man. This was not the time for him to think about it. "It's all lies about Harry. I promise."

"Maybe." His expression hollowed. "But I'm not sure what to think any more."

"George-san! Please." She moved to slip her arms around his waist.

He caught her forearms before she could. "I want to believe you. I do." He studied her, a vulnerable glint to his eyes. "Look, let's just meet up on Thursday, like we always do. We'll take it from there."

She rested her hands on his arms while something inside her dissolved into liquid. Maybe she'd hurt him enough. "I tell the truth, George-san. I don't care about any man but you. Please believe that, always."

He gave her a wan smile. "That's good to hear." He folded her into a passionless hug, then released her. "Thursday, then."

She did her best to smile. "*Hai.* I see you Thursday." Her voice seemed to come from somewhere outside her.

He turned and walked away. She stood, watching his departing shoulders for what was probably the last time. Feeling herself make a slow slide into a jet-black abyss.

A pair of boys in rumpled trousers scuffled toward her, jostling each other and laughing. One of them aimed a kick at the apple core George had discarded. It did an uneven roll along the sidewalk, landing among the muck and dead leaves in the gutter. A layer of filth crusted its pale flesh.

Wrapped in shame. Like her.

She stared into the gutter while the abyss engulfed everything around her—the smell of barbecue, the sound of passing traffic, the boys' voices. Nothing left but the winter sun on the apple core, the weight of her handbag, and the wretched ache in her chest.

Her handbag. The knives.

The meeting with Tsunada-san's man.

It took a supreme act of will, but somehow she took a step and then another. Somehow, she walked four long blocks to Namba Station. A quiet determination swelled inside her.

She was not going to stay in the gutter.

A weight that had been pressing on her chest lifted. There was a certain freedom in shedding her last real attachment. *Kataki-uchi* for Hiro-chan was her burden and hers alone. She'd use all the strength and courage her lineage had endowed her with to see it to its conclusion. If her miserable life had to shatter like a piece of worthless glass to accomplish that, so be it.

And if she loved George-san, perhaps the farther away he was when it all exploded, the better.

Tsunada-san's man waited in front of the station, cloaked in growing dusk. Miyako took a deep breath, made a low bow, and explained she hadn't come up with the money.

A scowl creased his face. "We went to a lot of effort for you. Tsunada-san won't be happy."

She cringed inside. She'd disappointed yet another man—this time a very powerful one. "Forgive me, sir. Please forgive me."

He brushed past her and stalked away.

Her feet, still heavy as mountain boulders, carried her up the broad cement stairs and into the station.

Five minutes to wait for the train. She reached into her purse for a cigarette and her fingertips grazed the knife's handle. She let them linger.

So, there'd be no poison now. But she still had her little armory.

Chapter Thirty-Seven

Sunday, January 2, 1949
Osaka, Japan

THE MIDOSUJI LINE BROUGHT MIYAKO TO Namba Station. It was too early to move on to the church—it might make her conspicuous. So she took twice as long as needed to pick out a small *bento* box. She sat on a bench, pulled out the chopsticks—and couldn't eat. The chopsticks trembled too much between her fingers. She set the box aside.

She let a few minutes pass, then started along the broad street. After a half-dozen blocks, the First Evangelical Lutheran Church loomed in front of her—at least that's what the sign declared. But there was no *torii* gate to mark the church as sacred. No garden. No gong. Just a standard door decorated with a pine wreath. Dozens of people streamed through it. She'd never imagined that so many of her own people would contaminate themselves with a foreign religion. Half the faces were Japanese.

No incense greeted her at the door. Instead, a Japanese woman wearing cloying perfume gave Miyako a bow and a handshake. The woman thrust something that looked like a playbill at her.

The bile mounting her throat threatened to choke her.

The buzz of small talk filled the building's airy interior. A row of stained-glass windows cast filtered light on a platform at the front, which displayed an unadorned podium and a piano. A banister separated the platform from the rest of the room. A pair of Marines stood at either end, candlelight glinting off their holstered pistols.

A shiver ran through her. Their guns, her knives. Hardly an even match.

She picked a seat at the aisle, about a third of the way back. She had no idea what Christians did in their churches, so there wasn't much she could do to plan. It all came down to one simple problem. Get close enough to drive one of those knives into Delham's soft flesh. The less she thought about what would happen after she did it, the better.

She bit at her lip so hard she tasted blood.

A door at the platform's side opened. She craned for a second, then deflated. A Japanese man in a business suit crossed to the podium, not Delham. A procession of men and women in long robes followed him—also Japanese.

The man behind the podium beamed his welcome. "We have a special treat for you tonight, as you know. But we'll start with prayer and worship, ah?"

Miyako took her cues from a pair of girls next to her. Bowed her head and clasped her hands. Stood and picked up a songbook from a rack in front of her. Sang along with the others, an anthem about shepherds in a field who apparently expressed themselves in Latin arias.

The choir filed off the platform and the reverend—his name was Kagawa—returned. "Thank you, choir. And now let's welcome our special guests, Reverend and Mrs. Delham. A story that's inspired us all, yes?"

An expectant murmur swelled through the hall. The door behind the platform opened, and Delham walked in. Sound died in her ears. Time screeched to a halt like a braking train.

She absorbed every detail of his appearance. His jaunty grin and smart tweed jacket. The self-assurance all Americans seemed to adopt as their unquestioned birthright. Rich waves of chestnut-brown hair receded slightly from a tall, frank forehead above arresting hazel eyes—the same eyes she'd seen in his photo. He held the door open for his wife, a striking woman with brilliant copper-colored hair. A young Japanese in a well-tailored suit drifted through the door in their wake.

"Please welcome another special guest," Kagawa said. "Matsuura-san has recently, ah, repatriated. He will translate for Reverend Delham tonight."

Matsuura-san? Her own name.

She took a hard look at the newcomer. What she saw sucked the air from her lungs.

Tall. Slender. Square jawline. Chiseled cheekbones. A younger version of Papa-san, except for a patch of scarred skin stretching from one side of his collar to his hairline.

"Akira-san?" she whispered.

But how?

Delham stepped to the microphone. *"Konnichiwa."* He gave the crowd a crocodile grin, followed by a couple sentences of sloppy Japanese.

"Matsuura-san, if you please." Kagawa's furrowed forehead conveyed a hint of urgency.

The man who looked like her father's younger copy took his place at Delham's side and bowed. "I am honored to assist my great friend, Reverend Delham, with the translation."

Great friend. Each word reverberated through her chest like the knell of a huge temple gong. A voice whose every nuance she knew so well.

It was all she could do to stay in her seat. Her brother could not be here. Miyako had carried it herself, that white box a Navy captain gave them. Smaller than a shoe box, it had contained her brother's ashes—all of Akira-san the war returned to them.

He anchored his eyes on the lectern's slanted top, flushing. So uncertain. Not at all like the eldest son who'd cut a swath through all the best schools. Her esteemed brother would be twenty-six now. This man looked older than that. More weather beaten, even ignoring the scars. And certainly, he lacked Akira-san's air of command.

Still...

She could not accept what her eyes and ears were telling her. Was he some kind of apparition? She shifted in her seat. Her rayon skirt slid across her knees—the second-hand skirt she'd bought to replace the clothes she'd left at a brothel.

Haji consumed her. The man on the platform couldn't be Akira-san, simply because she couldn't face him. After Papa-san, Akira-san had been the idol of her girlhood. She couldn't bear knowing she would only disappoint him, the way she'd disappointed Papa-san.

Recently, ah, repatriated. An explanation began to unwind, ever so slowly, in the matted cocoon that had taken the place of her mind. She'd heard a few improbable stories of "two-legged ghosts." Men who'd been declared dead in battle, but through some act of cowardice had actually survived the war.

Perhaps she and Papa-san were no longer alone.

Delham went on. Something about the anger the *gaijin* felt when Nippon attacked Pearl Harbor. Miyako had no use for anything he had to say. Her thoughts turned to a single problem—how to bury one of those knives in his belly.

Whatever happened, she would do her duty for Hiro-chan.

After what felt like an age, Reverend Kagawa returned to the platform and clapped Delham on the shoulder. It seemed the American was wrapping up.

She shifted her handbag from the floor to her lap. Her palms left a faint moist imprint on its sides.

"Do you know what I said then?" Delham looked around the room. "I said, 'No man set me free. Jesus Christ did that, over a year ago.'"

Someone clapped up front, and then the room erupted with applause.

Reverend Kagawa bowed repeatedly to Delham as the American found a seat. The Japanese pastor had to wait before he could make himself heard over the din. "Thank you, Reverend Delham. What an inspiring testimony." He paused a moment longer for the crowd to calm. "Before we close, Reverend Delham has asked our friend Matsuura-san to share a bit of his story and his very important prayer request. Matsuura-san?"

Matsuura-san stepped to the microphone.

"My name is Matsuura Akira. When we embarked on the war in the Pacific, I had recently graduated from Eta Jima. I was assigned to the *Nitto Maru*, one of a line of vessels charged with guarding our Pacific coast."

The *Nitto Maru*. Akira-san's ship.

So it was true.

He gazed at the lectern for a few seconds before he went on. "We discharged our duties. In April 1942, the *Nitto Maru* was destroyed by the enemy. I woke up in traction in their ship's infirmary. The sole survivor. *Horyo*." He looked around the room. "A prisoner of war. The last thing I ever imagined for myself."

Her brother. Wounded and captured, not dead. And standing in front of her.

But...*horyo*. Barely human. How could he ever look her

in the eye? How could he look *Papa-san* in the eye? After he'd fallen so far short of the ideal of Japanese manhood Papa-san had laid before them.

The acrid taste in her mouth crept down her throat and became a sour churning in her belly. She should leave. Before they had to confront each other—the captive and the whore. It was the kindest thing she could do for them both.

The two-legged ghost went on with feeling. "When the war was over, I could not bear to face my countrymen, especially my family. An American officer I met in the camp arranged a position for me with American President Lines. I spent a year and a half sailing their cruise ships to South America. But my heart called me to Nippon. At last, I signed on for the voyage home."

He paused and cast a solemn look around the room. "It will be very difficult to see my family again. But I wish it now with all my heart. I once believed a defeated life had no value. But I look now at *Iesu* and I see that a defeated life can have value."

He stood, talking that way, with the stained-glass image of the Christians' *Iesu* behind his shoulder. The deity they worshiped, his bloody head bowed in defeat. His downcast face was etched with pain, not the fierce triumph of a victor. The look of a man who'd lost everything.

She snorted. A weak god, for weaklings. Had her brother somehow become one of them?

Akira-san laid a fist on the lectern. "I've searched everywhere, but so far, no news of my family. Our old neighborhood in Tokyo is nothing but ash. Please pray I'll be able to get in touch with my father, Matsuura Saburo, who was captain of the *Aoba*. My mother, Matsuura Ayako. My brother and sister, Hiroshi and Miyako." He cast his eyes down and bit his lip. "And please, pray they'll accept me when I do."

She felt the heat on her face so distinctly she was sure it was visible.

For a moment, he seemed to stare straight into her face. "No matter how deep your *haji*, how complete your failure, I believe God still has a use for you."

She froze.

He stepped back and dropped his eyes. It seemed he could say no more.

The silence thundered.

Akira-san made his way off the platform. She sat very still, locked in place by an irrational fear that any tiny movement would turn every eye her way. That she'd become the target of the scorn every heart in the room had to be feeling for her brother—at least, every heart that was true to the Yamato ways.

After a moment she ventured a furtive glance past the girls beside her at their mother. The woman's lips wore a soft smile. She pulled a delicate embroidered handkerchief from her purse and dabbed at one glistening eye.

Miyako looked at girls' father. Then a Japanese man across the aisle. Stared at more faces, stunned. Broad grins and approving expressions wherever she looked.

Akira-san had spoken of the gravest possible dishonor. And they approved?

Reverend Kagawa directed them to bow their heads in prayer. After the prayer, she shifted in her chair, replaying her brother's words. *Defeat. Failure. Shame.* Such things— unendurable things—had happened to them all. The emperor had used that word himself the day he announced Nippon's surrender. She could still hear him saying, "...endure the unendurable," his strange brittle voice cutting through the radio static.

She'd learned in the years since that nothing was unendurable except *haji.* Capitulation. Prostitution. A death unavenged. Akira-san could wallow in his *haji* if he wished, but she would accept hers no more.

The prayers finished, and voices rose again in song.

"Sleep in exceeding peace. Sleep in exceeding peace." Soft strains, mellow harmonies, soothing lyrics. At least everyone else was probably experiencing them that way. All in complete opposition to the bedlam in her soul.

The chords faded. "Reverend Delham and his wife will be here for a few minutes after service. Come up if you'd like to greet them, ah?" Kagawa gazed around with a beatific expression. "Otherwise, may you go in peace."

She rose and pushed forward. Her pulse throbbed in her

ears like a great *taiko* drum. There was an air of inevitability about the way her feet conveyed her toward the platform. As if she had no more will in the matter than an iron shaving at the mercy of a magnet. Or Kamura-san's plum blossom drifting on the surface of an icy brook.

Clusters of chatting parishioners blocked her path. She threaded her way around them. Churchgoers had formed a queue, all eager to speak with the Americans. The icy brook deposited her at the end of it. Akira-san stood in front of the platform, lost in conversation. He had his back toward her, at least for the moment.

Delham and his wife leaned over the banister, exchanging comments with well-wishers.

Miyako rested her fingertips on her purse's clasp. She mentally rehearsed wrapping her right hand around the large knife's hilt and concealing it in her purse until the precise moment came to raise it for her thrust.

Only three people stood in line before her now. *Almost there. Almost—*

Delham looked up from the man he was greeting. His hazel eyes met hers. Sheer malevolence coursed through her body like an electric shock. Before she could move, a weight dropped on her shoulder from behind—a gnarled hand. It gave her a forceful jerk around. She ran her eyes up a row of silver buttons to a pair of braided epaulets and a knowing smirk. She muffled a cry.

Captain Oda.

Chapter Thirty-Eight

ODA HAD A DEATH GRIP ON her shoulder. "So, Matsuura Miyako. You have a habit of turning up in surprising places, ah?"

She hugged her handbag to her, wishing with her entire being that she could drive one of those knives into his barrel chest. But then she'd get no chance at Delham.

His lips twisted with growing amusement. "Normally I wouldn't soil my hands with such a matter. But there's someone here you should meet, yes?" He closed his other hand on her upper arm and squeezed so hard she winced. "You'd have been better served to stay in the red-line district, where you belong. But I'm glad you came." He cocked his head toward Akira-san. "Because in a profound way, the two of you deserve each other."

A grey-haired Japanese gentleman stood watching them. "What's this?" He shifted a large leather-bound book from his right hand to his left and took a step toward them.

Oda made a low bow toward him and the missionary. "I have found the sister of Matsuura-san," he said in English, in a voice designed to carry.

"Really?" Delham's wife trilled. "Right here? How wonderful!"

Delham looked over at Miyako, a grin spreading across his features. Akira-san spun to face her. A moment of uncertainty passed before her brother's eyes widened. In three decisive strides, he stood before her, eyes locked on her face. "Mi-chan?"

"There is a slight complication Matsuura-san will want to hear about." Oda reverted to Japanese. "I assure you this is your sister." He sniffed. "But there is a small matter of her profession, ah? She's a prostitute." He dropped her arm with a wrench that nearly made her cry out.

She opened her mouth to deny his accusation. Or at least explain it. But in the face of Oda's scorn, she couldn't.

A hundred ears listened to their words. A hundred eyes focused on them, all seeing how filthy she was. She withered inside.

Akira-san froze. "Is this true?"

It was like she was a girl again—one who'd earned a scolding. "*Onii-san*," she whispered, the old honorific title for an older brother springing to her lips.

He clasped his hands on her shoulders, and she noticed with a start that the rough brown scarring on his neck extended to his left hand. "My baby sister, here. I don't believe it." Then, nose crinkling slightly, "But you're so different."

She spat out a retort. "You aren't exactly what I was expecting either. They gave us your ashes, *Onii-san*."

"My ashes, ah?" His turn to look shamefaced and shift his weight. He let a very un-cremated hand slip from her shoulder. "I didn't know, Mi-chan. But I did use a false name during those years in America. I assumed you'd rather believe me gloriously dead."

"We'd rather not have spent six years believing a glorious lie."

A pinched expression crossed his features. "*We'd* rather? Where is everyone else?"

She answered in a softer tone. "Papa-san's in the hospital."

"The hospital? With what?"

The withered place inside her grew. She led him a few steps away from the press of people around the Delhams. "Leukemia."

"Leukemia?" He gave her a blank stare.

"They sent him into Nagasaki."

"Ah." He sucked his breath in hard. "*Hibakusha?*" His forehead wrinkled, as if *explosion-polluted* was too much to take in. A beat passed. "And Mama-san?"

"*Gaijin* bombing raid." She shot a glance at Delham. "You have no idea what those firestorms were like."

A wounded look lodged on his face. "Hiro-chan?"

She took a small step around him, placing his back toward the missionary. "Another bombing raid. The night you 'died.'" She went up on tiptoes to whisper in his ear. "Your friend behind you, ah? Your Delham?"

"*Hai?*"

"He dropped the bomb that killed your brother."

"What?" He took a step back, like she'd punched him. He lowered his voice. "You know this?"

"*Hai.*"

His features folded in pain, as if his own gut had been slit with a blade.

She anchored her eyes on his face and watched for some sign of the outrage he should feel. A change of expression that would tell her he knew his duty now and was prepared to do it. Some hint that he remembered who he was.

She didn't see it.

He stood very still, eyes going wider. After a few seconds, he gave her a long, slow shake of the head.

Papa-san's words repeated in her ears. *It's you and me, Mi-chan. We two can't pause, even to retrieve our weapons.* It was still up to her. Akira-san might come to himself in time, but she couldn't pause for that. Somehow the Christian demons had duped her brother so badly he forgot everything he stood for.

Delham's wife called out to them. "Akira-san, won't you bring your sister over and introduce us?"

Akira-san leaned toward Miyako, concern creasing his features. "Are you all right? Maybe I should see you home now?"

"I'm fine." Miyako flashed her teeth. "I'll meet your new friends." She strode toward the banister.

Akira-san caught up with her and laid a hand on her arm. "Mi-chan." He searched her face. "What exactly are you doing here?"

"I could ask you the same question." She shrugged his hand off her shoulder, stopped in front of Delham, and made a low bow. She straightened and smiled.

Delham extended a hand toward her. "Pleased to meet you."

Still smiling, she slipped her right hand into her purse as if she were after a pen. Her fingers closed on the hilt of the six-inch knife. And that was it. She clenched the weapon in her right fist, let the handbag drop to the floor, and drew the knife above her shoulder. Six years of bitterness and tortured shame uncoiled in a pouncing strike. She drove the knifepoint straight at the space below Delham's ribcage.

Akira-san moved faster.

Her blade bit into flesh and met resistance. The weapon sliced, then twisted from her grasp and clattered to the floor. Delham's wife screamed. Delham stood with gaping jaw, blood spattering his jacket.

Akira-san slumped against the banister between them, hand pressed to his neck, face contorted in pain. Blood oozed between her brother's fingers. The truth sank in as pandemonium erupted around the room.

She gasped. "Akira-san! What have you done?"

Oda smashed into her. Got her in a chokehold that had her gasping and clawing at him until he pinioned her wrists behind her.

The *gaijin* missionary vaulted the banister and grabbed Akira-san, supporting him from behind. "Doctor! Is there a doctor here?"

Both Marines leveled their pistols. The closest one ran up to her. "Freeze!"

Oda jerked at her arms. A pair of clicks and the feel of cold steel on her wrists. He sucked his breath in softly behind her. "*Che!* So you are your papa-san's daughter."

Except Papa-san would have succeeded. Akira-san should have succeeded, but he was too lost to try. And now he slumped in front of her, bleeding.

Commotion reigned throughout the building. But she focused past the Marine's shoulder at her brother. He lifted his fingers from his neck and studied the blood smeared across them.

"*Onii-san!*" She forced the words around what felt like jagged glass in her throat. "Forgive me, please."

He winced, pressing his fingers where his neck met his shoulder. His eyes were wide in his contorted face. "Mi-chan, not this way. There is a better way."

Delham eased her brother onto one of the long benches. Delham's wife followed with a wool muffler. She pressed it against Akira-san's neck, and crimson bloomed around her fingers.

A Japanese man with thinning hair ran toward Akira-san. "Keep the pressure on it."

"Dave-san." Akira-san gasped out his words, grabbed at Delham's arm. "Forgive her. She doesn't know. You must tell her."

Oda wrenched Miyako's arm so hard she teetered. "Guess you're going back in, Matsuura-san."

She shrank inside, but only for a second. She'd barely survived her last round at Oda's office, but what happened to her now didn't matter. This was her *gyokusai*, her suicide charge. She'd done all in her power to spend herself for honor, her own and that of her *samurai* ancestors.

Akira-san moaned. She looked at him and a chill wrapped her heart. The brother she'd venerated. Yet she was leaving him with these *gaijin*, bleeding from her blade.

Oda pushed her toward the door. She resisted with all her strength, twisted to look up at him. "Captain Oda. Please, please. Not yet." The police captain frowned and gave her an overpowering shove. "Let me talk to Akira-san!" Her voice rose in pitch.

The captain set his jaw. "Move, Matsuura."

She stared over her shoulder. Her brother rested with his eyes closed, his features etched with pain. A rich ruby-red stain suffused the gray muffler Delham's wife pressed to his neck.

Like the blood in the cement dust around Hiro-chan's battered little corpse.

The old sick angry feeling jolted her. With everything she'd lost, this *Onii-san* she neither knew nor understood was all she had. Had she killed him—like she had Hiro-chan?

"Akira-san," she called out. "Please forgive me. It wasn't meant for—"

His eyes flicked open and locked on hers. She couldn't hear it, but his mouth shaped words. "Mi-chan. You must listen to Dave."

Before his eyes drifted shut, she saw it. In the midst of his pain, his concern for her.

Oda pushed her through a side door.

Chapter Thirty-Nine

Vertical bars. How long could you stare at vertical bars? They stretched from floor to ceiling across the full four-foot front of Miyako's cell. Like the *shoji* that had formed an entire wall of her chamber at the brothel—but an implacable steel version.

The bars separated her from a narrow hallway. The wall on its far side boasted patches of peeling paint that added some interest to her view. If she squinted, she could make one patch resolve into a horse trotting. She imagined its mane flowing free. She could picture another as a brazier, like the one in the common room at the Oasis. In her unheated cell, her eyes lingered there. She chafed stiff fingers and summoned the most vivid image she could of those glowing coals and the warmth they suffused through that cheery room.

But the physical discomfort wasn't the worst of it. What tortured her, beyond all else, was not knowing. Had she killed Akira-san?

Firm footsteps sounded on the hallway linoleum. She thrust her hands into her lap and jerked into the only allowed position—*seiza* posture, the formal kneel. Back straight, gaze level, as befit a courageous daughter of *daimyo*.

The policeman strode into her field of view. He was tall and unnaturally thin, with jutting cheekbones. He stopped and fixed his eyes on her. They seemed to take on a glow. As he studied her, the cell seemed colder. She didn't know his name, but at that moment she gave him one. *Zugaikotsu*—the Skull.

His hand went to his wood baton. "Sit straight. Look forward, *horyo*."

She lifted her chin, stretched a quarter inch higher, and anchored her eyes on the middle bar.

"Better." He moved directly into her line of sight. He slapped his baton into his other palm and made a grimace that might have been intended for a grin. "Come."

The interrogation room was a windowless box with a single door. The light came from a bulb in a dented fixture dangling from the ceiling. The room was just big enough for a battered table and four simple wooden chairs.

Stern-faced policemen occupied two of those chairs. A third policeman with more elaborate epaulets leaned against the wall, appraising her.

Is Akira-san dead? These men could tell her.

One of them stood and yanked out a chair. Zugaikotsu shoved her into it. The second policeman grabbed two pairs of cuffs from the table and knelt. He clicked the first cuff shut around her right ankle, then secured it to the chair leg.

She shifted her gaze forward and worked to keep her breathing steady. She'd done her duty. She would face the consequences as a daughter of *samurai*.

The second set of cuffs clicked around her left ankle and the other chair leg.

Epaulets-san nodded his satisfaction. "Bring in Suzuki-san."

Suzuki-san. Her other interrogators had not identified themselves. He'd be the first man here with a name.

"*Hai.*" Zugaikotsu disappeared.

She bowed to Epaulets-san. "Pardon me for troubling you, Officer. Please, how is my brother?"

His lips quirked. "Ah. The esteemed brother you knifed? It would be best if Suzuki-san answered that one."

Weariness washed over her, and she closed her eyes. It was a long moment before she opened them again. Studying the items on the table was easier than meeting anyone's gaze. A manila folder—her dossier, no doubt. Three mugs of coffee. Four *bento* boxes filled the room with the tangy odors of broiled fish, seaweed, and soy sauce.

The door opened. Zugaikotsu held it for a man in a subtly striped flannel suit with threads of silver running through his hair. He exchanged bows with the three policemen.

The one with the fancy shoulders introduced her. "Suzuki-san, allow me to present Matsuura. Matsuura,

Suzuki-san. Your prosecutor."

Her prosecutor. This man would evaluate the evidence against her and recommend her sentence to the judge, a recommendation the judge would inevitably accept. Suzuki-san would, effectively, decide her fate. She made the deepest bow she could from her chair.

He gave her a perfunctory head-bob, took a seat, and made a show of examining her dossier. This gave her a chance to study him. The intensity of his focus and the authoritative set of his jaw. A man accustomed to getting what he wanted. Which, in this case, would no doubt be a lengthy sentence.

He shook his head before looking at her. "So. You got yourself in a little trouble, ah?" He let out a dry laugh. "Attempted murder. Assault with a weapon. Fifteen years. How does that strike you, Matsuura? How old are you?" He glanced at the paperwork. He leaned back and studied her face. "Thirty-five years old before you'll know freedom again, yes?"

That would be a long time. Forever, in prisons like this one.

"Too old for a husband. Too old for children." He paused, no doubt to let her absorb this. A frown etched its way into his forehead. "Shame." He sat up with a brisk nod. "Well, let's get started. Naturally, I have a few questions for you."

"Please pardon me for the trouble, Suzuki-san." She gave him another bow from her chair. "Could you kindly tell me about my brother? Is he in the hospital? Is he all right?"

He shared a smirk with Epaulets-san, then looked at her. "You need to know, ah?"

"*Hai*. Please."

"I could do this for you—this thing you need. In fact, there are many things you probably need." He gave a pointed look at the stack of *bento* on the table between them. She tried not to focus on the delectable odors drifting from those boxes. "But if I'm going to do something for you, you'll have to do something for me first."

"What do you want? I confessed to everything."

"Come now. You don't expect me to believe you came up with all of this on your own, do you?" He pulled a pack of

Chesterfields from his pocket. He lit one and leaned toward her. "Why should you take all the blame, ah? Just some names. That's all we want. Who else was involved in your little plot?"

He handed the pack around to the other two. They each took a cigarette and lit up.

She stared at Suzuki-san. "But there was no one else."

"The sooner you tell us the truth—the full truth, Matsuura—the easier things will be for you." He jerked his head at the policeman on his left. The man stood, stalked around the table, and loomed over her.

"The truth, Matsuura!" Suzuki-san said.

The policeman grasped her forearm. He jerked it toward him and twisted to expose the soft flesh of her inner arm. He poised his lit cigarette a quarter inch from her skin. She pulled away from the spot of heat it created. He squeezed her wrist tighter.

Suzuki-san's expression was stoic. "You should also understand that the better you cooperate, the better recommendation we can give the judge." His voice went deep with menace. "Believe me, we will pry the truth out of you. It's up to you to decide how long—and how unpleasant—the process will be."

And so the first interminable day of it began.

Morning. Her third day in detention. The law stated Suzuki-san had to bring her before the judge that day, outline the case against her, and request a warrant to keep her in detention.

It would all be for show. He could keep her there as long as he wanted.

Footsteps echoed at the end of the hall. Panic crept up from her belly. She forced it away, straightened her spine, and braced herself for Zugaikotsu and his leer. She was going back to that room.

He strutted into view. She screwed her eyes shut and worked at summoning the strength of will to endure what would come next. Several more hours of Suzuki-san. And the police rotation. No name badges. No introductions. Different voices, different faces, different volume levels. But again and again the same questions. Taking it by turns and wearing her down.

There was nothing more to tell them—except about the *yakuza* and the poison she never bought. She'd let enough people down already. She wasn't going to add one more broken promise to the list.

"*Horyo.* Hurry."

Her gut went as watery as her rice-porridge breakfast. "*Hai.*" She tried to stand but her right leg wouldn't straighten beneath her—bruised and stiff from a vicious kick the day before. She made a second wobbly effort and lurched onto her feet.

Zugaikotsu conducted her up the usual corridor, past a row of identical cells. He ushered her into a room she hadn't seen before. The visitation room. Long and narrow, divided by a windowed wall. A stained counter ran along her side of the dingy glass, with two mismatched chairs. And on the other side—

Akira-san. With a generous swath of blood-stained gauze taped across his neck, but alive.

Zugaikotsu, the detention center, the beatings. All of it disappeared in a wild rush of joy and relief. "*Onii-san,*" she breathed. She took a half-step toward the glass before she registered his companion and froze. *Delham?* The *gaijin* pilot—here? Her heart hammered. They'd brought him in to accuse her. And Akira-san was part of it.

Zugaikotsu pressed a heavy hand on her shoulder and pushed her into the chair. Which was a good thing, since her legs no longer seemed inclined to support her weight.

Delham caught her eyes and bowed in his seat. A wave of disgust flooded her. She dropped into a deep bow to disguise it. If she'd done what she was supposed to, he wouldn't be there. Confucius said not to share the same sky with your enemy. Here she was under the same roof.

She lingered with her face to her lap and took long breaths, working to compose herself. Zugaikotsu settled into the chair beside her. A second guard stood on the visitors' side of the room, just inside the door.

Zugaikotsu addressed them. "I will remind you of the

rules concerning this visit. You will confine your conversation to approved matters. You will not attempt to communicate with the *horyo* by gesture, in writing, or"—he directed a pointed glare at Delham—"in any foreign tongue. The visit will last no longer than thirty minutes." He encompassed them all with a withering gaze. "I am authorized to conclude it at any time I deem you've violated these rules. Understood?"

Akira-san bobbed a bow. "*Hai.* May I translate this to Reverend Delham?"

The guard grunted his agreement. Akira-san spoke a few sentences to the *gaijin* in English. Delham nodded as he listened, then gave the guard a brisk nod and a "*Hai.*"

"You may proceed," Zugaikotsu said.

She took another deep breath, anxiety roiling her gut. "Please forgive me, brother. I am very happy to see you. I hope you know I never meant to hurt you." She kept herself from looking at the *gaijin*—at his chest, which that knife should have punctured.

"Mi-chan." Akira-san's throat worked. "I've been trying to come to talk to you." He glanced at the guard at the door. "But it was nearly impossible to get clearance."

She spoke quickly to Akira-san, confident the *gaijin* wouldn't understand. "It's wonderful to see you. I'm so relieved. But tell me the truth, ah? Why is *he* here?"

Akira-san responded slowly, enunciating each syllable, clearly for Delham's benefit. "Reverend Delham asked to come. He has something he wants to say to you."

"To me?"

Akira-san gave the *gaijin* a slight bow.

She sat straight, lifted her chin, and looked Delham in the eye. She might be a prisoner but that didn't mean she'd yield.

Delham leaned toward her, his broad forehead gathering into furrows. "I for—"

The guard half stood, brows knit. "*Japanese!*"

"Sorry—uh, *sumimasen.*" Delham started again. "*Wata...ah...Watashi ha anata...woyurusu.*"

I forgive you. At least she thought that was what he was trying to say. His Japanese was barely comprehensible. But something in his hazel eyes caught her—a soft light she didn't expect. And this from the enemy she'd done everything in her power to bury a knife in.

A wave of warmth rose to her cheeks.

Delham turned to Akira-san. He opened his mouth as if to speak, then shot a glance at Zugaikotsu and closed it. "Please," he said to Akira-san, and extended a hand in her direction.

Akira-san nodded. "Here's what Reverend Delham came to say. I can perhaps express it better in our language. It's true he piloted the plane that bombed the Sumitomo Aircraft Factory. But he is broken-hearted about"—he closed his eyes for an instant, making a visible effort to swallow—"little Hiro-chan. Sometimes bombs kill the innocents." He looked into her eyes, his own glistening. "Reverend Delham wants you to know that's not anything he wanted."

She stared at him. *Sometimes bombs kill the innocents.* He had no picture at all. Those long nights of furious orange rain, followed by days spent filing past rows of blackened corpses, looking for anything she could identify. The sickly-sweet smell of charred flesh that stayed on her for a week.

"Ten thousand dead, Akira-san. Ten thousand, here in Osaka. One hundred thousand in Tokyo. I walked and walked, day after day. Never found them. Not Mama-san. Not our grandparents." She fixed her eyes on a stain on the counter, trying to push the unspeakable memories from her head.

Delham stood and bowed, low enough to grace a baroness. "*Watashi o yurushite, kudasai.*" *Please forgive me.* To her surprise, moisture glistened on the missionary's lashes. "*Senso wa warui kotodesu.*" *War is a bad thing.*

She bowed in her chair but said nothing. What could be said? One could forgive a child for breaking a plate. Or accept a friend's apology if her words offended. But this man had taken the life of her little brother, before he'd even had one. Other than a death for a death, nothing could atone for that.

"Mi-chan," Akira-san's voice was soft. "I don't know what those firestorms were like." He took a wry glance at his scarred hand. "I've had my own experiences with American bombing, but I don't know what anything was like here. I forgive you for anything you had to do. And I hope you can forgive me for not coming home."

The silence grew heavy.

"You know some of my story. I know so little of yours."

"Really?" Irony blistered her reply. "I was sure Captain Oda would tell you all about it."

Akira-san winced. "*Hai.* He told me a few things, but here's the important one—you've been taking care of Papa-san ever since the war. Alone." He leaned toward the glass.

She managed to bring her eyes to his face. It was taut with regret.

He gave her a faint smile. "Here's a lesson I've learned, Mi-chan. Hatred is a prison. Forgiveness is God's gift that frees you from it."

Zugaikotsu's expression hardened with suspicion. "Foreign religion. Not approved topic."

She looked back and forth between her visitors, trying to decide how to feel. Her brother forgave her—that was wonderful news. But what did some foreign deity have to do with that?

As for Delham. Was an enemy's forgiveness supposed to mean something?

"We've all been through so much, sister," Akira-san flexed his scarred hand, probably not realizing he did it. "Many wounds. Deep wounds. But now it's time for healing."

Healing. "Your neck, *Onii-san.* Where I stabbed you. Does it hurt much?"

He gave her a rueful smile. "It hurts a lot, little sister. But bodies mend."

Of course. Bodies could mend or die. But honor—honor transcended death. Duty to family transcended death. She choked back those words. "Please forgive me, Akira-san."

His smile was like sunlight beaming through the dingy room. "I forgive you. I told you that."

"*Arigato.*" She bowed, still not sure how to feel. She had so much more to ask him. And they had to be running out of time. "Did you see Papa-san? How is he?"

And how did he react to his not-so-glorious, not-so-dead son?

Akira-san's back went stiff and his smile dissolved.

"Captain Oda told me the doctor felt seeing me would be too great a shock for Papa-san in his current state."

"I am sorry," she said in a soft voice. "I'm sure that was painful to hear. But Captain Oda does know Papa-san well."

"I hope I can see him soon. I hope he can find some forgiveness in his heart for me."

She snorted. "He found none for me."

Akira-san turned to the American. "*Kudasai?*" He gestured at the door.

"*Hai.*" Delham gave her another genteel bow. "*Sayanara, Matsuura-san.*"

The guard let the American out. Akira-san waited until the door had closed. "You can't do it, ah?"

"Do what?"

"Grant him your forgiveness."

"Of course not. What would it even mean?" Irony wormed its way back into her tone. "But apparently you can."

"I couldn't have, five years ago. But when—" He glanced at Zugaikotsu. "Let's just say I see a lot of things differently now."

Clearly.

"In the hospital, and in the prison camp, I heard things and saw things that gave me a great deal to think about. There's strength and discipline in the Yamato ways, Mi-chan. But there's also a very real power our way doesn't teach us. A real freedom."

"And you're learning this power? From your Delham?"

"*Hai.* You think you can honor Hiro-chan's death through another death?"

"Approved subjects," Zugaikotsu growled. "I won't warn you again."

Akira-san made a quick bow in the guard's direction. "Forgive me." He looked into Miyako's eyes. "It doesn't work that way."

"How does it work, then?" She lifted her chin. "You and your new friend are wiser than Confucius, ah?"

"There's been a death already. It's paid for already. *Iesu's* death, Mi-chan."

Zugaikotsu glowered. "Enough. Approved subjects only. The visit is done. *Horyo*, come."

She heaved a sigh of exasperation. *Iesu* again. And he'd gotten their visit cut short over this madness.

"Mi-chan." Akira-san clenched his hand into a fist and rested it on the glass between them. "You know I loved Hiro-chan, too."

She rested her palm on the glass over his fist, tears hot behind her eyelids again. "I know."

Zugaikotsu grabbed her wrist. "*Horyo.* Come." He yanked her off the chair and propelled her toward the door.

Akira-san's voice echoed behind her. "I love you, sister. And I'll find you a lawyer."

She stared at him over her shoulder until the detention center swallowed her.

Chapter Forty

ZUGAIKOTSU DELIVERED HER TO HER CELL. He watched her for a moment, eyes aflame, tongue snaking over his lower lip. "Thought you were the forty-eighth *ronin*, ah? Little girls shouldn't play with knives. Or they wind up worthless *horyo*." He gave her bars a shake, then walked off.

She slumped onto the floor and lay still. A wave of revulsion washed over her. *Worthless horyo.* Worthless whore had been bad enough.

After a long moment, she pulled her aching legs beneath her and pushed herself painfully up into *seiza*, eyes on the bars. A dingy light from the small window behind her filtered through them. It stamped a pattern on the squalid wall across the hall. A rectangle of dim light striped with—what else?—vertical bars. Nothing to do but mark its slow progress down the wall and try to stave off sleep.

Nothing left for me but a lot of empty years.

Her mind drifted to Akira-san. One soul in all the world had shown some interest in what happened to her. What did he mean by these words? *There's been a death—already. It's paid for—already.* What did a foreigner's death centuries ago have to do with their brother?

He rejected their need for *kataki-uchi*—for blood to pay for Hiro-chan's blood. She was in prison for nothing, according to him. And this Delham was teaching him a better path.

The temperature dropped, and the light faded as she mulled this over. She went back to studying the peeling paint and imagining herself at the Oasis. The coals would glow in the brazier. There'd be that bowl of apples, and she'd sit with a newspaper. It would be lovely to have something to read.

Something to read. Delham's brochure. It might hold the key to Akira-san's madness. She brought it to mind as clearly as she could.

Solitary confinement. Hunger and weariness. Anger and

fear.

It all hit close to home.

In stories of spiritual awakening she'd heard, release from the turbulence of life came through meditation. *Obliterate self. Become empty.* Oh, she'd tried all that. Delham's story didn't seem to involve any of it. Only a simple plea for forgiveness to this *Iesu.*

She supposed she could try that. She'd prayed to the ancestors and to many *kami-sama*—Shinto gods. Perhaps this wouldn't be so different. It did feel like a betrayal, though. Certainly Papa-san would think so. But she felt an unexpected little lift at the realization that Akira-san would be pleased.

She prostrated herself to the floor. "*Iesu, kami-sama* my brother speaks of. If you can hear me, help me. If you please." She stayed there a long moment, forehead on the floor and eyes closed, waiting to see if anything would happen. Weariness swelled. Thoughts faded.

Spiritual awakening required patience.

An indeterminate period of time passed, and something did happen—boots echoed on the floorboards. She jerked into her best *seiza*, spine bamboo straight.

Not Zogaikotsu, please. An involuntary shudder rippled over her shoulders.

The guard came into view. Not Zogaikotsu, but one of the others, the stolid one with the square head. He paced to the center of her barred panel and stopped. He glanced up and down the hallway, tension written across his face.

What was he up to? Her stomach soured. He turned his focus to her, and she dropped her eyes to the floor.

"*Horyo.*" The word came in a stage whisper.

Che. What did he want?

She looked up to see him holding an apple between the bars. Plump and lovely, its rich red skin dappled with soft gold.

"Come." He took another furtive glance up the hall. "Quick."

He was taunting her. A sick joke. He'd pull it away when she reached for it. Or worse. Club her for leaving her *seiza* posture.

But the lure of the apple was too strong. She stood and took a hesitant step toward him. To her amazement, he held the fruit steady until she grasped it. It was firm and round in her hand, its dappled skin unblemished.

"*Seiza*, please. And eat fast." He bobbed a hasty bow and was gone.

She stood, frozen. "*Arigato*," she said, too late.

She got into *seiza* and held the apple to her nostrils. The fragrance it gave out was as tender a promise as a betrothal vow. *Eat fast.* She sank her teeth into it. It came apart with a satisfying crunch. Her mouth filled with what must have been the sweetest juice she'd ever experienced. She stripped it of every morsel of edible flesh and dropped the bare core into the latrine. The fruit's delicate scent lingered on her fingers, carrying images of soft spring skies and blossom-laden branches.

Stolid had taken a real risk to do this for her—a prisoner. Why?

A realization hit with such force that she gasped. The guard's bold act of kindness. Toward *her*, a mere *horyo*.

She'd prayed, and something had happened that looked like an answer.

Help me, Iesu? Perhaps you did.

It proved nothing. There'd been times she'd prayed to Kannon or the ancestors and things had gone her way. She smiled a little, remembering Yamada-san's face when she turned up the three cherry cards.

Shu Iesu, if you truly hear me, please show me.

Her eyes drifted closed. She wrenched them open. The succession of sleepless nights had worn on her. She had to keep herself awake, somehow, or risk another beating.

There'd been more in Delham's brochure—a few lines of their Christian writings. Perhaps she could work at remembering those. She bent all her powers of concentration to the task. She dug the words out of the murk at the base of her memory in hard-won snatches.

*...mata nanji kokoro...*What's more, with your heart.
*...yomigaerashishi...*Back from the spirit world.
*...shinzeba...*Believe.

That was it. Nothing else.

Fading again. She shifted her weight and tried to think of a peppy song she could hum to stay awake. She picked up a tune, but it trailed off.

Drifting... Had to...stop...drifting...

Your eyes. Open them. Miyako did, with a start.

Nothing new to see. Bars of solid steel in front of her, bars of shifting light and shadow on the wall beyond them. The box of light had traveled down the wall a bit. It rested now on the spot where her imagination kept conjuring a horse. On his mane.

And all at once she saw that mane, a fringe of pale gold against his rich chestnut coat. He tossed his head and the fringe flipped. He snorted, looked up at her with great liquid eyes and pawed the ground.

She stood, full of wonder, and he came to her, nickering. He nuzzled her ribs and burrowed his nose into the leather at the side of her breastplate.

Breastplate?

Hai. *The filthy skirt and sweater she'd worn since Sunday were nowhere to be seen. She was dressed in armor as splendid as one of her ancient ancestors arrayed for battle. Silk flowed beneath it, in all the hues of spring.*

She stroked the stallion's neck. Felt the power of his muscles beneath the warm velvet of his coat. She mounted him with a fluid motion.

He pranced and reared. Flung that pale gold mane.

Elation broke over her and she laughed out loud. Conforming her body to his motion felt like the most natural thing she'd ever done. She knew, somehow, he was eager to take her on a grand adventure.

But those bars. They blocked the path forward, stretching into the clouds as high as she could see. The bars surrounded them, confining them to a space he could cross in three paces.

Trapped. The stallion neighed, snorted, and arched his neck.

Their barred enclosure stood on a tiny island. Craggy cliffs fell away into roiling surf on every side. Forbidding precipices confronted them from across a broad chasm.

Pray. Ask.

It was a faint impression before, but now the words came full and distinct—a real voice. A man's voice, except that it seemed to come from everywhere at once.

The voice echoed again. What is it you need?

"Please. We need to get out, sir."

A half-dozen bars melted away. The stallion capered, pranced through the opening and stood, breathtakingly close to the point where the cliff plunged. She stared down the granite face at the thin rocky strand, the churning water.

What is it you need, Daughter?

Daughter?

Ask.

It wasn't Papa-san's voice. And the feeling that enveloped her at its sound was something she'd never experienced in Papa-san's presence. A sense of being absolutely known, yet completely accepted.

"Please. A bridge, sir."

A bridge appeared. But not like any she'd seen. A perfectly smooth rectangular surface. No arch. No guardrails.

But how could it bear their weight? No support—no piers, no cable.

The place-less voice. Shinzeba.

The sense of being known—and loved—to the very essence flooded her again. "Believe? Please, sir. Believe what?"

A jarring noise thundered from somewhere in the distance. A clanging sound, like the clash of weapons. She jerked—

Awake.

Cheek against worn *tatami* mat. Body sticky with filth—reeking. Belly screaming for something substantial.

Zugaikotsu loomed over her. Eyes aflame above sepulchral cheeks, he pushed at her ribs with his baton. "No sleeping, *horyo.*" He delivered a kick to her diaphragm.

Pain exploded through her torso. She folded and sucked at the air in a vain effort to fill her lungs.

"*Seiza.*" He towered over her, pounded his baton into his other hand.

She managed to take a breath. Blinked back unwelcome

tears, stifled a moan, and pushed herself into the requisite kneel. Straightened the stained sweater that had taken the place of her silk finery.

He stood with his unnerving leer and watched her collect herself. "Come."

Out into the dingy corridor again. Miyako wheezed for breath. Her eyes anchored on the peeled-paint steed. But he remained flat and motionless, all the color leeched from his pale gold mane.

For an instant, she let herself drift into the bright world of her dream. Pictured herself free, thundering along on the stallion's broad chestnut back over brilliant green meadows starred with tiny pink flowers. The weight of a firm, fragrant apple in her hand.

Zogaikotsu's baton struck her spine. A pang of loss squeezed her chest. It was only a dream, and a lie. This squalid hallway was her brutal truth.

They turned right out of the cellblock. The interrogation room door loomed a few feet down the hall. Zogaikotsu prodded her along with his baton. His arm snaked past her to open the door.

Another ten or twelve hours of questioning? Bile burned up her throat. She was in no condition for this. She stepped in.

Just one man sat behind the table this time, his cane propped behind him. *Oda?* Her gut went hollow. The police captain looked up at Zogaikotsu, his expression dour. "Leave us."

Zogaikotsu bowed and left.

Alone with Captain Oda. She willed her legs to hold her steady.

"Sit."

She sank into the chair, and he studied her for a long moment, his expression unreadable. She sat very still, almost not daring to breathe. What new doom was he about to unleash into her life?

"You failed, ah?" he said at last.

"*Hai.*" That was beyond dispute.

"I am prepared to give you a chance to succeed."

She stiffened. "What?" The sound bounced off the bare walls. She lowered her voice to a whisper. "Why? Why would you do this?"

"For your father, of course. To live to see his *haji* removed, by his own offspring." Oda stared somewhere behind her shoulder. "It's clear your brother won't do it. I would never have guessed it, but it seems you're the one who inherited Captain Matsuura's spirit, yes? In spite of the fact you're a woman. And in spite of the, ah, unfortunate turn your life has taken." He produced a pack of Chesterfields and offered her one. "All the more reason, yes? You can make amends for all that."

She reached for the cigarette. "Pardon my asking, sir, but how?"

"Ah." He settled into the chair and relaxed his shoulders. "We have it worked out. Your escape. Your next attempt." A smug smile played at his lips. "We've procured a weapon you can handle. I'll provide the details later. But you can trust we've worked it through a bit better than you did last Sunday, yes?" His smile evaporated. He leaned forward, fixed his eyes on her face. "You needn't fail again, Matsuura-san."

She sat a little straighter. Her dream... What if it came, not from the Christian god, but from the Matsuura ancestors? A fresh invitation to her moment of greatness?

Oda drummed his fingers on the table. "It's not without risk, young lady. But there's a chance you'll escape with your freedom. If not, what is that, in the face of such a glorious opportunity?"

Glorious. A sense of inevitability gripped her, as it had that night at the church. "What indeed?"

Oda's features shone with the nobility of his ideals. "Of course, you must be ready to spend yourself, should it come to that. Like any true-hearted soldier, yes? Prepared to go to the grave with honor."

Spend herself. She'd been born for that. Like a soldier. Like her father. Like her father's father. Like—

George-san. Her mind served up an image of her blond lover. And of that apple core, wobbling across the sidewalk. Nestling into the muck and dead leaves in the gutter.

Pain twisted her chest. Spend herself? She'd been doing that for years. To the very core.

Oda leaned toward her. "Your father wants this more than he wants his own life. I wish you'd seen the pride on his face when he heard about your first attempt, ah? When you succeed, you'll have done everything a daughter should." He sat back. The light caught the braid on his epaulets. His braid and brass had gleamed the same way in the hospital the day she ceased to be Papa-san's daughter.

She stabbed her cigarette into the ashtray. That moment was engraved on her mind like carving on jade. *Daughter.* Another voice had called her that, minutes before. A placeless voice. She could still hear its echo, still sense the comfort and acceptance that had flooded her at that word.

God still has a use for you. Those were Akira-san's words. The dream may not have been real, but Akira-san was. And Delham. And the guard she'd nicknamed Stolid, with his apple.

Oda studied her from across the battered table. "You'll be the faithful daughter your father needs now, ah?"

She looked into his face—her father's old friend. Deep gullies seamed his skin, cemented there through decades of ruthlessness. Driven by what?

Honor. The quest that had fueled the old Japan. That still drove her father. But that Japan was gone. More than gone—incinerated. And in the Japan that replaced it, women had sold her. Men had violated her. Soldiers reeking of sweat and whiskey, with enormous freckled fingers wrapped around brothel tickets, had used her like yesterday's merchandise.

She'd been as trapped out there as she was in here.

Perhaps there was a higher sort of honor. A duty to a different Father.

Oda shifted in his chair. "Are you ready to go ahead with this?"

She looked into his weather-beaten face and swallowed. "It will be difficult."

"What do you mean?"

"What I mean, Captain Oda"—she paused and took a deep breath—"is no."

Miyako sprawled where Zogaikotsu had flung her, face down on the hard floor of her cell. His voice growled from above her. "*Seiza, horyo.*"

Hai, she'd kneel. The second she could get up. She squeezed her eyes shut, tried to focus her energy past her pain and into her muscles. Blood pooled in her mouth. She swallowed it, tasting salty copper.

His boot squelched the straw floor mat beside her. It took everything she had, but she pushed herself into a kneel. She brought her forearm up to wipe a bit of moisture off her mouth. It left a vermilion smudge on her sweater.

He stood over her, baton raised. He watched her for a second or two, a slight smile parting his lips. He spun on his heel and clanged the bars shut behind him.

She sat motionless until the echo of his footsteps faded. Wiped her mouth again. She looked around the dismal cell. Holes like this were going to be her home for a long time to come.

Daughter. The memory of that voice flooded her with warmth and peace. She breathed a sigh and closed her eyes.

As long as she had her Father in heaven, a cell would be home enough.

Now. Where to start? She bowed her head. "*Lord Iesu,*" she began.

Chapter Forty-One

Tuesday, February 22, 1949, Osaka, Japan
Fifty-Second Day in Police Custody

MIYAKO STOOD IN A SUNNY TILED vestibule, blinking and rubbing her wrists.

The guard she'd nicknamed Stolid grinned, the handcuffs he'd just taken off her dangling from his hand. He bowed, smiled, and opened the door in front of her. "We're done with you, Matsuura-san. This way."

Done? Was it a prison transfer, or the trial where they'd make her incarceration permanent?

After weeks in her tiny cell, the lobby beyond that door seemed vast. And radiant—so bright she couldn't lift her eyes from the floor. She could see two pairs of shoes. Two men, one standing and one seated on a battered wooden chair.

All that space. Those men. She fought the urge to shrink into a corner.

"Go on, Matsuura-san. Unless you don't want to be released."

She shot Stolid a sharp look. "Released?" She glanced down at her filthy clothes. Shame settled on her like a weighted blanket. *Released!*

The standing man took a step toward them. "Mi-chan!" She knew the voice.

She squinted at him, eyes adjusting to the glare. "Brother?" Was this real, or another dream?

That beloved voice again. "Excuse me, sir. Can my sister come out here?"

The guard gestured her forward. "*Hai.* Please proceed, Matsuura-san."

Her knees, wobbly from so many hours in *seiza*, went even weaker. But she managed to take one hesitant step.

Akira-san strode to her, caught her up in his arms, and swung her in an exuberant circle. He put her down, and the room spun. She braced herself against his chest, giggling like a schoolgirl. She took a breath. How long had it been since she'd laughed?

"Akira-san, are they releasing me?"

He smiled. "*Hai.* Let's get you out of this place. We can talk more in the taxi."

The smell of sandalwood in his aftershave and wool in his jacket convinced her it wasn't a dream. She clung to him for a long moment, then took a half step back, shame pressing her feet into the floor. She brushed his lapel, possessed by a compulsion to remove a layer of invisible filth she'd left there.

"Congratulations, Matsuura-san."

She stiffened. She'd forgotten the second man. Another voice she knew all too well.

She forced a smile and bowed. "Suzuki-san. *Arigato.*"

Her prosecutor responded with a perfunctory head-bob. "The judge has agreed to release you into your brother's custody. He has your parole instructions. Mind you follow them to the letter."

"*Hai. Domo arigato.*"

Akira-san gave her shoulders a one-armed squeeze and picked up a package from a chair. He held it out to her with a small bow. "I brought you new clothes."

"Ah, so thoughtful." She clutched it to her chest as if the package itself could hide her soiled garments. "How is Papa-san?"

A deep shadow crossed his features. "We'll talk, Mi-chan. Go ahead and change. The ladies' room is over there." He gave her a wan smile. "I'll wait."

Her heart caved in at the look on his face. But he was right. There would be a better time and place to hear his news. She took the package with her to the ladies' room.

Clean, white porcelain fixtures glowed in filtered light. A small square of mirror hung above the basin. The hollow-cheeked, grimy creature who stared at her from its surface was someone she hardly recognized. A wave of nausea hit, making her steady herself against the sink.

She took deep breaths until the feeling passed, then fumbled the package open. A blue rayon dress with a modest white collar. A toothbrush and tooth powder. A comb, a lipstick—not her usual vibrant red, but it didn't matter—even a bar of scented soap and a washcloth.

Her brother had thought of everything. At least everything a man could be expected to think of. She held the soap to her nose and filled her lungs with its pleasant crisp scent of gardenia.

Cleaning up in the bathroom carried her thoughts to her old place. An image of Papa-san lying on his futon slammed into her mind's eye. A pang of longing struck her. To see him, and perhaps be rewarded with some glimmer of recognition of how much she'd sacrificed for him. To go on serving him, if he'd let her.

She let the thought go. She'd never stop loving him with all her heart, but she weighed her actions now through the eyes of a different Father. She had to.

It took a few minutes of scrubbing to make herself presentable. The process left her skin red and the washcloth streaked with gray-brown dirt. She slipped the dress over her head, fighting an undercurrent of irrational fear that she'd re-emerge in the lobby to find Akira-san vanished like a mist. She felt at the waistband where the fabric hung loose. The white linen cuffs flapped around her bony upper arms.

She frowned at her reflection. *So much weight lost.*

She retraced her steps to the lobby. True to his word, Akira-san stood where she'd left him, in animated discussion with Suzuki-san.

"They'll understand she's not—" He saw her and stopped, his face relaxing into an approving smile. "That's much better. We can go shopping tomorrow, ah?"

Suzuki gave her a glance and a perfunctory nod before returning his attention to her brother. "I need to be able to tell them we asked her, Mr. Matsuura."

Akira-san winced and faced her. "It seems someone leaked news of your release to the press, Mi-chan. Quite a few reporters are waiting for you."

"Reporters! Akira-san, no. What would I say?"

Stolid spoke from the vestibule door. "If I might make a suggestion?"

"Please."

"Suzuki-san could keep them occupied out front, ah? There's a fire escape at the rear. I can take you two through the back office."

Suzuki-san acknowledged that with a brisk nod. "Fair enough. I'll give you a couple minutes to get through the building, then I'll hold their attention as long as I can."

Akira-san held out a simple trench coat for her. She slipped into it.

Her prosecutor dropped into a real bow, from the waist. "Best of luck, Matsuura Miyako."

"*Arigato*, Suzuki-san."

Stolid led them through a double door on their right, then on past a row of lockers. Up a flight of stairs. A brisk walk along a narrow corridor with peeling paint led them to a double-paned window. Stolid shoved it open.

"Through here. Hurry."

Akira-san clambered over the sill and half-lifted her into a gray day. A bracing breeze pushed tendrils of hair across her cheek. An overgrown plum tree spread a cloud of delicate pink above her head, its branches invading the fire escape's steel banisters.

Pinks, greens, brick reds. For the first time in months, something other than dismal browns and grays. She took it all in, giddy with the realization she was about to walk free. She'd lost all but the slimmest thread of hope this could happen.

She had to wait until her legs steadied before she could bow to Stolid. "*Arigato*, Kusumi-san. I'll never forget you."

Akira-san touched her shoulder. "Shh! I hear them." He gestured toward the rusted steel stairs.

Indistinct voices echoed from the front of the building. She gave the guard one last bow then hurried down, her brother behind her. She did her best to walk so her worn shoes wouldn't clang on the steel. Plum branches brushed against her clothes and caught in her hair.

The stairs deposited them in an alley, where fallen flowers dusted pocked concrete like pale pink snow. Akira-san hurried her toward the far end. He stopped at the edge of a busy sidewalk, keeping her hidden behind him, and took a good look around. The heady fragrance of jasmine from a hedge at her feet lay heavy on the breeze.

Much of the tension drained from his shoulders. "I think we left them behind. Although I know we haven't heard the last of them." He glanced at her and broke into a laugh, then plucked something from her hair and held it out to her. A perfect pink blossom nestled in his palm.

She lifted it from his hand and stroked one unbelievably fragile petal. She couldn't take her eyes off it. A plum blossom. Vanguard of spring. Symbol of new life, in triumph over hardship. The tiny stamens and pollen grains picked up its soft shade in a vibrant magenta hue. She silently thanked *Iesu* for the gift.

Akira-san spoke, his voice soft with wonder. "I always knew God had a better plan for you than rotting away in that place." He guided her down the sidewalk, putting the police headquarters with its squalid memories farther behind them. "Is there anything you'd like before we get you settled at home?"

Home. She gazed into his face—even his scars were precious now. She shook her head. That single word encompassed everything she yearned for.

Her focus sank to the pavement. She still had something to tell him. She couldn't imagine he'd want to give her a home once he knew.

They settled into a cab. Of all the things they had to talk about, Papa-san was the topic that seemed easiest, given that the driver might listen.

"How is he?" Miyako said.

"He's not good, I hear." Akira-san snorted. "Still indomitable. He won't see me. But he might see you."

"Do you think so?"

His lips twisted with irony. "We'll find out, ah? You may have redeemed yourself, in his view."

She winced. "To think I once saw life his way."

"We all did, once."

She followed his eyes out the window, to a lot filled with charred rubble.

Akira-san's flat was two levels above the street, modest but clean. He hung her coat on a coatrack next to his and showed her a few more things he'd purchased for her— another demure dress with a high collar, a handbag that didn't look too worn, a housecoat. "To get you by until we go shopping," he said. And finally, he bowed and handed her a box covered in silver foil.

"Another gift? I'm overwhelmed, Akira-san."

"It's the most important thing I have for you."

"*Domo arigato*, then." She slipped the top off the box. A thick book nestled inside, bound in blue leather, with "Holy Bible" etched in silver on its cover. "It's beautiful. But what is it?"

"This is the book that will teach you what it means to be a *Kirishitan*."

She caught it to her chest. Tears filled her eyes. "You are so thoughtful."

He rested a gentle hand on her arm. "I can't believe you're finally here. What would you like to do? Eat? Sleep?"

She sniffled and almost laughed. "*Hai* and *hai*. A little something to eat first, please."

"Do you want to go out for *udon*?"

The street. The crowds. Her pulse surged, proving she wasn't ready. She bit her lip and shook her head. "Maybe later. But if we could have something light here, that would be perfect."

He made a grand gesture toward a cushion next to the low table. "I'll make tea and we can catch up, ah? Without a guard or a driver listening in."

The words *catch up* sent a ribbon of fear twisting through her breast. *If only I didn't have to break the spell. If only I could stay.*

She settled onto the cushion. Feeling something soft beneath her knees for the first time in weeks lent extra magic to the moment. The tiny plum blossom still nestled in her hand. She did what she could to straighten two crumpled petals. She placed it reverently on the corner of the table, trying to ignore the anxiety chewing at her gut.

Like her old place, the flats on Akira-san's floor shared a single kitchen down the hall, but he kept a few kitchen things in a cupboard in the corner. He switched on an electric teakettle, then fished around and produced a box of rice crackers, a plate of pastries, and a jar of sweet pickled plums. He placed a pair of cups on a tray and organized the snacks in dishes.

She watched his every movement, trying to memorize the moment. The gentle homey rumble of boiling water filled the room.

No reason I have to tell him right away, ah?

Delaying the inevitable. "How under heaven did you get me out of that place?"

He turned with a smile, knelt across from her, and placed the tray on the table between them. "Our friend"— emphasis on *our*—"Reverend Delham was responsible, Mi-chan. He pled your case very persistently with Suzuki-san."

She stared at him, astonished. "He did? After what I tried to do to him?"

"*Hai.* He told Suzuki-san you sincerely asked for forgiveness, and he insisted you should get it. He wouldn't give up. He used all his connections. He's a war hero, after all."

Tears blurred her vision again. "That was so kind of him."

"*Hai.* He's an amazing person, Mi-chan. I didn't tell you sooner because I didn't want to give you false hope." The teakettle whistled. Akira-san stood and returned with a pot of tea. "Shall we pray over our first meal in your new home?"

She shot him a smile. "You can't imagine how much I would love that." *The prayer, and the home.* She bowed her head.

Akira-san prayed. "*Shu Iesu*, thank you for the miracle you worked today in giving my sister back her freedom. May we always walk in freedom, and in the light of your presence. Please bless this meal together. Amen."

And may it not be our last. Amen. Maybe she could put off telling him until the next morning. Enjoy a few precious hours with him, at least.

Her eyes lingered on the porcelain teacups. One for him and one for her—like those his-and-hers bowls of sweet bean soup. That must have been another lifetime.

She picked up the teapot and poured for him.

"But your release comes with a price tag, Mi-chan."

She caught her breath and stopped pouring.

"You are going to have to talk to the press. Tell them what

a gracious thing the Americans have done for you."

She sighed. "I suppose that's fair. It will be painful, but I've endured worse." She looked into his face. "Far worse."

His eyes went soft with sympathy. "I'm so sorry for everything you've been through."

Something inside her shouted *now*. She tried to ignore it. But it had reached the point where it was harder not to speak about it, than to speak about it and accept the consequences.

She finished pouring. "*Onii-san*, there is something you need to know."

He chuckled and lifted his cup. "I'm sure there are a lot of things I need to know. Everything about your life. And vice versa."

"No. This is serious."

"All right, Mi-chan. Tell me."

She sipped at her tea. It did nothing to moisten the dry sand that seemed to have invaded her mouth. "When you invite me to stay, you need to know it's not just me."

He peered at her, teacup frozen in midair. "I don't understand."

The clock on his middle shelf let out a loud tick. Then another.

Out with it. "I'm pretty sure I'm pregnant, *onii-san*."

He set his cup down and blinked, like he thought it might help if he cleared his vision. "Ah." That was all.

She ran her forefinger along the fluted rim of the bowl of plums. "I guess I'm in my third month."

Air whistled as he sucked it in through his teeth.

She took a deep breath. She fixed her gaze on the tiny blossom by her sleeve so she wouldn't have to read the disappointment on his face. "There are other places I can stay. I think my friend Kimi would probably—"

"No." His hand landed on top of hers. "No, Mi-chan."

She looked up into eyes that shone with tears. "I've waited years to find you," he said. "You are not leaving now. No matter what."

"No matter what?"

He gave her a level gaze and shook his head.

"No matter if I don't know who the father is?" *Not for sure.*

George-san's face hovered in her mind, laughter crinkling the corners of his ocean-colored eyes.

"No." Akira-san's voice was quiet but emphatic.

"No matter"—she gathered all her courage and pushed the worst part out in a rush—"if the father might well be American?"

A shadow crossed his face. "No." The response took longer this time, but it was just as emphatic. "Mi-chan, whatever happens, we will deal with it together."

"Really, *Onii-san?* A mixed-blood child?" The words seemed to rip half her heart out with them.

He stood and took measured steps to the window. He stared down at the street for a long moment, pressing both fists into the sill. "Your child. My nephew or niece." He swiveled and faced her, tears glistening on his cheeks. "A person *Iesu* died for. That's all that matters, Mi-chan." He gave her a thin smile. "I may be just a two-legged ghost, but I'm not going to vanish. This ghost is here for you. And your child."

He knelt at the table, beside her this time, and gave her shoulders a squeeze. He pushed the bowl of pickled plums toward her. "Now. Please eat."

She leaned into his chest. Warm and solid, not ghostly at all.

She shot a relieved smile up at him. "*Arigato.* For everything." She dabbed away her tears and lifted her chopsticks. She was ravenous. "Now, you must tell me all about how the war went for you. I want every detail."

"Of course." He toyed with a pastry, then looked at her with an expression she couldn't read. "But not every detail. I'll stick to the interesting parts, if that's okay."

I'd Love to Hear from You

As an author, I place tremendous value on your feedback! If you enjoyed this novel, could you please consider leaving a review? Many readers weigh reviews heavily when shopping for books. If you leave one you could help another reader experience the power of this story.

If you're willing, it's easy to leave a review on Amazon by simply swiping left from the last page of an Amazon Kindle book. The reader's bonus page on my website (www.lthompsonbooks.com/plum-blooms-bonuses) provides quick links to leave reviews in other venues.

More Ways to Connect with Linda and *Brands from the Burning*

I have some exclusive reader's bonuses for you that will enhance your experience with *The Plum Blooms in Winter*! Please click over and claim them at this page on my website: www.lthompsonbooks.com/plum-blooms-bonuses

You can also sign up to receive updates on *Brands from the Burning Book Two: The Mulberry Leaf Whispers*, where Miyako's and Akira's story continues.

Other ways to connect with me:
Find my blog at: www.lthompsonbooks.com/blog
Like my author page on FB: @lthompsonbooks
Follow me on Twitter: @lthompsonbooks
Follow me on Instagram: @lthompsonbooks
Follow me on Pinterest: lthompsonbooks
Follow me on Goodreads:
www.goodreads.com/author/show/18168157.Linda_Thompson

Author Note

Thank you so much for letting me share this story with you. It's my fond hope it will jump off the page and come to life as vividly for you as it has for me.

After I read a historical novel, I'm always curious to know how much of what I read is fiction and how much is fact. I feel it's important to answer that for this book. This is a work of fiction, but the bones of the story are true. And quite honestly, I'm humbled I've had the privilege to capture a story that centers on such heroes.

A POW-turned-war-hero did feel led to show the love of Christ to the nation that tortured and nearly starved him. In 1948, he returned to Japan as a missionary.

And a Japanese woman did determine to assassinate him, because a bomb his B-25 deployed killed a young man she loved. When she learned the former airman was slated to speak in her city, she showed up at the service with a knife in her purse, hoping to find a way to kill him. But she was so moved by his message of forgiveness that she gave up that idea, ultimately deciding to follow Jesus instead. (She did not make an actual attempt on his life.)

Here's a bit more historical background. On April 18, 1942, a mere six months after Pearl Harbor, eighty men took flight from the U.S.S. *Hornet* on a perilous volunteer mission to bomb Japan. The Doolittle Raid was a brilliant military success. But it left fifteen B-25 crews stranded in enemy-occupied China.

Thirteen crews were smuggled to freedom, at great risk, by the Chinese underground. Two crews were captured by the Japanese. The entire crew of *Bat Out of Hell* and the three who survived the crash of *Green Hornet* enjoyed Japanese prison "hospitality" for the duration of the war—forty months.

As you read in the novel, only four of those eight men came home. Lieutenant William Farrell, pilot of *Bat Out of Hell*; Lieutenant Dean Hallmark, pilot of *Green Hornet*; and Sargent Harold Spatz, gunner on *Bat Out of Hell*, were executed by firing squad in Kiangwan, China, on October 15, 1942. Lieutenant Robert Meder died of malnutrition on December 1, 1943.

In the novel, I've got the men from *Green Hornet* (Dean Hallmark, Robert Meder, and Chase Nielsen) playing themselves. Although, as the legal disclaimer states, events and characters are used fictitiously, and this novel should not be construed as representing an accurate historical narrative, I've done my best to depict these heroes in keeping with historical records I located in my research. Many of the details are drawn from the account of their imprisonment in *Four Came Home* by Carroll V. Glines[1], arguably the Doolittle Raid's foremost historian.

The Pensacola Payback is a fictional plane with a fictional crew. Dave Delham is an invention. However, his spiritual journey was inspired by that of a real (but very different) man—Jacob DeShazer, the bombardier on *Bat Out of Hell*. Reverend DeShazer's prison conversion and subsequent return to Japan as a missionary are documented in a couple of biographies: *DeShazer* by C. Hoyt Watson[2] and *Return of the Raider* by Jake's daughter, Carol Aiko DeShazer Dixon, and Donald M. Goldstein[3]. Both biographies include numerous excerpts from Jake's own comments and notes.

Sadly, the prison conditions this novel depicts are as true to the Raiders' actual experience as I know how to make them. I didn't invent the tortures, the physical abuse, the privation, or the long months of solitary confinement. Nor did I invent the Morse code, the mental exercises Lieutenant Meder led the men to undertake to preserve their acuity, the names scratched under tin cups—or the impact of the books.

Glines' account includes a moving joint statement on what receiving a copy of the Bible after so many months in prison meant to these men. All four airmen acknowledged that, while they had attended church as children, they had never fully grasped the gospel message, and never understood the meaning behind the Bible verses they had memorized. They credited the Bible, and the trust it led them to place in the God who authored it, with bringing them through their "valley of the shadow of death"[4] (Psalm 23:4).

Chen and the other Chinese villagers Dave meets in the

novel are fictional. No Raider participated in any kind of firefight in China. The Raiders were proud to say later that not one of them fired a shot in his own defense on the ground—which is why I don't have Dave fire that Colt .45. Dave's fictional interlude with Chen and Pete and Chen's family was a bit of my own thought experiment. It's estimated that the Japanese army slaughtered as many as 250,000 Chinese people in Zhejiang and Jiangxi provinces in retaliation for aiding the Raiders. An entire region was decimated. Whole towns destroyed. Men, women, and children indiscriminately slaughtered. Bacterial warfare agents—anthrax, cholera, typhoid, and paratyphoid—deployed, compounding the misery and devastation for any who tried to return.

If the Raiders could have foreseen the price their Chinese friends were going to pay for bringing them to safety, how would it have affected them?

As far as I know, Jacob DeShazer never attacked a guard. The guards did push some of the others past their limits. George Barr, the *Bat*'s navigator, threw a punch at a guard in Nanking. They gave him the straitjacket torture I make poor Dave endure. George described it as "the most harrowing experience of my life."[5]

Miyako and her family and friends are fictional, although the knife in her purse was real enough. She's a composite of three different women Jake describes in his biography. I did my best to make her a fair reflection of the plight of many young women in turbulent post-war Japan. It's estimated that 100,000 Japanese women were forced into prostitution during the desperate years following the war.

As for the historical woman who once purposed to take revenge on Reverend DeShazer, her name and the rest of her story are lost. We only get a glimpse of her in snippets Jake and his colleagues captured. She attended Jake DeShazer's meetings with the intention of plunging a knife into him. But his marvelous message of God's forgiving love spoke to her, to the point where she ultimately decided to follow Jesus Christ instead.

About midway through writing this novel, an early reader—my mother—asked why I felt it had to be written.

Why dredge up such excruciating stories from a generation past?

In my view, any novel worth writing (or reading) needs to be about something bigger than that particular story. Something timeless. On the surface, this one is about how a group of individuals survived a certain war and its aftermath. But on another level, it's about two clashing worldviews. Both Dave and Miyako are doing what they believe is right and noble. It puts them on a deadly collision course.

But they have more in common than it might appear. Both must come to a crisis of faith. And both must surrender the flawed ideas they grew up with about what creates a person's worth and what makes a hero. "And be not conformed to this world: but be ye transformed by the renewing of your mind, that ye may prove what is that good, and acceptable, and perfect, will of God" (Romans 12:2). This is true in any culture.

The sordid situations this novel portrays—armed conflict, abuse of power, abuse of women, thirst for vengeance—have existed throughout history. And sadly, they won't go away until history as we know it ends. They're part of the human condition. As long as flawed humans are in charge of things on this planet, we won't be rid of them.

So why did this story need to be written? Because it's such a powerful illustration of how God's grace pierces through to the darkest places our world can devise.

You might be interested to hear how Jacob DeShazer's story actually ended. In his last weeks in prison, God told him to return to Japan, to teach the Japanese people about Christ's love for them. Jake, a farmer and lay pastor's son from Oregon, came back to the U.S. after the war. He stayed just long enough to acquire a Bible college degree from Seattle Pacific University. And a wife—Florence Matheny of Toddville, Oregon, who also completed a B.A. at S.P.U.

In 1948, Jake returned to Japan with his new wife and baby son, Paul. The little family eventually settled in Nagoya, the very city Jake bombed from *Bat Out of Hell*. Their thirty-year ministry in Japan bore fruit in twenty-three church plants, numerous changed hearts, and many stories as miraculous as this one.

Jake's decision to return to Japan wasn't as unique as I first assumed. General MacArthur, commander during the U.S. occupation of Japan, recognized the spiritual void left by the demise of Japan's prewar militarist ideology. He begged the major denominations to send missionaries. Thousands of people responded. Many of these were men who'd battled the Japanese across the Pacific, then felt called to serve them in ministry after the war.

Jake had a vision to see Japan become a "Christian nation." While this didn't happen, millions of Japanese individuals responded to the good news of Jesus Christ. The Bible became a bestseller there in the years following the war. So did *The Bells of Nagasaki*, a personal testimony of the power of Christian faith authored by Japanese Christian Nagai Takashi — while he lay dying of radiation poisoning.

God found Gideon in a hole. He found Joseph in a prison.
He found Daniel in a lion's den.
Where the world sees failure, God sees future....
He tends to recruit from the pit, not the pedestal.
- Jon Acuff

FOOTNOTES

1. Glines, Carroll V, *Four Came Home* (Missoula, MN: Pictorial Histories Publishing Co., Inc., 1981).

2. Watson, C. Hoyt, *DeShazer* (USA: Carol Aiko DeShazer Dixon, 2002).

3. Dixon, Carol Aiko DeShazer and Goldstein, Donald M., *Return of the Raider* (Lake Mary, FL: Creation House, 2010).

4. Glines, 164.

5. Glines, 106.

Discussion Questions

1. Most of us will never have to endure anything resembling Dave's prison experience. But we all have our "prisons"— our bad days and difficult situations where we feel imprisoned and there's no way out. What about Dave's reactions and responses to his imprisonment enlightened you about yours? What takeaways do you have from his story?

2. Have you met people who react to their "captors" (difficult marriage, unfulfilling employment, children on the wrong path, addictions to food, alcohol, internet, etc.) in ways similar to Dave (rage, hatred, contempt, dehumanizing)? What can you learn from Dave's errors? From his good choices? How can you pass that along to others?

3. The Bible is filled with conversion stories. We read about others' conversions and are challenged to consider where we are with our own. Are we "all-in" with Jesus? Believe in Him, yet still behave as if we are in control of our lives? Do we talk the talk, but fail to walk the walk in some ways? Have you ever had an opportunity to mentor a new Christian? If not, can you think of ways you might be able to get involved in the lives of people struggling in their faith?

4. How does Miyako's conversion story compare to Dave's? Does hearing about such dramatic conversions solidify your faith journey? Boost it? How, or why not?

5. Think about a time when you needed to ask for forgiveness. Did you do it? Or did you justify your actions, as Dave does through much of the novel, so you could sidestep your need to humble yourself and seek forgiveness? If you did seek forgiveness, how did the person respond? How did you feel afterward?

6. Dave discovered that there were areas where he needed,

not just the forgiveness of other people, but God's as well. We all have those. Have you met anyone like Dave, who struggled to forgive? How could you help or advise someone like that? "For all have sinned, and come short of the glory of God" (Romans 3:23). "For the wages of sin is death; but the gift of God is eternal life through Jesus Christ our Lord" (Rom 6:23). "If we say that we have no sin, we deceive ourselves, and the truth is not in us. If we confess our sins, He is faithful and just to forgive us our sins and to cleanse us from all unrighteousness" (1 John 1:8-9).

7. Think about a time when you were offended, when someone hurt you or did something against you. Did they ask for forgiveness? Did you accept it? Was it easy to forgive, or did you find it difficult? What would you share with someone facing the same challenge?

8. Is there someone who has offended you who never sought forgiveness, but you forgave that person anyway? How did that feel? If you have not forgiven them, even if you believe what they did was wrong, can you imagine how it would feel to let it go, as Dave did with his captors and torturers? Talk about a time you showed compassion for an "enemy." What enabled you to do it?

9. Feeling God's love is sometimes difficult, especially when we look to it to assuage a loss as great as a father's love. Talk about a time when you felt the presence of God's love...and a time when perhaps you wanted to but didn't. What do you do to draw closer to God? When you don't feel His presence, what do you cling to, to keep your faith that He's a good Father?

10. Many books and movies have been set during World War II. Here we see it through a different lens: life in vanquished Japan, after the war. What struck you most? Did experiencing Miyako's world through her eyes have an impact on your view of how the war ended in the Pacific theater? Do you agree or disagree with the U.S.

decision to deploy atomic bombs in Japan? (Bear in mind that U.S. military planners at the time projected that a land invasion of Japan would cost 1.7 to 4 million Allied casualties, and 5 to 10 million Japanese casualties.)

Now, a Sneak Peek at Book Two

The Mulberry Leaf Whispers

Chapter One

Saturday, April 18, 1942
Pacific Ocean, 650 Nautical Miles Off the Japanese Coast

SUB-LIEUTENANT MATSUURA AKIRA PACED THE OPEN bridge of the
Nitto Maru. He had the dawn watch—as usual. Captain
Yoshiwara wasn't much good before noon. Like his vessel,
the captain had seen better days.

Rough seas that morning. It wasn't raining hard, but the
swells stood tall as the mast. A stiff morning breeze drove icy
spray into Akira's face. He filled his lungs, relishing the
bracing tang of sea air. It smacked of everything he loved
about life in the Imperial Navy. Rigor. Discipline. And with
his nation triumphing against the U.S. and British fleets, a
golden opportunity to follow Papa-san in glorious deeds. To
prove himself worthy of his long line of ancestors, the ancient
lords of Hirado domain.

There hadn't been a more exciting time to serve in
Japan's Navy since his sixteenth-century forebear, the great
Matsuura Shigenobu, led Regent Toyotomi's army against
Korea. Akira should have every chance to mark a path his
little brother, Hiro-chan, would be proud to follow. Not to
mention his own sons, when he had them. And he would give
the Matsuura women—Mama-san and his sister, Miyako—
full right to stand tall.

He'd been born for the emperor's navy, although this first
assignment would give him little opportunity for glory. This
former fishing trawler stationed off the coast of the Land of
the Gods wasn't exactly the finest ship serving the emperor.

The thirty-meter boat crested a swell. Akira raised his
binoculars and scanned the strip of oily light that shone on
the horizon, beneath a thick layer of pewter-gray clouds.

The fourth day on patrol. Everything was as expected.

Ensign Nagai ambled onto the narrow deck ten feet below him. Akira's cabin-mate, making his rounds, reliable as rain on the China Sea. Even his round face and solid frame conveyed a sense of something immovable.

About midway across the deck the ensign turned and stared up at Akira, the wind whipping the end of his thick muffler. He grabbed at it and mouthed something. With an exaggerated gesture, he pointed at the sky, then cocked his head and brought one hand to his ear.

Listen.

Akira cupped his hands behind his ears and stood still.

Wind. Waves. Spars thrashing. The iron mast in front of him creaking. And above it all—the whine of a propeller in the clouds.

He let out a soft whistle. *Odd.* Especially considering the transmission they'd received two days earlier. Command had raised the alert level.

They'd have to radio this in.

He scanned the dull gray clouds, wondering for about the twentieth time what piece of intelligence had made Tokyo wary. With the Americans still nursing their wounds from Pearl Harbor and the British recently trounced at Ceylon, what could the threat be?

About half a nautical mile to the east, the cloud cover thinned a bit.

There. A cross-shaped fleck against the sky. She was exposed for just seconds, then banked immediately and vanished, bearing east-southeast.

Nagai loped across the deck toward him, bounded up the ladder, and saluted. Akira returned his salute. "Did you identify the aircraft, Ensign?"

Nagai bowed. "Maybe a Zero out of Yokosuka, sir. But I didn't get a good look."

Akira heaved a sigh. "Nor did I. And I didn't see the insignia. We'll call it in to *Kiso.*"

"I'm very sorry, sir. The radio's giving Onishi-san trouble."

Of course. Akira swore.

"Shall I give Onishi your order, sir?"

"*Hai,* alert him. I'll join you there." *After I do the dirty work of waking the captain.*

Nagai descended the ladder to the deck and disappeared into the radio room beneath the bridge. Akira followed his ensign to the deck, then took another ladder below. He strode through the hold, past three seamen snoring in their hammocks, and along a narrow corridor to the captain's cabin. He pounded on the door and braced himself for Yoshiwara's displeasure.

Nothing.

He knocked louder. "Pardon the interruption, sir. We've sighted a plane. Shall we report it to *Kiso?*"

The captain coughed a couple of times. He said something Akira couldn't quite make out.

"Permission granted, sir?"

This time the harrumph from the other side of the door was more distinct.

"*Hai.*" Akira bowed at the closed door. He retraced his steps, thoughts flicking from the *Nitto Maru*'s captain to his own father, Matsuura Saburo. Captain of the heavy cruiser *Aoba*. Six-hundred-fifty men under his command.

What Yoshiwara had been five years earlier.

Akira certainly wasn't the only one imagining himself with a better assignment. But where Akira's career lay ahead of him, Captain Yoshiwara's was adrift in a backwater. No wonder the man pounded down the whiskey every night.

The brisk sea air struck Akira's face again, a vast improvement over the reek of fish offal that filled the hold. The old fishing trawler would never lose that stench, no matter how much the Imperial Japanese Navy overhauled her.

He strode into the radio room. A gust rattled the door he'd closed and buffeted the windows. Midshipman Onishi, at twenty-six, the oldest among them save the captain, was prodding around inside his equipment. He stood and saluted.

"Onishi," Akira said. "We have a job to do. What seems to be the problem with that radio?"

"My apologies, sir. The solenoid went out. I'm replacing it."

"How long?"

"It's almost ready, sir."

Akira gave him a brisk nod. "Get it done."

This simple surveillance mission, this foul-smelling vessel—they were his duty. And he would not see it carried out in a manner one whit short of stellar. Even if it was routine.

It meant something to carry the blood of the Matsuura, the ancient naval power of Hirado Island. He would not dishonor Papa-san or all those generations of formidable ancestors for anything. He turned his attention to Nagai. "Ensign, stand watch on the bridge."

"*Hai.*" Nagai saluted and left.

Akira helped himself to a cup of lukewarm tea from the thermos. He perched on a stool and observed Onishi as he poked around the radio's entrails. The precision work would clearly be easier with a steady surface. But nothing for seventy nautical miles in any direction was steady that morning. The man was doing all he could.

Akira stood and buttoned his coat, preparing to relieve Nagai. Before he could take a step, the ensign burst back in, his round face flushed from the wind. He saluted.

"Sub-Lieutenant Matsuura, sir. You might be interested to look outside. Two of our beautiful carriers are on the horizon."

What's this? Akira should have been informed of any operation in their area. He set his cup down so firmly tea sloshed onto the table, and strode past Nagai onto the deck. "Where?"

In the distance, gray water met gray sky. He spotted them there—two darker flecks near the horizon, almost due east. He focused his binoculars. The flecks resolved into enormous vessels with elongated decks. Planes clustered in neat rows at their sterns like lines of jacks. Both vessels boasted commanding island structures, which towered above their flight decks.

Two carriers, indeed. *Enormous* carriers. Along with two—no, *three*—smaller vessels. Cruisers.

Bearing toward Japan.

He focused on one of the carriers and took a slow, deliberate breath. This ship looked like nothing he'd seen. He'd toured the emperor's newest carrier, *Shokaku*, in the shipyard at Kobe. Its island sat like a stack of blocks. It had a conventional curved prow. The vessel in front of him boasted a dramatic, squared-off prow. And its island stretched above its deck, graceful as a *geisha*'s neck.

She was *not* the emperor's.

The *Nitto Maru*'s situation swirled into focus in his mind like the optics had focused the scene between his fingers. Only three nations in the world boasted aircraft carriers. His own, and two nations at war with Japan.

He was witnessing something that hadn't happened in seven centuries. No enemy since the Mongols had dared venture an invasion of the Land of the Gods. And a *kamikaze*, a divine wind, had risen up to destroy that fleet.

Generations of ancestral spirits, all of them bred as warriors, breathed the truth into his soul. He was facing an enemy for the first time. And very likely the last. The *Nitto Maru* had one purpose—to radio an alarm to Japan. When his crew accomplished that, the enemy would hear them and almost certainly hunt them. Barring another divine wind, this was a battle they would not win.

His pulse took up a drumbeat in his ears.

Calm your own mind. The foremost act of war. Ancient wisdom Papa-san had taught him. He took a deep breath and wrestled back a tendril of fear. Tore his gaze away from the enemy warships and focused on Nagai. "Those carriers are beautiful. But they are not ours."

The ensign's eyes went wide. "Sir?"

"Call the men to battle stations. I'll alert the captain."

Nagai saluted. "*Hai.*"

"And Ensign."

"*Hai.*"

"Inspect the crew. Make sure every man has his life preserver."

Early Summer, 1587
Sakaguchi, Hizen Province, Kyushu Island

Omura Sono plucked the last arrow from the bucket beside her and nocked it. She took a deep breath and raised the bow and arrow just above her head. She brought her left arm down in a strong arc while drawing the bowstring back past her ear. Then farther back, in time with her slow exhale. The polished bamboo shaft glided across her knuckle until everything from her right fingers to her left forearm burned.

She stared down the shaft at the painted target a quarter *cho* away. Cicada song throbbed from the stand of mulberry trees behind her.

"Steady." Captain Fujita's voice over her shoulder was a silken whisper of guidance rather than his customary thunder of command. "Calm your own mind. *That* may be called the foremost act of war."

Sono focused on the center of the target, a wooden plaque that rested at chest height on an easel at the far end of the field. The hum of cicadas and the wheeze of the captain's breath disappeared as she let the target transform into a fearsome Shimazu warrior charging her on horseback, in full armor, with his *naginata* pike aimed at her heart.

She parted her fingers. The bowstring thrummed. The arrow hissed past her ear and whooshed above the brilliant green rows of tea bushes, and...

Buried itself in the earth bank behind the target. The bow vibrated in her left hand.

"*Che!*" she swore. She couldn't help a little stomp of her foot. Only four of her fifteen arrows had pierced the target. The first three had fallen into the bushes well short of it.

"Patience, Sono-chan," Captain Fujita said. "Your muscles need time to grow accustomed to the longer bow."

She huffed out a sigh. "It seems so, *sensei*." She'd recently graduated to this bow, which stood nearly her own height. Not as long as the bows the *samurai* used in mounted archery, but long enough to make her a formidable enemy, once she mastered shooting through a port in a castle wall.

She glanced back at him. Was that a hint of a smile crinkling the leathery corners of his eyes? A flush of pride swelled her breast. She smothered it. The nail that sticks out gets hammered, ah?

Fujita gave a brisk nod to a page standing behind them. The boy trotted off between the rows of bushes to collect her arrows.

She moved her right arm in a slow circle to ease the knot in her shoulder. Had the crinkle at the corner of Fujita's eyes deepened? She dropped into her humblest asking-for-a-favor bow. "Since I'm progressing with the way of the bow, *sensei*—"

Footsteps crunched the gravel path behind them. She glanced up to see her younger brother, Nagayoshi. Only thirteen but, annoyingly, he'd come back from the Jesuit school standing as tall as she did at sixteen. Each time she saw him, a jolt of surprise ran through her at how grown-up—and handsome—he looked in his new *samurai* uniform, with their family crest bold on both shoulders.

At the same time, a familiar twinge of envy twisted her belly at everything *he* got to do and see and experience because he was a boy. Sadly, that feeling always lasted longer.

She dropped her eyes, ashamed.

Nagayoshi bowed to the captain. "Greetings, *sensei.*" And a shallow bow to her. "Honored sister. I thought I'd see how you're coming along."

Sono bowed back. "I'm sorry, but I'm afraid you missed today's entertainment." Annoyance prickled in her voice. She regretted it instantly.

Fujita greeted Sono's brother then turned back to her, one thick gray eyebrow cocked. "You had a question?"

She glanced at Nagayoshi and swallowed hard. She'd have preferred to do this without an audience. "I was asking, *sensei,* whether you thought I might be ready to train with the firearms."

Nagayoshi let out a barking laugh. Fujita sucked air past his teeth in a cautionary hiss. "That is not a weapon for a noble lady, Sono-chan. It lacks the accuracy of the bow. That's why we train the men to fire in ranks. A job for foot soldiers, lady. And the arquebuses the men didn't take on campaign are needed by the guards." He clamped his mouth closed as if that were the end of the matter.

"I can come out early. Or late. Any time they aren't in use, ah?" She bobbed him a second bow. "Please, Captain. I want to learn."

Nagayoshi took a pointed look down the rows of bushes,

where the boy was busy plucking her arrows from the leaves. "Arquebus pellets can't be collected like arrows, sister," he said with a superior smirk. *He'd* been training with the Portuguese guns since he got back—in spite of everything Fujita said about their accuracy.

Fujita gave her a penetrating look. "I can ask your older brother when the men return from the southern campaign."

"But that could be weeks. Papa-san..." The thought of him brought a catch to her throat. Trapped by disease inside the elegantly paneled walls of his mansion. Withering away under brocade bedding, that horrible cough pulling blood from his lungs.

Just what she was trying not to think about.

She went on in a muted voice. "Papa-san told Father Rodrigues I should keep applying myself to the weapons training." In fact, he'd insisted on it, even though the *padres* deemed weapons practice unbecoming for a *Kirishitan* lady. "I'll ask *him*. Assuming, of course, you agree."

He grunted. "I don't recall your older sister being so interested in the warrior's way, Sono-chan."

And your father saw her *married well.* No doubt that was the captain's thought, although he didn't say it. The question of how well Sono would marry had hung over her for as many of her sixteen years as she could recall. Anxiety squeezed her chest. This problem soon would be her older brother's to manage.

She pushed that thought away—hard. Her fingers went to the cross at her neck. "I want to be ready in case—"

"In case you have to take on the whole Shimazu clan alone?" Nagayoshi folded his arms across his chest.

"*Hai.*" She lifted her chin and squared her shoulders. "Or the Matsuura—cursed pirates—while you're out on campaign. If the enemy lands a day's march from my castle, I wish to know everything about how to defend it."

Not only how to find my own throat with a dagger if things go poorly. The first lesson Papa-san had given his daughters on warfare. And it was all Sono's well-married sister had been willing to learn.

Captain Fujita pinned Nagayoshi with a glare. "Don't mock your sister. You may not be old enough to remember how hard your father fought to repulse the Ryozuji when they attacked us, but your sister does. And before that? It was the Goto and the Saito with the Matsuura. And before that?" The captain took a ponderous step or two, lurching on his bad leg. "The Matsuura had the gall to board the Portuguese Black Ship itself. In *our* harbor."

"I do remember, *sensei*. I remember Mama-san tending to that thigh in the castle courtyard." She could never rub out those memories. How they carried Captain Fujita in from the field of battle, blood from an angry gash in his leg dripping through the cotton stretcher.

"Sono," Mama-san had barked. "Fresh water."

They had a cauldron going over an open fire near the kitchen. Sono ran for it. When she got back with a bucket, Captain Fujita lay with the other wounded in one of the long rows that stretched across the courtyard. Mama-san had his armor unlaced, cleaning his wound.

Sono wandered among the wounded until hours after dark, kneeling to lower a cup to one blood-stained face after another.

"Water!" The memories still haunted her nights. The sound of their groans. The smell of their blood. And the fear that ran through it all. If the enemies who'd done that to Captain Fujita got past the castle walls, what would they do to her? To her mother?

The captain shifted his weight, bringing her back to the present—and the question of guns. "Alliances can be fluid. Your father knows this as well as anyone. His stance as a *Kirishitan* hasn't won him many friends. And bigger and bigger *koi* seem to find their way into our pond. So you never know..." His eyes rested on Sono for an instant. The furrows around his mouth softened. "You never know when one heart full of courage can make all the difference."

Nagayoshi's smirk faded. "Of course, *sensei*." He directed a bow at her. "Forgive me, honored sister."

"It's nothing," she said, finding it as easy to forgive him as she always did.

Fujita inclined his head toward Sono. "Nice work this morning, lady. Why don't you let me know what your father has to say? Then, ah...then we'll see."

"Hai, sensei." There was something odd in the way he let his gaze slide off into the fields. Almost evasive. Had he heard something?

She didn't envy her father and older brother this game of *Go* they were playing with everyone's lives. As a marriageable daughter, she was a critical stone to place.

But unlike *Go* stones, daughters aged. Lost their marriageable luster. Had her father decided it was time to put her on the board? While her value was at its peak?

If so, she'd have no more say as to where he placed her than a stone had. Her gut folded with ire at the knowledge that the voice of her older brother's wife would carry more weight than her own.

"I'd best go back to the mansion," she said. "Papa-san might need me."

Nagayoshi's irritating smirk reappeared. *"Hai,* look to our lordly father. But please be careful not to frighten him with your warlike ways."

"Funny, Naga-chan." She pushed her stockinged feet into the wooden sandals she'd left neatly lined up on the gravel beside the platform. "Are you going back?"

Before he answered, one of their father's servants hurried from the trees, not stopping to bow but calling out as he came. "Please excuse me, Omura-san. Please excuse me."

She took in the boy's short breath and wide eyes, and everything around her froze. A sound like ocean breakers swelled in her ears.

"Papa-san?" Nagayoshi's voice, barely audible through the roaring.

"Hai." The boy looked at Nagayoshi, then at her. "Lady Omura summons you both to the mansion. Right away."

Made in the USA
Coppell, TX
10 March 2020